T0161856

BEFORE. AFTER. ALWAYS.

What Reviewers Say About Morgan Lee Miller's Work

All the Paths to You

"This book made me, a self-proclaimed hater of sports, care about sports. Even sporting events that were purely fictional. That in and of itself is impressive. …My god, Kennedy and Quinn are such a cute couple, I love them!! I ship them so much it isn't even funny. Their chemistry is through the roof to be honest."—*Day Dreaming and Book Reading*

All the Worlds Between Us

"This book is really sweet and wholesome and also heartbreaking and uplifting. …I would recommend this book to anyone looking for a cute contemporary."—*Tomes of Our Lives*

"[*All the Worlds Between Us*] deals with friendship, family, sexuality, self-realization, accepting yourself, the harsh reality of high school and the difference between getting to tell your own story and having your own story exposed. Each character plays a vital role…and tells the story of this book perfectly."—*Little Shell's Bookshelf*

"If you're looking for an easy, quick cute f/f read, you should give this a try. …This was a solid debut and I can't wait to see what else this author publishes in the future!"—*The Black Lit Queen*

"This book took me straight back to all of my gigantic teenage emotions and got right down to the heart of me. I'm not a swimmer and I wasn't out in high school, but I swear I was right there with Quinn as she navigated her life as a competitive athlete and a queer kid in high school. Experiencing love and betrayal and triumph through her story was bananas. Morgan Lee Miller, you ripped my heart right out with this brilliant book."—Melisa McCarthy, Librarian, Brooklyn Public Library

"I'm always up for fun books about cute girlfriends, and *All the Worlds Between Us* was certainly that: a super cute ex-friends to lovers book about a swimming champion and her ex-best-friend turned girlfriend. ...*All the Worlds Between Us* is a great rom-com and definitely recommended for anyone who's a fan of romance." —*Crowing About Books*

"[*All the Worlds Between Us*] has all the typical drama and typical characters you'd find in high school. It's a tough, yet wonderful journey and transformation. The writing is divine. ...It's a complicated tale involving so much pain, fear, betrayal and humiliation. *All The Worlds Between Us* is a terrific tale of taking what you want."—*Amy's MM Romance Reviews*

"Morgan's novel reiterates the important fact which should be repeated over and over again that coming out should always be done on one's own terms, and how this isn't a thing that any other people, straight or queer, should decide."—*Beyond the Words*

"Finally, a sporty, tropey YA lesbian romance—I've honestly been dreaming about reading something like this for a very long time!"
—*Day Dreaming and Book Reading*

Hammers, Strings, and Beautiful Things

"There's more going on than first appears and I was impressed that Ms. Miller won me over with a well written book that deals with some more serious issues."—*C-Spot Reviews*

Visit us at www.boldstrokesbooks.com

By the Author

All the Worlds Between Us

Hammers, Strings, and Beautiful Things

All the Paths to You

Before. After. Always.

BEFORE. AFTER. ALWAYS.

by

Morgan Lee Miller

2021

BEFORE. AFTER. ALWAYS.

© 2021 By Morgan Lee Miller. All Rights Reserved.

ISBN 13: 978-1-63555-845-6

This Trade Paperback Original Is Published By
Bold Strokes Books, Inc.
P.O. Box 249
Valley Falls, NY 12185

First Edition: May 2021

This is a work of fiction. Names, characters, places, and incidents are the product of the author's imagination or are used fictitiously. Any resemblance to actual persons, living or dead, business establishments, events, or locales is entirely coincidental.

This book, or parts thereof, may not be reproduced in any form without permission.

Credits
Editor: Barbara Ann Wright
Production Design: Susan Ramundo
Cover Design By Jeanine Henning

Acknowledgments

This story was my first ever attempt at NaNoWriMo, and as someone who takes a long time to write stories, this one came pouring out of me. I was so excited by how quickly I was able to write this story and excited to partake and succeed at NaNoWriMo.

Then the pandemic hit, and I struggled to finish it. Like everyone else, I grappled with the immense anxiety and stress of watching this virus claim so many lives and turn life as we knew it inside out. On top of that, the US elections weighed heavily on me, and health issues arose in loved ones and family members. I felt so hopeless. I wondered how I could finish this book when I was mentally and emotionally exhausted, and how I expected people to read a story about grief during such a dark, uncertain, and unprecedented time.

But then little moments of light started to seep through the darkness, and it was then when I was reminded of what *Before. After. Always.* is really about: capturing moments of light in unwavering darkness. Much like the story, these moments found me when I least expected them, and it came in the form of so many wonderful people who entered my life and kept me laughing, kept inspiring, and kept believing in me.

To Erica, Sabrina, Lily, and Kris: 2020 brought me you, and I will always be grateful for that. Your friendship and support mean so much to me, especially during times of self-doubt and increasing anxieties.

To my wonderful family and friends who support and love me just the way I am, and constantly encourage me to embrace all the things that make me me.

A big thank you to Rad and Sandy for allowing me to write my stories and making me feel like I have a purpose, even when I've spent a year in nothing but my pjs. To my wonderful editor, Barbara, who makes me a better writer with each story, and always approaches my manuscripts with kindness and humor.

And mostly, to all my readers. I can't wait to meet you when life returns back to normal so I can tell you in person how much you mean to me.

Dedication

To Mom, Julie, Karlee, the Rudolph family,
and anyone navigating life in their Afters.

CHAPTER ONE

The high-pitched screech of the flatline cut through the tension in the operating room.

Eliza and her team quickly switched gears, abandoning the tools in their hands to begin chest compressions on the nineteen-year-old boy.

Eliza couldn't lose him. She gave him CPR until sweat beaded her forehead, and her triceps burned.

This was all too familiar. Tears threatened, and when she tried to swallow them back, a pain tugged at her throat.

After several minutes, she was out of breath and pronounced him dead. The realization tore through her body. As the anesthesiologist removed the mask, Eliza observed the patient's lack of facial hair under the bruises and lacerations. He'd never been given the chance to grow it.

She stepped out into the hallway and rested her head against the blue-gray wall. The same thirteen-year-old memories flooded her mind at a time when she needed to hold it together. She wondered if Tess's doctors had thought the same thing right after they'd pronounced her dead. She'd still had a lip ring that she never had the chance to grow out of, newly straightened teeth from the retainer she'd used nightly, and random zits that had broken out on her forehead.

Now came the hardest part of her job. She had to tell the family of her nineteen-year-old patient that their loved one had died. She would witness their lives split into a Before and an After. She had done this before but never for a patient this young, as young as Eliza had been when her life had split in two.

As she walked to the waiting room, she ran over the words in her head. Telling the family that their son had died from hypovolemic shock before she even had a chance to save him tore her in two. It was all too real. The mother and father broke down, and the two preteen siblings stared at their parents as they slowly processed Eliza's words. The throbbing in her throat became stronger, making it almost impossible for her to offer sympathetic words.

The clothes underneath her white coat suddenly weighed a ton. She needed air.

When she stepped outside, she let the warm early July air fill her lungs as her emotional seams burst. She couldn't believe she hadn't been able to save him. She couldn't believe the first week of her last year of residency resulted in losing a teenage patient.

Memories flooded her mind again, tossing, turning, and mixing with the fresh ones. She rested her back against the building and cried.

Deep breaths. That was what she'd learned from years of therapy dealing with her own trauma. Deep breaths. Grounding herself in the present. But it was all too real. Her mind glitched and sent her back to the hospital when she was eighteen, hooked up to machines that prevented her from running all over the building to try to find and save Tess.

"Dr. Walsh?" a familiar deep voice said. Without opening her eyes, Eliza knew it was Dr. Norman. His warm, giant hand rested on her shoulder for a moment. "Are you okay?"

She wanted to remain professional and tell her superior that she was fine, that she was able to continue her eighteen-hour shift without being an unstable mess, knowing that this was the extremely unfortunate and hardest part of her job. But there was still a part of her that worried he would cite her for unprofessional conduct. She was supposed to keep her emotions in check so they didn't get in the way of patients' health and safety.

"I'm so sorry, Dr. Norman," she said, wiping her face with the collar of her white coat. "This is so unprofessional of me—"

"Grieving is a healthy reaction to sadness." Underneath his professionalism and stoicism, Eliza could still hear the immense empathy in his voice. It was enough for her to open her eyes and expose her tear-stained face.

"It all happened so fast," she said as fresh sobs bubbled in her throat. "I couldn't even start...he was so young." A cry flew out of her, and she covered her mouth to prevent any more from filling the space around them. "God, I'm so sorry, Dr. Norman. I shouldn't be reacting like this."

"Real doctors cry, Dr. Walsh."

She'd always admired Dr. Norman for a myriad of reasons. His knowledge, his experience, his guidance, but she especially admired how he carried himself through the toughest days and surgeries. Many surgeries were successful, but of course, some weren't, and he was always able to remain calm during the tumultuous emotions surrounding failure and death. He was able to deliver news sympathetically and with kindness, but he never cried. He didn't have to. He showed his emotions in his words and his reactions. Eliza was taken aback by his admission now. "What?"

"Don't let any other doctor fool you. We see the worst of the worst. How can you not feel something when it goes wrong? I would be lying if I said I've never cried after losing a patient."

"He's my youngest patient who..." She paused and considered her next words carefully. "I'm sorry. This one really hits close to home."

"Would you like to talk about it?"

She didn't expect him to ask, but as he did, her heart swelled with so much respect for him.

"Let's just say, I've been on the other side of it," she said, picking at her thumb cuticle. "When I was eighteen. I lost my girlfriend in an accident. I was the driver."

"Oh, wow. I'm really sorry to hear that, Dr. Walsh," Dr. Norman said and rested a comforting hand on Eliza's shoulder again. "I had no idea."

"It's what made me want to be a doctor. I lost the most important person to me, so I wanted to save lives and make up for the one I couldn't. And now…I couldn't save another kid. It's just…it really hit me."

"This was a hard one, even for an old doctor like me. After a while, you get used to the downsides of our job, but that doesn't mean it can't really get to you. You're allowed to be sad. I still am with every patient I lose. You're an incredible surgeon, Dr. Walsh. You have a bright career ahead of you. You did everything you could. You need to know that. Feel free to take as much time as you need. I'm always here if you want to talk about it more."

"Thank you, Dr. Norman. I really appreciate that."

He patted her shoulder one last time before he headed inside.

Eliza took advantage of those extra minutes he'd given her to process what had happened. She needed them to push through and care for the rest of her patients until her shift was over. But she couldn't shake the kid out of her head.

It was morning by the time she got home. Her roommate Allison sat at the kitchen table drinking a large mug of coffee. Eliza couldn't understand why she woke up at six a.m. during her summer vacation. She felt like most teachers took advantage of the freedom they had in the summer. But not Allison. She was an early riser and probably the only millennial to subscribe to a physical newspaper. She drank her coffee and had *The San Diego Union-Tribune* spread across the table with her glasses perched on the end of her nose as if she was a sixty-five-year-old trapped in a thirty-one-year-old's body.

"Hey. How was the shift? I'm about to make eggs and bacon. Want some?" The caffeine seemed to have already hit and sped up her words in her perky accent.

Eliza possessed no culinary skills—on top of working long hours—so Allison usually left her some dinner during her day shifts or cooked breakfast after her night shifts. Even though Eliza's stomach growled, she shook her head and tossed her purse and keys on an empty kitchen chair.

"Everything all right?" Allison asked.

"Bad night," Eliza said, opening the fridge to pour a glass of water. "A teenager died right before we started surgery. Car accident."

Allison lowered her mug. Her stare was so intense, Eliza felt it wrapping her up in a hug. "Oh, Eliza, I'm so sorry."

"I just need to process it. It's making me think too much about Tess."

Allison looked at her sympathetically. The two had met during the hardest moment of Eliza's life. Two weeks after Tess died, Eliza had to continue on with life, the life she and Tess had spent a year planning together. She'd moved cross-country to start her freshman year at USC, and she'd done it alone. Instead of having Tess as her roommate, the school had reassigned someone: Allison Cassidy from Santa Cruz.

Eliza had felt bad for Allison, who was all excited to start college, looking forward to befriending a new roommate and everyone else on the floor, but it had been so hard for Eliza to match the enthusiasm of the other freshmen as they'd started their new lives. She'd started a new life too: her After. Poor Allison had tried so hard to get to know her, and after two weeks of trying to coax Eliza out of her shell, Allison had gotten hold of a handle of Smirnoff vodka, and Eliza had drunkenly confessed and sobbed during their first heart-to-heart. Once Eliza had opened up about everything, becoming best friends was easy.

The two had lived together for all four years of their undergrad and had been living together since they moved to San Diego right after Eliza had finished medical school five years ago. Over the course of their friendship, Allison had learned exactly the right things to say and do to calm Eliza down from her tumbling. Besides Eliza's older sister, who still lived back home, Allison was the one constant in Eliza's life. They'd met when she'd felt the most alone in the world. Waking up every day to continue living after losing almost everything had seemed impossible. But befriending Allison, who was always there for her, saved her.

She would always be grateful for her best friend.

"You sure you don't want me to make some breakfast?" Allison said. "I can make pancakes. I need to use those blueberries before they go bad. I promise to make them extra fluffy."

"I don't know. I think I just need to sleep—"

"No," she said and got up. "You worked eighteen hours."

Eliza went to tell her that she'd eaten her leftover Indian food and had stolen a Jell-O cup from the kitchen, but Allison raised a finger and said, "That little bit of leftover Indian and your usual Jell-O doesn't count. How are you a doctor and still eating like shit?"

"I'm a surgeon. Not a nutritionist. I'm useless in the kitchen, but if you suddenly need an appendectomy, I'm your girl."

"Please let me make some pancakes?"

Eliza shrugged. "Fine. Let me get changed."

Inside her room, she flipped the light on and looked at the picture on her nightstand. She sat on the edge of the bed, picked up the wooden frame, and ran a thumb over Tess's beautiful face. Seeing the youthful, innocent features of her patient, Eliza had been reminded of how young she and Tess had been when the car accident happened, how much life they'd still had to live together. The picture had been taken at the end of their junior year in high school, before life and families had twisted their relationship into a knot so tight, they'd spent a year trying to untangle themselves.

But they'd never fully gotten out of it. Time ran out.

Eliza reached for her necklace, the one she'd worn every day since she was eighteen. She swung the ten-dollar, white-marbled, resin ring side to side on the silver chain, staring into Tess's beautiful hazel eyes and her glowing smile that was so contagious, it got Eliza to smile every time.

"Tell me when it's supposed to hurt less," she said, caressing the frame with her thumb. "Because today felt like the night I lost you."

Talking to Tess had become less of an occurrence than right after she'd died. But it still helped her on the bad days like this one, when she was reminded, yet again, how death didn't discriminate. It didn't care about age or how wonderful the person was.

How to separate a patient's death from her own loss was the one thing in med school she didn't learn. She wondered if the doctors trying to save Tess had been as upset as she was after losing her teenage patient or if Tess blended into their memories of the other patients they'd lost.

Eliza would remember the nineteen-year-old, the youngest patient she'd lost, reminding her of the very reason she'd decided to become a surgeon: to save lives and make up for the life she couldn't save thirteen years ago.

And like that fateful night, she'd failed yet again.

CHAPTER TWO

It was official. Blake had landed in hell.

She'd always had a sneaking suspicion that if heaven and hell existed, she would make it to hell because of everything she'd put her parents through as a teenager in her rebellious phase, though she hoped she'd redeemed herself since. And also because of that one girl she'd briefly dated who'd tried so hard to pull her into the world of Christianity. Blake couldn't fathom how a very gay woman wore a cross every day, went to church every Sunday, and even had a cross above her kitchen table. Once she'd seen the cross in the kitchen, she was done. Out the door, and now, surely the girl had made a deal with God to forbid Blake from entering the gates of heaven.

And also because there was nothing straight about Blake Navarro.

Not even her fractured tibia.

She slowly opened her eyes and traced the path of tubes connecting her arms to the machines surrounding her, and goddamn, was she inhaling flames from an inferno? It hurt every time she took a breath.

Then her mother appeared from the fiery pits with that scowl she'd given Blake thousands of times throughout Blake's thirty years. Jaw set, lips pursed, eyes drilling into Blake's half-open ones. She flinched at the sight of her mother, father, and younger sister Jordan, and when she did so, she felt the neck brace and noticed her left leg resting in an elevated sling.

"Blake Maria Navarro, what the hell have you gotten yourself into?" her mother said.

She thought about it, trying to find the last memory floating around. Yup, there was more pain. A familiar throbbing banged against the walls of her brain like a pinball. She knew this pain all too well from suffering a handful of concussions back in her high school softball days. Her mother had a valid question. What the hell did she get herself into?

The last thing she remembered, she was zipping down Cabrillo Memorial Drive in Point Loma, enjoying the dusk falling on the peninsula while the wind rippled through her faux leather jacket. A few people lit fireworks in a belated Fourth of July celebration. It was a beautiful evening, one that screamed for her to take her motorcycle out for a joyride to enjoy the perfect temperature, the ocean waves, and the sunset falling on the Pacific.

And now she was in hell.

"What's going on?" Blake muttered and regretted it as the fire inside her rib cage ballooned when it met with the oxygen filling up her lungs.

"You're in the emergency room," her father said, and then gestured to something behind her. "Getting a blood transfusion for your internal bleeding."

"You got hit by a car, dumbass," Jordan said.

Leave it to Jordan to continue to give her major sass despite her being hit by a car and ending up in the ER. Wasn't it supposed to be the other way around? Wasn't Blake, older by three years, supposed to be "bullying" her younger sister? It had always been Jordan teasing her, all throughout their childhood and into adulthood.

Blake flipped off her sister and noticed her right hand was covered in gauze. Every time she moved, she found a new injury, like an Easter egg hunt all over her body.

"Road rash," Jordan said. "It's gnarly. You don't want to see what it looks like under there."

"The doctor said once your internal bleeding has resolved, you'll need surgery for your leg," her mom said. "How many times did we tell you to get rid of that bike?"

A million times. She bought the bike when she became the head chef at the family restaurant, something to treat herself with for getting the title when she was only twenty-seven. That deserved a celebration, and the fact that her Uncle Hugo and her older cousin Marc trusted her enough to take on the executive chef job at their upscale Mexican restaurant. She had no regrets for buying Gisele, not even after all the nagging her family gave her.

Until now. She had a few regrets.

The pain forced her back to sleep.

The next time Blake awoke, she was in a different room, and the sun colored the sky outside the window. She wasn't sure how she'd slept through the night. Maybe it was a combination of pain and medication. She felt loopy, like her mind was a ball tumbling down a hill. She could barely open her eyes, and the stabbing pain every time she breathed didn't encourage her to speak up.

As she started dozing off again, a team of doctors came into the room. She didn't have the energy to engage with them, so she pretended to be asleep. She knew her parents would speak on her behalf.

"Hello, I'm Dr. Walsh," a female doctor said. "I'll be Blake's doctor today—"

"Please tell us everything is okay," her mom said with a shaking voice. "She's going to walk out of here?"

"We want to make sure of that, yes."

Most things didn't sound soothing early in the morning, like her mom's frantic voice, the obnoxious humming of the machines surrounding her, or the constant chatter and screech of shoes against the waxed floors in the hallways. But the doctor's voice *was* soothing. Blake wanted to see where the calm in the middle of the chaos was coming from. When she opened her eyes, she spotted a beautiful face above a white coat looking down at the computer on a rolling table at the foot of the bed.

"You're my doctor?" Blake asked weakly, the pain medication encouraging her to speak.

The doctor glanced over from the computer and gave her a warm smile. "I am."

My doctor is a babe, Blake thought, widening her eyes to take in more of her. Her blond hair fell in slight natural waves to her shoulders, and those sapphire blue eyes made Blake's insides swarm. She didn't think beautiful doctors like that existed outside TV shows like *Scrubs* and *Grey's Anatomy*. Surely this had to be a dream…or the strong medication making her see things.

"How are we feeling right now?" Dr. Walsh asked.

"Like shit," Blake muttered. "But if you're my doctor, things are looking up."

"Oh my God," Jordan said through a laugh, and the medical team joined in. "Are you seriously hitting on the doctor right now?"

Her mom elbowed Jordan, and more muted laughs from the other doctors ensued. She might not have shown it, but on the inside, Blake smiled, not only because she was able to make the doctors laugh so early in the morning but because her doctor was gorgeous. It was basically a large dose of visual endorphins.

Ignoring the snickering as if nothing had happened, Dr. Walsh turned on the illuminator on the opposite wall and pinned Blake's CT and X-ray results up for everyone to see.

"Blake has some pretty serious injuries," she said. "A tibia shaft fracture and three broken ribs. You can see here." She pointed to the cracks in the bones. "You got hit pretty badly, Blake. You have multiple fractures all up and down your tibia. That's going to require surgery to fix."

"Blake, what did you do to yourself?" her mom said, shaking her head before turning to her.

Dr. Walsh turned off the illuminator. "The blood transfusion worked. Your body has healed enough to stop any internal bleeding on its own. Now we can go ahead and prep you for surgery as soon as possible. What we're going to do is realign your tibia, and that will be done by inserting screws and rods."

"Screws and rods?" her dad said.

"It sounds like a lot, but because of her multiple fractures, I assure you, this is the best way to heal her leg. I'll be one of the doctors performing surgery on her—"

"How long is the surgery going to take?" her mom asked.

"Several hours. Due to her other injuries, we're going to want to keep her here for a couple of days to monitor her. Luckily, her leg is the worst of her injuries. She'll be in a cast for probably four to six months and will require physical therapy, but it could be much worse. I consider her very lucky."

"We do too," her mom said and then looked at Blake. "This is why we didn't want you to have the bike."

Blake closed her eyes to pretend like she didn't hear.

"That is one of the consequences of riding a motorcycle," Dr. Walsh added, which would only encourage her parents' nagging. "Cara, your nurse, will be coming in shortly to prep you for surgery, and I'll see you right before, okay?" Blake gave a thumbs-up. "Great. We're going to put you back together, and you're going to be almost as good as new."

An hour later, Blake was in the pre-op room answering the nurse's questions about her medical history, and the anesthesiologist walked through the drugs she would be given. It had her nerves going. She'd only had surgery one other time, but this was going to be her biggest one yet. Screws and rods were now going to be part of her skeleton? Was she going to light up at the airport? What happened if they fell out? Did these screws rust? How the hell did they work?

She should have waited to ask her doctor these questions because it would give her a reason to talk to her. But Blake wasn't thinking as sharply as normal. She thanked the pain, the concussion, and all the medication for that.

"Hello, Blake," Dr. Walsh said as she walked into the room. "Are you still feeling okay?"

"I'm okay. Just nervous."

"You're in good hands, I promise. The orthopedic surgeon has done this surgery plenty of times. I'll be assisting him and will make sure nothing goes wrong."

"Like waking up in the middle?"

Dr. Walsh laughed. "Dr. Cindy, your anesthesiologist, will make sure of that. You'll sleep right through it like a baby."

"I trust you. Don't let me down."

"I won't. I promise. Do you have any last-minute questions? Concerns besides the nerves?"

Well, if she hadn't asked her nurse all her stupid questions, she would have had a list for Dr. Walsh, but maybe it was a good thing she'd gotten the stupid questions out of the way so she didn't look clueless.

Blake attempted to shake her head but forgot yet again about the neck brace preventing her from doing so. "Is this brace even necessary?"

Dr. Walsh let out a small chuckle. "I know it isn't comfortable, but it's going to support your neck while your tissues heal. Your neck would hurt a lot worse without it. You'll only need it for a few days if everything goes as planned."

"What about the inferno in my ribs?"

She smiled again. "Unfortunately, the best thing for broken ribs is time and rest."

Blake grunted. "This sucks."

"I know, but my job is to fix you and make you feel as comfortable as possible given your situation. And we're going to start by fixing that leg. I'll be marking your leg for the surgery site. Does that sound good?"

A thumbs-up added to Dr. Walsh's smile as she used a marker to draw the incision site.

"Do you have any other questions?" Dr. Walsh asked when she finished.

"No, Doc."

"Your anesthesiologist will be in shortly. I'll see you when you wake up and your leg is put back together."

A part of Blake was scared to go under, but Dr. Walsh's face would distract her from the pain and give her something to look forward to in the gloomy hospital. Silver lining to all of this.

Blake Navarro's surgery was the definition of successful; the lower residents and medical students could jot down in their mental notebooks how a smooth and successful external fixation went.

After giving Blake two hours to recover from the surgery and anesthesia, Eliza went to her room to check on her, finding Nurse Cara attending to her.

"How are we doing in here?" Eliza asked. She walked over to the computer and typed away to pull up her charts.

Blake's eyes were half-open, and she winced through the pain as she tried getting comfortable in bed.

"She's loopy and numb," Cara said.

"What did you do to my leg?" Blake asked in a groggy voice.

"I fixed it. I should ask what you did to your leg."

"I went out on a joyride."

"A joyride straight to the hospital?"

A smile twitched Blake's lips. Eliza glanced at her vitals, making sure they were where they needed to be. As she did, she could feel Blake watching her every move, and when Eliza looked down, she noticed that Cara had wrapped Blake's arms and hands in new gauze, probably after putting on more ointment to help her road rash. Given her circumstances, it was a miracle that the only injuries to her head were a mild concussion, proof that wearing a helmet really did pay off.

"Do I get to leave soon?"

"No. We're going to keep you here tonight. Make sure your leg heals the way we want it and monitor those broken ribs to make sure you don't develop pneumonia."

"This isn't fun."

Eliza gave her a sympathetic smile. "The hospital isn't really a known hot spot of the town."

"What are you talking about?" Cara played along. "We have high quality food like yogurt and oatmeal." She gestured to the tray scooted to the side of the bed.

Blake held up a finger. "I'm a chef, and I can assure you, this is not high star quality."

Eliza feigned shock. "You haven't tried our Jell-O cups, then. Our signature dish. Plus, we have quality entertainment." She gestured to the turned-off TV.

That tweaked a laughing grunt from Blake. Then her gauze-covered hand clutched her ribs. She winced.

"Easy," Eliza said. "You're not allowed to laugh. Your vitals are looking great, Blake. I just want to check your ribs to make sure your chest is sounding good, all right?"

Blake gave a thumbs-up. Eliza positioned the stethoscope in her ears and held up the chest piece to warn her. "Might be a little cold."

She placed the chest piece over her thin hospital gown, instructed Blake to take deep breaths, and listened for any signs of pneumonia, an unfortunate side effect of broken ribs. As she listened, Eliza caught Blake's dark brown eyes looking straight at her, and there was a sudden jolt to her midsection, causing her to look away in order to really focus on how Blake's lungs sounded. It was probably the unexpected eye contact. Usually when she listened to lungs and hearts, the patient never stared directly at her.

After a few moments of moving the chest piece around Blake's back and chest, Eliza determined that her lungs sounded fine.

"Your lungs are good," Eliza said. "You're lucky your broken ribs didn't puncture them. *And* you're lucky that you only have a mild concussion. But imagine if there had never been a motorcycle, all the amazing food and entertainment you'd be getting right now if you stuck to the car or public transportation."

Blake's smile faded, and Cara flashed a knowing grin across the bed.

"No, no more nagging. I'm already getting that from my parents."

"But you still have to get one from a doctor. How about this, I'll save the lecture for evening rounds. In the meantime, rest up, and I'll see you soon, okay? If you're nice enough to Cara, she *might* sneak you our award-winning Jell-O cups."

"You're going to get me in trouble one of these days," Cara said to Eliza.

"I'm trying to make our patient feel a little more comfortable. We just got a negative rating on Yelp."

"We all have our weaknesses," Blake said. "Just don't go around spreading the word about the chef craving a Jell-O cup, all right? It will damage my reputation."

"We'll keep it a secret," Eliza said and zipped her lips. "You're looking good, Blake. Let's keep this up."

Blake cocked an eyebrow. "Don't hit on me, Dr. Walsh," she said jokingly, but the blunt comment sent a heatwave through Eliza, and the warmth hit her cheeks. She didn't remember the last time she'd received so many compliments in one day.

"I meant your vitals," Eliza said, forcing a steady tone to hopefully erase the blush on her face. "Your surgery went well. You're on the right path to recovery. Remember, blue Jell-O from this one." She hooked a thumb at Cara.

When it was time for Eliza to do evening rounds, a bunch of Get-Well balloons greeted her when she entered Blake Navarro's room again. A bouquet of flowers and several cards took up all the space on her nightstand. Blake had her bed propped up and scooped a spoonful of blue Jell-O into her mouth very slowly, cringing as she did so. But when she noticed Eliza, a smile took over, and two dimples popped out. Eliza wasn't prepared for that smile to stop her in her tracks on her way to the computer. She blamed the dimples. Apparently, she was a sucker for them, she found out at that exact moment.

There was no question that Blake Navarro was attractive, and as the day progressed and Blake livened up, her beauty was able to shine through the pain and discomfort contouring her features. Her smile was beautiful enough for Eliza to steal a second look. Blake's dark mocha, sideswept hair was all disheveled, and those dimples were cute—

Eliza shook herself out of the very inappropriate thought. No, it wasn't okay. Instead, she acknowledged Blake's attractiveness, and that was that. The second any desire sprouted, Eliza instantly ran over it like a lawn mower over a weed. She came here to do rounds with her medical team, not soak up the attractiveness Blake Navarro possessed.

"How is the fine dessert?" she asked.

"Absolutely delicious. Best part of the day."

"You're a child," her sister said.

"You're just upset because you don't have one."

"You're an award-winning chef. Act like it."

Eliza checked out her charts on the computer. "Award-winning chef?" She looked at Blake from the computer only for a split second, afraid of her body reacting to Blake's dimples and smile.

"She's the head chef at my brother's restaurant," Blake's father said proudly, a wide smile on his face. "Mezcal Cocina."

"You're the head chef at Mezcal Cocina?" Eliza asked with piqued interest.

It was a high-end Mexican restaurant in the Gaslamp Quarter and was always on San Diego's lists for best tacos, best Mexican cuisine, and was one of the top restaurants in the city. She and Allison had been there quite a few times for their delicious margaritas and tableside guacamole, and their tacos were truly some of the best Eliza had ever had in Southern California.

"I am," Blake boasted.

"I've been there before. My roommate and I love that place."

"Doesn't the Jell-O ruin her reputation?" the sister asked.

"Oh, shut it, Jordan," Blake said.

"We all have our guilty pleasures," Eliza said. "The restaurant is amazing. Really, one of my favorites."

"Does that mean you can discharge me a little earlier?" Blake asked. "Think about all the people who want that delicious food—need the delicious food—and I can't be there to make sure they get the quality al pastor tacos they need and deserve."

"Great pitch. A-plus for effort," Eliza said. "But, no, that's not going to qualify you for an early discharge. You had a pretty nasty accident, and I want to make sure one of the top chefs in San Diego leaves here as healthy and put back together as she can be. For all of our sakes, all right?"

Blake let out a deep sigh and then grunted in pain. "Goddamn, I keep forgetting my ribs are broken. It hurts to breathe and laugh and do anything really."

"Let me see how the leg is doing, and then we'll check on the ribs."

Blake's thumbs-up must have been her signature move, and Eliza hated how involuntary her smile formed whenever she did so.

She suppressed the smile as she pulled the bed covers up to check on Blake's leg. She gently undid the bandages to take a look at the incision site. "Leg looks great," Eliza said. "Let's check out those ribs."

"Go for it, Doc."

Blake set her finished Jell-O cup on the table, and Eliza pushed it out of the way before lifting the hospital gown to inspect her ribs. The first thing she noticed on Blake's left ribs was a dog tag tattoo with beautiful shading, all black ink, and precise detail on the chain. On the tag, it said, "Adrian 11-11-04." Right below the tattoo were a few dark red bruises.

"Does this hurt?" Eliza asked and glanced up at her.

Blake had an unusual eye color. It wasn't a simple chestnut brown or honey. It was a rich espresso color. Almost the color of her dilated pupils from her mild concussion.

"Yes," Blake said with a light breath as if holding in the pain.

"Are you taking shallow breaths?"

"Yeah, because breathing normally hurts."

"Okay, then. I'm going to have your nurse bring you something called an incentive spirometer. You're going to use it about five times an hour. Since you're taking shallow breaths, your lungs aren't filling up with air, and you could develop pneumonia. This device will help prevent that. Your nurse will go over how to use it."

She gave another thumbs-up. "Okay, Doc."

Eliza lowered the gown. "Your ribs are going to be sore for a few days. Unfortunately, we can't do much to fix them except have you rest, take deep breaths a few times an hour, and we'll give you some medication to help with the pain."

"Sounds good, Dr. Walsh."

"I see you enjoyed the Jell-O?" Eliza gestured to the demolished cup.

Blake laughed, seeming surprised by the question. "It hit the spot."

"It's known to do wonders. A medicinal treat. I try to prescribe it as much as I can." She put the stethoscope in her ears. "I told you that Cara will give her favorite patients anything they ask. Within reason, of course."

Blake put her gauzed-covered hand over her heart. "I take great pride knowing that I'm a favorite patient. I should ask her for some chocolate next. A gooey chocolate chip cookie sounds amazing right now. Fight away the hospital blues."

Eliza laughed and wiggled the chest piece as a warning. "Chocolate is morphine in the culinary world. Now, I'm going to listen to your lungs again, make sure that we're still pneumonia free."

Eliza pressed the chest piece to Blake's back, listened for any irregularities, and then moved to her chest. She felt Blake's eyes trying to hold hers, and it took everything in her willpower not to follow the force, knowing exactly what would pass through her if she caved. Eliza's skin prickled just feeling Blake's gaze on her.

When she deemed Blake's lungs crystal clear, she wrapped the stethoscope around her neck and walked to the foot of the bed to plug her observations into the computer.

"Any signs of pneumonia?" Blake asked.

"What?"

"Pneumonia. You just checked me for pneumonia?"

Oh, right. Yes. That.

Eliza put on a cordial—and professional, emphasis on professional—smile. "Like everything else, your heart and lungs sound great. You're recovering as I'd like."

She focused her attention on the computer. It was a great excuse to avoid looking at Blake with the lustful thoughts still taped to the front of her mind.

"So, discharge tomorrow?"

"Blake," her mother chimed in. "Stop it."

"Your recovery is going very well," Eliza said. "I'm very impressed by how you're doing given the severity of your accident. You were hit by a car twenty-four hours ago, sustained some pretty bad injuries, and just because I'm happy with these results and everything is looking great, your ribs are still broken, and your skull is still swollen. We need to get some blood flowing to your leg, so you'll see a physical therapist tomorrow and practice walking on crutches. You had a serious accident. You're lucky you only have these injuries. I've seen so much worse. We can have that motorcycle lecture right now or save it for tomorrow morning."

Blake grunted. "Definitely tomorrow morning."

"Great. I'll add that to my notes. Must lecture...Blake Navarro...about...motorcycles," Eliza said, literally typing it for herself...and maybe for some comedic relief. It garnered smiles from the Navarros at least. "There. Added."

"It should be every time you see her," her mother said. "We've been trying to get her to sell the bike for years."

"That's my goal by the time she leaves. Those things are death traps."

"Listen to the doctor," her father said.

"Not gonna happen," Blake said.

"Then maybe I need to keep you here until you open your mind to the idea."

"Ha," Jordan laughed.

Blake frowned. "I don't think you can do that?"

"We will definitely chat tomorrow morning. Until then, you have a good night. I hope you get some rest, and remember to breathe."

The second Eliza stepped out of her room, she exhaled slowly. There was a seed of excitement buried deep in her that looked forward to tomorrow's rounds. It was another thought she had no control over, and the second it rang, she looked at the charts for her next patient: the middle-aged man who'd contracted osteomyelitis after suffering a severe puncture wound to his leg. That would make her forget about her cute first patient.

Until the next morning.

Blake wasn't a morning person. Never had been. Before she'd adulted and gotten a full-time job, she was one of those people who could sleep until one in the afternoon with zero regrets. Now that she had a kitchen to run, her one p.m. wake-up days were long over, but she still couldn't function until she had a cup of coffee as a warmup and then another cup to help her stay awake.

But waking up to Dr. Walsh stepping inside her hospital room for morning rounds made a morning without coffee almost worth it.

"Good morning. How did you sleep?" Dr. Walsh asked and went straight for the computer to view her charts.

"Better than expected," Blake said with a groggy voice, barely awake. After giving Dr. Walsh several moments to glance over the charts, she asked, "Am I leaving today?"

Dr. Walsh looked at the computer. "Ah, perfect timing to begin the motorcycle lecture," she said, causing Blake to roll her eyes, and the medical team chuckled to themselves. She'd totally forgotten about the looming lecture. "Your exact situation is what happens when you ride a motorcycle. You get hit by a car and need to spend some time in the hospital. And that's just the case for lucky ones like you."

"I've had the bike for three years. Haven't gotten a scratch until now."

"Well, you sure made up for lost time." As Dr. Walsh walked along the side of the bed, she reached into her white coat and handed Blake a small paper bag. When Blake glanced inside, she found a chocolate chip cookie, one she'd been craving for days. Her eyes widened.

"Something to cheer you up," Dr. Walsh said. "From the bakery down the street. It never disappoints."

"It's not even from the hospital? Oh wow. Dr. Walsh, this is great. I didn't actually think you would get me a cookie."

"Long hospital stays are tough. Figured you needed something to liven your spirits. Now, I really expect you to consider ditching the motorcycle. You want to know how many patients I've seen who've been in motorcycle accidents? A lot. And oftentimes, they look worse than you. Both legs broken. A few were paralyzed. Many died. Consider yourself very, *very* lucky. If you don't like staying in the hospital, it's something you need to really think about."

"You're the best part of the hospital, Dr. Walsh," Blake said, trying to ease the severity of the conversation.

But Dr. Walsh wasn't having it. Her stare remained firm. "I'm being serious. I strongly recommend you ditch the motorcycle unless you love staying in the five-star resort that is this hospital."

Dr. Walsh made the hospital close to a five-star resort, Blake thought. She made sure Blake was always comfortable, recommended and distributed the best treats and medication, and the views were amazing—all from her gorgeous face and smile.

"You'll be meeting with the physical therapist today to walk around on crutches. If all goes well, we can start looking at discharging you tomorrow at the earliest."

"So I can get back in the kitchen soon, right?"

"Wrong."

She deflated. "What?"

"You really need to take it easy. You can't be working in a crowded kitchen and rushing to get orders ready when your leg is starting to heal. Enjoy the rest."

"I can't. I have a kitchen to run. Tacos to make. Stomachs to please."

"And you can do all that once your leg heals. Let's see how today goes, and I'll start the discharging process once I talk to your primary care doctor. We can most likely get you out of here tomorrow morning."

Blake accepted defeat and eased her sorrows with her cookie. It was everything she was craving. Soft, gooey, with half-melted chocolate chips.

Walking around with her physical therapist was so much harder than she'd originally thought. She had to get used to the crutches because her therapist warned her that she would have to use them for at least three months until her physician switched her to a walking cast, which she could be in for another three months.

"So my Christmas present will be getting my cast off?" Blake said as she maneuvered through the hallways with crutches. The therapist stayed close to her side with his hands extended, ready to catch her if she fell.

"I think so," he said. "A fractured tibia is a serious injury. A big bone like that takes a long time to heal."

"Well, that's great." Okay, now she was officially annoyed. The crutches hurt her armpits. Her whole body still hurt. The fucking neck brace was the bane of her existence. The hospital food sucked, with the exception of the Jell-O Cara treated her to for lunch. Her bed was uncomfortable. She was bored out of her mind. The girl she had been casually dating for the last several weeks, Carrie, had yet to visit her. Everyone else had. Her parents, sister, uncle, cousin, her best friend Malai, and some of her employees. Everyone except for the girl she'd been sleeping with for six weeks.

She was really considering her future.

By the time of evening rounds, Blake had already made up her mind about Carrie. It was time to forget about her. If Carrie didn't care enough to see Blake after being hit by a literal car, then she didn't care about their relationship, and Blake wasn't about to waste time. She might have when she was younger and wanted someone to fill the empty spot in her bed, but she was done with that era of her life.

A knock on the door signaled her turn for Dr. Walsh. She lifted herself in bed as Dr. Walsh stepped in, flashing a beautiful smile that took up her whole face.

"How are we doing? I heard that your walk went well today?"

"It did. I'm practically a pro at crutches."

When Dr. Walsh checked her lungs, Blake watched her listen through the stethoscope, hoping that Dr. Walsh's dark blue eyes would meet hers so they could share that secret moment, like they had a couple of times before. She sat so close that Blake could smell either her perfume, shampoo, or bodywash. Blake considered holding her breath to create some kind of disturbance in her chest that would make Dr. Walsh stay, listening to her body for longer than a quick minute.

But unfortunately, Dr. Walsh studied something on the ground, completely wrapped up in the sounds of Blake's heart and lungs, all business, no pleasure.

It was very disappointing.

Dr. Walsh wrapped the stethoscope around her neck and walked to the foot of the bed without a single glance. "Okay, Blake, you're looking good for a possible discharge tomorrow morning."

"Really?" Blake asked, excited for the next day.

"Really. I'm going to talk to your physician. I'd like you to leave the neck brace on for a few more days—" Right as Blake deflated, Dr. Walsh raised a hand. "I know. They're not comfortable. But I assure you, it's beneficial for your recovery. If you take it easy when you go home and take the recovery seriously, your neck, ribs, and leg will heal faster. Remember that when you're getting the urge to get back on the motorcycle or cook."

"My motorcycle and I are on a break," Blake said and loved that her stupid joke caused Dr. Walsh to break her stern lecture to smile.

"Well, I'm very glad to hear that. Hopefully, the break turns into a permanent breakup. You take care tonight. I hope you sleep well, and we'll cross our fingers that tomorrow is the day we set you free."

It wasn't until Dr. Walsh left that the thought of never seeing her again really bummed Blake out. Sure, she'd only known Dr. Walsh for two days, but there was just something about her. Women were beautiful, but then there was that level of absolute gorgeousness where Dr. Walsh was. Blake couldn't shake off that kind of beauty the moment she crutched out of the hospital.

Her ribs had hurt consistently since she'd woken up in the hospital, and when Dr. Walsh stood in front of her, Blake completely forgot about the pain.

That was something worth noting, right?

CHAPTER THREE

I have something for you," Cara said as she walked alongside Eliza in the hallway the next afternoon. She pulled a folded piece of paper out of her scrubs pocket and handed it to her. "From your not-so-secret admirer."

"What?"

"I didn't read it. I was told to deliver it."

All she had to do was mention a secret admirer, and Eliza knew it had something to do with Blake Navarro. It was bad enough that her team had witnessed Blake's flirting, then referred to Blake as the Denny to Eliza's Izzy, and no matter how many times Eliza directed glares at her snickering team or punished them with extra paperwork, they still smiled whenever Blake Navarro's name was mentioned. Eliza hated how she couldn't tame her damn cheeks to stop warming up.

And now Cara knew about it? She would about die if word traveled to Dr. Norman.

"Do not tell any of the other residents or med students about this," Eliza said and buried the note in the deepest part of her coat pocket. "They're already taunting me."

Cara zipped her lips. "My lips are sealed."

"Or I tell the kitchen you're sneaking patients extra Jell-O."

She feigned shock. "You wouldn't dare."

"Try me." She bumped into Cara's waist.

"Well, open it."

"Hell, no. I have no idea what this says. Plus, I'm on my way to a gastrostomy. I'll read it later."

"But I need to know all the juicy details."

"Absolutely not."

Cara grunted. "You're ruining the fun, Dr. Walsh. I would let you read a love letter I got from a patient."

"Maybe you're next."

Throughout the afternoon, when her mind offered space for a thought, Eliza wondered what the hell was in the note. Several ideas crossed her mind, and every thought sent heat through her. She felt guilty. Was the cookie too much? Did it give Blake the wrong impression? She'd snuck other patients Jell-O cups and little treats throughout their stays, a little something to liven their spirits since hospitals did a good job draining them. All she expected in return was a smile, a clue that the treat went a long way.

She didn't expect a personal letter.

After her last surgery of the day, Eliza scurried home, the only place she felt one-hundred-percent safe reading whatever was on the paper. She could talk to Allison about it without a problem, but she didn't want to encourage Cara or any other of her medical team in their playful banter. She wanted to remain strictly professional at work. Her personal life was off-limits. She wanted her colleagues to think that she didn't have a life outside of work. She wanted everyone to think she was like one of the Sims who went home and stared at the wall as time sped up until the next shift. She thought that was much better than any colleague knowing any details about her love life.

Once Eliza had poured herself a glass of wine, she got comfortable on her couch and opened the note that had been weighing on her mind ever since Cara had handed it to her.

She wished Allison wasn't at a work happy hour because she needed her best friend for some analysis.

Eliza texted Allison, *Get home ASAP so you can pick apart this note a patient left for me.*

She stared at the paper as if something would burst out when she opened it. She wasn't clueless. It was probably a phone number, and the thought of a cute woman going out of her way to leave her a note only encouraged the pulling in her gut.

She held in a breath as she finally read it.

Since you're not my doctor anymore, I would love it if you stopped by Mezcal Cocina. I could whip up anything on the menu (or off) as a treat for being an amazing doctor. Or since the best doctor at Bellevue hospital told me to stay away from the kitchen, I can order you anything from the menu.

Consider it payback for the cookie and the Jell-O.

You definitely made a two-day hospital stay tolerable. Feel free to call or text whenever you want to cash in the offer. Hope to see you sometime - Blake Navarro

She ended it with her phone number.

Eliza blew out a breath, and then took a long swig of wine as her body temperature rose. She had been running in the opposite direction of any love life for years. But she couldn't remember the last time a woman made her insides feel like a butterfly exhibit.

She really needed advice from her older sister, Violet, to take advantage of her career as a therapist

"Emma! My favorite person," Eliza said when her five-year-old niece picked up her FaceTime.

She and Violet had a weekly FaceTime date that they never missed. Even though Violet was four years older, she was still one of Eliza's best friends, her confidant, and the only one in her family to know all the details about her life. Any time Emma snatched the phone away from her mother, it was an absolute treat for Eliza. She hadn't seen her favorite little person in two years, the last time Violet and her husband, Jonathon, had come out to visit. So much had changed. Emma was speaking full sentences that Eliza could actually understand. She'd just finished preschool. She was learning to cause trouble, like stealing her mother's phone when it went off.

"Aunt Wiza," Emma said with a giant, toothy smile.

"How are you?"

"Good."

"Are you ready for kindergarten to start soon?"

"Yeah."

Deep conversations with a five-year-old.

Emma quickly lost interest and tossed the phone on the couch. Violet laughed and picked it up. "Guess she's over you."

"Guess so."

Their weekly chats had started as phone calls. They hadn't missed a week in the nine years since they'd started. Violet was Eliza's window to all things back home, letting Eliza know how her parents were despite their estranged relationship. Even though she hadn't spoken to them in nine years—excluding sparse and forced holiday text messages—she still cared about how they were doing. There wasn't a day that passed when she didn't wish things were different between them. She really wished she could find the strength to forgive them for all the hurt and betrayal.

So Violet was the only family member she trusted, and she was so grateful for their weekly chats. They were the highlight of her week, and it was even better when she got to see Emma, who looked more grown-up every week.

"What's new in your life?" Violet asked. "Besides the usual studying."

"I officially started my last year of residency."

"Oh, yeah. That's right. How's it going?"

"Well, I cried last week because a nineteen-year-old died in the OR. It was horrible. And then this week happened, and it's been... interesting to say the least."

Violet raised an eyebrow. "Interesting in a good way or a bad way?"

"Have you ever had a patient hit on you?"

Violet laughed and sunk into her couch as if getting comfortable for the tea. "What?"

"I hear that's a common thing in therapy. Patients falling for their therapists."

"Did you make someone fall in love with you?"

"I think I did."

Violet's sapphire eyes widened. She loved the gossip. "Oh, tell me. First, how juicy is it? Do I need to pour myself a glass of wine?"

"Yeah, you do. Ten-out-of-ten juicy."

"Fuck, yes. One second." She set the phone on the couch, and in the background, Eliza heard her yelling, "Jonathon. Jonathan? Can you put Emma to bed? I'm talking to Eliza. She made someone fall in love with her, and I need the details." Jonathan said something, and then Eliza heard opening and closing of the cabinets, the pop of a wine cork, and uneven footsteps scampering back to the couch. Violet took over the screen again, smirk wide and eyebrows risen with intrigue. "Okay. Spill."

"A patient asked me out."

She choked on her first sip. "What? Seriously?"

"Seriously. She wrote me a note after hitting on me for two days straight. In front of my medical team, mind you, so for the four rounds we did, they referred to her as Denny and me as Izzy."

"I don't get it."

"It's from *Grey's Anatomy*, and it's mortifying."

Violet rolled her eyes. "Okay, Eliza, don't be so dramatic. Was she not hot or something?"

Eliza faltered. Her brain defaulted to medical ethics and how she couldn't fully bask in the attraction she had for Blake Navarro, but now that Blake was no longer her patient, Eliza finally allowed her body to react, completely unhinged and with no censor. She thought it was truly adorable whenever Blake gave the thumbs-up. It was quirky and unique, and Eliza loved quirky and unique. She was a sucker for Blake's dimples and thought her dark—almost black—eyes were beautiful.

Eliza grunted and tossed her head back until it hit the couch. She knew she was being dramatic, but she rolled with it. "See, that's the thing. She was very attractive, and most patients...well...aren't."

Violet squealed. "Oh my God. And she asked you out. How does that make you feel?"

Typical therapist question.

"Guilty. My whole team knows about it because they witnessed her flirting. One of the nurses gave me the note, so now she knows too. I swear, if it spreads around the department, I will die of embarrassment. I'm very content with people thinking I'm only a doctor and that I only do doctor things."

"You do realize you're bright red?"

Eliza checked herself on her phone screen, and damn it, her sister was right. She wiped her face as if that would do the trick. "I blush anytime someone hits on me. I react easily."

"Mm-hmm, sure," Violet said in a disbelieving tone. "But I'll pretend like that's true. Carry on. What did the hot patient say? I want all the deets. I'm happily married with a five-year old. The most exciting part of my day is when Emma counts to one hundred in Spanish."

"That's actually really impressive—"

"Stop. Spill. What did she say?"

"She asked me to come to her restaurant, and she gave me her number."

"Her restaurant?"

"Apparently, she's the head chef at this really amazing Mexican restaurant, like one of the best in San Diego."

"Hot. Are you gonna call her?"

"Absolutely not. Put yourself in my shoes, Mrs. Therapist. A hot, former patient of yours asks you out. What do you do?"

"Totally different."

"No, it's not."

"Yes, it is. I know everything about their life and then have to guide them through it. And I develop *long-term* relationships with them. How long was she your patient?"

Eliza counted in her head. "Two days."

"And what do you know about her besides her injuries?"

"That she's a chef and has a motorcycle." She grumbled at the motorcycle part.

"Exactly. You don't know her life story, and you've only known her for two days. Now, if I had a patient and only saw him for three sessions, and he looked like Jason Momoa, and my insides caught on fire every time he looked at me, and then he decided not to see me as a doctor anymore, *maybe* I would consider it."

"When I say I want to get to know someone on the inside, I didn't mean it literally. I've literally seen her insides. I screwed her leg back together."

"And you can tell your children that it was love at first internal sight."

"Shut up." Violet roared with laughter as Eliza's face became hotter. "You know how I am about dating."

"Yeah, you don't do it enough. So come on, you think she's really hot. Tell me more."

Eliza hesitated and shook her head at the truth she was about to reveal, knowing she was going to regret it. "Being around her made me nervous. How is that even possible? I don't even know her, and I was nervous."

"This never happens to you. Text her, damn it. This means something."

"It means nothing."

"I thought you told me you wanted to start dating again?"

Eliza had said that, but she was hoping Violet had forgotten that despite the fact that it had happened a few months ago. Yes, Eliza wanted to date. Her love life consisted of sparse dates and shallow one-month things with women. Not even flings because a fling was more of a commitment than those encounters.

It wasn't because Eliza was afraid of commitment. There was nothing she wanted more than to find the love of her life and spend their lives together. She wanted that so much. It was just that the process of finding that woman was so much trial and error, which meant disappointment and heartbreak.

The thing was, her heart had never fully mended from the loss of Tess. It still ached daily. Lowering her guard just the slightest bit to share a part of her life with a woman terrified her because she didn't want to go through the devastation of losing someone she was so in love with again, a woman she'd planned the rest of her life with.

"I do want to date again," Eliza said. "But not a former patient. Literally anyone else."

Violet let out a deep sigh, and that indicated the mood change. "Eliza," she said sternly, and Eliza braced herself for tough love from her older and much wiser—and happier—sister. "I thought you were ready to move on."

"I do want to move on."

It was the first time Eliza had said the words out loud. After all these years, it was like Tess's heart was still threaded around hers the way it had been when they were together. It never untied after her death. She was still very much a part of Eliza like she was back then, as if Eliza could feel her heart beating in a different dimension.

She hadn't been able to open her heart fully since, and she wasn't sure how to let another woman in when Tess still had a hold on her. Eliza was ready to find out the answer. She was ready to share her life with someone, and something as little as texting Blake Navarro, her little crush, was huge for her. She'd dated women in the past, but they'd never made her nervous or made her stomach swirl. Taking initiative and acting on her feelings was a step she had yet to take.

"I think it's time, Lize," Violet said, much softer this time. "It's been so long."

"At the same time, it feels like it was yesterday."

"You're allowed to move on, you know. It doesn't mean you loved her any less. It means you're trying to live."

The emotion started balling up in her throat when Eliza looked back on the last thirteen years and realized she hadn't accomplished anything. She still let the PTSD kick her around like a useless pebble in the way. She was still terrified of opening up to someone else and then losing them. In college, Eliza had believed that by the time she was thirty, she would be engaged, married, or dating the woman she would spend the rest of her life with.

But now, she was a million miles away from what she'd wanted her life to be when she was thirty. She was thirty-one and so fucking alone. She'd done a really good job of using the pain of her accident and her broken family to build a sturdy wall around her heart to make sure no woman would have the chance to ruin it.

And in return for not taking the risk of falling in love, she was probably the most alone she'd ever felt in her life.

"When was the last time a girl made you nervous?" Violet asked.

Eliza actually considered. When was the last time she'd noticed a woman looking straight at her, and a spark had zipped through her gut like a comet piercing the night sky? It was simple. It was Tess.

"I was a teenager," she answered.

"If this patient makes you feel something, you should follow it. And if it doesn't go anywhere, at least you put yourself out there. You need to take that first step to get your love life in motion again, to allow yourself to be the tiniest bit vulnerable. You should follow those feelings. I would think being nervous around someone means something, and it's a good thing, Eliza. What you're feeling is something that is exciting and should be celebrated."

Violet had a happy marriage to her college sweetheart, an amazing daughter, a relationship with their parents. Literally everything Eliza wanted but didn't have.

Maybe that was a sign Eliza should listen to her. Maybe she needed to plow through those walls, stop listening to her scarred brain, and follow her heart for once. Her brain was terrified of falling, but her heart was so lonely; it wanted a partner. It had wanted a partner for years.

She had nothing to lose at this point. Then what was holding her back?

❖

Blake was confused.

When Carrie had come over two days after Blake had been discharged, Blake thought she'd made it clear that they were done. Her blood had boiled when Carrie had tried excuses, and Blake had told her to leave the apartment.

What the hell was Carrie thinking coming to Mezcal now?

Blake had come to the restaurant to check in with her staff and do some budgeting while being barred from the kitchen and forced to stay off her leg. But as she stepped into the dining room, she spotted Carrie's curly red hair at the bar.

What the fuck?

She quickly hobbled to the bar to see why the hell Carrie was at the restaurant. Did she forget? Did she lack so much respect that she chose to ignore what Blake had told her?

"Hey, you," Carrie said, sliding her fingers across Blake's back.

"What are you doing here?"

"I was out with one of my friends and saw your car parked in the back."

"Where's your friend?"

"Across the street grabbing us a table. Though I should tell her to come over here—"

Right as she reached into her black side purse, Blake stopped her hand. "It's okay."

Carrie frowned. "It's okay? What do you mean?"

"I thought we had this conversation three weeks ago?"

Blake was annoyed. She thought her time with Carrie was done. If Carrie couldn't connect the dots and see that not visiting the woman you were fucking for six weeks when she was in the hospital was a pretty shitty thing to do, then Blake didn't want to waste more of her time.

"Yeah, but...I missed you." Carrie squeezed her wrist as if to coax her to change her mind, but if anything, Blake was more adamant about her decision.

Blake pulled her hand away and fought against the cringe that snaked through her. "You need to go, Carrie. Go join your friend."

Right as Carrie opened her mouth, one of Blake's favorite customers greeted her. "There's my favorite chef," Henry said and gave her a hug.

He and his wife were frequent customers, usually coming to Mezcal for their Friday dates. He'd become such a part of Mezcal that he and Uncle Hugo even golfed with each other occasionally.

"How are you? And the leg?"

Blake rested her cast on the footrest of the barstool for Henry to get a better look. "Getting better. It's a wicked break, though. Apparently, I'll be in this thing until, like, Christmas."

"I can't believe a car hit you," he said, shaking his head. "When your uncle Hugo told me and Barb a couple weeks ago, we couldn't believe it."

"I couldn't believe it either, but hey, I'm almost as good as new."

Almost being the key word. All the spare time she had sitting around her studio and "taking it easy," was making her extra irritable, anxious, and bored, but once she got herself back into the kitchen, then yes, she would be a brand-new woman, ready to conquer the kitchen and hopefully the dating world—sans Carrie. And she was okay with that.

"When can you get back in the kitchen? I bet that's driving you crazy."

"Henry, it's killing me, but the doc says I need to get into my walking cast before I get back in there, and even with that, I need to be mindful." She buzzed her lips. "What he doesn't know won't hurt him." She winked.

Then something from her peripheral caught her eye: a blond with slight waves in her hair weaved around the tables, and her dark blue eyes pierced through her.

She barely recognized Dr. Walsh without her white coat. She looked like a real human being in a light blue top that accentuated those beautiful eyes and short jean shorts that pulled Blake's gaze to her smooth, toned legs and held it there.

Damn, her legs were sexy. They pinned Blake right to the spot.

Three weeks after leaving her a note, Blake had given up hope that Dr. Walsh would stop by. It was a huge risk asking her doctor out to her restaurant, but Blake had to. She was insanely attracted to her and had nothing to lose if Dr. Walsh didn't accept. It was worth the risk because the rewards would have been astronomical. And finally seeing Dr. Walsh in her restaurant, Blake was stunned yet victorious. Maybe she had a shot after all.

"Oh, hi. What are you doing?" Dr. Walsh said flatly and pointed to Blake's cast still resting on the barstool.

"This lady just got out of the hospital," Henry said and patted Blake's arm. "Nasty crash, but now she's looking almost as good as new."

"You think I can get another ride on the bike soon?" Carrie asked and slid a hand into Blake's.

But Blake wasn't having it. She retrieved her hand yet again and waved at Dr. Walsh as her face started to burn. She put her foot on the ground and positioned her crutch underneath her armpit as if trying to undo the scene.

"I'm not sure if I'm allowed to ride my bike anymore," Blake told Carrie. "Doctor's orders." She hooked a thumb at Dr. Walsh.

"Your crutch is under the wrong armpit," Dr. Walsh said.

"Shit." Blake threw it underneath her left, the side of her cast.

"And where's your other crutch?"

Blake glanced behind her shoulder at the bar where her crutch rested against the wall. She faced Dr. Walsh again and made an "I'm in trouble" face. "It's back there," she replied, sounding like a dog with its tail between its legs.

"Why?"

"Looks like someone's in trouble," Henry chanted and hid his grin behind his beer bottle.

"She is," Dr. Walsh said. "And why wasn't your bad leg on the ground?"

"I was showing Henry the damage."

From the corner of her eye, she could see Carrie scoping out Dr. Walsh as if she were her competition.

"Hey, Lize, our table is ready," said a brunette, placing a hand on Dr. Walsh's shoulder and nodding to an empty table behind her.

Blake wondered if she was a friend, a date, or a girlfriend. She couldn't quite tell based on the brief interaction. It was probably too good to be true. One of the most beautiful women she'd ever seen coming into her restaurant to see her did seem wildly unrealistic.

"Use the crutches," Dr. Walsh said with a last point, and despite not knowing if the brunette was a friend or a date, the demand pleasantly tugged on Blake's chest. It made Dr. Walsh even sexier. "Your insurance is paying good money for that."

Blake watched the two sit and decided that she had to find out about the brunette. She suspected that based on the invitation to Mezcal, Dr. Walsh wouldn't have brought a date. But she also wanted to take advantage of the fact that Dr. Walsh had showed up.

Plus, talking to her meant she could ditch Carrie.

"Who's that?" Carrie said in a snarky tone, following Blake's gaze.

Blake rolled her eyes. She wasn't about to dedicate another night to Carrie drama. It was over. She'd made it very clear. "You need to go back to your friend," Blake said as she grabbed her second crutch. "I've got things to do. Bye, Carrie."

She left the bar and made her way to Dr. Walsh's table. When her bright eyes looked up, Blake couldn't contain the smile growing on her face.

Had the letter actually worked?

"Hey, you came," Blake said. "I didn't think you would actually show up."

Was that a little bit of blush dusting Dr. Walsh's cheeks? Was she making Dr. Walsh blush?

"I was craving a jalapeno margarita," Dr. Walsh said and focused on the menu.

Blake noticed the brunette sucking in a growing smile.

"Is that what you'd like to drink?"

"Actually no. I would like a very stiff old-fashioned."

Her friend cocked an eyebrow. "I thought we came here for margs."

"I need something stronger."

"I'll get whatever you two need," Blake said.

Seriously, whatever would make Dr. Walsh stay or would help her buy some time to sneak in a conversation. She would tell the kitchen no rush on the order, though.

"Don't we have a server?"

"Yeah, but I can get you the drinks faster."

"With crutches?"

Blake waved a hand. "It's not a problem. I've had lots of crutch practice. So, a very stiff old-fashioned and what about you?"

"A jalapeno marg, please," the friend said, alternating a glance between them.

Brie came up alongside Blake and took the drink orders. "How about some food on the house?" The friend's eyes widened as if she was pleased with the offer. Blake turned to Brie. "Let's put in two orders of al pastor tacos, tableside guac, and queso blanco."

"Wow, that sounds amazing. Thank you so much," the friend said.

"You didn't have to do that," Dr. Walsh said softly.

"It's all good."

"Hi, I'm Eliza's best friend and roommate, Allison," the friend said once Brie took the order to the kitchen. "And how do you know Eliza?"

Eliza, Blake said in her head, almost as if she'd forgotten that doctors had first names. The name suited her. It made her even more intriguing.

Blake tossed a glance at Dr. Walsh, trying to read how she should answer the question. By her firm stare and tight jaw, she knew she had to wing it.

"We matched on Tinder," Blake said.

"Oh really?" Allison looked back at her friend. Thank God she was just a friend. "You're back on the dating apps, and you didn't tell me? Why the hell did you invite me on a three-way date?"

Blake's grin grew, absolutely flattered that Dr. Walsh's best friend assumed that they were on a date. It boosted her confidence. Plus, watching Dr. Walsh's cheeks darken with a blush was highly entertaining. Blake tried her best to tame her budding grin.

"Forgive my best friend for this lapse in judgment," Allison said. "She's quite the catch, I promise. Please, take my seat—"

"Allison!"

Allison didn't listen. She offered Blake her seat. "And woo her. I'll entertain myself at the bar. Maybe chat with the redhead over there who's been eyeing us this whole time."

"Oh, the redhead is harmless," Blake said. "If you can get her to go back across the street to her friend, the next two rounds are on me."

Allison smiled. "Challenge accepted. Now sit. I insist."

Blake wasn't going to fight. Allison already pulled out the seat, and maybe sitting with Dr. Walsh would send Carrie the hint that they were really over.

Blake sucked in her grin as she watched Eliza struggle to make eye contact. A full-on blush on her cheeks traveled to her neck.

Blake couldn't believe she could make her blush like that. The extra red made her more adorable.

"Hi," Blake said and rested her cheek on her propped-up hand. "What a pleasant surprise."

"I'm sorry about Allison—"

"I like her. She makes you squirm. It's fun to watch."

"She's been making me squirm since freshman year of college."

Brie came back over and handed Blake a bottle of Corona with a lime wedge on the rim while Johnny, the tableside guac guy, pushed the cart over.

"This is Johnny," Blake said as he mashed three avocados in the mojocate before tossing in small bowls of pre-cut jalapenos, cilantro, tomatoes, and red onions. "One of my finest staff members. King of the Mojocate. Protector of the Freshest Guacamole Ingredients. First of His Name."

Eliza laughed and glanced at her old-fashioned as if trying to hide her smile, and the fact that Blake accomplished the feat made her proud of herself.

Johnny squeezed in two lime halves. "You're just saying this because you want me to take Alyssa's shift on Monday," he said with a grin.

"Maybe. We'll chat later."

He set the guac and the basket of chips on the table, winked at Blake, and pushed the cart away.

"Dig in," Blake said and gestured to the food.

Eliza grabbed one of the homemade tortilla chips that they made daily from corn tortillas fried and tossed in lime juice before being sprinkled with the perfect amount of salt. Eliza closed her eyes briefly at the first bite.

"Wow, this guac is delicious," she said and reached for a few more chips. "Allison might come back to no chips, and quite frankly, that's on her."

"She should know better. A basket of chips is everyone's weakness."

"Especially mine," Eliza said, reaching for another.

Blake laughed and pulled a sip of beer. "You haven't commented on my lack of a neck brace."

Eliza smiled as she studied her, and Blake had to take a large sip of Corona to ease the wave of warmth washing over her. "You look like an almost normal person outside of the hospital."

"Does Dr. Walsh approve?"

"Eliza. Call me Eliza. No white coat, no doctor, and I'm no longer your doctor."

Thank God because as much as she loved having Dr. Walsh as her doctor, she wanted to get to know her beyond the title and white coat. She hoped admiring her piercing eyes and the adorable curl in her blond hair didn't come off as creepy.

"Okay, Eliza," Blake said, and she liked how the informality sounded on her lips.

"And yes, I approve," Eliza said. "I hope you're taking it easy, which you probably aren't since you were on one leg earlier."

"You came in during a weak moment."

Brie brought out two servings of al pastor tacos, and the scent wafting from the plates smelled amazing. Blake was proud of her taco recipe, straight from Mexico City and the masterminds of her grandparents, who, in her eyes, had perfected the Mexican cuisine. Her love for cooking came from them. Every summer growing up, her brother, sister, and she had spent two weeks with their grandparents in Mexico City, and it was always the highlight of their summer. They would help out at Tito and Bela's food stall, and since Mexico City thrived on street food, it was how her grandparents made their living. Bela had taught them how to make homemade corn tortillas and how to perfect the tamale, though Blake still had yet to nail Bela's recipe. She would rather have her grandma's tamale than her own. Tito's al pastor tacos had been a hit in the city for three decades, and people from all over came in droves to taste them.

Blake caught Allison tossing a glance at them as if asking permission to come back. Luckily, Carrie was gone, and Blake had a safe path to the kitchen to finish the work that needed to be done before she went home. As wonderful as it was to see Eliza, she'd come with her friend, and Blake didn't want to take up too much of their night.

"I hope you and your friend enjoy," Blake said and gestured to the food. "I should let you continue your evening. But maybe you and I could resume our chat over drinks? Or dinner? After your next shift?"

Eliza thought about it for a moment. Blake held her breath waiting for her reply. This was her throwing herself out there one more time, and God, would she be disappointed if Eliza wasn't interested.

"Under one condition," Eliza said.

Blake's stomach dropped. Was she going to agree to drinks? Hopefully one-on-one this time so Blake could learn all the things she wanted to know about her. "What's that?" Blake asked.

"You can't call me Dr. Walsh and two feet on the ground at all times."

Blake stretched her hand across the table for a shake. It gave her a reason to touch Eliza, gave her one more thing to hang on to until they met again. Eliza hesitated for a moment, and when she accepted, her soft, gentle hands made something pass through Blake like a pinball zipping through a machine.

"Deal," Blake said. "Can I have your number so we can coordinate? I'll put you in as Eliza, I promise."

"I get off at eight tomorrow," Eliza said after they swapped numbers. "If that works for you."

Blake was shocked that Eliza was the one to suggest the next day. She'd made it three weeks. Twenty-four hours was nothing.

Blake snatched her beer bottle and hoisted herself back onto her crutches. "I'll find a nice bar near the hospital and will have a very stiff old-fashioned waiting," she said with a wink.

CHAPTER FOUR

Two surgeries, three hours of conferences, tons of paperwork and calls, and two rounds of fourteen patients later, Eliza met Blake at the bar.

The fact that she had something to do after her shift excited her. Something different than going home and eating some microwave meal while diving into studying for her boards. She had something to look forward to, and it helped guide her through her busy workday.

Blake didn't lie. She had an old-fashioned waiting for Eliza at their table. And God, did she look sexy, and she probably didn't even try. As Eliza walked over, some fluttering lodged in her gut. Blake wore a maroon, short-sleeved button-down, black jeans, and her hair was absolutely flawless. She'd thought the same thing when she'd stepped into Mezcal the night before. Now that Blake was free from a hospital bed, her transformation from recovering patient to normal person was clear, and she was stunning.

Blake Navarro smashed any bullshit belief that women had to be feminine in order to be beautiful. Her short hair was buzzed on the sides and textured on top; the longer hair parted to her left and dangled halfway down her forehead. It was thick and voluminous, and Eliza wondered how soft it would feel if she ran her fingers through it. When Blake smiled at her approaching the table, the smile had so much glow that little sweat beads formed on the back of Eliza's neck.

She was simply gorgeous, and somehow, Eliza had to get through a few rounds of drinks without sounding like an idiot. She'd been out of the dating scene for so long, she was rusty. How did she make conversation? How did she stop herself from staring at Blake's face for too long? How did she tame the blush?

"Wait, you really just worked a fourteen-hour shift?" Blake asked as Eliza slipped into her chair.

"I did. It was long, and this drink is going to do wonders." She took a sip of her strong old-fashioned. The warmth igniting her throat felt wonderful, easing the stresses of the day.

"And yet, you still look amazing."

Yes, the compliment joined forces with the whiskey and heated Eliza's cheeks. But she knew it was a line, one Blake probably used on a lot of women. Someone as attractive, charismatic, and confident as Blake had a not-so-little black book. Eliza was sure of it.

"Do you use that on all the girls?" Eliza asked and cocked an eyebrow.

Blake pulled back as if shocked by the callout. "What? No, I'm absolutely serious. I bet you're one of those women who glows after a grueling workout too."

"No, I look like a monster."

"Doubtful."

"How was your day?" Eliza said, trying everything to move on. Speaking of rusty, she'd never learned how to take a compliment, but she didn't have time at that moment to start. She needed her cheeks to go back to a normal color, and that was only possible by changing the subject.

Blake shrugged. "Good. Hugo and I drove down to Tijuana to grab food for the restaurant."

"In Tijuana?"

"Yeah. All of our ingredients come from Mexico. I want the experience to be as authentic as possible. We drive down once a week to pick up the purchase orders."

"So that's the secret of why those al pastor tacos are everything."

"It is." She winked, and Eliza felt it in her chest. "My grandparents had a taco stall at La Merced Market, which is one of the biggest and oldest markets in the city. It's like the beating heart of the Mexico City food scene. They bought all their ingredients from produce vendors at the market. They wanted the most authentic Mexico City taste, and you can't get more authentic than that. And I really liked that aspect of the food. I want to give my customers the same authenticity."

Eliza smiled. She loved that answer. Passion for what she did poured out of Blake, and Eliza was there to collect it. Passionate people intrigued her. "That's actually really cool," Eliza said. "Those tacos are phenomenal. I've been thinking about them all day. I can't imagine how great they tasted at your grandparents' stall."

"Amazing, and I'm glad you liked them."

"Allison texted me at work saying we needed to get them again soon."

"I wish I could take the credit for the recipe, but I can't. It was my grandparents'. I stole it from them."

"Are they the reason you got into cooking?"

"Definitely. My brother, sister, and I would spend two weeks down in Mexico City every summer, and our grandparents put us to work. There were so many customers at the market every day, it was like an adrenaline rush. You never stopped cooking. My brother and sister didn't like working at the stall, but my grandparents said it would teach them business, customer service, and history, and I'm so glad they gave us that experience because that's when I fell in love with it. The rush, the smells, the tastes, and enjoyment on people's faces as they ate what you cooked. It's amazing."

Eliza grinned behind her lowball glass at all the passion and enthusiasm Blake had when talking about her job and her family. "It seems like you really love your job."

"Oh, I do." Her smile was so wide and genuine. It was contagious. Her face glowed, and it highlighted her beautiful facial features: her straight white teeth, sparkling black eyes, and her perfectly shaped eyebrows.

The sweat beads on Eliza's neck grew larger the more Blake's smile grew. "It seems like the restaurant is doing incredibly well,"

Eliza said. "Have you told your grandparents that their al pastor tacos are the top tacos in San Diego?"

"Oh, yeah. They're ecstatic. We actually flew them up about three years ago to see for themselves. Got a stamp of approval, and that's more important to me than rankings from magazines." She took a sip of beer and ran her hands through the long part of her hair, pulling Eliza's gaze. Her hair fell perfectly back in place. For a simple movement, Blake sure made it look sexy. "So why a doctor?"

The comment snapped Eliza out of the trance. "What?"

"Why did you want to be a doctor? That was my story on why I wanted to be a chef. Surely you have a story on why you wanted to be a doctor."

Eliza sipped her drink to kill the pain that came with that loaded question. She hardly knew the woman and didn't want to spill her baggage and the trauma she'd gone through as a kid. That was the last thing she wanted. She wanted to hear more about Blake's love for cooking, more about her time in Mexico City. The last thing she wanted to do was talk about her past.

"That's a loaded question," Eliza said through a cough. She eased it with another taste of her drink.

"Oh God, I'm sorry. I didn't mean—"

Eliza raised her hand. "It's fine. Really."

"I expected an answer like you've always dreamed of it since being a kid or something."

"I think I wanted to be everything but a doctor when I was a kid. A teacher. A marine biologist. A lawyer. I was almost set on majoring in business because at eighteen, I thought owning a business as a woman defined badassery. Also, you can do so much with a business degree."

Blake hesitated for a moment, and her eyes softened. "But you didn't."

"But I didn't. I chose twelve years of schooling instead."

Eliza tried to ease the tension with a laugh, anything to shift them away from the memories taking over her mind. Anything that reminded her of her accident still had the ability to drown her thoughts and squeeze her throat and chest. She'd assumed that after years of therapy and even a bout of outpatient therapy she would have the ability to control the triggers. But she couldn't. Although the therapy had helped, it didn't eliminate it.

"I was in a really bad car accident when I was eighteen, and that really influenced it," Eliza said and pulled an encouraging sip.

"Oh, I'm so sorry. I didn't know—"

"It's okay, really."

Blake glanced at her bottle and picked the label. Eliza blamed herself for letting the accident dim Blake's vibrant, infectious grin so early in the night.

"I almost became a marine," Blake said.

"What?"

Blake chuckled and glanced back. "Yeah, I still can't believe it either. My older brother, Adrian, was a marine, and I idolized him. He was seriously the coolest, chillest guy I ever knew. When he joined, I wanted to join, which was crazy because I was twelve. Even after he died, I was still set on joining. Even talked to recruiters when I was seventeen—"

"He died? Oh my God, I'm so sorry."

"Yeah, he was killed in combat. Phantom Fury to be exact, the deadliest battle of the Iraq War." Blake shook her head. "He was twenty."

Eliza remembered the beautiful dog tag tattoo on her ribs. "Is that what your tattoo is? On your ribs?"

Blake nodded, and there was another shift, except something about this sullen moment was different than the one before, like the shift clicked them back in place. Eliza felt like she'd been camping out in left field since her accident, and then Blake unexpectedly joined her out there.

The smallest smile found its way to Blake's lips again. "You were supposed to be observing my broken ribs. Not my tattoo."

"Couldn't help it," she said, feeling the blush consume her face. "It was a beautiful tattoo." She took a moment to reflect on the newfound knowledge. How both their losses seemed to string them together in a way Eliza wasn't expecting at all. So she decided she would give Blake more. Maybe for the first time since the accident, she could talk to someone who was fluent in heartbreak and loss. "My girlfriend was in the car with me. I was driving. She was the passenger, and...well...she didn't make it."

Blake's face dropped. "I'm so sorry."

"So that's why I wanted to become a doctor. To make up for the life I couldn't save."

Blake reached out to grab Eliza's wrist. A jolt passed through her at the touch. It was comforting, the way Blake's stare held hers with empathy. She made Eliza feel seen for the first time since the accident. Violet and Allison were always there when she needed comfort, but they didn't know what it was like to go through something horrible like that. Violet could read all about it in the "Diagnostic and Statistical Manual of Mental Disorders," but it was one thing to memorize and another to know and understand.

Eliza raised her glass, and Blake retrieved her hand to join her. "To Tess and Adrian." Once the two cheered and took a sip, Eliza said, "So you never became a marine?"

Blake laughed and ran her hand through her hair again, and Eliza's stomach did that tugging thing. She wished she could rewind, watch, and repeat. What the hell was that hair thing about, and why did it affect her like that?

"No, turns out they didn't like gay people. Who would have thought?" Blake said facetiously. "Plus, I don't think my vision is good enough to drive a tank."

"You wanted to drive a tank?"

"Yeah," she said it like it should have been obvious. "How badass would that be?"

"Of course you wanted to drive a tank."

"But a tank is much safer than a motorcycle, right? All that bulletproof armor. The sheer size of it."

Blake was a few inches shorter than Eliza. Her hospital records listed her as five-three, a hundred and thirty-four pounds. A little thing in control of a monstrous tank? Eliza couldn't imagine it, but it was humorous to picture a small woman woman-handling a beast of a vehicle like that.

"Speaking of which," Eliza said, "how's the motorcycle? Dusty, I hope?"

"Gisele is doing fantastic. Want to go on a ride sometime?"

"Absolutely not."

"Oh, come on, we can take a nice cruise up the PCH. Watch the sunset."

Eliza lowered her drink. "Did you seriously bike over here?"

An impish grin grew over the bite on her lip. "You're cute when you get frustrated, you know that?"

Eliza knew Blake had noticed the heat crawling up her neck because she released her lip and allowed the smile to fully consume her face. Eliza attempted to cool herself down by taking another drink, then remembered whiskey did quite the opposite of that to her insides, so she sucked on the remnants of the ice cube.

"And when you blush," Blake added.

But apparently, the ice cube didn't help her one bit.

"I can't believe you named your motorcycle," Eliza attempted to divert.

"Gisele. She has a name, Eliza. Treat her with respect."

"Not when she did you dirty like that."

"But she's pretty. She can get away with it."

"I think you can do better."

"I have an Audi. Is that better?"

Eliza considered this. "Depends. What's the Audi's name?"

"Audo. Spelled A-u-d-o."

She laughed. "Clever."

They ordered another round of drinks, an old-fashioned for Eliza and another Corona for Blake, plus bruschetta for an appetizer. The second old-fashioned hit her quickly, and she celebrated and welcomed the feeling. Talking became easier. She had a list of questions to ask that she genuinely wanted answered. Blake's favorite food to make. Her favorite food from Mexico City. When was the last time she'd visited her grandparents? Where the hell had she grown-up?

Blake answered all her questions. Her favorite food to make was carne asada, and the food from Mexico City that she craved for days were tlacoyos...and Bela's tamales. She last saw her grandparents three years ago when they visited San Diego and said she was long overdue for a trip. She was born and raised in San Diego, went to culinary school in LA, making another thing they had in common that had less emotional weight tied to it.

"Hey, maybe we crossed paths in college," Blake said after Eliza told her that she went to USC. "Where did you go out?"

"I didn't," Eliza said with a laugh. "Premed kicked my ass. But the few times I caved and said, 'fuck it,' Allison and I went to Hollywood, West Hollywood, Venice—"

"If you were out in the Hollywoods, we had to have been at the same place at the same time. I even went to USC a couple times for some parties on the Row."

"I'm proud to say that I never went to a party on the Row."

Blake widened her eyes. "You missed out then. I had some of my most memorable—well, and not so memorable—nights over there. That's when the 'straight' sorority girls wanted to experiment, and I was there for it," she said, air quoting straight.

Eliza smiled, and she wasn't sure if it was because she was impressed with Blake or because she knew she was right about her and that little black book.

"And ninety-nine cent beers at 9-0?" Blake said while waggling perfect eyebrows.

"Okay, I did do that," Eliza said with a point, basking in the tipsy feeling that loosened her up. "I needed some incentive to bury myself in books to pass my tests. Ninety-nine cent beers were that incentive."

"I love it," Blake said.

Eliza leaned back in her seat and let out a pleasant sigh. Thinking about how much time she'd devoted to studying in college and comparing it to the fun she was having currently, she wondered if she'd missed out on a lot of fun, fun she really needed at that dark time in her life. "God, I don't remember the last time I got all liquored up on a Tuesday," Eliza said, feeling the smile take over. But she didn't hold it back. She let it roam wild.

"Well, I'm flattered that you decided to get liquored up with me," Blake said. "Doctors need to have fun too."

"Not when they have boards to take next summer."

The server brought the check, and Eliza had to admit that she was bummed at how quickly the night had flown by.

Blake pulled out her wallet and placed a card on the receipt.

"No, no, no," Eliza said and snatched it, but Blake's reflexes were quick. When she grabbed the checkbook, her fingers grazed Eliza's, but Eliza didn't flinch. Maybe without the two drinks, the spark that passed through her would have jolted her from the sudden touch and scared her back into her seat. But the whiskey had turned into confidence, like a chemical reaction, and the feeling that zigzagged through Eliza didn't scare her at all. She welcomed it. "Let me contribute, please," she said.

Blake pulled it out of her grip, and Eliza was more upset about the loss of Blake's fingertips than losing the check she really wanted to help with. "No. I told you I wanted to treat you to a drink."

"You already did. Last night, remember? And you treated me to tableside guac and the best tacos I've ever had, plus two drinks tonight—"

"You're a little chatterbox when you're tipsy, huh?" Blake closed the book with her card popping out, keeping it protected on her end of the table. "Now I know how to get you out of your shell."

"Stop changing the subject. Please let me pay."

"Nope."

"You already got me a drink last night."

"Yeah, but now I'm treating you tonight because you worked fourteen hours and deserve it. Now humor me and accept the drinks."

Eliza crossed her arms when the server took the receipt, adding a little pout for comedic relief, hoping she could see Blake's dimples again and hear her laugh. And it worked. She considered that as much of a victory as contributing to the check.

"How are you getting home?" Blake asked when the two stepped outside. "You need a ride?" She dangled her car keys. "Courtesy of Audo, not Gisele."

"I'm taking the bus—"

"The bus? No. Let me drive you home. It will save time."

Eliza thought about it. For years after her accident, she'd had panic attacks whenever she got into a car, so she avoided them like the plague unless there was no other option, like taking a cab to the airport. It wasn't until she'd started therapy and spent three months in outpatient therapy the summer after college that she'd learned to at least outgrow her fear of being a passenger in a car. She'd been in a car plenty of times at night since her accident, but there had yet to be a time when her heart didn't race, or she didn't find herself clenching the hand grips.

But when Blake offered, Eliza swallowed the fear that had lodged in her throat. The extra ten minutes with Blake was worth the threat of a heightened pulse. At least this time, it wouldn't only be fear racing her heart. She had the excitement of being around Blake—being closer to Blake—to dilute the aching.

They took their time as Blake crutched through the parking lot. Eliza was grateful for the slow pace because it bought her more time. She wished they could have had another hour. She never felt like their conversation was forced, and even during the brief lulls, Eliza never felt awkward. Talking to Blake was easy, and if Eliza had found that with other women, she wouldn't have stayed away from dating so much. Just two rounds with Blake made her more open to the idea of dating.

You should ask her out, Eliza told herself as she opened the driver door for Blake since both her hands were out of commission.

"What a gentlewoman," Blake said, hopping on her good foot to get inside.

Eliza took the crutches and placed them in the back. "I try."

In between directing Blake, Eliza tried distracting her brain with another thought, one that would push back the fear to the forgotten part of her mind, encouraging her to muster the confidence to ask Blake out. *Ask her if she wants to get drinks again. Tell her that you owe her a few. Or maybe a dinner. It's not that hard. It's all in your head.*

As Blake pulled into Eliza's apartment complex parking lot, Eliza exhaled and loosened her grip. As she flexed her tight fingers, the words she'd prepared danced on the tip of her tongue. This was why she avoided women and dating since Tess. In all of Eliza's thirty-one years on Earth, she'd never made the first move.

"I'm glad we did this," Eliza said once the car was in park. "Most interesting Tuesday I've had in a long time."

She faced Blake, and the close proximity made it possible to catch the scent of her cologne. A subtle woodsy smell that had her wanting more. But she stayed rooted in place.

"We need to get you out more," Blake said.

"We really do. Maybe, um…" *You can do this. Just ask. Stop acting like an inexperienced teenager.* "Maybe we can find another time to get me out. Distract me from studying for my boards."

Blake smiled, Eliza's perfect reward for putting herself out there and suggesting another meetup. "You have my number. My work is very limited these days, so I have almost all the time in the world to distract you from studying. Or if you need help, I'm free as well. I'm free to do whatever."

Eliza blushed and glanced at her lap as her smile widened. "Okay, this is all good to know."

She didn't know why she hesitated before opening the passenger door, but she did. The moment that passed through the Audi reminded Eliza of the thrilling anticipation in high school, sitting in a car after a wonderful night out, wondering what the hell it all meant. Blake's stare lingered on her, taking in her features, and Eliza's grin grew with each passing moment.

"You have the best smile," Blake said softly.

A compliment like that should have filled Eliza up and colored her neck and face in a blotchy red. Instead, it felt like needles dipped in fire pricking up her back until it choked her chest.

"You have the best smile," Tess said. Eliza peeled her focus off the road to look at her. Eliza kissed the back of her hand, and a spotlight highlighted Tess's face in white.

Eliza opened the passenger door, desperately needing air to untangle the knots coiling inside her. "Um…thanks again for the drinks," Eliza said, her words staggering out all at once. "I'm sorry, I have to go."

She bolted out of the car and had a panic attack in her room.

❖

August 6, 2007

Sheets of rain pelted the windshield, competing against track six of the mix CD Tess had made Eliza at the beginning of the summer. "Stolen" by one of their favorites, Dashboard Confessional, blasted through the speakers. The energy from the concert still ran through their veins, they belted the chorus of the song in their horrible singing voices, and the smell of summer and rain permeated the car. Tess loved the rain and always insisted on cracking the window to smell it.

"This song is much better than 'She Will Be Loved,'" Eliza said, catching Tess's reaction before she flitted her eyes back on the highway. She knew that would cause Tess to react, and Tess did. Her bottom lip with the lip ring hung at the same time her honey-colored eyebrows furrowed. She playfully hit Eliza's arm.

"This is a really good song but so is my song," Tess said. "You're just biased because you think Adam Levine is overrated."

"I do. All his songs sound the same, and I'm shocked you're not with me. Are you sure you're not straight?"

"I'm one-hundred-percent positive. How many times have we watched the second season of *The OC* solely to watch Olivia Wilde make out with Mischa Barton?"

They spent too many nights at the library, tucked away in the history section watching the box set on Tess's portable DVD player. It was one of the few places they could be together in their hometown. It was practically their home base for not only planning scholarships and where to go to college but for simple things such as watching their favorite teen soap together.

"Probably at least ten times," Eliza replied.

"And why is that?"

"Because Olivia Wilde is single-handedly the most beautiful woman in the world. Well, second to you, of course."

Tess smirked. "Nice save. You know, every time I hear this song, I think of you."

Eliza stole another glimpse at her. "I think of you too."

"And how much I love you."

She smiled before looking back at the road. "I love you too."

"Makes it even better that Olivia Wilde's in the music video, right?"

"It was like Dashboard Confessional made that music video for us."

"I think they did."

Eliza exited the highway onto the dark, country roads. Exit 22, the one she always took. She'd been on this road so many times that she knew every twist and turn, stop sign, and stoplight. The rain cascading sideways made her decelerate to fifty miles an hour, the speed most people went on the route. The rain was heavier than when they left the concert, and if Eliza had known how hard it would pick up, she would have waited it out in the parking lot, enjoying Tess next to her, the CD, and the wonderful smell of the rain. They could have probably gotten away with a steamy make-out session too.

The one thing they'd both said they would miss about Ohio was the rain. Before their parents found out about them, and they'd been allowed at each other's homes, Tess would pull Eliza outside to dance around in it. Eliza secretly hated it. She hated the feeling of wet fabric sticking to her skin, but she did it because Tess loved it, and she loved Tess. She loved watching her girlfriend stick her arms out, twirl around, and allow the splattering raindrops to fall on her face as if there were no problems in the world that could ruin the moment. Honestly, those moments shielded the dark reality that lurked around the corner.

Ever since Tess's mom had caught them kissing the summer before, the Wares had forbidden them from being together, and Eliza's parents had told her to respect their wishes. They had no choice but to sneak around now, and that meant that Eliza couldn't watch Tess enjoy something as simple and innocent as the rain.

Until now.

They knew that moving to California meant sacrificing the rain, but Tess had said, "Dancing in the rain will be more special then." And Eliza couldn't wait for their first California rainstorm.

The country roads were dark even on the clearest night, but the rain made Eliza anxious. They were about three miles from the

K-Mart where she and Tess always met up, a neutral spot so their parents wouldn't ever find out they'd been together.

Tess cranked the window down an extra inch, and it pulled Eliza's attention so she could watch her stare out the window and take in the sights of the passing trees, wiggling her fingers out the window. Tess's smile was wide, and her long, honey-colored hair blew behind her, giving Eliza a perfect view of all the beauty that made her insides swell like a balloon. Seventeen more days until they finally embarked on a new journey, a life out of their parents' control. Then, they would be free from living a life confined to their parents' insular—and heteronormative—expectations. Seventeen more days until they could breathe in a world that would finally be theirs.

"I still can't believe we did it," Eliza said as she combed through all the progress they'd made in the last year.

"Can't believe what?"

"That we got all our scholarships, we worked our asses off to get good grades, to get into the same college, and to convince USC to let us be roommates. We did it without our parents finding out."

Tess laughed. "My parents think that you're going to Ohio State. My little Buckeye." She grabbed Eliza's hand and kissed it.

"And mine think you're going to Bowling Green."

"Wow, we really did it, babe," Tess said. "Little do they know, we're going to be roommates and have all the privacy in the world to fuck."

Eliza's cheeks warmed, and she squeezed Tess's hand as the thoughts of unlimited privacy washed through her. She was eighteen, hormonal, and her girlfriend was the most beautiful girl she'd ever seen. One mention of sex, and Eliza considered finding a secluded spot to squeeze in a session. "Stop it."

"Can't and won't."

Eliza wished so much that they could hop on that plane tomorrow and go. California was so close yet so far away. That "exotic" world they'd grown to love and fantasized about from watching *Laguna Beach* and *The OC* was about to be a short drive away. After their hell of a year, they were both so ready to leave. Eliza smiled thinking about everything they'd overcome. Together.

"You have the best smile," Tess said softly. Eliza peeled her eyes off the road to look at her. She kissed the back of Tess's hand before lowering it to the center console, rubbing her thumb over the Claire's ring on her left finger.

Seventeen days until they started their lives. One more year until they flew to Massachusetts—the only state that allowed gay marriage—to celebrate their fifth anniversary by getting married.

Bright white lights cut through the thick darkness and highlighted Tess's gorgeous face. Her hazel eyes and her lip ring sparkled. Her beauty warmed Eliza. She squeezed Tess's hand, telling her that she loved her without words, and when Tess squeezed back, Eliza's smile grew even more.

When Eliza finally processed what the white lights were, she swerved the car to the right and felt the rain carry them off the road.

Every August sixth, Eliza went to the beach. All nineteen songs Tess had put on that last mix CD aged into its own playlist on Spotify and played through her headphones. She'd been there for an hour and had listened to the playlist once already since claiming her spot in the sand. She closed her eyes and felt the breeze rolling off the waves and into her hair. She imagined it was Tess's fingers combing through her hair like they used to when Eliza laid her head on Tess's lap. Cotton candy clouds hung overhead against the bright yellow horizon, meeting the indigo night sky. That was what Tess used to call those types of clouds. They had been her favorite kind, and it had been the first Eliza had ever heard of someone having a favorite kind of cloud.

So why on this August sixth, the thirteenth-year anniversary, were they out in full bloom?

Eliza had never been a religious person. The Wares were. They'd even forced it on Tess by making her repent for her gayness. During the summer they were broken up, Tess had spent three full days a week shadowing the priests and the nuns at St. Teresa of Avila, where she'd learned all about how the sinners—aka, the homosexuals, according to the clergy—went straight to hell. Eliza had never seen herself as a sinner, and neither had Tess, until the clergy took turns brainwashing her with sacred hate. All Eliza had wanted to do was love her, brighten her day, cuddle her when she was feeling down, make her laugh and smile, protect her from pain and sadness.

How was that so wrong?

If there was a God, why would he take an eighteen-year-old in a blink of an eye? Any questions she had about the existence of God were crumpled in her Honda Civic that night.

However, the thirteenth anniversary brought a rare rainy morning and a cotton-candy-clouded evening, sparking a flicker of wonder of something beyond this world. The rain and clouds had to be more than a coincidence, and in those moments on the beach when Eliza started to feel like she was pulling away from the world again, she refused to believe it was anything but a sign. In those moments, she truly wanted to believe something more powerful existed because whatever that thing was, it gave her Tess in the form of soft breezes, morning rainstorms, and cotton candy clouds.

She wondered if Blake's compliment had hit her so hard because she was already mentally preparing for the anniversary. She had been for weeks. She could feel the weight threatening from a few days out. When late July came around, the anxiety started snaking around her spine and heat squeezed her lungs, and the feelings gradually became more painful until August sixth came. During that time, the nightmares became more frequent and vivid too. She didn't remember the accident. One minute she was holding Tess's hand, and the next, she was in the ICU hooked up to machines, her neck in a brace, her body writhing in sharp pains. According to doctors, she'd only been knocked out for a few minutes and had been talking to the EMTs and the firemen as they'd used the Jaws of Life to extract her from the vehicle after it had hydroplaned into a tree. But no memory remained. Her only snapshots of the accident came in the form of nightmares.

And now the guilt continued to weigh on her over how quickly she'd ran out of Blake's car the other night. Eliza couldn't be too surprised. Anytime a woman gave her some kind of compliment, her walls went up. She couldn't help but wonder if her subconscious had triggered a panic attack as a way to push her away from Blake right as they'd started to share a moment. Or was it because August sixth was around the corner, and whenever the date loomed, she felt connected to Tess more than at any other time of the year.

By the time she was ready to leave, the cotton candy clouds had morphed into dark reds and purples, a sign from Tess that she should be getting home. She had to leave the beach before the night fully encapsulated her. Although she'd made significant progress over the years toward being able to ride in a car at night, it was all thrown out the window in early August.

How was she ever going to find love again if she couldn't handle someone telling her that she had a nice smile?

When she got back to her apartment, she floated around the kitchen, half her mind in the present and the other half in Tallulah, Ohio, circa 2007. Somehow, she was able to make a cup of chamomile tea, a remedy that would hopefully ease her anxiety and treat the insomnia that had been troubling her for the past couple of days. It was her first resort before she took a prescribed Xanax.

She was so zoned out nursing the warm tea that cascaded down her throat so soothingly, she didn't even notice Allison slip into the seat across from her until she said her name.

Eliza covered her racing heart and set her mug down. "Jesus, you scared me."

"I'm sorry. You were somewhere else."

"Yeah, sorry."

"How are you doing?"

Eliza forced herself to snap back to the present in an apartment in Hillcrest, San Diego, a much safer place than 2007 in Tallulah, Ohio. She shrugged. "Not well."

This was Allison's twelfth August sixth with her, and she was a pro at handling it. Her lips thinned as she grabbed Eliza's wrist. "You want to talk about it?"

The tension balled in Eliza's throat. She eased it with another sip of tea and shook her head.

"Need me to make you anything?"

"I think that would make it worse, honestly."

"Hey." Allison playfully pushed Eliza, who forced the smallest grin at her attempt at teasing. "I was going to suggest some takeout. Like Indian or Chinese. Oh," she said as if something came to mind. "We could always Grubhub Mezcal. Eh? Those delicious tacos and guac whipped up by a hot chef?"

Eliza rolled her eyes. "No, that's definitely not an option."

"You still haven't texted her?"

"And say what? Sorry for the awkward moment after you told me I had the best smile?"

"Well, not quite. I was thinking more along the lines of asking her to get drinks again and then explaining yourself. Eliza?"

Allison snapped her out of a tumbling path into the dark corners of her mind. "Hmm?"

"You're here, and you're okay, all right?"

Eliza wrapped her hands around her forehead. This was so pathetic. Thirteen years later, eight years of therapy, three months of outpatient therapy, and she was still broken.

She clutched the Claire's ring that hung on her silver necklace chain. It was the only thing she had left of Tess, and she'd felt it resting against her chest the whole day. She'd been wearing the ring since Tess had given it to her two months before she'd died on the night of their high school graduation, the night they'd made the promise to get married.

"It's hard to even think about Blake right now when I can feel Tess," Eliza said, moving the ring back and forth on the chain. "This weight in my chest has been here for a week. I keep having dreams about her. She still has a hold on me."

"Maybe you should stop listening to that playlist she made for you. You're just encouraging all those memories."

"Yeah, you're probably right."

"And I still think you should text the hot chef."

Eliza slid her hands down her face, grunting as she did. "The accident shouldn't be intertwining with Blake. She has nothing to do with it or Tess or my fucking hometown, yet it's squeezing itself in the way. It always pops up when I'm trying to get to know someone."

"You're being too hard on yourself," Allison said. "You said Blake lost her brother, right? I'm sure she would understand if you were honest with her."

"I don't want to talk about the accident. I just want to have drinks with a woman without it pulling up a seat next to us."

"Then don't let it hold you back. I bet that you're dwelling on it much more than she is. Don't run away from this one. Not until she at least gives you a reason."

"Yeah, you're right."

"I know I am." Allison slid Eliza's phone over. "It's been three days. If you wait any longer, it might be too late."

After so many lectures from Violet and Allison about lowering her guard, allowing herself to be vulnerable around other women, and stopping herself from running away, this was another test to see if she was truly committed to having a love life. The fact that she hadn't stopped thinking about Blake since she'd first stopped by Mezcal was a sign.

So for the first time in a long time, Eliza acted on her feelings.

❖

When Blake had gotten a text from Eliza the day before, asking to meet at Mezcal, she was excited and relieved.

She'd been wondering about Eliza ever since she'd awkwardly scurried out of the car the other night. Blake wasn't really sure what that was about, but she was starting to come to terms with Eliza's endearing awkwardness and quirkiness. She didn't really think anything of it until three days passed without a single text, and then she'd started to worry what she'd said or done that had made Eliza uncomfortable. But then out of nowhere, Eliza asked to meet Blake after her shift, and Saturday got that much more exciting.

The hostess directed Eliza to a circular booth tucked in the back of the restaurant where Blake was waiting and resting her foot. She had an old-fashioned waiting for her.

"You're spoiling me with these drinks," Eliza said as she situated herself.

"Honestly, I have no idea what else you drink. You care to share so I can change it up?"

When Eliza bit her lip and looked skyward to think about it, Blake forced herself to suppress a grin. Somehow, after operating on people, caring for a number of patients, and being on her feet for hours, Eliza Walsh was still able to pull Blake's gaze and hold it tightly. Blake was truly astonished that someone could still radiate beauty after working ten-plus hours. She knew what she looked like after working in the kitchen all day. There was a reason she wore a black chef's uniform: to hide all the oil and stains that collected on the fabric. Her feet would be sore, she'd smell of oil, the day would be detailed on her face with dark circles under her eyes and a long frown. Eliza Walsh was an anomaly.

"I love margaritas," Eliza replied. "Any kind of beer. I'm a sucker for craft beer. I don't care if it's polarizing. I like what I like."

A sucker for craft beer? Blake's heart tugged pleasantly.

"I dropped the ball with the old-fashioned," Blake said. "I can drink it and get you something else."

Eliza raised her hand as she laughed. "It's fine. Trust me. Working fourteen hours and ending it with an old-fashioned hits the spot too."

Right as they took their first sips, Blake's Uncle Hugo came trotting over with a wide smile etched onto his face. He could have waited at least five more minutes to meet the famous doctor who'd saved her life, but it seemed he couldn't contain his excitement. Once Blake had told him she was coming into the restaurant to meet up with the doctor, his dark brown eyes went big, and he'd warned her that he had to meet her.

"You must be the miracle worker," Uncle Hugo exclaimed once he reached the booth. His voice was heavy and distinct. It could travel like his laugh.

"Eliza, this is my uncle Hugo, the owner."

She smiled and extended her hand. "Oh, hi. It's nice to meet you."

Hugo clasped her hand with both of his. "No, it's nice to meet you. Thank you so much for sending her back to us. Really."

Eliza stole a glance at Blake and then turned back to Hugo. "That's what I'm here for."

He retrieved his hands and placed one on Blake's shoulder. "I don't know what we would have done if we'd lost another Navarro. I don't know what your parents would have done, Blake."

Her family really loved reminding her of the terror her accident had put everyone through. She already felt bad for creating another scare. It didn't matter if seventeen years had passed since Adrian had died, there wasn't a day when they weren't reminded of the hole in the family.

Uncle Hugo was like her second father. Her cousin Marc was her second brother, and Marc and Adrian had been best friends, practically brothers. Her family was so tightly knit, without one of them, their family crumbled, and that was what had happened when Adrian died. Now that they had most of their lives restacked, Blake's accident had been like a bottom Jenga piece that had been pulled out. She already felt awful, and constantly getting nagged about it wouldn't undo anything.

"Uncle Hugo, let's save the sullen moments for later on in the evening," Blake said and forced a thin smile to ease the awkwardness.

Hugo turned to Eliza. "Whatever you want, it's on the house."

Right as Eliza opened her mouth, Blake said, "How about two orders of the al pastor tacos and another round of the IPA we have on tap? She's a big fan of the tacos."

"My parents' proud recipe," Hugo said. "I'll put in an order."

He winked and headed into the kitchen. Once they were alone again, Eliza's jaw set, causing Blake to laugh. She was starting to love how animated Eliza was. Seeing her react quickly, getting embarrassed over little things that she shouldn't have been embarrassed about, was highly entertaining.

And freakin' adorable.

"No, this is *not* on the house," Eliza insisted. "I'll be buying these tacos and these drinks myself."

"Okay, whatever you say."

"What? Why are you saying it like that?"

"Because you're not going to convince my uncle. I come from a very stubborn family, you know."

"Great, there's more of you," she said with a teasing eye roll that made Blake snicker again.

"And I'm one of the easiest ones to deal with. So what's up? You wanted to talk?"

"I do." Eliza pulled a sip as if she needed it to get her words out. "I, um, I came here to apologize."

Blake frowned. "Apologize for what?"

"For the other night." She focused on the orange peel floating in her drink. "For running out so awkwardly and abruptly. I'm really sorry."

"You mean in the car?" Blake asked, and Eliza nodded. "It's fine. I didn't really think anything of it, but since we're on the topic now, was something wrong? Did I say or do something wrong?"

"No, no, no, not at all. Nothing was wrong."

"Then why apologize?"

Eliza considered this for a moment. "It hasn't been a good week. I'm just a little sensitive right now."

Blake furrowed her eyebrows. She'd seen Eliza twice during the week and each time, she'd seemed perfectly fine. "Did something happen?"

Eliza looked at her lap. "Remember that accident I told you about?"

"Yeah…"

"The anniversary was yesterday. It's always a really hard time for me, and, well, it really hit me all at once the other night. That's why I ran away. I can't really explain it."

"Hey, you don't have to. It's okay," Blake said. As a reflex, her hand moved halfway to Eliza's arm to give her an empathetic touch, but Blake stopped herself. "I'm really sorry. You want to talk about it?"

She gave Blake a thin smile. "Thank you, but no, I don't. I've been thinking about it for weeks, and it's the last thing I want to do."

"For what it's worth, I know what it's like. When my brother's anniversary comes around, it messes me up too. It's like it knocks you down all over again."

"Right? How many anniversaries have to pass for us to be somewhat stable on that day?"

"When you find out, let me know."

She flashed Blake a knowing smile. "I will."

Blake struggled the whole month of November. The month started with Día de los Muertos, which was the easiest day because in Mexican culture, they celebrated the belief that loved ones who passed awoke and spent the day alongside them. It was a celebration of life, not death. It wasn't until Adrian had died that her parents had decided to fully embrace their heritage.

Blake's mother, Sandra, was third generation Mexican on her father's side and German on her mother's side, so the day didn't hold as much significance until she'd met Blake's father, Luis, who grew up celebrating the day with his parents. After Adrian died, the Navarros turned the mantel in the dining room into the ofrenda, an altar that honored the dead and provided what they needed for their spirits to continue their journey.

Although Adrian's marine photo, folded American flag, and dog tags sat on the mantel all year long, the Navarros added their favorite pictures of him, lit candles, and left out a pitcher of water at his table seat along with a plate of pan de muerto, Bela's tamales, and his favorite food, sopes. While the rest of the family ate, they shared their favorite Adrian stories. It was a day Blake had learned to appreciate. She felt connected to Adrian more than ever, rediscovering those lost pictures she'd avoided the rest of the year, allowing herself to reminisce on her favorite memories of her brother, and watching her family laugh at the mention of his name rather than become silent.

On Día de los Muertos, Adrian filled the room. Her family felt complete again. On November eleventh, Veteran's Day, and Thanksgiving, the Navarro household felt even emptier than it was on the normal days of the year. All of November held significant weight to her and her family.

Eliza didn't need to explain herself. Blake completely understood.

"How about we enjoy these drinks then?" Blake said. "Let's try to end this week on a somewhat positive note."

"And that involves drinking?" Eliza asked with a small smile.

"Yes. Do you have a better idea?"

She thought about it. "No, I don't. An old-fashioned always hits the spot."

"I'm just glad I get another drink with you. Lucky me."

"This is why I need to buy you a drink."

"You're going to have to fight Hugo on that. He'll insist this is all on the house."

"Blake, this can*not* be on the house again."

Blake smiled, completely amused at the live entertainment that was the blush crawling up Eliza's neck.

Hugo emerged from the kitchen, eyes rounded and smile wide. Blake loved her uncle dearly, but sometimes, he had no clue of when to stay away. Couldn't he see how gorgeous the woman across from her was? He should have known better than to keep interrupting his lesbian niece when a gorgeous doctor was sitting with her.

"Blake, I just got off the phone with your father," Hugo said. "I told him that the miracle doctor is having drinks with you. And now he wants to treat her to a dinner. Right here."

"What? No, I can't accept that," Eliza said. "I'm not a Good Samaritan off the street. I'm just a doctor—"

Hugo patted Eliza's shoulder. "But you're not just a doctor. You saved our Blake. We're forever in your debt. I won't take no for an answer."

"But it's literally my job—"

"You know he's not going to leave until you accept, right?" Blake said, laughing.

"We can make you whatever food you like. We have a very versatile chef." Hugo hooked his thumb at Blake, and she smiled and waved.

"Hugo, that's really sweet of you. But you guys have already treated me. This is the fourth offer—"

"I don't know how many times my niece has treated you, but the family has yet to do it. So that doesn't count."

"He has a point," Blake said.

Eliza's face was bright red. "I can't accept it—"

"If you don't accept the dinner right now, I'm going to have to call Blake's parents, and they're much more difficult than me."

"Much," Blake added. "Worse than both of us combined. Take the settlement."

Finally, Eliza let out a defeated sigh. "You do realize you're climbing up the ranks as one of the most difficult families I've dealt with?"

Hugo put a hand over his chest. "We'll take that with great pride. I'll tell my brother you've accepted."

When Hugo walked away, Blake let out a bellowing laugh as Eliza shook her head and took a long gulp of her drink.

"Stop," she said, directing a finger at Blake, trying to hide her smile behind her lowball glass.

"I can't. It's funny."

"It's not."

"But it is. I see that smile of yours. And your face is brighter than a fresh tomato."

Once the tacos came, Blake noticed how she and Eliza squeezed into the center of the half-circle booth. Apparently, Eliza was too preoccupied with the delicious tacos and round of IPAs to notice that the space between them had disappeared, and at one point, Eliza's warm and smooth leg rested against hers. Blake didn't want to move, worried that Eliza would notice and retrieve her leg. She wanted to marvel at the feeling of the smallest part of Eliza brushed up against her body. She wanted to let herself cave into the strong pull. Just for a moment.

Eliza rested back against the booth, tapping out once she'd finished her last taco. "This is the last time I'm accepting free food. When can I finally treat you to something, huh?"

Blake rested her cheek on her palm. "I don't know. You tell me."

Eliza pulled herself up and imitated Blake with her chin on top of her propped-up hand, making Blake's insides catch fire. The tension between them was almost palpable, and she still had so much more Eliza Walsh to discover, so much more time for the tension to thicken, and she was ready for it.

"This dinner that you're being forced to cook for me doesn't count," Eliza said.

"Of course not. And I'm not being forced. I'm happy to do it."

"Okay, then." Eliza tapped her chin and looked upward. "What kind of food don't you like?"

"I like all food. Even vegan food."

"That doesn't help."

"No, it should be easy. I like all the foods. Now woo me and pick something good."

The chin taps continued, and the rush ballooned in Blake's midsection. It threatened to color her cheeks, and taking advantage of Eliza's skyward look, Blake cooled herself with another sip of beer to hopefully wash away the redness. She thought about how wonderful it would have felt to run into the freezer for a second to get some temporary relief from the consistent lust that had been pulsating through her ever since Eliza had sat down.

"It has to be nice enough to make up for all four occasions," Eliza said. "Because none of them were necessary at all."

"One of them was necessary. The second and third because I was in a good mood. The dinner is my dad and uncle. Don't blame me."

"Well, I'm going to. So now I want to take you out and make it up to you."

Blake sucked in her lip and sat upright. "Eliza Walsh, are you asking me out on a very nice date?"

For starters, she wanted to make sure this was where they were heading. They'd met up for two drink dates, plus whatever she wanted to call Blake's family organizing a dinner for Eliza. She wanted to make sure that what she was feeling was what Eliza was feeling: the push and pull of whatever was blossoming between them. Blake wasn't dumb. She knew the signs when a woman was attracted to her, but she'd been screwed over in the past, and it couldn't hurt to make extra sure she wasn't being led on.

And secondly, she asked the question because she wanted to see Eliza struggle with hiding her blush.

That kind of cuteness would never get old.

It worked like a charm; Eliza's face turned the color of a tomato again. "Um, well…" She paused and thought about it for a moment, and once it seemed to hit her, she straightened and met Blake's gaze again with more confidence than a second before. "Yes…yes I'm asking you out on a date."

Blake had to tame her pride. She'd somehow gotten the incredibly beautiful and adorable Dr. Eliza Walsh to ask her out.

"I gladly accept," Blake said as she felt her cheeks turn a traitorous red, refusing to remain coy during all of this.

"How about we talk about it whenever this dinner happens?" Eliza said and then pulled two twenties out of her purse. "You're taking this whether you like it or not. For the drinks and a large tip for Hugo."

"Don't boost his ego. And yes, we can talk about it at dinner. When is your next off day?"

"Saturday."

"Then I'll talk to my family, and I'll text you when we figure out the final plans."

"Sounds good. Just please, don't go all out."

Blake smiled, and her heart didn't stop skipping for the rest of the evening.

CHAPTER FIVE

Okay, Eliza did tell Blake to not go all out, but she didn't know it was impossible for Blake *not* to go all out when it came to cooking for someone she liked.

She got to Mezcal early in the morning to prep the food and challenged herself to whip up a feast even with her crutches. She had the whole kitchen to herself, a sparkling pristine kitchen that she made sure her staff cleaned diligently every night because she wasn't about to be exposed by the health department…or worse, Gordon Ramsay. An empty kitchen was like her blank canvas. With her travel mug of coffee following her everywhere she hopped, she blasted some seventies rock from her Bluetooth speaker, the kind of music her dad had always played when she was a kid: Pink Floyd, The Who, and Bruce Springsteen, plus some seventies folk rock like James Taylor, Simon and Garfunkel, and Bennett and Sons.

She knew Eliza wouldn't approve of her hopping around the kitchen to cook all the food, and her nagging did repeat in her head as Blake whipped up the mise-en-place. She was mindful of every step and pulled up a seat at the counter to chop, sauté, fry, shred, and marinate the ingredients, mostly while sitting down.

The menu needed to impress Eliza. She knew Eliza was already impressed with the al pastor tacos, and of course, those would be making an appearance, but she wanted to showcase more of her work, her art, her passion. Her grandparents showed their gratitude through their cooking, and that was something Blake had taken to heart. Eliza had asked for simple, but Blake wasn't going to give her that. No, she was going to make homemade corn tortilla chips, salsa roja, and queso fundido, and when dinner came closer, she would sneak back into the kitchen to make fresh guacamole. Eliza said chips were her weakness, so Blake made probably too many, but one of the many great things about chips was that they made perfect leftovers. She shredded the pork to make the al pastor meat, and the skirt steak soaked in her special marinade until it was time to grill. She whipped up Tito's delicious Mexican rice, cooked in caldo de tomate. Then it was time to grill the plantains, attempt Bela's amazing tamales, and then the sopes, Adrian's favorite. Every summer, Tito and Bela would greet Adrian, Blake, and Jordan for their two-week visit with plates of tamales and sopes, and Blake and Jordan had to fight with Adrian so he didn't eat all of them. He usually won. He was older, taller, stronger, and had a bottomless pit for a stomach.

Once Blake finished making all the food—plus churros for dessert—she plopped in her office chair to rest her leg. She'd conquered the kitchen with two crutches and one foot in a cast and no added injuries.

She loved being back in the kitchen. It gave her purpose again.

Her family took over Mezcal's second level that was mostly used for private parties, but for the evening, it was going to hold her family: her parents, Jordan, Hugo, and her cousin, Marc. When Eliza walked through the double glass doors in a royal blue sundress, Blake's breath hitched. Their gazes locked, and a fluttering started in Blake's stomach and bubbled up to her chest. Somehow, Eliza got more beautiful every time Blake saw her, and she wondered if she would ever reach the max limit of beauty or if she would constantly raise the bar.

Right as Blake gave her a welcoming smile and reached for the crutches to go greet her, her mom practically pranced over to Eliza with arms held wide and stole Blake's thunder.

"Oh my God, we are so thrilled to see you again, Dr. Walsh," her mom said and pulled Eliza in for a hug.

"Please, call me Eliza."

"Yeah, guys, she has a very strict rule," Blake said to her family. "If she's not wearing a white coat, she's not a doctor."

Eliza flashed her a small grin before letting her gaze fall back on Blake's mom.

"Then let's skip all the formalities together, Eliza. You can only call me Sandra, and I won't accept anything else. Thank you so much for saving my baby girl's life."

"Mom, you're being too much," Blake said. Her family was very affectionate, and it had benefited her growing up knowing she had so much love given to her, which meant she had so much love to give someone else. But at this moment, they needed to tone it down so they didn't scare away the guest of honor.

"I don't care," her mom said and waved. "This woman saved your life, and we're forever in her debt."

"That's not true," Eliza said. "It's part of my job." She lifted two bottles of wine out of her canvas bag. "I brought these so I wouldn't come empty-handed but then questioned if wine and tacos even went together."

"Oh, that's so sweet of you," her mom said and took the two bottles. "Wine goes with everything, in my opinion."

"I agree," Eliza said.

Once her mom moved out of the way, Blake crutched over, and the closer she got to Eliza, the warmer and more nervous she was. Eliza had this superpower, making Blake nervous, and all the words she wanted to say would turn to mush. Blake did well under pressure. It was part of her job, something she'd learned during culinary school and her externship at the two-star Michelin restaurant, Axis LA, where she'd worked under renowned celebrity chef, Serena DeLuca, and had cooked for a handful of celebrities. That experience had built her confidence when pressure weighed on her even outside the kitchen. It had expanded her tolerance for pressure and nerves.

But all of that came crashing down when Eliza stood in front of her in that beautiful sundress.

What was she going to tell Eliza again? Why was she standing in front of her?

"I told you that you didn't have to bring anything but yourself," Blake said softly, resting her hand on the small of Eliza's back as she leaned in toward a familiar fruity scent.

"I'm sorry, but I couldn't listen to your rules," Eliza said.

"Never took you for the rebellious type."

"I guess I have my moments."

They plucked themselves into their own secretive moment away from the Navarros, which would probably be the only time they had a moment to themselves all evening, knowing her family's track record.

"Look at all that food waiting for you," Blake said and slipped her hand off Eliza's back to point to the plates of food spanning half the length of the empty second-floor bar.

"This doesn't look like a simple dinner."

"Simple is boring. Plus, this is what happens when I can't be in the kitchen for a long period of time. I was planning on making the al pastor and grilled skirt steak, but then I got carried away with the plantains, sopes, tamales, and churros." Blake shrugged and made an, "I'm in trouble," face. "Oops."

"That doesn't sound like taking it easy."

"I did. Trust me."

Eliza cocked an eyebrow. "I don't think I do."

Blake handed her a plate. "You get first dibs, Doc."

She raised a finger. "No Doc."

Everyone sat at the other end of the bar, Blake and Eliza taking the corner. Eliza didn't hesitate when taking a first bite, and that made Blake excited that she was eager to try everything. It might have been creepy to watch her taste each item, but how was Blake supposed to wait for feedback when she'd spent the whole morning cooking the food to impress her?

At the first bite of tacos, Eliza let out a soft moan that had Blake's mind spinning.

"This," Eliza said, pointing to the tacos, but Blake's mind was still lagging from three seconds before, replaying the murmur. Something Blake had created had pulled that beautiful sound from her.

She had to cook for Eliza again. It was her newest mission.

As everyone devoured the food and had second and thirds, Blake sat back and watched her family grill Eliza with a bunch of questions. Mostly her parents and Hugo asking about med school and where she was from. Turns out, she was from some small town in Ohio, a place that none of her family had ever been. Blake didn't know people were actually from Ohio. It was just a flyover state to get to New York City.

"Don't worry, you're not missing out," Eliza said. "Unless you like rollercoasters. We have the best amusement park, a definite must."

"Uh, can we backtrack?" Blake asked. "Did you just claim that Ohio, cornfield capital of the US, has a better amusement park than all the ones in California? Not to brag or anything, but we have everything. Beaches, mountains, deserts, the film industry, celebrities, a bunch of national parks, sports teams that win championships—"

Eliza raised a finger. "Rule one of being around an Ohioan: you never bring up their sports teams. We are known for our failures. It's called the Cleveland Curse. It's an actual thing."

"Oh, I know. I've watched the *30 for 30* on it. And we also have Lebron now so…"

Marc reached out for a fist pound. Blake pounded it. "Yeah, we do," he said.

"Wow. Salt in the wound," Eliza said.

Blake shrugged. "It's the truth. So please, continue telling me about this amusement park that's supposedly better than California Adventure, Knott's Berry Farm, Universal Studios, and Magic Mountain."

"And SeaWorld," her mom added. "Before *Blackfish*, I loved going to there as a kid."

Blake patted her mother's knee. "Yeah, Mom, no one cares about SeaWorld anymore. It's a horrible place."

"This place is called Cedar Point," Eliza said, straightening in her seat as if getting comfortable for the pitch. "And you can't claim to be a rollercoaster enthusiast and not know about Cedar Point. It's ranked the best in the country, consistently, the world even."

Blake wanted to press her buttons. They hadn't even cracked the bottles of wine or mezcal yet, and Eliza was already loosened up and letting her rollercoaster passion spill out. If Blake wasn't already intrigued by her, this would have done it. She sat back and allowed Eliza to tell everyone about this mysterious place in one of the country's most boring states, a state she forgot existed until the presidential election rolled around, and somehow everyone's eyes were on Ohio. According to Eliza, this Cedar Point place was the only redeeming quality about the state, and when she started bragging about its seventeen rollercoasters, Blake pointed out that Magic Mountain had nineteen, the most in the world, just to watch her squirm. After quickly fact-checking on her phone, Eliza fought back, saying that Cedar Point had the second tallest coaster in the country, which outdid Magic Mountain's third tallest coaster.

"I've been to all of those parks in California," Eliza added. "And the only one that sort of compares is Knott's Berry Farm. You can't hate on a place that you've never been to, and since I've been to all of them, I think my opinion is more valid, therefore, I win this argument."

Blake loved every moment of it. Eliza had her family laughing even though they were set on Eliza being wrong. She spoke with so much passion, and God, that smile on her face the whole time and the little bouts of anger that furrowed her brows had Blake fighting to hide her smile.

"Even though she's completely wrong about amusement parks," Blake's mom said, putting an arm around Eliza. "She saved our baby, and that's what matters."

Eliza pointed a finger in the air. "And what also matters is that Cedar Point is really the best amusement park."

"It's not, though," her mom said, and Blake couldn't have been prouder. "But we still like you. We will like you even more if you help us reel this one in." She hooked a thumb at Blake. "She has a notorious injury rap sheet Luis and I thought she would outgrow once she became an adult."

"What are you talking about? I was an angel," Blake said and turned to Eliza. "They act like I have a criminal record or something."

"I'm surprised you don't," her dad said.

Hugo insisted they open a bottle of wine and gave Eliza the first glass, and her dad and mom continued telling Eliza about all the injuries Blake had accumulated throughout her thirty years on Earth. Shoulder dislocation from falling off the monkey bars when she was nine. Broken finger from playing kickball at recess when she was twelve. Broken ankle for kicking the side of their townhome when she was arguing with Adrian, and three concussions over her high school softball career.

"Okay, but I was an amazing shortstop and MVP from sophomore to senior year *and* scored the most home runs for the last two years," Blake said, finger pointed upward to emphasize the bragging. It was an important detail to add since her parents were ruining her game. Combing through her injury report was not how she impressed a doctor. "Those three concussions were worth it."

"Well, I don't know about that," Eliza said.

Blake shook Eliza's bare knee, and the touch sent a powerful hum all the way up her spine. "Come on. Just admit that it's impressive."

"It's very impressive," Eliza said softly as she glanced at Blake's hand. "So you were a jock?"

Blake grinned. "I don't know…maybe."

"She got into a golf cart accident right after she graduated high school," her dad added, snapping them out of the moment. Blake rolled her eyes, retrieved her hand, and went for her wineglass. She needed it to get through the rest of this conversation because unfortunately, there were still more injuries to unveil that would prevent any moments with Eliza. "Worked at a golf course," her dad continued, oblivious to everything. "Was flying down a hill for fun, another concussion and a broken hand."

Eliza's eyes widened. "Blake! What's wrong with you?"

"I have a need for speed."

"Golf carts aren't race cars."

"They are on rainy days when no one is golfing, and the grass is slick," she said with a wink.

"You're lucky you got a concussion and a broken hand," her dad said. "The cart did multiple flips and landed on the side."

Eliza took a large gulp of her wine. "This is really stressing me out—"

"A UTI that led to a kidney infection when she was in college," her mom continued, counting the injuries on her hand.

Blake playfully smacked her arm. "Mom, too personal."

"You spent the night in the hospital. I count it as an injury."

Eliza bit her lip as if to hide her grin. "You like going to the emergency room? You really do think it's a hot spot?"

"I'm an active human being. What can I say? I had a great injury-free streak for ten years." She needed more wine. The embarrassment had gotten to her, and she couldn't tell if that was warming up her cheeks or if it was her first glass of wine. She placed a hand on Eliza's back. "Can I get you another glass?"

"Only if you're having one," Eliza said.

"Well, then, I have to. Whatever makes you stay longer."

"Who said I was in a hurry to go home?"

"I just wanted to make sure my family hasn't scared you off yet."

"Your family is amazing. I'm having a great time. The only things scaring me are the long list of injuries on your record."

"But I had a great ten years of no injuries. Let's focus on that."

"Until Gisele did you dirty. Here, let me refill our glasses."

As the wine drained from the bottles, the rest of the family started cleaning up, and when Eliza offered to help, everyone insisted she stay in her seat. She then told them that Blake shouldn't help, to give her leg a rest, and of course, Blake didn't mind not helping. She'd prepared all the food, and she wanted an excuse to stay close to Eliza's side.

"I have a crazy idea," Blake said to her.

Eliza leaned in closer and rested her chin on her palm. "What's that?"

"Want to go to the beach? Watch the sunset? Leave them to clean up while we enjoy our buzz?"

Eliza tossed a hand over her heart. "I am a sucker for the beach."

"Then let's bail," Blake said. "They don't need us anymore. We're useless. The beach is calling us."

Eliza bit her bottom lip, nodding, and Blake's stomach swirled at the excitement that their night wasn't over yet.

❖

When the Uber dropped them off at Mission Beach, Eliza made sure to find a bench so Blake didn't have to crutch through the sand. A handful of surfers attempted to ride out the last waves of daylight while others took a stroll along the tide, played volleyball, or waited for the sunset on their blankets.

For the first few years of living in California, Eliza had taken advantage of the beach. Allison and their friends had made frequent trips out to Santa Monica and Venice for either an afternoon in the sun or when they were sick of the LA nightlife and wanted something different. But when medical school started, her free time had vanished, and she couldn't make it to the beach as often as she'd wanted to. Sitting on a bench now while her heart fluttered from being inches from a cute, hot, and sexy woman, she rediscovered her appreciation for the beach all over again.

She'd missed it.

"I was supposed to learn how to surf when I moved out here," Eliza said and nodded to the few cutting through the waves.

"What? No way."

"Way. My girlfriend and I made this whole elaborate plan to escape Ohio. We planned for a whole year, and when we decided on California, learning to surf was on our list of things to do."

"It's not too late, you know."

"Oh, I think it is. I've worked at a hospital for seven years. That does a good job stopping you from doing a lot of fun things."

"I could teach you," Blake said. "I'm not good by any means. My surfing is more like balancing on the board for a few seconds, riding the smallest wave, and then falling off. But still, it's considered surfing. It's really not too dangerous."

"Like the motorcycle isn't?"

Blake laughed and ran her hand through her fluffy hair. Eliza couldn't help but stare as she did so. "Surprisingly, I've never been hurt surfing. I also don't attempt the big waves. Adrian did, though. He was much more into it than I was, probably because he was really good at it. He taught me how."

She looked out at the water, and Eliza followed her gaze. Two surfers cut through a wave no more than four feet tall. The sun began its descent toward the horizon, splattering bold yellows and streams of thin pink clouds in the sky. The sunset was going to be beautiful, and she was grateful she could share it with Blake.

"Oceanside was our go-to beach since it was the closest to our house in Carlsbad," Blake continued. "Jordan and I never actually took surfing lessons like Adrian did. He taught us himself. He was so good. He could even surf at Black's Beach, which has some pretty sick waves, like over ten feet tall. I wasn't good enough for those, but I always tagged along with him because there were so many hot girls who surfed there. I cheered the girls on from the shore. You know, they needed emotional support."

"I can totally see you doing that."

Blake nudged her arm. "Had my first kiss from tagging along with him, so it worked out for me."

"Then it was worth it."

"Totally. So you had fun today? My injury list and my family haven't scared you?"

Eliza looked at her, and at the sudden eye contact, she peeled her gaze away and back to the ocean. She wasn't sure why she was nervous all of a sudden. Maybe it was the fact that they were alone, no family to interrupt them, and the feelings she'd tried to suppress finally claimed her body all at once. But she wasn't nervous enough to back out of planning that date she proposed the other night at Mezcal. If anything, spending the last few hours with Blake's hand touching her back and knee had made her more committed to it.

She wanted another night of that.

"I had a lot of fun today, and no, none of those things scared me away from our date."

Blake's stare dropped to her lips, and how quickly she looked to Eliza's eyes made it seem like it was an accident. But it didn't stop Eliza's lips from buzzing.

"Good, because I would really love to go on that date with you," Blake said, sucking in her lip as Eliza stared, and the heat curled inside her and aimed lower.

"You like sushi?" Eliza asked.

"I love sushi."

"I've been really craving sushi."

Blake bumped into her shoulder. "Let's do it."

Eliza wanted more than a shoulder bump, and she sensed that Blake felt the same. She couldn't remember the last time she'd barely known someone but had the urgency to kiss them.

The fact that they stayed at the beach until the sun dipped below the horizon inflated her with so much happiness, she wished she could bottle it for the next time she needed a large dose of endorphins. She'd thought her nights in California would involve many more sunsets, but given everything that had happened in her life, it hadn't worked out that way. Watching a sunset alone was like watching it in black and white, and witnessing one with Blake reminded her of how beautiful they could be.

The Uber headed to Mezcal to drop off Blake before it would continue north to Eliza's. As they approached the restaurant and the familiar sights of Fifth Avenue, Blake turned to her, and despite the darkness, her smile still had enough shine to light up Eliza.

"I'll see you next Saturday for our steamy date?" Blake asked.

Eliza felt a blush blossoming on her cheeks. "Yes," she said and tucked a strand of hair behind her ear. "I just have a really awkward question to ask."

"Your awkwardness has yet to disappoint me."

Eliza pushed her arm. "Hey."

"What? It's all endearing. What's your question?"

"Would you, um, would you be able to pick me up? I know this is supposed to be me taking you out but…well…I don't drive. You know…that car accident really did something—"

Blake grabbed her hand, and all the rambling disappeared. "I can drive. I'll pick you up whatever time you want."

"No Gisele."

Blake laughed. "But you would look so cute behind me. In a helmet, of course."

Eliza directed a point, but her other hand still clasped Blake's. "Don't do that."

"Because it makes you blush?" Blake rubbed her thumb back and forth against the soft part in between Eliza's thumb and pointer finger, and the sweat that stuck to the back of Eliza's legs glued her to the Uber's leather seats.

"Don't worry. I'll pick you up in Audo," Blake said. "Gisele is on sabbatical."

"Hopefully, she goes right into retirement."

The car pulled off to the side of the road in front of Mezcal, and Eliza's mind was already a week ahead and willing time to speed up so a moment like this could happen again.

Blake touched her arm, one last touch that would hopefully help her last another week until she got to see her again. When Blake retrieved her hand, Eliza felt the loss immensely, but she hoped all their stolen moments of the day would stay with her until next Saturday. "Take care, Eliza," she said, and once she stepped outside, she lowered her head as if to catch one last glimpse. "I look forward to next weekend."

Once she shut the door, the Uber shifted to drive. As the car drove away, Eliza stole a glance over her shoulder to find Blake watching the car drive down the street.

Chapter Six

"Oh my gosh, you have a date?" Violet muted her shriek, probably remembering she'd just put Emma down ten minutes prior. "And you're smiling. What the hell is this nonsense? Are you sleep deprived? Oh, Lize, you're sleep deprived and delirious. You poor thing."

Eliza bit her lip to stop her smile from growing, but it was too damn hard. With so many thoughts spinning around, it was hard to prioritize them.

"Sorry, I'm just really excited."

She filled her sister in on everything that had happened since the note. When she finished, she realized how warm her face actually was. "And I have no idea what to wear," she said and then let out a petulant moan. "Tell me what to wear."

"Lize, you've been on dates before. Find the sexiest dress in your closet, one that flaunts your assets."

"Great, the one black dress I wear to every first date. I feel like it's cursed or something because most of those first dates never make it to the second."

"Your dress isn't cursed, Eliza. It's because you run away after those first dates."

Violet was right. If the woman didn't send a spark through her, the connection wasn't there. Sure, she'd met a few women who'd given her a flicker of a spark. But it wasn't until she met Blake that she realized those sparks with other women were simply tiny particles of chemistry. They were nothing of what she was truly looking for: a powerful zap that would have her insides working overtime whenever she was around the woman or talking to her, the way Tess had made her feel all those years ago. And now, she'd finally found similar feelings whenever she was around Blake.

Eliza had a feeling that this wouldn't be the first and only date with Blake, and because she didn't want to take any chances, she decided to run out to the store to find a brand-new date dress, one that wasn't cursed.

She bought a burgundy skater dress with short lace sleeves, a V-neck that showed off the right amount of cleavage, a little teaser but still reserved. Allison lent her black dangly earrings and then gave her a seal of approval. She spent extra time curling her hair for the right amount of "beach tousle," fluffed it multiple times, and each time she assessed herself in the mirror, a new round of butterflies was unleashed.

Oh, and her palms were clammy. Great.

Once she got Blake's text that she was in the parking lot, she wiped her hands against her dress, sucked in one last breath in an attempt to manage her accelerating heart rate, and took the elevator downstairs. The summer heat didn't help the nerves warming her insides. And neither did Blake standing in front of her white Audi looking all dapper.

Holy hell. Eliza was going to turn into a sweaty mess before they even got to the restaurant.

"Wow," Blake said breathlessly, her eyes taking in Eliza's face and trailing down her body. "Dr. Walsh looks amazing in a dress."

She could say "wow" about Blake too. She was gorgeous, sexy, and handsome all at the same time. Her hair was styled, her eyes darkened with a touch of mascara, a black button-down shirt was cuffed around her biceps, and French-tucked into light gray jeans with her poor cast still in place. But even with a cast and crutches, she still rocked her whole date ensemble.

She could have rocked whatever she wanted, honestly.

Eliza raised a finger. "Any more doctor nonsense and I head back inside." Blake laughed and zipped her lips. "And you look really good too. Geez." Eliza caught the wonderful scent of woodsy cologne. She fanned herself, attempting to make it look as if she was playing along, but in reality, she really did need some air. "Making me all warm."

"Nah, that's just the sun."

"Yeah, you're right. My mistake. Now let me get the door for you."

Blake crutched to the driver's side. "I should be the one opening the door for you since I'm driving."

"This is what happens when you ride a motorcycle. You can't be the gentlewoman." She opened the door and gestured Blake in.

They ventured over to Pacific Beach, a couple blocks from the ocean, to an upscale sushi restaurant. Eliza spent more time than she probably needed trying to find a place that had everything she was looking for. She wanted romantic date ambience: mood lighting, good bottles of wine, amazing reviews, and bonus points for white tablecloths and being a few blocks from the beach so their night didn't have to end when *she* paid. She crossed her clammy fingers that they could squeeze in another sunset.

The restaurant didn't disappoint on the inside. White tablecloths, dim lighting, and a small candle in the middle of the table was everything Eliza was hoping to get.

"What? Why are you smiling?" Eliza asked as they settled into the booth.

Blake's cheeks turned bright red, and Eliza loved it. Blake possessed a lot of confidence, which was great and sexy, but it was also nice seeing that she had a vulnerable spot, and somehow, that involved Eliza calling her out on her beaming.

"I'm not allowed to smile?" Blake said.

"No, it's strictly forbidden."

"I'm just glad to be here. I've been looking forward to this night all week. It made the week drag by so slowly."

"Tell me about it."

"And you look absolutely stunning. Damn. Just to warn you, I might stare longer than usual. So don't think I'm creepy."

"I never thought you were creepy. A player, however, that's a different story."

"You thought I was a player?" Eliza nodded, and Blake coughed up a laugh. "What? How?"

"Carrie? All your lines."

"My lines?"

"Oh. You know exactly what I'm talking about."

Blake opened her mouth and closed it as if picking up and discarding rebuttals, seeming to be thrown off guard that Eliza had called her out. Since Blake was usually the one to say and do things to get Eliza to squirm, Eliza sat back in her seat and enjoyed giving her a taste of her own medicine.

Now she understood the appeal. It was highly entertaining.

"I think I really need to fix this impression you have of me," Blake finally said. "That's the last thing I want you to think."

"You've redeemed yourself a little bit."

"I don't know what you define as a 'player,' but I don't think I'm one."

"You're very attractive and charismatic. I'm sure you could get any woman you want."

The blush deepened on Blake's cheeks. "Yeah, I had fun in my twenties, but I'm thirty and over all that. Seriously. Ask my family."

"Your family? They know about your dating life?"

For someone who didn't have any sort of relationship with her parents, the news that someone was close enough to their parents that they knew the details of their dating life was shocking to Eliza... and she was a little envious.

"I'm very close with my family," Blake said. "Let's just say they're more invested now that I've taken dating seriously over the last few years."

"Taken dating seriously? Yup, that's something a player would say."

Blake threw her hands up in defeat, and Eliza laughed behind her glass of water. "How do I prove to you I'm not what you think I am?"

Eliza shrugged. "I don't know. You have charm. You can figure it out. I believe in you."

"The night you came by Mezcal, Carrie knew I didn't want to pursue her anymore, and then, the lesbian gods answered my prayers, and in walked this super gorgeous woman. I was so surprised you came. I'd been waiting for three weeks. I was starting to think you weren't going to show."

"I'm shocked I came by too. It's pretty out of character."

Blake tilted her head to the side. "What do you mean?"

"Work takes up all my time, and when I'm not working, I'm sleeping or studying."

"So you don't date?"

Eliza laughed at the confusion crossing Blake's features. "You sound disappointed."

"I'm not disappointed. I'm just shocked, that's all."

Eliza paused for a moment. Even though she didn't want to dive into the past, Blake needed to know some of the reasons why she didn't date. She didn't want that little bit of information to scare Blake away without any context. She knew if she wanted a second date, she needed to open up, offer a part of her. That was easier said than done because anytime she thought about her baggage, it balled up in her throat and prevented words from coming out.

But for Blake, she would really try.

"I've, um, the accident really messed with me. Losing Tess… it's something I've struggled with still to this day. It's easier to hide from dating so I wouldn't have to lose someone I love that much."

Blake's eyebrows furrowed, almost like she could feel the pain and heartbreak. "I'm really sorry, Eliza," she said softly while looking at her with sympathy.

"Yeah, me too, because it wasn't until recently that I realized hiding hasn't done me any good. I'm at a point in my life where I want to find a partner and share my life with them. It's been so lonely all these years, and I'm sick of it. I'm ready to move on."

Blake gave her a thin smile. She reached across the table and placed her hand on Eliza's wrist, and Eliza could feel the warmth in her chest. "Well, then, I'm extremely lucky that I'm on this date with you," she said.

"You charmed your way into it," Eliza said to put them back on track for a lively conversation that didn't dive too deeply into their traumatic pasts.

They debated for the next ten minutes on which sushi rolls to get. Blake suggested they order their favorites and then one of the restaurant's specialty rolls. Eliza wasn't going to argue with that. The more sushi, the better. Eliza chose her favorite dynamite roll, Blake got her beloved spider roll, and they both decided on one of the restaurant's specialty rolls: Hokkaido roll that had tempura baby scallops, mango, avocado, and a jalapeno garlic dill aioli. They ordered a bottle of wine that would pair perfectly with their sushi: a Grüner Veltliner that would go well with the avocado in all of their three rolls.

"So your mom gave you all androgynous names? I just realized that," Eliza said once the server walked away after filling up their wineglasses.

Blake waved her hand. "She gave us 'unisex' names, not androgynous names. My mother wasn't that progressive when we were born. She hated all the girl names."

"She seems pretty progressive to me."

"Yeah, maybe she is now, but growing up, she wasn't. Both of my parents weren't. Voted for Bush. Supported both wars. They didn't like it when I would wear Adrian's clothes as a kid and told me to dress like a girl. I told them I had a crush on a girl when I was twelve, and my mom cried, sent me to Sunday school."

"Really?" Eliza was shocked. That was something she expected her own mother to do. Not Sandra. Sandra had all the qualities she wished her mother had, mostly the acceptance part. She didn't seem to care at all about anyone's sexuality or like she would judge anyone from living a life outside the "status quo." "I can't picture your mom doing any of that."

"Yeah, well, she did. You should see the awkward photo of the three of us when Adrian graduated from bootcamp. My mom practically forced me into a dress. She wouldn't allow me to wear dress pants, so now there's this awkward photo of us in the foyer. It didn't really change until after Adrian died two years later." She studied the stem of her wineglass. "We didn't really address my fashion or my coming out until I came home for Thanksgiving during my freshman year of college with my hair short. Mom asked if I still liked women. I told her that I had a girlfriend, and she said she was happy for me. That she loved me no matter what. Jordan told me that she and Mom were talking one night, and Mom told her that she'd already lost one kid, she didn't want to lose another. Life was too short to judge, and she wanted her kids to be happy and find love, even if it meant cutting my 'precious locks off,'" she said with a small laugh.

"Wow, that's quite the progression. I'm glad she was able to do that."

A surge of envy ran through Eliza, and she wished so much that she had the same experience with her parents. She was so glad Blake got an apology. She wanted that.

"Me too," Blake said. "It's weird how death changes the perspectives of some people. I think the only silver lining of Adrian dying was that my mom became more open-minded, and now she's the most supportive mom out there. I even got her to go to Pride last year with me and Jordan, and she wore this 'proud mom' shirt with a rainbow on it. It was everything."

Eliza smiled, genuinely happy that Blake got to experience that. "You seem really close with your family," she said.

"I am. My family is everything. I don't know what I would do without them. What about you? What about your parents? Your family?"

A laugh flew out of Eliza and hung awkwardly between them. Blake frowned, probably hearing the sarcasm. She couldn't look Blake in the eyes while her memory spun all the things her parents had said and done about her "lesbianism" when she was a teen.

"What did I do wrong?" her mother had wept after the phone call from Mrs. Ware that outed her relationship with Tess. "I just don't understand where I went wrong."

"Honey, there are plenty of other fish in the sea," she'd said to "comfort" Eliza when she couldn't stop crying after Tess had broken up with her…well, when the Wares had forced Tess to break up with her so she could date the nice church boy, Jake Kozlowski. "Maybe if you start befriending some boys, you will discover you like them."

"When will you ever be over this girl phase?" she'd asked Eliza at the end of the summer when she didn't have a boyfriend like her mother had hoped but was still heartbroken over Tess.

Plus, the printed online articles her parents had left on her bed that claimed that being gay could be fixed.

Those words had devastated Eliza. Her parents had chipped her away bit by bit every time they'd made those comments and with every article they'd put on her bed. They'd chipped away so much of who she was, there had been nothing left. She'd had no other choice but to free herself from them if she wanted to be comfortable in her own skin. She hated that her parents were weights in her life, but constantly hiding who she was for fear of them making a comment had prevented her from building her life from the rubble. If Eliza had never given herself that space from them, who knew if she would have ever learned to accept herself?

"I take it they're not as accepting?" Blake asked in a soft voice.

"Uh, no they're not. I, uh, I don't have much of a relationship with them."

Blake's eyes grew. "Really?"

"It's um, it's a long story. Too much of a downer for tonight."

"I have all the time in the world tonight, but if you don't want to dive into it, I totally understand. We can forget I even asked."

"Well, besides the long story, I have nothing else to say about them. I haven't seen them in…" She looked at the ceiling as she counted the years. *Damn, it's really been that long?* "Nine years."

Blake choked on her wine, covering her mouth. "Nine years?"

Ever since Eliza had moved to California, she'd mostly stayed clear of her hometown. She'd spent Thanksgiving at Allison's parents' house in Santa Cruz during her undergrad and med school. She'd gone home for Christmas but only for a few days. She'd bitten her tongue while with her parents and had played along with the whole let's-sweep-all-of-our-issues-under-the-rug game. She'd really only gone home to see Violet and then had spent the rest of the break at Allison's.

The wounds of high school had cut so deep and were still so fresh. Her lack of going home had caused their relationship to dangle on a string. Her parents had offered to pay for some of medical school, which she was grateful for, but she'd known that she'd unfortunately needed to separate herself from them in order to fully come to terms with herself and her new life. She hadn't accepted the money because she hadn't wanted them to dangle it over her head and use it to pressure her into having a relationship with them. With enough scholarships to pay her way through med school, she'd been ready to take out loans to pay for the rest. She'd told her parents after her college graduation that she was staying in LA for med school, that she didn't need their money, that she would never forgive them for what they'd put her through after learning that she was gay and not accepting her for who she was, and how they hadn't been there to comfort her when she'd needed them the most after the accident.

That was the last time she'd seen them in person.

She would have gone about it a little differently at thirty-one. She would have spoken to them more reasonably and maturely, a conversation with less angst, but at twenty-two, she'd still been so raw from the accident, from losing Tess, from her parents' betrayal. Despite minimal and shallow text conversations during those nine years, she'd never found the energy to reconcile with them, and she hated that they hadn't tried…that she hadn't tried either.

"Yeah, I know it's bad," Eliza said. "We send each other the occasional text for holidays and birthdays." She almost tricked herself into believing that lessened the blow. "More wine?" She reached for the bottle and topped off her glass without waiting for a reply. Anything to change the subject. Her parents had ruined her love life in high school, and she refused to let them ruin a first date with a woman who lit up her insides for the first time in thirteen years.

"You have any siblings?" Blake asked cautiously as Eliza refilled her glass.

"Oh, yeah, my sister Violet. She's four years older than me, lives right outside my hometown. We talk once a week. She's my best friend, and I'm absolutely in love with her daughter, Emma. She's everything."

Blake smiled. "You're an Aunt Eliza?"

"I am. I haven't seen her in about two years, but sometimes she picks up my FaceTime calls with Violet."

Blake's phone buzzed on the table. She checked it, typed out a text, and a few seconds after she set it down, it went off again.

"You're a popular woman," Eliza said through a laugh, nodding to her phone.

Blake rolled her eyes and flipped it over to hide the screen. "Sorry, it's Jordan not understanding boundaries."

"Oh, yeah?"

"My whole family may or may not know that I'm on a date with you right now." She made the toothy "I'm in trouble" smirk.

Eliza raised an eyebrow. "You keep anything from them?"

"I kept Gisele from them for a long time. I'm pretty proud of that."

"Don't be proud of that."

"My mom has been on my case about my dating life. She didn't really like the last couple of women I dated. She said she's questioning my ability to find a partner."

Eliza choked on her drink as she attempted to hold in her laughter. "Geez, what girls are you bringing home to Mom?"

"None of them. I don't tell my family about the first few dates because they can go either way, but I had to tell them about this one. For bragging rights, you know, since they love you."

"Did you get any points from them?"

"I did. You're worth, like, a hundred. I think my mom sees a little ray of hope that I can find the good ones."

"Keep telling them good things about me. My reputation is on the line."

"I will. Now, what about you? What's your dating story? I know you said that you don't date much, but there have to be a few women."

The lump threatened to bloom once again at the prying into her past. Eliza hated how her body reacted to anything that had to do with her Before.

"Isn't talking about dating history against the rules of a first date?" Eliza said.

Blake shrugged as if she didn't really care. Eliza should have known better. Blake bending the rules wasn't a secret. "Maybe. You don't have to talk about it if it's too much. I'm kind of an open book, and sometimes I forget that not everyone is like that."

Eliza liked open books. Since she was the exact opposite, she could ask open books questions as quickly as they popped into her head, and they would answer. She was good at asking questions. It came with her job. The more she asked, the less she had to answer.

As far as her dating story, Eliza could hardly fill a page. Maybe a Post-It if she took out Tess. Calli for a month during her sophomore year of college. Janie for a month and a half during med school. Hannah on and off for three months during her second year of residency. And Sofia for three months the summer before, the most significant relationship since Tess but hardly significant enough to push past her wall.

"My dating life is nonexistent," she answered and eased the bitter taste of those words with another sip of Grüner Veltliner. "There's not much to really say."

Blake shook her head. "I find that very hard to believe."

"I guess I don't really try. Does that ruin my shine?"

Blake grinned, dimples out, and Eliza's body hummed at the sight of them. "No, not in the slightest."

The server brought out their food. Eliza had a good feeling about the three plates of sushi, and finally, her intense craving for it would be relieved. Each roll made her melt in her seat. They were everything she'd been craving. The Hokkaido was now her new favorite, and she was so disappointed that it was a specialty roll, the scallops, the mango, the aioli, all of it. She wished it was a regular so she could find it anywhere.

"I can always attempt to make you one," Blake said as she plucked a dynamite roll off the plate. "I'm no sushi chef, but I can certainly try."

"I'm willing to be the guinea pig in your sushi experiment."

"Maybe it could be the second date?"

Eliza smiled at that promise. "Maybe."

No sushi or drop of wine was left behind. Once Eliza had the pleasure of finally paying for the meal, they stepped outside with the rest of the night ahead of them. Although her stomach was so happy and Eliza had the perfect buzz, she didn't want to go home. The night was too young, and Blake was looking too sexy.

Blake caught a glimpse at her watch. "It's almost seven thirty. It's way too early…unless you want to go—"

"I definitely don't want to go home. I'm having a great time."

"Good. Me too. Let's not end it, then."

Eliza glanced down the street and noticed the orange and yellows in the sky, signaling that another beautiful sunset was in store. She wanted to relive the moment after Mezcal and hoped so much that watching the sunset would ramp up the tension and give Eliza the courage to make some kind of a move. Whether it was holding Blake's hand or kissing her. She was desperate for her touch to erase all the loneliness she'd lived in for a long time.

They found a spot on the sand this time, right off the sidewalk. Eliza helped Blake ease into a sitting position with her cast resting straight in front of her. Eliza took a seat next to her, making sure she sat close enough to encourage Blake to touch her…in whatever form she wanted.

"You know, if I wasn't in a cast, I would have asked you to go salsa dancing," she said. "There's a club down the street."

"I found the silver lining to you being in a cast," Eliza said. "I don't have to go dancing now."

"What? You wouldn't have tried it? Come on."

"I'd probably make a fool out of myself. I'm really not coordinated at all."

"You're a surgeon. Being coordinated is a requirement."

"I'm coordinated with my hands. My body, not so much."

Blake bit her lip, but a smirk still grew. "That's hot."

The warm blush rushed to Eliza's cheeks. "Not what I meant at all."

"I know, but just run with it, okay?"

Eliza nodded and straightened her back. "Okay, I'll run with it."

"You're coordinated with your hands. I know how to salsa. Therefore, I'm coordinated with my body." She gestured to herself, salacious inflection prominent in her tone. It hit Eliza hard. She loved how Blake oozed confidence even when she was making light-hearted jokes like that. "I think we're a perfect match. Maybe once I get out of this thing, I can teach you."

"That would definitely ruin my appeal. Trust me."

Blake shook her head. "I don't think there are many things that would ruin your appeal. You have an exorbitant amount."

Eliza swallowed the flutter in her chest. She took in Blake's beautiful eyes that held hers so steadily, she could feel them wrap her up.

"I'm sorry, was that a player line?" Blake asked, waggling her perfectly shaped eyebrows and nudging Eliza's arm.

"It's a line but a good one."

"Oh yeah?"

There was going to be a point in time where Eliza couldn't handle the dance around her immense desire for Blake. She was sure that the limit would be the end of the night. Even with all of her lines, Blake was able to make them work, make Eliza feel like they were specifically crafted for her, and she believed it.

"You know, I haven't had a first date go this amazing in a long time," Eliza said.

The corner of Blake's mouth tugged upwards. "Really?"

"Really."

"Yeah, me too. You're pretty good at treating a lady. Maybe I should let you do it more often."

"I'd love that."

Blake's stare dropped to her lips, and right as Eliza felt a tickle in her bottom lip, Blake tore her gaze away and back to the sunset. For once, Eliza wished the sunset would turn black and white so she could be the color that stole Blake's attention. She wanted those eyes back on her lips, and she wanted so much for Blake to satisfy every need pricking at her skin.

"Blake?"

Blake faced her, and finally, she saw the desire sparkling in her dark eyes. Eliza stared at her lips and how femininely shaped they were. She bet kissing Blake Navarro was out of this world. She wanted to feel that confidence on her lips. She wanted Blake to blanket her with it. She wanted Blake's lips to hold her. She imagined they were soft, delicate, yet sturdy when they needed to be. Just like the way Blake's stare gave her so much when Blake listened to her.

Eliza watched Blake's gaze fall to her mouth, and it made her grin. Blake's thoughts became public knowledge. Eliza's heart hammered from how close they were, how sturdy Blake's eye contact was as she skimmed Eliza's face. They were a whisper away from each other. Blake's pull was so strong that the next thing Eliza knew, she was grazing her fingertips along Blake's cheeks, feeling the tingles vibrating low inside her. The cool ocean breeze that had greeted them absorbed their heat and sparked a rare charge around them. Eliza let her hand wander toward Blake's lips, feeling them with a thumb, and something exploded in her when Blake parted them, almost as if she had no control over her own body, but Eliza did. The electric charge spread further, all over her body, deep into her muscles and bones, and her skin caught fire.

Enough was enough. Instead of waiting, Eliza just wanted to *do*. She slowly leaned in, giving Blake enough time to escape if she wanted. But she didn't. Instead, she closed her eyes, waiting for Eliza to kiss her, and when Eliza finally captured those lips with her own, she reveled in Blake's grip around her mouth. It was gentle and sweet. A simple kiss that was reverent but eager to explore. A wave whirled up from Eliza's midsection to her chest as Blake gently raked her fingers through Eliza's hair and secured a hand on the back of her head, and the way she held her so gently, yet firmly forced Eliza's mouth to open. Their tongues met and moved with gentle hesitancy, learning the patterns and rhythms until they fell in sync.

Kissing Blake was everything Eliza imagined and more. She was soft and gentle, yet hungry. She took over the kiss but didn't dominate it possessively. It was like her lips and tongue guided Eliza through a wonderful dance that she'd long forgotten.

Realizing they were out in public, Eliza pulled away and refilled her lungs with much needed air. Blake's untamed grin sent Eliza's heart into a marathon sprint, and for the first time in a long time, a first kiss with someone settled in her instead of alerting her to run away.

"I want to keep doing this," Eliza said with ragged breaths. "Because I've been wanting to do that all night, but we're kind of in public."

"Then let's find somewhere less public so we can resume."

They drove back to San Diego. Blake held her hand the whole time, and even though a part of Eliza wanted both hands on the wheel, something comforting swaddled her as her anxiety begged to take hold. Eliza wasn't sure if Blake reaching over the center console to grab her hand was because she wanted to keep touching her or if it was because she sensed her fears about being in a car. Either way, wanting Blake pushed the anxiety to the back of her mind. Though it was still there, slightly squeezing her chest, the surge of need was a more powerful force than the anxiety, and she chalked that up as a win.

Blake parked in the most desolate spot of Eliza's apartment parking lot, tucked in a corner underneath a palm tree where nothing would shine a spotlight on them. Once the car shut off, they both leaned in to resume right where they'd left off, except this time, the kiss didn't start off slow and shy like the first round. It was hot and passionate, as if the drive had depleted the relief of their first kiss and then some. The temperature in the car quickly rose as their tongues collided and danced together. Blake placed a hand on Eliza's knee and slowly skimmed her fingertips up her leg. Eliza's skin burned and pleaded at the touch. Blake crawled her hand underneath the hem of Eliza's dress, and every inch gained sent her heart beating faster and heavier. Blake's kissing skills had her melting into the seat. Sweat glued her legs to the leather, even more so when Blake grazed up to her inner thigh, lighting up her center in ways Eliza hadn't felt in years. Blake made her feel like a teenager again. The warmth buzzing through her felt like a secret collection of teenage hormones erupting, and moments of secretly making out in a parking lot had her heart thrumming with a thrill she'd forgotten she'd liked at a distant point in her life.

Eliza pulled away to catch her breath, holding Blake's face in her palms. She was breathing raggedly too—Eliza could feel it on her lips—and it was wonderful that Eliza was able to do the same thing that was being done to her. The light a couple of spaces over offered the right amount of brightness for Eliza to catch a glimpse of Blake's red, swollen lips and satisfied grin. She was very proud of herself, to say the least.

"God," Eliza said, running a thumb down Blake's lips. She really wished her brain and heart could agree with what her lower half wanted. Currently, they were feuding, and it was all because of Blake's amazing kissing talents and the fingers resting on her inner thigh, a few inches short of where Eliza wanted her. So badly.

"What?" Blake said through her smirk.

"You're just making me feel a lot."

"Good a lot?"

Eliza bit her lip and nodded. "Very good. Maybe too good."

"This is all really good feedback," Blake said and squeezed Eliza's thigh.

Blake leaned in, but Eliza stopped her with a hand to her chest. This was where Eliza had to stop Blake's inner player…or the retired player. Unfortunately for her throbbing center, Eliza had to listen to her brain and heart, and that meant pulling Blake's hand from her thigh. It had been such a long time since she'd slept with someone. A year to be exact. Sofia, much like the other women who'd come and gone, had been someone to fill the void in her bed but not in her heart. Although Eliza desperately needed the release, she could already tell that Blake was different from those other women. A simple look or touch sent her body spiraling, and for a person who struggled to find that spark, Eliza didn't want it to burn out from getting caught up in the moment and rushing things. The type of feelings Blake caused had to be cherished. They were delicate because they were so rare.

Blake flashed a defeated smile as she took back her hand, tilting her head forward as if disappointed.

"I'm sorry," Eliza said, and she meant it.

Blake looked back, a thin smile still intact. "It's okay."

"It's not like I don't want to continue. Trust me when I say that I really want to take you to my room and continue this...preferably horizontally."

"Ugh, you're killing me," she said and rested her head on her seat.

"I'm just not ready to do that yet. It's...um, well...it's a long story."

Blake turned her head and held Eliza's hand. "You don't need to explain. It's okay, really."

"I had a really amazing time, though."

"I did too. I would love to take you out again."

"I would really like that. You promise we can make that happen?"

Blake kissed the back of her hand. "Promise."

After kissing each other good-bye, Eliza slowly meandered to her apartment, lost in a daze. The nerves in her lips were inflamed, celebrating hard, and she hadn't realized she was resting against the front door, fully swept up in the aftermath that was kissing Blake Navarro until Allison snapped her fingers.

Allison was right in front of her with a wide smile. "What. The. Hell."

Eliza ran her hands down her face because she could feel a smile claim all of her, and how easily it came was embarrassing. Allison would be teasing her for days. Instead of saying anything, she tossed her purse on the kitchen table and floated through the apartment.

"Uh, no you don't," Allison said and whisked her around. "What the hell is on your face? Is that a bashful smile?"

Eliza tried hiding it like it was a hickey and turned in the other direction, but that only caused Allison to roar with laughter.

"Give me something, damn it."

Eliza fell onto the couch and stared at the wall. "We just made out for such a long time. Like teenagers."

"What?" Allison plopped right next to her. "Holy shit."

"I…I don't know what else to say except for it was wonderful. Everything was wonderful. God!" Eliza hid her face in her hands.

"Ah," Allison shrieked. "You're blushing like a little schoolgirl."

"I know, and it's so embarrassing."

"Lize, this is great," Allison said, pulling Eliza's hands down. "I've never seen you so glowy. I think I need sunglasses."

Eliza rolled her eyes, but her mouth didn't get the memo. It still curved upward.

"Tell me this, did you feel it? The spark?"

Eliza bit her lip and nodded. "I felt it the whole night. I didn't even need to kiss her to feel it."

"Wait. You kissed her? You? Eliza Walsh initiated a kiss?"

Eliza smiled, proud of an accomplishment she thought was impossible. "I did. I had to. It was getting…overwhelming."

"Oh my fucking God. This is, like, the biggest news since you decided to sign up for the dating apps."

"I know, and now that we kissed, that spark…it shows no signs of flickering off."

Allison's mouth dropped. "Damn, Lize. You, like, really kissed someone. I'm imaging a steamy make-out session with messy hair and *Titanic*-fogged-up windows."

"Yeah…something like that."

Allison cocked an eyebrow. "Are you going to be in a daze for the rest of the night?"

Eliza smiled as she replayed the sensual way Blake's mouth moved against hers, and Blake's hand sliding up her thighs. She snapped herself out of the memory, but the grin didn't dim. "I think I am."

She saved the daze until she lay in bed, and it was a wonderful way to fall asleep.

Chapter Seven

"Earth to Blake." Malai reached over the table to snap Blake back to reality. "Does the financial analysis look good to you?"

Blake flinched and directed her focus to her business partner and best friend. "Hm? What?"

She had totally zoned out, ruminating on every part of her date. Not even her second caramel macchiato from the coffee shop had been able to keep her weighted in the present. She thought about that steamy make-out session in her car, and every time the memory replayed, Blake felt it zip down her chest and throb in her core. She couldn't shake it from her head, even when she and Malai were working on finishing their business plan so they could start accruing restaurant capital for their food hall. Thinking about Eliza's lips and heavy breathing was much better than going over numbers for the millionth time.

"Do the numbers look correct?"

"Haven't we gone over them, like, ten times?"

"Yes, but they need to be spot-on, or we're not going to get the capital. Where's your mind at, huh? You've been in la-la land all morning."

Blake took a sip of her drink and pushed her glasses up the bridge of her nose. Blake was easily distracted, and Malai was one of the most organized, thorough, and focused people she knew. She was going to be a great business partner, always snapping Blake back to the present.

"Sorry," Blake said and focused on the charts in their business plan in Google Docs. She wasn't good with numbers. That was all Malai. They'd met at culinary school in LA. Malai had been studying restaurant and culinary management while Blake had studied culinary arts. Malai was the brains behind Blake's creativity. She deferred to Malai on the numbers, and when Malai asked Blake to look them over, she'd asked Marc to assist as a third pair of eyes on the most important document she would probably ever have in her life. This was her ticket to her dream of opening up a restaurant. She'd spent the last twelve years working for this very moment, and everything had to be perfect.

"Marc said they looked great," Blake said. He had his MBA in business, so she trusted him. "Malai, we've looked over this plan so many times. I think we're ready to share it with investors."

Malai relaxed in her seat. "I know, I know. I just want to make sure there's no mistakes before our meeting next week."

"There were hardly any issues when Marc looked at it, and we've combed through these three times since. I think this business plan is ready to make some money. We're ready to give life to this dream."

A good feeling settled in Blake. The more she reviewed the business plan, the more she was ready for investors to look at it, sign their checks, and cheer them on as they created a restaurant they'd been dreaming of since culinary school.

Malai sighed and took a sip of iced latte. "Okay, fine. This is the last look."

"Great."

"What's got you in a daze? What's more interesting than reading our business plan for the twentieth time?"

Blake rested her arms on the table. "I had the best first date on Saturday."

Malai's eyebrows rose. "Who's the girl?"

She couldn't control her grin. "A surgeon."

"A surgeon? You wooed a surgeon?"

"Why does everyone keep saying that? You sound like Jordan."

"I've known you for ten years. I'm pretty sure you've dated all of San Diego's queer women."

"That's not even true."

"Probably could have conquered LA if not for Lindsey."

Blake scoffed at the mention of her ex-girlfriend. She'd had one serious relationship. She and Lindsey had met sophomore year at culinary school and had dated all throughout college. It was so serious that Blake had considered proposing. The only thing that had prevented her from buying a ring was the fact that Lindsey was from New York, and no matter how much convincing both of them did to get the other to live in their home state, they weren't going to budge.

Blake was able to ignore the underlying issue that was never going to go away no matter how many times Malai told her to be careful. Young, naive Blake had actually thought she would be able to accomplish the unthinkable, getting Lindsey to ditch her home state for California. Wasn't everyone's dream to move to California? It seemed like it from all the people she met at culinary school. When she'd brought Lindsey to meet her family, Lindsey had kept saying how beautiful San Diego was, had talked about where the two of them might live, how Blake could teach her to surf. All that future talk had led Blake to believe that Lindsey was starting to consider it. She didn't realize that she'd been strung along until Lindsey broke up with her a week before graduation.

Blake had felt so betrayed and blindsided. It had absolutely destroyed her. She'd felt as if she'd wasted three years of her life committing to someone who'd had no plans to commit to her at all. She'd missed out on all the time in college when she could have explored the dating scene, figuring out who she was and what kind of partner she needed in her life. Once she'd moved back to San Diego, she'd spent the rest of her twenties dating and sleeping around. She'd numbed her broken heart through casual sex, but with every new woman, Blake had felt more doubtful that she would find that perfect person to settle down with.

"Okay, well, I'm done doing the whole casual thing. I've turned over a new leaf."

"Weren't you dating some redhead a month ago?"

"Carrie is long gone. She didn't even visit me in the hospital."

"Ugh. Well, I'm glad you kicked her to the curb. Old Blake would have been, 'whatever, as long as she's good in bed.'"

"That's not even true." Okay, she knew what Malai said was half-true, but she was still too embarrassed by her younger self and how she was easily fooled. She had too much pride to let Malai get away with saying "I told you so," even though Malai was right the whole time.

"How many times did I warn you about Lindsey? For like two straight years, I told you to be careful because there was no way that girl was going to stay on the west coast, and you told me you'd worry about it when the time came."

"Okay, the point is, I'm not that naive person anymore. The redhead is gone, and the surgeon is in, and she's amazing."

"Then don't screw it up."

"Thanks for the support."

Malai winked. "Now, let's finish looking this report over."

Hours later, after she and Malai officially gave their plan the stamp of approval and practiced their pitch, Eliza, the date, and that kiss still lingered, taking turns with the business proposal throughout the day on what would occupy the forefront of her mind. Blake had just plopped on her couch and was debating what show to binge on Netflix, when a single chirp grabbed her attention. Her heart sprung out of her chest when she noticed a message from Eliza.

When she opened their text thread, she found a picture of a premade salad with a text that read, *Rate my dinner on a scale of 1-10.*

She smiled as she wrote a response. *I give it a solid 2. The only thing preventing it from being a 1 is because of convenience. You deserve a real salad.*

Eliza: *Do I lose my appeal if I admit that I don't know how to cook?*

Blake: *Nope not yet. If anything, it means I need to cook for you again. And sometime soon.*

Sooner is better, Eliza replied with a winking emoji.

Blake: *Would you be interested in coming to my place? Next free night you have? Please tell me we don't have to wait too long.*

Eliza: *I'm off on Thursday. Is that soon enough?*
Blake: *No, but I'll try to manage. Please come over?*
Eliza: *It's a (second) date then.*

She lowered her phone and smiled at the ceiling. Her heart swelled with the anticipation and all the ideas floating through her head on the next meal she could make to woo Eliza.

Three more days. She could do it.

"Oh, hey," Blake said when she opened her front door. She skimmed Eliza's face and then her shorts flaunting her sexy, toned legs. "I've missed your face."

"Oh, have you?"

"I have. It's been pretty hard to forget about that first date. Now, come on in."

Eliza stepped inside her apartment: an open studio, concrete floors, exposed columns, and large windows illuminating the space with exposed sunlight. Planks of wood made up the ceiling. Blake's queen bed was tucked in the farthest corner, on the opposite side of her gray couch, right next to the windows.

Eliza nodded to the bowls of various ingredients scattered along the kitchen island. "What's for dinner, chef?"

Blake smiled, hoping her idea for their second date wasn't too far-fetched. She rested her back against the island to balance so she could hold Eliza's waist. It was much better than holding crutches. "I have an idea," she said.

"What?"

She wanted to kiss Eliza so badly. The curve of her smile and the slight bite of her lip had Blake's mind glitching, forgetting what she was going to say. As much as she wanted to reacquaint herself with those lips, she knew that it would distract both of them. Kissing would come later.

"I've already cooked for you, and you already treated me, and I thought that maybe, since you said you don't know how to cook and that salad you sent me looked super pathetic, we could cook a meal together."

Eliza's eyes rounded. "You know that I've burned Kraft macaroni and cheese. And that wasn't in college. That was a few weeks ago."

No, she had no idea that beautiful, intelligent Dr. Eliza Walsh burned boxed mac and cheese. Blake thinned her smile, a little disheartened at the new information. "You did?"

"I did."

"How?"

"Obviously, I cooked it too long."

"Did you not read the directions?"

Eliza furrowed her eyebrows. "Did you lose some hope?"

"A little bit. That makes this more of a challenge. I guess we're going to have to role-play: teacher." She pointed to herself. "Student." She poked Eliza's cheeks.

"I've never had a crush on a teacher before. I might get distracted."

Blake was totally improvising this whole role-play thing, but it wasn't a bad idea at all. A way to flirt, fuel the flames of their chemistry, and have a bit of fun even if Eliza burned down her kitchen.

"You'll be rewarded for every assignment you complete," Blake said.

Eliza grinned as if she liked the sound of this game. "What's the reward?"

Blake looked skyward as she thought about it. "Strip cooking?"

A streak of pink washed across Eliza's cheeks. "Too bold?"

"No, uh, no, not at all. I just was expecting, like, a kiss or something. But I'm completely fine with this."

"I give you a task, and if you ace it, I take an article of clothing off. You fail, I put it back on."

"Even better that you're doing the stripping. Just be careful when we finally get your pants off."

Blake had no idea what she'd gotten herself into. Heat crawled up her spine, her neck, and wrapped around her face. Eliza must have noticed because right as it all set in, she laughed.

"My guest, my idea, my stripping. Now, step inside my office and be my sous chef. My mobility is limited."

"Yet you went against doctor's orders by cooking a whole feast at your restaurant."

"I did most of the work sitting down." Blake crutched to the fridge, asked Eliza to grab two Coronas, and she opened the bottles for both of them while Blake turned on her Bluetooth speakers and played the seventies rock Spotify playlist she loved so much.

She cracked her knuckles for dramatic effect. "Chef Navarro is going to teach her student, Dr. Eliza Walsh, how to make carne asada tacos. And yes, we're going to make the corn tortillas. None of that packed flour shit."

"I'm good with my hands, remember?" Eliza said, flexing and wiggling her fingers.

Blake swallowed. She couldn't wait to see how great she was with them. She pulled a sip of Corona to ease her arid mouth. Not right now. They had dinner to cook.

"Task numero uno," Blake said and gestured to two raw skirt steaks resting on the chopping board. "We have to marinate the steak."

She directed Eliza each step of the way. She held open the gallon-sized plastic bag and instructed Eliza to juice two limes. Blake bit back her laughter as Eliza struggled to slice the limes, slicing them in half the wrong way, but she wasn't going to dock her points for that. Orange juice, olive oil, salt and pepper, and Blake taught Eliza how to mince garlic and chop up cilantro. Eliza was thorough with each slice, and Blake couldn't help but observe her fingers and how slow and precise she minced the garlic and cilantro, as if she was using a scalpel in the operating room. Slow and precise was the right approach in the OR—and sometimes in bed—but in the kitchen, time was of the essence, and chefs learned how to dice and slice at impressive speeds.

After spending twenty minutes on the marinade, Eliza plopped the skirt steaks in the fridge and smiled proudly.

"I think you owe me an article of clothing," Eliza said and motioned for her to pay up. Blake raised her good foot and motioned for Eliza to take off the sock. Eliza acquiesced after an eye roll. "Lame," she said.

"Still plenty of time, my dear student. While that marinates for an hour, we're going to do task numero dos: make the tortillas. Gives you a chance to show off your supposed hand skills."

Just like with the marinade, Blake stood to the side and guided Eliza through making the dough, directing her to mix masa harina and warm water together.

"I think that when I ace this task, I get to pick the next article of clothing," Eliza said, wiggling her eyebrows and drinking beer while they waited for the dough to sit for five minutes.

"I'm a strict teacher, and that sounds a little like extra credit. You should be glad I didn't criticize you for cutting the limes the wrong way or taking too long to mince the garlic."

"Oh, now the truth comes out?"

"I wasn't going to hold it against you, but maybe I should? I can't be too easy, can I? I have to withhold a little bit to keep you around."

The next step was to knead the dough, and as it started to come together, Blake helped Eliza by adding a bit of water to make it less dry. Then she joined in rolling the dough into golf-ball-sized balls.

"This is a tortilla press," Blake said, gesturing to the circular, cast aluminum appliance. "This is where the magic happens."

After pressing all the tortillas, Eliza demanded Blake take off her black, short-sleeved button-up with the white windowpane pattern, leaving her in a white V-neck, jean shorts, and her bra and underwear. She obliged, knowing that task three, cooking the tortillas, would result in several errors.

And it did. The first one turned out black. With the second, one side was black while the other was raw. Finally, the third tortilla was almost perfect, and they gradually improved with each one. Eliza studied the finished product with amazement sparkling in her eyes.

"Wow, I actually made those," she said and pointed to the stack of fresh corn tortillas.

"With only two and a half failures."

"I think that results in an article of clothing."

"No, failures equal clothes back on."

"But I made fifteen tortillas and only got docked two and a half points, which is eighty-three percent, a B grade."

Blake pretended to care and grunted as she took off her V-neck. Now she was only in her bra, shorts, and underwear. Eliza's eyes brazenly skimmed over every inch of exposed skin as she finished the rest of her beer. It was as if Blake could feel where her eyes looked—from her collarbone down to her breasts and to her stomach—as each part of her torso lit up. Eliza's emboldened eyes practically undressed the rest of her, and it sent a shiver down her spine. But she didn't care at all. She loved how she caught Eliza stealing glances at her stirring the Mexican rice while she coached Eliza through grilling the steak.

By the time dinner was ready, Blake had lost her shorts since Eliza had grilled the steak almost perfectly, a little more on the medium-well side instead of the medium-rare that was best for skirt steak. But she gave up the point…and the shorts.

"Let me help you," Eliza said while Blake's back rested against the kitchen island. She undid the button, slowly lowered the zipper, and Blake had to seal her lips together so a murmur didn't slip right out of her. That was how much she ached for Eliza to touch her.

Blake loved watching Eliza's face move lower with the shorts. Her fingers skimmed Blake's legs, and from the smirk on her face, Blake sensed that she did that to purposely tease her.

When the shorts were off, Eliza stepped back and observed her progress, sucking in her lips as she did so. "You look absolutely great right now," Eliza said, not even trying to hide the fact she was staring straight at Blake's breasts.

"I feel like a piece of meat," Blake said not too seriously.

"Oh, stop. It was your idea."

They took a seat at the table, and Blake spotted Eliza's failed attempts to steal secret glances, and when Eliza seemed to realize it, the blush blossomed yet again.

Eliza took her first bite of the tacos and hummed her pleasure. "Wow, I did a fabulous job."

There was that sound of approval again. Blake drank her beer to add moisture back to her throat.

"You really did."

Eliza snapped a picture on her phone before flipping it over, screen to the table. "I have to show this to Allison. Pics or it didn't happen."

It was a good thing Eliza got proof of her creation because the two of them devoured it, leaving no trace behind. Eliza gave Blake permission to put her clothes back on after Blake ate her second taco. They both slumped in their spots, started drinking their second beer, and sat in perfect silence as their stares locked, and their smiles widened.

"What's the ultimate goal?" Eliza asked. "In your career? I mean, being the head chef at Mezcal is amazing. I was wondering if you've achieved the dream or if you have any more plans?"

"Well, actually, the ultimate dream is in the works right now."

Eliza raised an eyebrow. "Oh really?"

"My friend Malai and I want to open a food hall with vendors that represent amazing food from cities from around the world. Different sections of the hall for different continents, and each section will have decor and music to match each area. So it's like you're visiting Tokyo without really being in Tokyo. But you'll get a similar ambience, the food, music. We still have to nail down what cities depending on what vendors we lease space to. But obviously, Mexico City will be one and since Malai's Thai and some of her family still lives in Bangkok, that will be another city. We actually have a meeting next week with a bank. We're going to go over our business plan and see if they're interested in giving us a loan."

Eliza leaned forward. "Oh my God, Blake, that's so amazing. I'm sure you will do great next week. Keep me posted?"

"For sure, especially if it's good news. We need a loan, some investors, and then we can start looking for the perfect spot."

"Where are you looking?"

"San Diego for sure. We have a wonderful food scene here, we have a lot of connections that will help us fill up space, plus my family is here. I can't leave them."

"And what's the hall going to be called?"

Blake smiled, loving so much how impressed and excited Eliza seemed to be about the idea. She remembered telling Carrie about it on one of their dates, and Carrie couldn't care less and only asked if that meant she could get free food. "Vagabonds," she replied.

"That's a really great name for a really great idea. I'll be there on opening day, if you invite me."

"You're already invited."

Cleaning up would be a problem for Future Blake, and instead of doing it, they moved over to the living room couch with a fresh bottle of malbec. Blake brought over the Bluetooth so the background music could continue, and they sat close together on the couch.

"Okay, I'm not allowed to talk anymore," Blake said as she patted Eliza's knee, loving that she'd worn shorts so Blake could feel her silky-smooth legs.

"But you're so good at it. I like listening."

She shook her head. "Nope. I've done enough, and I want to learn more about you. Tell me about work."

"Work is work. Lots of patients, lots of surgeries. I'm actually finishing my trauma rotation, and then I'll be starting a new rotation at the beginning of September at the VA hospital."

"Oh really?" The mention of the VA hospital encouraged her to have a big drink of wine. "Are you nervous?"

"Not really. It will mostly consist of things I already do. It will be interesting, that's for sure. Haven't had a rotation there yet. But other than that, work is work."

"Saving lives, the usual boring thing."

"If I actually got into the weeds of my job, it would be boring."

"Okay, if you think your work is boring to talk about—which I don't—I can think of something else." She tapped her chin, pulled an inspiring drink, and then asked, "Okay, what's one thing you haven't done that you want to do?"

Eliza laughed. "What? What a random question."

"What? You're a closed book. I only know a handful of things about you. Gotta start somewhere."

"It makes me extra alluring, right?"

Blake sensed Eliza's walls stacking back up. She wanted to know everything about her, but Eliza made it a little challenging. Blake had dated quite a few people in her past, some she wished she hadn't, but none of them were quite like Eliza. Not as beautiful, not as quirky, and definitely not as protective of their own heart. Eliza had to be the biggest closed book Blake had ever met, and she wanted to know why.

Eliza looked upward and blinked through several ideas before settling with, "I want to go to a concert."

That was something Blake wasn't expecting at all. But then again, this was Eliza Walsh. She'd made it pretty clear she wasn't the bungee jumping, cage diving, or skydiving person. Riding the tallest rollercoaster in the world, maybe. That might have been something she was expecting from Eliza. But not something as simple as going to a concert.

Eliza scratched the back of her head. "Yeah, um, that kind of flew out of me. I'm sorry, I didn't mean to say that." Her eyes went somewhere far away, and her walls were so sturdy, they created a strong presence in the living room.

"Eliza, you okay?" Blake asked and rested a hand on her knee.

She exhaled a staggered breath and met her gaze. That was when Blake noticed the tears brimming and her fun conversation-starting question had triggered something in Eliza that she'd never meant to bring up.

"I haven't been to a concert in a really long time," Eliza muttered and glanced at her lap.

Blake scooted closer, ready to catch her if the seams broke. "I'm...I'm sorry. I didn't mean for it to bring up a bad memory or anything." She kept her focus on Eliza, searching and begging to find out what the hell she did wrong, but Eliza remained focused on her lap.

"I, um, I haven't been since the night of my accident."

"Oh God, I'm so sorry." She should have never asked. It was a stupid question anyway.

"I don't want you to feel like I'm a closed book," Eliza said and whisked away the tears. "It's not like I do it on purpose. It's just that the accident has invaded almost every aspect of my life, and sometimes, I don't want to deal with it. It's too much." She sighed and finally looked back. "We were coming back from a concert. It was two weeks before we were supposed to move here. It was raining really bad, and I took my eyes off the road once, hydroplaned, hit a tree—"

Blake grabbed her hand and squeezed it. Eliza was opening up, and she had to be reassured that she was safe.

"Eliza—"

"I've never gotten over it," Eliza said, shaking her head and wiping her face with her free hand.

"I wouldn't expect you to."

"I haven't been to a concert since because it brings back too much. Hell, I haven't driven a car since that night because...the anniversary was earlier this month. I'm sorry. This is an extra emotional time and—"

Blake met her gaze. God, the pain in her eyes sliced Blake in two. "You don't need to apologize. I know how the anniversaries are. They're debilitating. That's how November is for me. I get it, Eliza. I really do."

"Yeah, they really are," she said. "It's just really hard because her parents, they told me it was my fault, and—"

"Wait, they what?" Her voice cut through the sullen moment, but she didn't care. She was infuriated.

Eliza seemed taken aback. "They told me it was my fault."

"Why the fuck would they say that?"

As her anger hung between them, a blink sent tears down Eliza's face. Her beautiful sapphire pupils were lost in thick gloss of vivid, traumatic memories. Blake knew exactly what was happening to her. All the memories of Tess were washing over her like a tsunami, and she was probably half in the present and half tumbling back in time. Blake had those moments too.

"Because Tess and I weren't supposed to be together. Her mom caught us kissing the summer before, and she literally screamed. It was, like, eleven at night, and we heard a shriek from the garage. And she called my parents and told them. She outed me, forced Tess to break up with me, and made her spend her summer getting brainwashed by their fucking church." She wiped her face again, and Blake held her hand tighter. "We weren't supposed to be around each other anymore, and obviously, we didn't listen. We applied to the same college, requested to be roommates, had everything planned to move out here together, worked day and night on scholarship applications so if our parents disowned us, we didn't have to worry about their money—"

"Jesus," Blake muttered under her breath. She couldn't imagine planning her life in such intricate detail because she was afraid of her parents disowning her for being gay. Sure, her mom hadn't been a fan of Blake dressing in Adrian's clothes, hadn't liked it when she'd first chopped off her hair to rock a pixie cut, but she'd never worried about her mother disowning her, especially after Adrian had died and her mom had cared less about Blake's androgynous fashion. And now? Her mom was so invested in Blake's love life that she knew some details a mother probably shouldn't have known.

It started to make sense why Eliza was so guarded. She was scared. She'd been betrayed and blamed, the heavy weight of the accident thrown on her back all because she was the driver. There wasn't anything Blake could have said or done to erase that. But she was going to fucking try with every fiber of her being.

"You know it wasn't your fault, right?" Blake asked, tilting her head to catch a glimpse of Eliza's eyes.

Eliza shrugged. "I think I know, but it's like part of my mind is frozen at eighteen, and the blame keeps ringing through that part every day. And all my parents did was tell them to 'knock it off,' but it was in such a submissive way. They acted like it never happened. They hated confrontation so much, they couldn't even acknowledge that I was screamed at and blamed for it. They were too scared to defend me at the worst moment of my life, and that really stayed with me."

"I'm so sorry."

Blake pictured two grown adults screaming at an eighteen-year-old who had not only survived something traumatic but had lost her girlfriend in the process. What the hell had they been thinking? Why the hell hadn't her parents done more to get that horrible accusation out of their daughter's brain?

After a few silent moments of reflecting, Eliza swiped away the last bit of moisture on her face and downed the rest of her wine.

"I feel like my life hasn't been normal since the accident," Eliza said. "I have PTSD, no relationship with my parents, every late-July and August gets me extra emotional. Exhibit A." She gestured to herself. "I don't know. Going to a concert might sound simple, but for me, it's a big, giant leap. I'm so tired of being scared of everything. I have so many regrets, and it only took me a couple of months ago to realize everything I've been missing out on. Maybe going to a concert again is a small step to feeling normal. They seem really fun."

"They are, but don't feel like you're not normal just because you haven't been to one since. I haven't attempted to surf since Adrian. I usually isolate myself in November. Try not to make too many plans with friends because who knows where my emotions are going to be. What does normal even feel like? Is anyone really normal? I'm definitely not."

"You seem normal to me, but I get what you're saying." Eliza shrugged, seeming embarrassed. "I really didn't want to unleash all my baggage tonight…at least not all at once."

"Hey." Blake leaned forward and palmed her face. "I asked you out because I find you genuinely interesting and because I want to get to know you. You shouldn't feel ashamed to share anything with me. I want to know all of it, even the bad parts. Every part of our lives—good, bad, and tragic—makes us who we are today. And who you are is a woman I find extremely sexy and beautiful and intriguing and intelligent and—" She was shocked when Eliza leapt up and straddled her. She was surprised by the gesture, but she wasn't going to complain. "What are you doing? I'm being serious—"

Eliza pressed her finger against Blake's mouth, causing her to hush, which was okay because her heart started racing, and she wasn't sure if she could form words right away. "I know you're serious," Eliza said, her stare holding Blake's tightly. "Thank you for…I don't know, just being there. For listening."

"Why wouldn't I do any of that?"

"I don't know."

Eliza stared at Blake's lips, and Blake's center awoke. God, Eliza was so incredibly sexy, even if her eyes were still red and swollen.

"When you, um, when I ran out of your car, it was a few days before the anniversary," Eliza said. "You told me I had a great smile and that…it was the last thing Tess ever told me."

Blake felt gutted, and she could feel the blood drain from her face as she processed the knowledge. "I'm…oh my God, I'm so—"

Eliza forced a smile and placed both hands on Blake's cheeks. "Don't apologize. It was very sweet. It's just that my mind was already teetering with the anniversary."

"I had no idea—"

Eliza silenced her with a soft kiss. "I know," she said against Blake's mouth. "I wanted to let you know, and I hope that doesn't scare you from giving me more compliments."

Blake tilted Eliza's chin up so she could get a better look at her and the faint smile curving her lips. She'd meant every word. "You do have a gorgeous smile. You walked into my hospital room when I was all drugged out on pain meds, and when I first saw your face, it jolted me awake."

"Lies."

Blake laughed. "Not lies, all truth."

The smallest smile let Blake know that she was okay for now. "I would very much like to leave that behind and enjoy the rest of the night."

"We can do whatever you want to do."

When Eliza sucked in her bottom lip and gently bit it, Blake leaned in to kiss her, sweet and simple, to let her know that she was all right and that she was safe.

"Are you sure you're okay?" Blake said after a few moments of tame kissing. "You don't want to talk about it anymore—"

Eliza silenced her with another finger to her lips. "I'm really good at not talking. You should try the same."

Blake smiled and nodded, and Eliza captured her mouth, diving straight into a kiss that heated Blake's spine. Pushing Eliza's head to the side with her cheek, she sucked and kissed the nape of her neck and slowly moved her fingers underneath the hem of Eliza's shirt, touching her smooth, soft skin for the first time. It sent goose bumps all over. Eliza's breasts pressed against hers, and she wondered what it would be like to slide her hands up Eliza's shirt and feel those breasts perfectly in her palms, or even better, in her mouth. The thought of it prompted her to rake her fingertips up Eliza's back. As she inched closer to her bra, she felt the goose bumps on Eliza that begged her to continue. Blake retrieved her hands and methodically undid the buttons of Eliza's blouse, slowly, allowing Eliza to tell her to stop at any point. But her ravenous stare demanded she continue. After undoing the last button, the shirt pooled to her side, and Blake's breath hitched.

God, Eliza was so beautiful.

Blake savored each inch of her body, skimming along her collarbone and watching as Eliza closed her eyes and let out the softest hum that ignited a throbbing in Blake's core. She moved from her collarbone down to her black bra, tracing invisible circles around the swell of her breasts. When Blake glided her tongue along the top of her breasts, Eliza held her there with a firm grip in her hair. The erotic tugging at the back of her head had her entire body aching for more. She couldn't take it.

She plopped Eliza on her back and hung her casted leg off the side of the couch. It was uncomfortable, but the desire taking her over was much more potent than the discomfort.

Balancing on her knee in between Eliza's legs, she tugged on Eliza's shorts, paused, and looked up, silently asking permission. When Eliza responded by lifting her hips, Blake freed her from the shorts and tossed them on the ground. With that barrier out of the way, Eliza was now in a black bra and pink-lace underwear, looking up with so much vulnerability and desire in her eyes. Blake lowered herself to kiss Eliza's inner thighs and swirled patterns along her skin that elicited more whimpering.

They spent the next half hour making out like teenagers, with Eliza rocking her bottom against Blake. Blake felt her arousal from it and decided it was time to relieve it and relieve Eliza's muted moans so she could fully bask in them.

She kissed Eliza's lips, neck, and then her collarbone before working her way down. Eliza's moans became more frequent, encouraging her to continue. Blake took her time kissing those sexy thighs, probably toned from hours of standing in the hospital. When Blake pressed her thumb into Eliza's center, and Eliza groaned, Blake's pulse quickened at the reaction, and she loved how she could feel Eliza's arousal through her underwear. She couldn't wait to yank them off and finally taste her.

"Blake?" Eliza said.

She lifted her head. The look in Eliza's eyes had changed from moments before. The desire was no longer there, and instead, what looked to be regret had taken over. Blake frowned as she pulled herself up from in between Eliza's legs.

"I...I don't think I can. I'm so sorry. I don't think I can. At least, not right now."

Blake thought about it. Damn, she'd misread all of those signals. She sat straight up. "Oh. Okay."

Eliza reached for her knee. "I'm really sorry."

"It's fine."

She wished she'd disguised her disappointment better, and it wasn't until the words left her mouth that she could hear them linger. She'd really hoped that they would go further. She'd thought that was a clear indication of what Eliza wanted.

"I'm sorry," Eliza said with a cracked voice.

Blake grabbed the hand still resting on her knee. "Eliza, it's okay. Really. I want you to enjoy it, and if you're not ready, then I'm okay with waiting. I just want you to feel safe."

She meant it. As much as Blake would have loved to finally have her way with Eliza, she wanted it to come naturally. Blake was someone who went at life at a hundred miles an hour, and Eliza was someone who went slowly and cautiously. Maybe going slow was exactly what Blake needed to experience. Whatever Eliza wanted and needed to feel safe, she would do. Eliza deserved to feel that way because Blake had a sneaking suspicion that she hadn't felt it in a long time.

And that wasn't right. She deserved the world.

"I do feel safe with you," Eliza said. "I don't know why I get terrified right when we're about to go further."

"You don't need to explain why you're not ready. You're not. End of story, and that's completely okay. I mean, don't get me wrong, you're sexy as hell, so of course I want to go further. But I'd rather have that happen when you're ready. It will be better for the both of us." Blake kissed her cheek. "How about this: we can have another glass of wine, sit and talk, or watch a movie. Whatever you want to do."

"I want to kiss you," Eliza said firmly. "That's what I want to do."

Blake laughed. "Okay, if that's what you want to do, then kiss me."

God, did Eliza kiss her. She stripped Blake's pants off because she said she needed to feel more of her, and even though Blake knew she would probably secretly combust if the grinding from before resumed with less layers, she still let Eliza take off her shorts. As the kissing progressed, their hips started undulating in sync, and it was so brutal without another layer over her underwear. Talk about feeling like a teenager: allowing someone to grind on her to the point she almost came several times, and in order to stop it, Blake had to rearrange them or pause for a sip of wine to calm herself down.

They kissed like that for another hour, and by the time Eliza left, Blake had to coat her lips in peppermint ChapStick. But even with chapped lips, she lay in her bed with the biggest smile on her face, and she hadn't even gotten laid. A make-out session with Eliza Walsh made her feel as good as if she had.

Her heart was soaring, and she worried it would fly right out of her chest. She couldn't remember the last time she'd felt that way. Come to think of it, had any woman made her heart race as much as Eliza did?

When she thought about it, the answer was no.

CHAPTER EIGHT

Ever since Blake moved back home after culinary school, Sunday evenings were dedicated to the family.

For the past few Sundays, Blake's mom had kept checking in with her about Eliza. Blake had brought that upon herself when she'd bragged about their first date, and then she'd made the mistake of telling them they'd had a second date. It'd been two weeks since their second date, and Blake had only seen Eliza twice since she had one day off a week when she wasn't on call. Each time Eliza left Blake's apartment, Blake lay in bed in a dizzy bliss with chapped, swollen lips. Apparently, the smile lingered on Sundays when she saw her family, and now her mother wouldn't stop asking about how things were going.

So Blake invited Eliza to dinner, a bold move when they'd only been talking for a month and a half and hadn't even slept together yet. Jordan kept referring to Eliza as Blake's girlfriend, even though they'd never had the conversation, and she assumed that Eliza wasn't seeing anyone else, but she couldn't be too sure. Someone with Eliza's beauty and smarts was quite the catch, and Blake still believed it was too good to be true. But with whatever they were still questionable, she went with what her heart wanted, and that was for Eliza to join her family's Sunday dinner.

The doorbell rang, and Blake swiftly crutched to the front door to try to sneak in a moment with her before her mother swooped in. Her mom had been on the edge of her seat for the last hour, and Blake had to remind her to calm down because Blake and Eliza had only been talking for a month and a half, and she didn't want her mom's enthusiasm to scare Eliza away.

Blake found Eliza on the other side of the front door wearing the same maroon dress she'd worn on their first date. The curls in her hair were more pronounced than usual, and her makeup highlighted all her best features. Blake pulled her in for a long kiss and properly greeted her with a quick tongue graze.

Eliza pulled away, laughing. "Oh, hello. That was a greeting."

"Sorry. I had to kiss you before my mom whisks you away and ruins my chance for the rest of the night."

"You do realize that you've set the bar incredibly high now for greetings," Eliza said. "I'm going to expect a kiss like that every time."

"It won't be a problem, believe me."

"Is that Eliza?" Blake's mom called from inside.

It was a good thing she got that kiss in.

Her mom scampered down the hallway with a smile as wide as her arms. "Our favorite doctor is here," her mom said and nudged Blake to the side so she could give Eliza a hug. It was official. Her mother loved Eliza more than her own daughter, and Blake was completely okay with that, knowing she was lucky her family loved the woman she was dating. Seeing? What the hell were they exactly?

She'd worry about that later.

"How are you, hon?" Blake's mom asked as she gestured Eliza into the house. "We've been trying to get Blake to invite you over for weeks now."

"You do know she's a doctor," Blake said. "Saving lives and studying for her boards. She's a busy woman. It's even hard for me to get penciled in."

"Thank you for having me, Sandra," Eliza said. "I'm glad I could join."

"Oh, please, the pleasure is all ours. Now come on in and make yourself at home. Dinner will be ready in a few minutes."

As Blake's mom scurried back to the kitchen, Eliza glanced at the wall of family pictures. "Oh my God, am I about to see that picture of you in a dress?"

Blake took the bottle of cabernet out of Eliza's hands. "Maybe."
She watched Eliza observe each photo leading down the hallway toward the kitchen. Each Navarro kid had their own picture frame that held their school pictures from kindergarten through eleventh grade, all encircling their senior picture in the middle. Blake's was in between Jordan and Adrian's. She'd gone through the biggest transformation. From a toothy little kid to a feminine middle schooler with pigtails and long, thick locks past her shoulders to high school when she started shedding some of her femininity as each year progressed.

"Nice blue hair," Eliza said and pointed to her eleventh-grade picture. It was the only picture where she had short, bright-aqua hair fresh from the dye box.

"Oh, thanks," she said proudly. "My parents really pissed me off two days before this picture, so the night before, I dyed my hair. I was grounded for a month, but at least we have this gem. Took my mom a few years to finally add it to the frame. It used to be an empty spot."

"I understand why. That's a hideous color."

Blake laughed as she nudged Eliza's arm. "She shouldn't have pissed me off if she wanted the beautiful photo she paid for."

"I'm not at all surprised you were one of those teenagers."

"What do you mean? I was a perfect child."

At the end of the hallway were Adrian's pictures, and Eliza stopped to study his frame for as long as she'd studied Blake's. He was an adorable kid who'd grown into quite an attractive guy in high school. Girls had always fawned over him, which had made Blake jealous a couple times because she'd wanted some of those older girls to do the same with her. He looked like Blake and Jordan: the same tan skin; dark brown, almond shaped eyes; that wide smile that would cause someone to take a double glance at the photo. Plus, he had his father's dimples like all three Navarro kids.

Next to Adrian's frame was a photo of him at boot camp graduation wearing his short-sleeved Marine khaki shirt tucked into blue trousers, and a white Marine hat covering part of his shaved hair. Compared to his senior picture, he'd shredded the rest of his baby face and had toned up. A middle-school-aged Blake stood next to him with shoulder-length hair, narrow glasses, and that gaudy lavender dress. Then came an elementary-aged Jordan on the other side of Adrian who looked like she'd bought out Limited Too with her hot pink dress and pigtails. It was amazing what a transformation Adrian had undergone in just a year. He looked like an adult in his uniform while standing proudly with his sisters under his arms.

"Ah, there's the picture," Eliza said and tapped the frame. "You look adorable."

"I look hideous. Look at my nerdy glasses and that ugly dress."

Eliza glanced back at the photo. "Adrian looks really happy."

"He was. My parents were so happy that day too. They weren't angry anymore."

"What do you mean?"

"They didn't want him to enlist. They knew it was a death trap, at least for their son. They supported the war up until Adrian died, but just because they supported it didn't mean they wanted their son to enlist. He was supposed to go to college, study architecture like he said he wanted to throughout high school. Out of nowhere, he decided to join the Marines instead. My parents were so upset. Mom was really worried about who he would become after going to war, seeing things no one should see. Her brother went to Vietnam, and it changed him, and she was terrified that it would do the same to Adrian. But he did it. Four months after this picture, he was deployed, and two years later, he was killed." Blake faced the picture and stared at her brother, at how much youth and innocence shaped his face. "Anyway, shall we head to the kitchen? Open this bottle?"

The smell from the charcoal grill perfumed the kitchen. Her dad had just finished grilling the burgers and marinated chicken breast, and when he came in, he gave Eliza a welcoming hug.

As everyone fixed their plate, her mom asked Eliza about work. Blake knew she'd started her shift at the VA hospital two weeks ago at the beginning of September, but whenever Blake asked how it was going, Eliza was always brief and said it was going well, typical surgeries, mostly older people. She got the feeling that when they were together, Eliza didn't want to discuss work, so Blake always dropped it after that. She didn't want to force her to talk about something she didn't want to.

"It's good," Eliza said after swallowing her first bite of chicken. "I'm doing surgery at the VA hospital."

Blake's parents perked up. "Oh really?" her dad said. "How are you liking it?"

"It's going good. It's mostly gallbladder, hernias, and appendix removals."

Blake furrowed her eyebrows, sensing Eliza was holding back. She'd never met anyone who walled herself so quickly, and the more Blake hung out with her, the easier it was to detect when she did so: avoiding eye contact, brief responses, and the tension thickening around her as she retreated.

"Do you get mostly older patients?" Jordan asked.

Eliza hesitated and took another bite. "I've had some younger ones too. I've seen every age."

"Are they…you know…messed up?"

"Jordan," her mom said.

"What? Okay, I didn't mean it like that. I just meant, like, do they have, like, PTSD?"

"You shouldn't be going around calling people with PTSD 'messed up,'" Blake said and snuck a glance at Eliza to make sure her sister's lack of class hadn't affected her too much. She didn't seem too fazed by it, but Blake guessed it was because she'd walled herself up moments ago. "They've seen some serious shit, and they don't need people like you thinking they're fucked-up because of it."

"I'm sorry for my choice of words," Jordan snapped at Blake. "I didn't mean it like that. I just wanted to know if…I don't know… the younger ones had health problems. That's all."

Great, and now an awkward silence covered the kitchen table like a fancy tablecloth. Blake stabbed the potato salad with her fork, quickly searching for something to kill the silence. Something to make them get off this topic. Eliza probably clung on to the stupid PTSD comment and how Blake's parents and Jordan were thinking about Adrian, trying to gauge how he would be if he'd survived the war. The dinner was supposed to be fun without everyone's baggage lying on the table like a side dish.

Right as Blake was about to change the subject, Eliza spoke up. "Most of them have PTSD, yes. But I only know that when I read their files. Most of them don't show visible signs when I interact with them."

Jordan nodded and went back to her food.

"Have you ever played Catan?" Blake said. "It's the game we're playing tonight."

After dinner, Blake set up the board while Eliza helped Jordan and her mom with the dishes. Eliza sat next to Blake when she was finished, resting a hand briefly on her thigh as if to sneak in a moment with her. Blake looked at her, and Eliza smiled back, squeezing her thigh before retrieving it to drink some water.

"We should have brought out Operation," Jordan joked as she took her seat.

"Maybe you can get that after you lose," Blake said. "Since you never win in Catan." Jordan elbowed her side. She yelped. "You can't elbow me in my healing ribs," Blake said. "She's going to yell at you, know you." She pointed to Eliza. "Lectures are her specialty."

"They really are," Eliza said. "Speaking of lectures, have you ditched the bike?"

Jordan bellowed. "Ha. No, she hasn't."

"Everyone shut it, and let's play this game. You can watch me knock that cocky smirk off Jordan's face when she loses."

Ten minutes into the game, everyone had at least three victory points, and Blake put the robber on Jordan and their parents' eight-wood spot. Then she stole a resource card from Jordan. She pumped her fist when it was a valuable ore that she needed to upgrade a settlement to a city on her next turn. Any time Blake rolled a seven or played a Knight card, she targeted one of Jordan's spots and stole a card from her.

Jordan pounded her fist on the table, and it was Blake's turn to toss her head back in laughter.

"This is some bullshit," Jordan yelled. "Stop putting the robber on my stuff."

"But your reaction is everything," Blake said. "Punishment for sucking at this game, Ms. Three Victory Points."

"Because you keep robbing me. I would have had at least four by now. Eliza has five, and Team Parents have six. Go after them. They're more of a threat to you."

"Nah, I'd rather go after you and watch you cry about it."

Their mom shook her head. "Welcome to family game night, Eliza. Where my precious, adult daughters act like children."

"Just wait until she loses," Blake said to Eliza. "She'll storm off."

"Please, you do the same thing when I kick your ass at President," Jordan said.

A few rounds later, Blake reached the needed ten victory points to win. She celebrated by tossing her hands in the air, and Jordan grunted as she leaned back in her seat, crossed her arms, and pouted. Eliza left the room to go to the bathroom…and probably hide from the nonsense that was Blake and Jordan playing games together. Once the bathroom door shut, Jordan quickly got over her loss, rounded her eyes, and leaned against her propped arm.

"So you and Dr. Walsh?"

"Her name is Eliza," Blake said.

"Is she your girlfriend yet?"

Her mom beamed across the table. "She's a very sweet girl, Blake. You two have been talking for what? A little over a month now?"

Heat claimed Blake's face. She'd never seen her family so invested in a woman before. Even her dad grinned as he waited for her to answer.

"We've been talking for a month and a half," Blake said.

"Have you kissed her?" Jordan wiggled her eyebrows.

Blake started to sweat. Was the air-conditioning even on? She'd told her family about her dating life, but she'd never told them details about kissing or anything, obviously. Jordan only got those details on occasion…when she behaved. But ever since she and Malai had blown away the banks and investors with their Vagabonds business plan and had acquired the restaurant capital needed to open, when Blake wasn't with Eliza, she was either at Mezcal or working with Malai on their must-haves, would-likes, and deal-breakers for a venue. She'd forgotten to text her sister all the juicy details about her dates with Eliza, and she wasn't about to tell her parents about making out for hours and desperately wanting to sleep with Eliza while at the same time respecting the pace Eliza wanted.

Jordan sunk back in her seat as she plastered on a victorious grin. "You totally have. Your face is bright red."

Blake wiped her cheeks as if that would erase the embarrassment. Her mom applauded. Blake wasn't in the mood for the conversation. Not when Eliza was only a wall away and could walk back in at any time.

She stood and planned to steal a moment with Eliza without her family watching. "We're seeing how things go."

"Oh, Blake," her mom said, lowering her voice and leaning into the table. "She'd be so perfect for you."

"She's quite the catch, mija," her dad added. Even her dad had opinions. He was usually quiet, especially during dating talk, which her mom bathed in. She loved the gossip and knowing that her kids were on track to finding a partner and settling down, despite the fact that not everyone's happily ever after ended with monogamy or marriage or kids.

"I know she's great. That's why we're enjoying whatever this is," Blake said.

Her mom shook her head. "Don't you think you should figure that out? Don't string her along."

"I'm not stringing her along—"

"Obviously, it's something if you brought her here tonight."

"Yeah, because you bring her up every chance you get—"

"And obviously it means something to her if she came."

"Don't get defensive," her dad said. "It's not fooling anyone."

Jordan snickered, and Blake grunted. Now was the perfect time to check on Eliza, steal a moment, and let her cheeks cool down.

As she entered the hallway, Eliza opened the bathroom door and flinched when she saw Blake. What Blake wanted to do was grab her hand and whisk her to the laundry room, the farthest room on the first floor away from her family. But given her damn crutches, she whispered, "Follow me."

Once they were in the laundry room, Blake used a crutch to shut the door. She leaned her back against the dryer, pulled Eliza in, and went for the nape of her neck, which she'd been eyeing during the whole game. It was long and smooth and begging to be sucked on. Eliza melted into her, letting out a soft murmur of pleasure.

"Blake," she breathed, half pleasure, half laughter. Blake traced circles with her tongue on all the right spots she'd recently come to know that unwound Eliza completely. "Your family is right outside."

"That's what makes it fun," she said against her skin.

Eliza caved and pulled Blake's face to hers. After a few moments of getting lost in her perfect mouth, Blake pulled away.

"I have a surprise for you," Blake said.

"Oh yeah? Does it involve a bed and ChapStick? Because that would be a great surprise."

She laughed and reached for her phone in her back pocket. "It can involve that, but it's not the main essence of the surprise."

"Then what is it?"

Blake went to the saved Safari browser and showed her the surprise. Pictures of a white, A-frame cabin with a beautiful wooden patio and ponderosa pines extending from the deck. She slid her finger on her phone to show her the interior, a bright and open cabin with bamboo floors, an open staircase leading to a loft and a queen-size bed, two log stumps that served as the downstairs coffee table, and a black steel fireplace with a batch of firewood next to it.

"This is beautiful," Eliza said. "But what is it?"

"You want to take a weekend trip with me? During your week-long vacation in a few weeks? Just us in this cabin and these woods?"

"Wait, really?"

"Really. It's right on Big Bear Lake, two and a half hours away. Unless you have plans that week—"

"I don't have any plans except for studying, but this is a much better idea." Eliza clasped Blake's face and silenced her with a grateful kiss. "Let's go. I don't remember the last time I took a trip, even if it was for a weekend."

"Then I'll book it now," Blake said.

Blake knew that they were still so new in…whatever it was that they were doing. Ever since Eliza had showed up with Allison at Mezcal, the two had seen each other once a week, spending the late afternoon and evening together. But since Eliza had to wake up early the next day, they hadn't shared a night together, and even if the trip didn't lead to anything, it would be nice to have someone to fall asleep next to.

Planning a weekend trip together might have been fast, but Blake also wanted to treat Eliza to an escape from studying. Eliza had said she hadn't traveled enough, and for the week off she got four times a resident year, she always stayed at her apartment. A break would be nice for both of them. Plus, Blake looked forward to three full nights with her, curled up in a log cabin, surrounded by the smell of pines.

She was so glad that Eliza was just as eager for the trip as she was.

Three weeks was going to be a hell of a wait.

CHAPTER NINE

Despite living in California since she was eighteen, Eliza had hardly seen the vast scenery the state had to offer. She'd visited the Bay Area with Allison, had taken a spring break trip to Lake Tahoe her junior year, and had introduced Violet, Jonathon, and Emma to Joshua Tree two years before when they'd visited.

But it wasn't enough. She wanted to see so much more of her new state. Hell, she wanted to see so much more of the world.

She rolled back the Audi's sunroof as she and Blake ventured east, and once they got to the San Bernardino Mountains, the temperature dropped ten degrees. Evergreen woods surrounded them, and the smell of pines and crisp bonfires permeated the air. It was the first weekend of October. Fall was right around the corner. A few trees had already started turning gold, crimson, and amber. Eliza was reminded of the one thing she missed about Ohio: fall had been her favorite season. She'd loved walking home from school, wearing a sweatshirt and jeans, going out of her way to step on crunchy leaves. She'd loved drinking warm beverages like tea and apple cider and had loved it on autumn Saturdays when her mom had made a different kind of soup. Her soups were the best, from chicken noodle to white chili to chicken dumpling to even a cheeseburger soup. She'd loved the feeling of warmth in her stomach with the fresh crisp air outside.

She hadn't seen fall foliage in years nor had she enjoyed a big bowl of homemade soup since she'd left Ohio. She was sure that no one could make soup like her mom. Not even Blake, and Blake's cooking was phenomenal.

"This is the best idea you've ever come up with," Eliza said and twirled around the living room of their cabin. The pictures didn't do it justice.

"I was pretty proud of it myself," Blake said and paused to watch her spin. "Can I ask what the hell you're doing?"

"Enjoying this lovely cabin and all its perfectness."

"You know, I had a feeling you were a cabin girl."

Eliza stopped spinning and tried to gather her balance. "You're spot on. I thought about living in Denver, my second choice. I just love the mountains and being all cozy, especially during fall. It's the one thing I miss about Ohio."

"And that silly amusement park that's supposed to be the best?"

Eliza directed a point. "Hey. You're not going to win this, okay? Just because an amusement park is in California doesn't mean it trumps all other parks. Cedar Point *is* the best. Now I have two things I miss about Ohio. Don't get me going."

"But you're so cute when you get going." Blake gave her a soft kiss. "You know, there's a hot tub outside. I say, I cook up some steaks, and then we crack open a beer and get in the hot tub."

"I'm all for this plan."

"Plus, my leg can have a breather," she said and pointed to the new walking cast she'd finally gotten a week prior.

"You know, I barely recognize you without crutches."

"Just wait until I have no cast. I'll be a different woman."

Two grilled steaks and delicious, buttery corn on the cob later, Eliza opened the beers, changed into her bathing suit, and met Blake, who was already ahead of her since Eliza did the cleaning up. She should have known how she would react seeing Blake in a bathing suit. Given her year-long dry spell, why hadn't she prepared herself more?

Blake sat on the edge of the bubbling tub with her injured leg propped along the side and the walking cast on the ground. She wore a black bikini top and black boy shorts, and Eliza was amazed by how her body reacted. Her dating life had been so thin, she had no idea what her type of woman was or what her weaknesses were. Well, her weakness list officially started with women in boy shorts.

As Eliza took in her legs and butt, accentuated by the shorts, she noticed Blake do the same to her. She didn't even hide where her eyes went, scanning Eliza's breasts, down her stomach and to her legs. Eliza enjoyed every moment of it and the salacious grin that claimed Blake's face.

"I like this view," Blake said and gestured to Eliza as she cautiously lowered herself into the steaming water.

As Blake slid in, Eliza pointed to Blake's leg. "Be careful."

The occasional gentle wind brought a chill to the air, hinting that cooler weather, crunchy leaves, and cozy sweaters were looming. The outside cabin light flickered above them as the sound of crickets and night bugs filled the woods.

Eliza waded through the foamy water and straddled Blake.

"Oh, hi," Blake said, clutching her beer so it didn't spill off the ledge.

"Sorry, this bathing suit is making you really irresistible. I'm liking these boy shorts." She ran her hands up Blake's thighs, and they felt as wonderful as they looked.

"You don't have to apologize for touching me. I welcome it."

Everything about the scene was absolutely perfect. The perfect temperature with a beautiful cabin surrounded by trees, the sounds of the bugs, the smell of smoky bonfire in the distance, Blake's bare skin on hers.

"I have to say, all of this is very therapeutic," Eliza said while Blake ran her fingers across her collarbone. "I need to do this more often. Get away."

"You really do. You need to treat yourself more."

"It's hard when you're working eighty-something hours a week."

"You need to make room for it. Go treat yourself to a massage, go study in a park or the beach."

"You know that I've never gotten a massage?"

Blake stopped her fingers mid-collarbone. "You're joking."

"I'm not."

"Why not? I'm sure the massage therapist would have a field day with you and all those tense muscles."

Eliza shrugged. "I don't know. I never thought of it."

"Self-care is important. You should at least make some time to do things that you want to do. Go to the beach or the pool or drag Allison out for drinks."

"I *do* do things I want to do. That's why I spend my days off with you."

"I know I'm amazing and all. Maybe on one of those off days, we can get a couples' massage."

Eliza pulled her face back. "A couples' massage?"

After Blake said it, she closed her mouth and took a long swig of beer. Eliza slid off her lap as the tension piled between them. A cocktail of emotions filled Eliza. Excitement, nervousness, confusion. Two months into…whatever it was they were into…the fact Blake said "couples' massage" was a great segue into discussing what the hell they were because Eliza had been wondering. Allison and Violet kept asking her about it. Maybe it was time to get an answer.

"Is that what we are?" Eliza asked, tossing her question into the open like a fishing line and expecting to catch a shark. "A couple?"

Blake looked back at her, biting her lip and making an adorable, "I'm in trouble," face. "Yeah, um…" She scratched the back of her head. "Sorry, it slipped right out of me."

"Are you glad it slipped out of you?"

"I guess I'm just nervous about what you'll say."

Eliza was nervous. She wasn't going to deny it. Having a girlfriend meant she could lose that girlfriend, especially a woman who loved motorcycles that were a thousand times more dangerous than a car. But she wanted to try. She owed herself and her heart a partner, and every new day with Blake was exciting. It pumped new life into her. She wanted to wake up because that meant she could talk to Blake, and on the best day of the week, the one when she didn't have to work, she got to see her.

She wanted this. She wanted Blake.

"You really think I'm going to say that I'm not interested?" Eliza said. "I'm here with you. I've only been spending all my off days with you."

"Good point. I, well, I haven't had a girlfriend in a long time."

"I haven't had a girlfriend in thirteen years. I think I beat you." Eliza smiled as she resumed her position on Blake's lap. "That doesn't scare you, does it?"

"No, not really. Did my rambunctious twenties scare you?"

"It did at first, but it doesn't anymore."

Blake tucked a strand of Eliza's wet hair behind her ear. "Then can I start telling my family that you're my girlfriend? Because that would be really awesome."

The title was foreign to Eliza, but it came with a feeling she would always remember. For what seemed like half of her life, she'd desperately searched for the feelings to fill the voids punched out of her: a strong need to be loved, wanted, needed, and understood. And then here came Blake crashing into her life, effortlessly giving her all of that and more.

"Please do," she said and pulled Blake's waist into hers.

She'd loved being Tess's girlfriend, and there was no doubt that she would love being Blake's. She wanted to return everything Blake made her feel.

"My girlfriend is a surgeon. Damn, I did good."

"My girlfriend is a head chef and about to start her own business. Damn, I did good."

"I don't have MD after my name. So you have beaten me in the cool factor."

Eliza silenced her with a kiss and slipped her hands into her hair. She ran her tongue along Blake's bottom lip, teasing and warming her up before asking for more. As the kiss deepened, more heat bubbled in the tub of hundred-degree foamy water. Blake sucked on Eliza's tongue, eliciting a moan, and the two melted further into the kiss. The way Blake's tongue danced against hers, so delicate and precise, made Eliza feel like she was being methodically undone. There was nothing left to do except to glide her hand in between Blake's legs and skim her center through the thin boy shorts.

Blake pulled away for a moment, almost as if checking in to see if Eliza meant to touch her there. Eliza held her stare and pressed harder with purpose, proving that she meant everything she was doing. God, did it feel wonderful to touch Blake there, and it sparked a tingling in the same spot for her. She loved watching Blake react. Blake parted her mouth for a moment before latching on to Eliza's neck, swirling her tongue in delicate patterns in all the right spots to make Eliza weak. She closed her eyes and imagined those exact patterns right where she needed them while she stroked Blake without the barrier of the shorts.

She wanted to feel her, hear her, watch her, taste her.

She couldn't wait anymore.

"Can we go to the bedroom?" she whispered in Blake's ear and then nibbled it.

Blake moaned. "Really?"

"Yes."

She wanted Blake so badly, she didn't even worry about the walking cast. After Eliza had her way with Blake and undid her completely, she'd go get it and put Blake back together again. She was thankful she had a couple inches on Blake that made it easier to scoop her up so she didn't have to put pressure on the recovering leg.

By the time they went up the steps, Eliza's arms shuddered from the weight and her lack of upper body strength. She plopped Blake on the bed and resumed straddling her so they could devour each other. With one hand holding Eliza's back, Blake reached for the knot in her bikini top, untied it, and slowly peeled it off.

Eliza watched Blake absorb the sight of her naked breasts for the first time. Her heart hammered heavy and fast as the nerves spiraled in her gut. Ever since Blake had proposed the trip, of course Eliza had thought about what could happen. She and Allison had analyzed it at least four times. They'd been seeing each other for two months, and with years of practice walling herself off from deep emotion, Eliza's guard was tall and sturdy. Another part of her guard was tossed aside with each layer of clothing that Blake removed. Sex had just been sex with the short list of women in her past because there had been no feelings. But sex with Blake was going to be an overwhelming experience. It would be her first time with a person who made her feel some semblance of what Tess had. That terrified

Eliza because sleeping with Blake would be handing off the baton to crush her heart.

As much as Eliza wanted and craved her, allowing someone in was unnerving, pressing on old wounds that weren't completely healed. She trusted Blake. She knew that Blake would handle her heart and her body delicately in that moment, but she feared the future and what opening herself fully to Blake would mean when they hit a rough patch.

Blake's eyes had such a beautiful and expressive look as she absorbed the sight of Eliza's naked breasts, as if Blake was an artist painting small details on a canvas. She had a way of really looking, like Eliza was the most important person in the room. Like what she said really mattered. When Blake took in her naked body for the first time, Eliza's skin caught fire with each inch that met her stare.

Once Eliza had given herself permission to allow unfiltered feelings to blossom, falling for someone had become exciting. Blake effortlessly had Eliza completely caught up in her orbit, and she welcomed it.

Blake palmed Eliza's face and softly kissed her, almost as if she could feel how scared she was and wanted to ease the nerves. She was so gentle and delicate as she moved on to her neck, kissed down to her collarbone and breasts. When Blake captured a nipple in her mouth and swirled her tongue in the same precise patterns as before, a moan escaped Eliza's lips. Blake was undoing her without fully trying. Eliza was in trouble. Blake was dangerous because Eliza's heart and all the sensitive spots that comprised her body wanted and needed her.

For the first time in a long time, Eliza wanted the danger to excite her and awaken her. She wanted to feel something.

Blake had been so kind and patient that Eliza didn't want to wait anymore. So she pushed Blake on her back and crawled over her. She undid Blake's top and ripped her boy shorts down her legs.

Now it was her turn to consume the sight of Blake naked below her.

Her small breasts fit perfectly in Eliza's palms, and when Eliza captured one of her nipples in her mouth, they were already hard. Blake's breathing hitched, only encouraging Eliza to take in the other nipple. Eliza nibbled it gently as she rolled the other one between her fingers. Blake arched and groaned at the suction.

Eliza loved how she reacted to every touch. Apparently, despite her dry spell, Eliza was still able to light a woman up, and the feedback injected more confidence that propelled her lower, down Blake's stomach and to her inner thighs where she traced invisible patterns, slowly inching closer to the spot where Blake needed her the most. The sounds coming from Blake matched Eliza's rhythms and patterns. They were so sexy, she felt like she could combust just from listening.

That was it. She spread Blake's legs open and positioned her face in between them.

"Fuck," Blake muttered and tossed an arm over her mouth.

"No," Eliza demanded. Blake glanced down, and her stare begged Eliza to release her. "I want to hear you."

She slipped her fingers inside with ease, and Blake cried out. Her head fell back onto the pillow, and Eliza watched her mouth part while moving inside her. She circled her hips around Eliza's fingers, searching for the release. She was so unbelievably sexy that Eliza failed at the teasing game she wanted to play. Her plan was to warm Blake up before using her mouth to push her over the edge, but she couldn't even wait for that anymore. She needed to taste her. When Eliza captured her with her mouth, Blake moaned and combed her fingers through Eliza's hair, holding Eliza where she wanted her. Eliza obliged. The sounds she made were a preview to the wonderful noises she'd make when she came, and Eliza was ready to hear all of it. With a few more strokes, licks, and sucks, she got her there. Blake tensed, her cries becoming louder and higher until her body withered in Eliza's grip. She collapsed and left Eliza with her lips parted. It was amazing how sexy Blake sounded and how quickly Eliza made her come.

God, if she wasn't already wet, that would have been enough.

After taking a few moments to collect her breath, Blake opened her eyes and cupped Eliza's face. "Good God," she panted.

"You're unbelievably sexy—"

Blake leaned forward and kissed her so deeply that Eliza could feel the intimacy scorching inside her. Blake pushed her by the shoulders so she could fall on her back, and once she cautiously straddled Eliza, Blake resumed the kiss, and Eliza fastened her legs around Blake's waist. A surge of electricity sparked through her everywhere Blake kissed. Her collarbone, her neck, trailing down her stomach to her waist. When Blake ran her tongue along her hip bone, Eliza stifled a moan and gripped the sheets for support. She tried so hard holding in all the sounds begging to come out. When Blake pressed her thumb over her bikini bottom, Eliza was done. Listening to Blake already primed her for reciprocation.

"Blake," Eliza croaked. Blake looked at her, and her skin sizzled. God, she wanted that smolder on Blake's face between her legs and kissing her folds. "I need you."

"You do?" Her tone held a mixture of confidence and vulnerability. Like she knew how big of a deal this step was. "Are you sure?"

Once Eliza had heard and watched Blake climax, every tiny doubt had gone out the window. She knew what she needed and that was Blake to make her come.

"Positive."

"It's okay if you don't—"

The only way to stop her from rambling was to lean forward, grab her face, and slip a tongue in her mouth so she would know for certain that not only did Eliza want it, she needed it.

"Please," Eliza begged when she pulled away and lay back down.

Blake's eyes held on to her as she kissed down to Eliza's breasts, swirling around a nipple and grazing it with her teeth. Eliza tightened her lips, not ready to give her pleasure all away yet. She'd forgotten how sensitive her nipples were, and Blake's amazing kissing skills reflected in the way she caressed and teased her breasts.

She sucked each nipple into a hard peak and then continued planting kisses on her journey down, still setting Eliza's skin in a tingling fire. Blake straightened and ran her fingertips along Eliza's inner thighs, absorbing the sight of every inch and curve of her body. She made Eliza feel like the sexiest person in the world when she looked at her like that.

Blake replaced her fingertips with her mouth and softly kissed the inside of Eliza's knee, a part of her body she had no idea felt so wonderful against someone else's lips until Blake introduced the new erogenous zone. That was when she knew Blake was going to yank her out of her own body and put her in a completely different one. She sealed her lips to censor her moans. She was worried she would come across as being too easy—and maybe she was—but Blake made it so goddamn difficult while she skimmed her tongue up her thigh, closer to her throbbing center.

Eliza forgot how much she loved all of it: the tender moments, the intense and hungry moments, the teasing, the giving, the taking. She forgot the anticipative moment when a woman sucked her clit into her mouth, and the warmth and delicacy of her tongue that pulled her whimpers out in the open.

She was done for. With Blake's mouth and her fingers still driving her, Eliza grabbed Blake's free hand to feel more of her as Blake coaxed her body to unravel. And Blake squeezed back as if encouraging her to let loose. Eliza's mind became lost in the longing, her thoughts incoherent, every part of her dizzy. She cried out, rocking against Blake's mouth and fingers, and feeling herself starting to lose complete control. The pressure between her legs crawled up her spine in a buzzing warmth. She clenched the sheets and twisted with each feeling that zigzagged through her. Blake claimed her entirely. The orgasm rippled through Eliza so powerfully that her scalp tingled during and after. She cried out and rode out the aftershocks against Blake's mouth and fingers until she couldn't take it anymore.

Eliza buried her face in her hands while her body flickered and soared into a different dimension. She came so quickly, she wasn't sure whether to be embarrassed or excited. With the small handful of other women, it had taken her a while, adding another layer to Eliza's belief that she was forever broken. So broken, she struggled to climax. But with Blake, there wasn't a single struggle. Eliza had no idea how deprived she'd been until the orgasm ignited her body and released a bit of her brokenness. She'd missed someone seeing her—really seeing her more than a conquest for the night—and she'd missed allowing someone to see her. She felt so wonderful and light and appreciated and safe, feelings she hadn't felt in such a long time that the cocktail was foreign to her.

"Hey," Blake said softly, and there was a smile in her voice.

She kissed her way up Eliza's stomach and sucked on her neck. Eliza lowered her hands. She couldn't even form words. Her throat tugged, and a sting hit her eyes. Everything was so overwhelming. Years of longing to be loved, touched, and appreciated like that swelled a balloon of emotion so large, she wanted to cry. She'd truly believed that no woman would ever make her feel like that again. Blake had just reminded Eliza that sex could be so much more, and for that, she was so grateful.

Eliza held her face and kissed her tenderly, thanking her.

"How are you feeling?" Blake asked when she pulled away, the victorious smile still on her face.

Eliza wanted to tell her that her scalp still tingled, and she had a few tears brimming, but she saved all of that for herself.

"Fucking amazing," Eliza said. "I haven't felt this good in a really long time."

Blake brushed a stray hair out of her face. "You're really fucking sexy, you know that? So unbelievably sexy."

She shook her head. "No."

"Yes, believe it. You're even prettier when you come."

Eliza felt a streak of heat highlight her cheeks from the aftermath of her orgasm, but Blake's comment darkened it.

"I think we're going to need to do a lot more of this," Eliza said. "I'd truly forgotten how much I love sex."

"I think we can make that happen."

CHAPTER TEN

B lake woke up to kisses against her bare shoulder and soft lips that moved to the nape of her neck and sucked on her pulse point. When Blake rolled onto her back and opened her groggy eyes, even through the blurriness of her moderately bad vision, Eliza's beauty shined. Her hair was all messy from sleep... okay, mostly sex.

"Wow, this is a great way to wake up," Blake said, her voice hoarse and groggy.

Eliza hovered over her. "So this is okay?"

"More than okay."

Eliza quickly resumed. Blake's eyes shot open when Eliza kissed a path down, and she became fully awake when she felt that wonderful tongue in between her legs.

What a way to wake up, Blake thought.

For a woman who'd claimed her dating life was hardly in existence, she sure knew how to make Blake come. Holy fuck. The rumors were absolutely true. Eliza Walsh was really good with her hands. They had stayed up late into the night, not able to take their hands off each other. It was as if the sex seal had been broken, and after the first time, they didn't want to stop. Sleeping was so overrated when she had someone wildly attractive in her bed who wanted her.

When Eliza accomplished her task yet again, it was Blake's turn to return the favor, as if they hadn't already done it four times before they actually fell asleep. Blake always knew Eliza was reserved, so her hidden libido was a very nice surprise.

"I think we should get out of bed," Blake said, still panting from her second orgasm. Eliza kissed a way up from between her legs to her lips. "Have some coffee. Water. Electrolytes. Breakfast."

Eliza plopped on her side of the bed and rested her head on Blake's shoulder. "I feel like a heathen for having sex twice before showering or having any coffee."

"What have you been missing out on?"

"A lot, apparently."

"You really stayed away from it, didn't you?"

"Well, I mean, I had some fun nights with women over the years. But it was never a marathon. They weren't able to make me feel the way you do."

Well, after that feedback, Blake didn't need coffee. She was awake and ready to conquer the day. Or maybe scrap the plans altogether and stay in bed so she could make Eliza feel like a queen. She was torn, but either way, she knew she couldn't hide the red that probably claimed her cheeks.

"Don't boost my ego," Blake said.

"I can't help it. I speak the truth."

"I thought you were this shy, innocent woman, and well, you proved me wrong. Six times in the last nine hours to be exact. I'm proud of this new personal record."

Eliza ran her fingers through Blake's hair. "I'm sorry. I find you incredibly sexy, and you know what you're doing."

"You know what *you're* doing."

"I think you're blinded by my face."

Blake laughed. "No, it's a fact. A scientific fact. Eliza Walsh is really good with her hands in every aspect. What she says is true." Eliza playfully smacked her arm. "Now, come on. I wouldn't be a gentlewoman if I didn't cook you a mean breakfast after all that, right?"

She whipped up blueberry pancakes, scrambled eggs, and bacon, and even allowed Eliza to help with the eggs and steal a couple blueberries as an appetizer. Even with Eliza scrambling, Blake considered it a victory that the kitchen didn't burn down. Maybe when she grilled burgers for dinner later, she would upgrade Eliza's responsibilities to helping form the patties.

Maybe. It still was risky.

The cool fresh air smelled like a piney morning and warned her that it would heat up by the afternoon. Blake's body hummed as caffeine flowed through her veins, she enjoyed a delicious breakfast, and a beautiful woman sat across from her with the biggest heart eyes any woman had ever given her. Blake beamed. She'd finally found someone who looked at her the way Eliza did, like she mattered. All throughout her twenties, she'd disguised her heartbreak and betrayal by keeping her mind—and her body—busy with other women, but she realized now that by doing that, she'd made herself feel very empty and used. She wanted to fall in love. She wanted to get married, have a family, have a best friend and a partner by her side. She wondered if her struggle to find that woman had been karma for her casual dating and one-night stands when she was younger.

But Eliza was different. Blake had always known she was different. And now, Dr. Eliza Walsh, MD, was her girlfriend. She couldn't wait to tell her family.

"What are we doing today?" Eliza asked as they stepped out of the shower and started to change.

Blake stopped when a freshly showered and naked Eliza reached for a T-shirt. They might have gotten a little sidetracked during the shower, and she still wasn't over how great Eliza looked without clothes on. "You have a great body," Blake said. "I still can't get over it."

"Oh, stop sucking up, and tell me what we're doing."

She bit her lip to contain a grin. "I'll tell you if you promise me that you'll still like me after this."

"I already don't like the sounds of this." Blake placed her hands on Eliza's waist and planted kisses down her neck, sucking on the spot that always pulled a moan. "Yeah, I really don't trust you now, but I'll accept these kisses."

"Okay hear me out. What are your thoughts about riding ATVs?"

Eliza pulled back. "You're joking, right?"

"No. I'm serious. I did all this research and found a place a half hour from here with really flat land, and we can ride two people to a vehicle, and I can go really slow—"

"For one, you're literally in a cast—"

"I promise I'll be safe. I'll take it easy. We can go as slow as you want and avoid all the hills."

"Two, if you're doing reckless things in front of me, what the hell are you doing behind my back? Riding that motorcycle?"

"I haven't ridden Gisele since the accident. I promise, I'm being good."

"I'm not getting on an ATV. I see what those things do to people. They're atrocious."

"They're not atrocious if you go slow. Babe, I just don't want you to fear everything. I promise to take it easy and make it enjoyable."

"Anything with four wheels stopped being enjoyable for me when I was eighteen, and then I saw the horrific effects when I started working in a hospital."

Blake let out a sigh in defeat. She wanted to help Eliza experience life again. Eliza said before that simple things like going to a concert would make her feel normal again, and Blake thought that being cautious on an ATV would be something the two could enjoy together. It was stupid to ask her to get on a vehicle, and she wished so much she could reel in the idea and discard it like it never happened.

"I just thought that we could get you out a little more, that's all," Blake said.

"I'm not going on an ATV, Blake, and you shouldn't either. You're in a cast. Your leg is still healing. You just got hit by a car three months ago. Why hasn't that scared you or taught you to be more cautious?"

"It has. If you don't want to try it—"

"I really don't."

Blake shrugged. She was willing to accept defeat. Anything to unravel Eliza's frown and her firm words so Blake could see her smile, bask in her heart eyes, and hear her elevated, soothing voice. Blake wanted all of that back so Eliza's accident didn't suffuse in the space of their beautiful cabin—a place they'd rented to escape reality for a weekend.

Instead of putting up a fight, she kissed Eliza's forehead. "Okay, then we can do Plan B. Canoe and swim in the lake?"

Eliza gave her a small smile of approval. "I like that much better. I've never been canoeing."

"Then it will be an adventure."

And just like that, the disagreement about ATVs disappeared. Blake was glad that Eliza's defensive voice instantly stopped once the talk of ATVs ended. She didn't want Eliza to be upset about the risky proposal. At least she seemed excited to go canoeing and swimming in the lake, and that was all that mattered to Blake.

Eliza loved how the rest of the weekend consisted of driving through the woods and the mountains, a broken leg's hiking tour, as she called it. In the evening, Blake fixed delicious meals, they cuddled, drank beer around the fire pit, and had plenty of sex at night and in the morning.

The last night of their trip, they decided to go out. Much of the last day was spent naked in bed, and after a few sessions, they'd worked up quite the appetite. So they decided to be decent human beings, shower, put on nice clothes, and head into town for a nice dinner. Their table was outside with stringed lights hanging above, and they had a perfect view of the lake as boats and jet skis zipped through the water.

"I don't want this weekend to end," Eliza said once the server poured them their first glass of Sangiovese.

Blake reached for her hand. "I don't either."

"Can you build us a cabin in the woods?"

"I don't think I have that kind of craftsmanship."

"But you make a killer fire and a killer breakfast. Surely that's the same thing."

"I can only make you a fire and food. Unfortunately, not a cabin. I hope that's not a dealbreaker."

They were still so new, but Eliza doubted Blake had any secret dealbreakers. Maybe her love for ATVs and motorcycles, but given the fact Blake hadn't touched Gisele since the accident, she thought she was winning that battle. Blake surely checked all the boxes Eliza never even thought of until she met her.

"Your fluffy pancakes saved you on that," Eliza said. "I think I can manage."

Lobster and crab cakes for an appetizer, then another glass of Sangiovese to prepare them for their delicious ribeyes. The conversation reached another lull. Eliza looked forward to those moments with Blake the most. They shared the silent moment together, and her luminous eyes focused on Eliza and only Eliza. That long and concentrated look of hers had so much power to undo her. She'd honestly believed that no woman would ever look at her like that again, like she was perfect or at least, perfect for her. Even with Tess, it had been hard to feel that way when they'd been keeping their relationship from their families, and when their parents had found out, they'd tried keeping Eliza and Tess apart.

This was the first time Eliza allowed herself to bask in all the thrilling emotions that came with dating someone, and it made her feel wonderful, like she was wrapped in a thick warm blanket, and now that she knew what that was like, she never wanted to be without it.

"Can you promise me something?" Eliza asked.

"I'll try."

"Please be careful." Blake relaxed into her seat and reached to take a sip of wine. "On ATVs, on motorcycles, or just in general. You're my girlfriend now, and that makes me even more terrified of your adrenaline rush. I see some really awful things at the hospital.

I see the consequences, and I can't even imagine seeing you hurt again after losing Tess—"

"I'm always careful," Blake said seriously, and Eliza didn't buy it one bit. "What? I'm always careful. I always wear protective gear and—"

"It's so much more than wearing a helmet."

"I've been on ATVs since I was a kid. We have a family friend who lives outside of Anza-Borrego State Park who built a motocross track for his son. You should have seen Adrian, Marc, and Anthony on that. Much more careless than I was."

That explained a lot. Eliza knew from the way Blake talked about Adrian that she idolized him. He'd shaped her whole world, from surfing to considering joining the Marines, to her love for ATVs, and probably so much more Eliza had to learn.

"Now I know where you get it from," Eliza said.

Blake smiled, but it didn't reach her eyes. The mood shifted as she looked at her wineglass. "I didn't really get into it until after Adrian died. Marc, Adrian, and Anthony were all the same age, and Marc and Adrian were best friends. Practically brothers and inseparable, so it hit him hard too. Marc would drive Jordan and I out to the Ramoses, and it gave us time to forget about everything for a while. It's kind of therapeutic in that sense. But anyway, yes, I promise to be safe, extra safe for you now. No Gisele and no ATVs until the cast is off."

Eliza winced. Okay, she apparently still had a lot of convincing to do. "I would really love no ATVs. Go ride a rollercoaster instead. Hell, I'll even do that with you."

"Take me to that little amusement park you have in Ohio, and it's a deal." She studied Eliza for a moment and then furrowed her brows. "I've been meaning to ask something. Completely off topic."

"What?"

"What's that?"

It took Eliza a moment to figure out what Blake was talking about until she followed the path of her stare to the Claire's ring in between her fingers. It was a habit Eliza had: moving the ring back and forth along the chain to give her fingers something to play with. She did it so often that she never realized when she did.

She dropped the necklace and buried her hands underneath the table so she could nervously pick at them. It dawned on her that she'd never told Blake that she and Tess were technically engaged. The sudden realization sent a prickly heat snaking down her spine. "Um, it's a...ring."

"Does it have any meaning?"

"Um...it..."

The deep-seated guilt and dread ballooned inside Eliza. The memory of graduation night flashed through her mind, and she tried everything she could to skip over every scene until the memory shut off.

Panic collected behind her sternum, and the more she tried to suppress it, the faster it started to bubble up. Once it tugged in her throat, it would choke her, and Eliza knew if she didn't calm herself down, she was seconds away from choking.

I want to marry you, Eliza, Tess said. I want to live the life with you we always dreamed of.

"Eliza?" Blake asked, stretching her hand across the table. "Is everything okay? Your face is white—"

Eliza snapped back to the present, hot tears streaming down her cheeks like a burst pipe. No, she couldn't do this now. Not again. But the more she thought about how ridiculous the trigger was, the more she overworked herself. The memory colliding with the anger was like a wave smacking into a wall of rocks.

The next thing Eliza knew, she jumped up like the thrashing waves and drifted from the table to the toilet. The air in the bathroom was much cooler than outside, providing the smallest relief for her burning hot face, but it didn't shove the memories back. It didn't loosen the ball hanging in her throat or dry her face. The necklace dangled against her chest, warm from playing with it for God only knew how long. Feeling the warmth brought the memories to life. It brought Tess back.

And then, suddenly, Eliza was eighteen.

❖

"God, I just want to be in LA now," Tess said and looked over with those beautiful hazel eyes. The two of them lay in the middle of the deserted football field at Cavanaugh Park. At the top of the hill, the sounds of aluminum bats cracking against baseballs pierced the humidity while the stadium lights tangled up in the falling night. "We could be celebrating our high school graduation by lying out in Santa Monica right now next to the pier, making out, and no one would care because California is like fifteen years ahead of the shitty Midwest."

They'd graduated four hours before, finally done with high school and done with the hetero-vibe of Tallulah, Ohio.

Almost.

Eliza looped her fingers through Tess's and pulled her hand up to her lips. Tess's hands always smelled like fresh clean lotion from the Bath and Body Works hand sanitizer on her keychain. "Seventy-nine more days left in purgatory," Eliza said. "August twenty-third can't come sooner."

"Promise me that once we settle into our dorm room, we go to the beach and do exactly that. Make out for hours."

"You mean you don't want to christen our twin beds right away?"

Tess looked skyward as she thought about it. "Good point. But we can always do that after. I need palm trees, beach, and California sunsets."

Eliza smiled at how simple Tess wanted their first Californian night to be. "I've never been more ready. I would move there now if we could."

Tess pushed herself up on her arms and tucked some of Eliza's hair behind her ear. "Seventy-nine days, babe. Seventy-nine days until we listen to 'California' by Phantom Planet the whole flight. Nothing's going to be in our way, Eliza Grace Walsh." Tess leaned in to kiss her, and still, after four years of being together, kissing Tess made Eliza's stomach flip. "We'll be so far away that my parents can't force us to break up, I won't have to date a boy to convince them I'm not gay—"

Eliza hushed Tess with her finger. "I know it's been a year since you broke up with me and dated Jake Kozlowski for the most torturous summer of my life, but it's still too soon."

Tess laughed and playfully snapped her teeth at Eliza's finger. She quickly retrieved it. "Guess what? I didn't like him," Tess said.

"I think we only kissed, like, under ten times—" Eliza covered her ears with her hands and started la-la-ing a random melody. Tess grabbed her wrists to lower them, laughing as she did so. "Okay, I'll shut up. What I'm trying to say is that no one is going to get in our way. We planned this out perfectly, babe. All those nights in the library, working on scholarship applications, all the weekends we worked to save up money, it's all about to pay off. And then, when our parents find out the truth, we won't need them or their money. We'll already be sufficient on our own."

"God," Eliza said, grunting dramatically. "This is going to be the longest summer of our lives. I feel like we're in this awful limbo until August twenty-third."

Tess paused and took that silent moment to graze Eliza's cheek with the back of her hand. Eliza closed her eyes and basked in the way Tess made her skin catch fire. When she opened them, she had a front row view of Tess's famous mischievous smile.

"What's that look for?"

The smile grew, making her more afraid of Tess's next words. "I know how we can celebrate our fifth anniversary next year."

"How?"

"We elope."

Eliza hoisted herself up. "Elope?"

Up until they'd started dating, life was a tightrope Eliza cautiously walked, trying her best to balance in the world of chaos. She hated getting in trouble or disappointing anyone. She liked following the rules and didn't mind having the "goody two-shoes" title Tess and their friends called her. And then there was Tess, a hurricane-force wind, testing Eliza's balance and showing her the world she wouldn't have gotten to explore if she'd stayed on that rope.

They'd met in sixth grade when their elementary schools had merged into one of the two middle schools that made up the Tallulah school district. They were friends up until the summer right before their freshman year. Tess was the friend who'd inspired Eliza to bend the rules, helped her emerge from her shell to finally embrace life and the fun of being young. So Tess's sudden plan to elope on their fifth anniversary shouldn't have been a huge surprise given her track record. Having Tess in her life over the years warmed Eliza to some pretty careless and spontaneous ideas.

But unlike a lot of them, when she thought about this one, it actually made sense. Still crazy, but it didn't stir in her gut like sour milk, like some of them.

"Yes, we elope," Tess said and kissed her nose.

Eliza pulled away to assess her. "Did you just propose to me?"

"Yeah, I guess I did. Does it count when you're eighteen?"

"I think it counts when you're serious." Eliza paused and tried to gauge where Tess stood by the look in her eyes. She came up with nothing. She was too overwhelmed to study details. "Are you serious?"

Tess shrugged like this whole thing wasn't a big deal despite being the biggest deal they'd had yet to face. "Depends. What's your answer?"

"My answer is that you're crazy."

"That's your answer to tons of things I've proposed."

"And this is probably the craziest."

"We're moving to LA in seventy-nine days. We've been together for four years, and we're still crazy about each other. There's nothing we can't do."

"We can't elope, Tess," Eliza said. "No state except Massachusetts allows it."

"Then we get married in Massachusetts. Eliza," she said and tucked her legs underneath her. She held Eliza's hands. "We spent all of high school together. We survived last year with all the shit that happened, our breakup, our parents, those three months with Jake Kozlowski, and we got what we wanted. Same college, same dorm, a bunch of scholarships because we're fucking geniuses on multiple levels, and our parents are absolutely oblivious. Our love is that powerful, babe. We're that powerful together."

She imagined their courthouse wedding in Boston, kissing Tess passionately in front of the judge as a nice big fuck you to society and their parents.

Before Eliza answered, she said they needed to go to the mall. Once they parked, Tess grabbed her hand, and they bolted in, ran up the escalators, and into Claire's, the same place they'd gone to get their belly buttons pierced when they'd turned eighteen. When it had been Eliza's turn to finally get her belly button piercing, Tess had decided to get a lip ring. Eliza had been shocked by it, but Tess was able to pull it off, and Eliza had loved the thought of the Wares being mortified over it.

They only had thirty-four dollars in cash. Eliza found a ten-dollar, resin, white-marble ring, and Tess found a fourteen-dollar white-gold ring with a robin's-egg-blue stone. After they bought them, Eliza zoomed the fourteen minutes back to Cavanaugh Park, the place they'd had their first kiss that summer after eighth grade.

"Are we really doing this?" Eliza asked, standing under the red pavilion next to the parking lot, feeling the adrenaline rushing through her, her heart pumping faster than it ever had.

Tess twirled Eliza's ring in between her fingers. "Eliza Grace Walsh, I can only afford this ten-dollar ring from Claire's right now, but I promise you, once I save enough money, I'll buy you the ring that you deserve. I promise that our next year together will be the best one yet, in our new city, our new home."

Eliza held out Tess's ring and grabbed her left hand. "I promise to take you to Dairy Queen for your birthday, like we've done every year since we met, for your cherry-dipped vanilla ice cream cone. I promise to one day buy you Killers concert tickets so we can hear and dance to 'Mr. Brightside' in person. I promise to watch whatever movie you bring home from Blockbuster, but I can't promise to always like it."

"I promise I'll bring back at least one movie I know you'll enjoy."

"With Milk Duds, please."

Tess grinned and pushed a stray hair behind Eliza's ear. She always loved it when Tess did that. "I promise, babe. I want to marry you, Eliza. I want to live the life with you that we always dreamed of. I don't need anything grand. Not a big party, not a fancy white dress that neither of us can afford. I just need it to be with you. You're my high school sweetheart and the love of my life. Will you elope with me next year on our fifth anniversary?"

It seemed like Tess's goal had always been to elicit a rush from Eliza, but she really outdid herself when she asked Eliza to marry her. Eliza felt so much friction in her body, she thought she was going to skyrocket to the moon.

"I'll marry you next year, Tessa Lynn Ware. And I won't regret it. Ever."

It was crazy to think that at eighteen, four hours after they'd graduated from high school, they made a promise to marry each other. But out of all the crazy things Tess had made her do, this one was the most normal. It was the only one that didn't terrify her at all.

To this day, that ring was the only piece of jewelry she wore. It was the only way she could still feel Tess. When she wore it, it pressed against her chest. If she played with it long enough, it absorbed the heat of her fingers, and when she tucked it under her shirt, she could feel the warmth.

She could feel Tess.

Eliza's cries echoed against the bathroom walls. She sealed her mouth behind her hands, trying desperately to shove the scolding panic back in. Luckily, she was the only person in this room that spun and tilted on the Earth's axis while she tried to weigh herself in the present.

In Big Bear Lake, California.

With Blake.

On the other side of the country from Tallulah.

Thirteen years after all of this.

"You're safe," the soothing voice said.

"Tess isn't. She was never safe," the other voice said.

She only heard the blood rushing in her ears. She wrapped her hands around her head, attempting to secure her brain from tumbling into the dark corners. Her hands shook. The air in the bathroom felt thick and hot, and hot flashes sent a wave of sweat crawling up her spine and making her head tingle.

The outer door opened, and Eliza covered her mouth to mute the cries.

"Eliza? Eliza, are you in here?" Blake's boots pointed toward the stall.

"I'm fine," she blubbered and cleaned her face.

"No, you're not. Let me in, please."

"I…I just need a moment."

"What's wrong?"

She cried harder when Blake didn't leave as fast as she wanted. She could barely compose herself. She wasn't ready to talk, especially in the bathroom where anyone could walk in.

"Please, just leave," Eliza begged through her sobs. "I…I need a moment. Let me have a moment."

"But—"

"Blake!"

She hated the sound of her own lashing out ringing through the empty bathroom. She covered her mouth again when the anger bounced back, and Blake left. She worried that she'd scared her away, and once Eliza was able to calm down, Blake was the one person she needed to feel safe again.

After what felt like twenty minutes, Eliza was able to compose herself and her breath. When she stepped out and saw herself in the mirror, the aftermath of the panic attack remained on her face. Her mascara was smeared, which meant that she had to commit to taking it off with a paper towel and water. Burst blood vessels spotted the skin under her eyes like tiny red freckles. She couldn't walk out of this bathroom without people knowing she'd been sobbing. She wouldn't be able to keep this from Blake, even though talking about the night and the sudden flashback was the last thing she wanted. They'd had a wonderful weekend together, and Eliza was so pissed that their last night had drastically turned into this.

She walked back to the table and focused on the ground so no one could see the evidence of her crying. When she slipped back in her seat, she caught a glimpse of Blake, whose worried and confused stare drilled into her.

"I already paid," Blake said after a few moments of silence as Eliza guzzled the rest of her wine. "How about we head out of here and talk?"

The whole thing had ruined their date. All because Blake had asked Eliza about a ten-dollar Claire's ring, and her brain had decided that would be the perfect time to turn upside down.

They walked to the lake and found an empty bench in the midst of families walking around. Eliza took a seat and filled her lungs with the smell of young fall air. A few silent moments sat between them while she rummaged through all of her thoughts to figure out the right things to say with minimal tears. But as she searched and discarded sentences, the pulling in her throat resumed.

"Eliza?" Blake said softly and placed a hand on her knee. "What happened? Talk to me."

She deserved answers. All Eliza could do was shake her head. The tightness in her chest was like the ache that had been stored there for years was finally trying to break apart. She sucked in a breath and held it, hoping that would ease the heavy pang. When Blake clasped her hand, she was able to send some kind of painkiller through Eliza.

Eliza looked out at the stringed lights lining the pathway and slightly piercing the fresh darkness. The lake was a massive black blob in front of them. She was thankful for the darkness, censoring her sadness to onlookers. A breeze rippled through the air and gave her extra oxygen to say the words that it would take everything in her to say. Eliza wanted to believe that it was Tess empowering her to get through this. It gave her the courage to face Blake.

"I'm so sorry," Eliza said as a crying hiccup rippled through her.

Blake squeezed her hand tighter. "Talk to me. Please."

"I...I had a flashback." A pained look crumpled Blake's face. She brought Eliza's hand up to her chest and held it there. "I, um, I didn't realize that I never told you that, um, well...technically Tess and I were engaged."

The grip around her hand loosened, and their hands lowered. "Really?" Blake said softly, but she didn't look upset. Her stare still pleaded for Eliza to continue.

Eliza twirled the ring in between her fingers for a moment, then she unhooked the necklace. "I guess some people wouldn't consider it a formal proposal because it happened so spontaneously, and we were eighteen, and we could only afford ten-dollar rings from Claire's, but the promise was real. We were going to get married in Boston the next year to celebrate our fifth anniversary. I know it might sound crazy and careless because that meant we were getting married at nineteen, but the last year of her life, we went through so much together. Hell and back, and we still found a way to be together. If all of that didn't split us up, then what would?" She glanced at the ring. "I still wear it because it's all I have left of her. It's the only part of her I can physically feel."

Blake didn't say anything, but her hand never wavered from Eliza's, and she considered that a clue that her truth wasn't scaring her away.

"I don't want you to think that I'm emotionally unavailable, that because I still wear this ring and think about her all the time that I don't have room for you."

"I've never felt that way at all, Eliza. Sure, you're guarded, but you've been through shit. You've been hurt. But why would I think you're emotionally unavailable?"

"Because I've been told that from multiple women."

Sofia most recently, and being labeled as "emotionally unavailable" really stung. Eliza thought that if it was true, then why the hell should she date and drain more energy if other women would eventually discover the same thing? So she'd closed herself off even more until Blake had entered the picture.

"You're reserved," Blake said. "You have walls up, but I never thought you were emotionally unavailable. I find you to be quite the opposite."

"I want to move on. I've been in love before, and it was the best feeling in the world. Allison and my sister tell me I'm too picky when it comes to dating because I shut it down if I don't feel a spark, and never feeling it made me worried that I'm actually broken, that I'm never going to find that kind of love again. I want a partner and a family and a life, and just when I thought that would never happen, you walk in, and I felt something instantly. I had walls up with you because I knew there was something there, and I was so drawn to it. I guess I always stopped myself from falling for someone because I never wanted to experience that pain again. But you, Blake." She wiped her moist eyes, and when she met Blake's gaze, she noticed the stringed lights sparkling in her eyes. Eliza saw her pain reflecting back at her because she'd found someone who absorbed her feelings. "You make me feel so amazing and beautiful and loved and wanted, and I'm scared because I know I'm falling so hard for you, so quickly, and the last time someone made me feel that way, I lost them, and—"

Blake cupped Eliza's face. "Hey," she said softly. Her tone was so soft, and her energy was so light given the heaviness Eliza had dumped on her all at once. It was refreshing. "I'm right here, and I don't plan on going anywhere."

"And that's why I can't have you on Gisele or ATVs because I can't go through that again."

Blake kissed both her hands. "I won't ride Gisele or ATVs. I promise. I'll give all those up if that means you'll be happy. You want to know why?"

"Why?"

"Because I'm falling hard for you too."

"You...you are?"

She nodded. "I don't want you to feel like you have to carry all this weight by yourself anymore, okay? I'm your girlfriend, and

I'm going to be there for you whenever you need it. I hate knowing all the stuff that people have said to you because now you don't see yourself the way I see you, and I think you're so wonderful and perfect."

She exhaled. *Perfect.* When she and Blake were together, the two of them really did feel perfect, and the feeling settled pleasantly in her gut like an autumn leaf falling into place. "You do?"

"I do. You're patient, cautious, and compassionate. You're guarded, but when you let your walls down for someone, you really give them everything. You have the biggest heart I've ever known. Nothing about you has scared me away. You're going to have to try much harder to do that."

"That's not what I want. Not at all."

Blake forced a small smile. "Good. We're on the same page again." She kissed her softly on the lips as if stitching Eliza's broken seams back together. "Want to head back? I can make a fire, and we can drink some hot chocolate?"

Eliza nodded. "That sounds perfect."

When they got back to the cabin, Eliza snuck into the kitchen and tried to make hot chocolate while Blake made one last fire. The Swiss Miss packet and hot water kind, something impossible to mess up. But Blake caught her red-handed and sprinted into the kitchen. She smelled like fire and faded cologne, and it wrapped Eliza up in such a daze that she easily surrendered the hot chocolate so Blake could salvage the remains of it.

Apparently, when making spiked hot chocolate from the packets, you weren't supposed to use water. How was she supposed to know that?

As they sipped their boozy drinks by the fire, they buried themselves under a shared blanket and swapped stories about Adrian and Tess. Both of them seemed to realize how long ago they'd lost them. Looking back on all the things that made up Eliza's Before and all the things Adrian and Tess had never experienced or lived through, it was so hard to believe that they were still so much a part of their lives. Eliza wondered if there was a statute of limitations on grief. When the nineteen-year anniversary came around, did that mean she had to fully get over Tess because then Tess would have been gone longer than Eliza even knew her, longer than she was even alive? When was it going to stop hurting? When would the PTSD flashbacks stop? When would she finally let go of the scars the Wares and her parents had given her?

When would she forgive her parents and give them a second chance?

There was still so much Eliza wanted to do, and seeing how Blake processed her brother's death made her realize how she was the one holding herself back. She was ready and hopeful that she would be able to take her life back, and it had a lot to do with Blake breathing new life into her.

CHAPTER ELEVEN

D amn, this place looks like it could be the perfect venue," Malai said as she spun around the new construction.

The venue was barely even a structure. Blake and Malai had to wear helmets because it was an active construction site, and she smiled when she'd put it on, thinking about Eliza and how proud she would be of the safety protocols.

Blake couldn't deny it. The venue's blueprint and mockups were perfect: fifteen thousand square feet of space a few blocks from the ocean. They could turn the parking lot behind the building into a patio. They could even build private event rooms to host events and add another revenue source. The building had a gritty brick vibe on the outside and exposed brick inside but still left so much room for all the creativity Blake and Malai wanted to put into it. With this venue, Vagabonds could be much more than a food hall. It could be a destination that checked all the boxes for the perfect night out: amazing food; patio drinking; hell, a stage for a live band; and space for events like beer and wine tasting and pop-ups. It was limitless.

The only problem with the place was that it was in Huntington Beach, an hour and a half from San Diego. And that was on a good day with minimal traffic.

She followed Malai as she bounced around the space, painting an even more perfect space than what Blake envisioned in her head.

"We can rent out some of this space for private events," Malai said. Ambition radiated in her wide beam. "People love exposed brick. We can really utilize this."

After securing their restaurant loans, the next step was to find a venue. They'd both agreed that they wanted to stick to the San Diego area. That was where the majority of their connections were, and those connections would help them find the vendors they needed to pack the food hall with the best foods. But they also had some in LA from culinary school. A few of their former classmates had stayed in LA and had their own restaurants.

The Huntington Beach venue was the first venue of their search. But as great as it was, Blake wanted to stay in San Diego. She had her family and Eliza there. However, Malai didn't have anything weighing her down. Her parents lived in Queens, and her two siblings were scattered across the US in Philly and Chicago, so nothing was tying her to San Diego. She just wanted the perfect spot for Vagabonds that would make it an unforgettable experience.

On their drive back to San Diego, Blake thought long and hard about Huntington Beach. It was perfect, everything she and Malai had envisioned. Blake had initially shot down Huntington Beach, but Malai had convinced her that taking a look wouldn't hurt, so she'd agreed. But now she regretted that decision because she saw how perfect it was, and Malai had fallen in love with it. She knew her best friend. When Malai loved something, it would be hard to get her to forget about it.

"Downtown is so cute too," Malai said as she drove. "Don't you think?"

"I think we should keep this on the backburner. We were supposed to stay in San Diego."

"I know, and I know this is only our first one, and we still have other places to look at but…I really love that space."

"I know but…my family is in San Diego. I don't know if I want to move two hours away from them. Plus, things are going really great with the girl I'm dating."

Malai rose her eyebrows and looked over. "Oh yeah? The surgeon?"

Blake thought of Eliza, something that happened all the time now, and whenever she did, she always found herself smiling. She checked her phone to see if Eliza had texted her, hoping that she'd found down time during her shift to sneak in a text. Blake always enjoyed those texts.

"Yeah, the surgeon," Blake said. "Things are really great, and I really like her. Like, I haven't felt this way about someone in a long time."

"Since Lindsey?"

Blake thought about it as she dangled her hand out the window and played with the wind. "That's the thing. Eliza makes me feel things I never felt with Lindsey."

"Whoa. Are you in love?"

Blake laughed. "I don't know. But I think it could happen, and I really don't want to move two hours away and lose that. We just made it official a few weeks ago."

"Wait, you're telling me that Blake Navarro has a girlfriend?"

"Yeah, should be a clue as to how great things are going and how much I want to keep it that way."

"We'll look at other venues," Malai said.

"I don't want to look at any other venues that aren't in the San Diego area."

Malai thinned her grin and nodded. "Okay, we won't." A pause. "When do I get to meet this mystery surgeon?"

"Soon."

"Has the family met her?"

"They met her when I was in the hospital. I think my mom likes her more than me, and that's really saying something because I really like this girl."

"Whoa. So she's, like, your future wife?"

Blake playfully hit her arm. "Don't jinx it. She'd be an awesome one."

She loved how enthusiastic Malai was about the Huntington Beach venue. Blake loved it too; she just didn't love the distance. Lying in bed that night, she told herself it was a good back-up plan in case San Diego didn't work out, except the back-up plan would mean two hours from home. But then again, Eliza had mentioned several hospitals with trauma fellowships in LA that she was looking at applying to once she finished her final resident year in June. But if Eliza stayed put, she had no idea what that would mean for them. It would also suck being that far from her family. She loved her family's Sunday dinners, she loved working with her uncle and cousin, but owning a food hall didn't require her to be on location every single day. She'd be okay commuting out there once a week if that meant she got to stay with her family and Eliza the rest of the time.

Maybe she was extra sensitive to leaving her family because Adrian's anniversary was around the corner. She hated November and everything about it. Sometimes she even dreaded Thanksgiving because even though it was her favorite holiday, Adrian's death somehow squeezed into the day and forced out sadness and tears. There had yet to be a Thanksgiving in seventeen years where someone hadn't cried.

She remembered when Marc and Adrian had talked about what they wanted to be when they grew up. Marc had just declared his major in business when Adrian was back from deployment during the summer of 2003. Marc had said that he wanted to own his own business and that his dad was strongly considering starting a restaurant. Even though Blake was only thirteen, she'd already loved cooking with Tito and Bela, and being a chef was one of five things on her list of things she'd wanted to do. Adrian had told Marc how badass that would be if he and Hugo went into business together and had encouraged him to go for it.

In her last conversation with her brother, Blake had told him she was going to try out for the softball team, and Adrian's voice had lit up with excitement as he'd unleashed all his advice on what to practice on, and she'd taken it all in because he was a good baseball player. He was good at anything he tried, really.

She couldn't even imagine how proud Adrian would have been. Not only did Marc and Hugo own that business, not only was Blake the head chef by the age of twenty-seven with a prestigious culinary school and Michelin-star restaurant on her resume, but she and Malai were going to open up their own food hall. She was this close to accomplishing her dream.

She would have given almost anything to be able to tell Adrian that, to make him proud.

❖

November 11, 2004

Blake had the same routine coming home from school.

She bopped along to Avril Lavigne's second album playing from the discman tucked in between her jeans, pedaling through the quiet streets of their neighborhood until she reached the end of the cul-de-sac. She tossed her bike in the small patch of grass underneath a tree that had a yellow ribbon wrapped around the trunk. She'd passed by a lot of yellow ribbons that day since it was Veteran's Day, a day she didn't think twice about until Adrian had enlisted. But for the third year in a row, her parents had made sure there was a yellow ribbon on the tree, and she was proud to be one of the few kids who had a loved one fighting overseas. Her friends and teachers lit up when she told them about Adrian, and she loved that they looked at him like he was a hero, just like she'd been looking at him her whole life.

She bolted up the steps to where the family's Dell desktop sat in the nook in the upstairs hallway. She had about a half hour before Jordan rode home from the middle school. Her parents didn't come home until four thirty to five o'clock, which gave her two hours and fifteen minutes to hop on AIM and message her crush, Lauren Sanford. She logged in and let out a disappointed sigh when she didn't see Lauren's screen name on her friend's list. While she waited for BeachBrat717, Blake changed her away message, a lyric from "My Happy Ending" by Avril that she'd put up two weeks before when she was heartbroken that Carly Price didn't want to kiss her any more. It had only happened twice, but those two make-outs had been like labelling each other as girlfriends. She was over Carly Price and didn't want to waste the space on her away message for a lyric dedicated to her. No, she was going to change it to a lyric from "This Love" by Maroon 5, and she hoped Lauren Sanford knew it was for her.

By the time Jordan came home, Blake was already ten minutes into her conversation with Lauren. Jordan scampered upstairs and whined for the computer so she could play Rollercoaster Tycoon.

"Don't you see I'm busy?" Blake said and gestured to the computer that only showed her friend's list. She'd minimized her chat with Lauren because she didn't want her nosey little sister to see she was flirting with a girl.

Jordan stomped her foot. "You always get the computer."

"Ride your bike faster, then."

"I don't get out until three."

"At least I'm talking to people instead of making fake rollercoasters. Now go away."

"Your screen name is Sk8erGurl8. You don't even know how to skate."

"Jordan. Go. Away."

Fifteen minutes passed, and Blake was invested in her conversation with Lauren, which hadn't reached a lull once. Right as she was going to ask if anyone had asked Lauren to go to the upcoming school dance with them, there was a firm knock on the door. She expected Jordan to answer, but when she heard another knock, she grunted and yelled, "Jordan, get the door." A third knock. She rolled her eyes and stomped down the steps so Jordan could hear how pissed she was.

When she opened the door, two tall marines stared down at her. She felt her eyes round, and her veins felt like they'd been filled with cement.

"Hello, I'm looking for a Mr. Luis Navarro. Is he home?" the older marine asked.

Everything in Blake hollowed. Her feet felt nailed to the ground, and she forgot to breathe. This was the start of all her nightmares, the two marines in the olive-green alpha uniforms appearing at her front door.

The tears pooled. "Is this about my brother?"

"We need to speak to a Mr. Luis Navarro."

Blake glanced at the analog clock that hung above the TV. It was four twenty-two. Her parents were due to be home in the next half hour. "He's...they're not home yet. My parents are usually home by five." She studied the medals and ribbons on both uniforms that signaled they were important and had a lot of authority. She looked up at the steps and found Jordan on her knees, hiding behind the corner upstairs as if the marines were two monsters she'd found in her room. "I'll...I'll go call them," Blake said and walked into the kitchen to call her dad's cell phone. As the phone rang, the marines continued to stand in the family room, watching her every move with unwavering eye contact. A prickling heat pierced her back. "Hi? Dad? When are you going to be home?"

"Hi, mija. I'm just pulling into the neighborhood right now. Is everything okay?"

"Um, no. There're, um, there are two marines here waiting for you."

The phone went dead.

Two minutes later, her dad burst through the front doors, and when he saw the marines, he said, "No. No, no, no."

Witnessing the tears collect in her father's dark brown eyes for the first time in her life broke Blake. She started crying and sandwiched a throw pillow between her chest and her tucked-in knees.

"Are you Mr. Luis Navarro?" the older marine asked.

"No...no, we aren't doing this until my wife gets home. No." He pulled his Nokia phone from his back pocket, turned his back to the marines, and got a hold of Blake's mom.

Waiting for her mother to come home on that day was Blake's first taste of the relativity of time. She watched the clock tick seven minutes, but it felt so much longer than that. Her dad sat in between her and Jordan, his arms wrapped around both of their shoulders. Jordan curled up into his arms and hid her face in his chest. Blake sat straight up, staring at the marines and listening to the faint ticking of the clock. She'd forgotten all about her AIM conversation with Lauren Sanford. It no longer mattered. She would give up talking to

Lauren Sanford for the rest of her life—hell, she'd even give up her AIM, the computer, and her Avril Lavigne album—if it meant that the marines wouldn't tell her what she expected. She could feel the sorrow and heaviness emanating from them, filling up the house like poisonous gas. The longer they waited, the more painful it was to breathe. Her chest clenched, the air in her lungs heated.

Eventually, those seven minutes ended when their mom stumbled into the house, and when she saw the marines, she let out a cry. Her dad ran over to her as her mom reached for a chair to break her fall. Watching her mom bawl into her dad's chest was a scene burned into her memory. She didn't need the marines to say any words. She pinched the back of her arm and sealed her eyes shut so she could find herself lying in her bed, but no matter how hard she tried, she couldn't get out of her living room.

The marines took off their hats. "Mr. and Mrs. Navarro," the older marine said, low, stern, and rehearsed, like he'd done this plenty of times before. "The commandant of the Marine Corps has entrusted me to express his deep regret that your son, Lance Corporal Adrian Navarro, was killed in action in Fallujah, Iraq yesterday, on the eleventh of November. He died while engaging with enemies in hostile fire. The commandant extends his deepest sympathy to you and your family in your loss."

The tears poured freely from her as she bolted upstairs and went straight to Adrian's room. A Kobe Bryant poster taped to the front of the door greeted her as she ran inside, plopped on his bed, and clutched his pillow in front of her chest.

This couldn't be real. He couldn't be gone.

She stayed in the room for the rest of the night. Her parents tried getting her to come be with her family, but she couldn't pry herself away from Adrian. His room was still so full of life—so full of him—when she knew that his life wasn't anymore. She was just bragging about him to her friends and teachers. They'd talked on the phone two weeks ago, and she'd told him that she wanted to try out for the softball team in a few months, and he was so excited.

She never even thought that it would be the last time she heard his voice.

That night, Blake and Jordan slept in his room. For two sisters who couldn't even share the computer or barely a room, they managed to forget about the insults they'd thrown at each other earlier and squeezed into Adrian's full-size bed. While Jordan drifted to sleep next to her, Blake stared at his surfboard. When Adrian came back from his first deployment the summer before, he'd taken her to Oceanside to teach her more surfing and had promised that they would hit up a different beach to test her new skills. On their last phone call, Adrian had said that he would teach her everything he knew about baseball so she could be a, "badass on the field."

She wanted to learn everything from Adrian, her older brother, the coolest guy she'd ever met.

Her hero.

❖

Adrian had died on Veteran's Day, and the seventeenth anniversary of his death fell on Veteran's Day yet again.

She had just told Eliza about that awful day after realizing that she hadn't told her the horrible story until the moment they sat on the Oceanside beach, the very place she and Adrian always went to surf...or in Blake's case, flirt with surfer girls.

"It's weird to think that Adrian has been gone longer than I've known him," Blake said softly. "Sometimes I wonder if I'm even allowed to be upset now, which I know is ridiculous."

Eliza held her hand. "I know what you mean. Tess and I only knew each other for seven years, and she's been gone twice as long."

Blake saw the hurt and understanding reflected in Eliza's eyes. She was heartbroken that the woman she was starting to care so much about had gone through the same kind of immense loss. It was a kind of pain she wouldn't wish on her worst enemy. But having someone who knew and was truly empathetic helped hold Blake together when she wanted so much to fall apart.

"I wonder all the time what it would be like if Adrian survived, if he came back," Blake said as a breeze blew through their hair.

"What would he be like? Would he come back a completely different person?" Eliza didn't respond, but Blake didn't expect her to.

Blake kept her gaze on the surfers and the amber and gold sunset that painted bold colors in the sky as the sun dipped closer to the horizon. "After he died, I did so much reading about the operation he was a part of and the war. I'm so pissed off that all of that happened, and there weren't even weapons of mass destruction. What the hell was the point? And Phantom Fury was the bloodiest battle of the Iraq War. Is a Purple Heart supposed to make up for the fact that my brother died in a pointless war?" She ran a hand through her hair and picked up a handful of sand and let the grains fall between her fingers. "More marines in his battalion died by suicide than in Phantom Fury, can you believe that? Would Adrian have been one of those marines?"

"It's hard to say," Eliza said softly.

"But probably, right? You said it yourself, most of the vets you saw at the VA hospital have PTSD."

"Yeah, but PTSD is a spectrum. Not everyone who has it is suicidal."

Blake reflected on the time Adrian came back from the war. It was a few months after the US had invaded Iraq, and he was home until they deployed his battalion again in mid-2004. Even after a couple of months of active fighting, Adrian had already seemed different. He was once extroverted, but when he came home, he retreated to his room more. Sometimes he'd wanted to surf by himself, and one time Blake had asked to tag along, and he'd snapped at her. He'd never snapped at her like that before. He was so calm, chill, and reasonable before the war. He had a wide, dimpled smile that was hard to shake off. He was always cracking jokes and was the life of the party in whatever room he was in. But after his first deployment, he was quieter, more irritable, and liked being alone either in his room, on a walk around the neighborhood, or on a trip to the beach.

"Sometimes I forget that I ever had a brother," Blake mumbled, shaking her head, and looking at her lap. "It's only for a brief moment, but it scares me that those moments even happen. I forget what his voice sounded like. I forget his personality. I only remember it in certain memories, and if it weren't for pictures, I wonder if I would start forgetting what he even looked like."

"I completely understand. I only brought a few pictures of Tess with me, and her face is so faded. I barely remember the sound of her voice."

Blake looked at Eliza with sympathy. "Yeah, it really fucking sucks. I really miss him."

Eliza wrapped a tight arm around her and pulled her in, planting a long, soft kiss on her temple. "I know you do."

Blake didn't know how she would tackle the rest of the month by herself. Surely, it would be like the sixteen Novembers before this one, but now that she knew what it was like to have someone by her side who completely understood everything she was going through, she'd realized just how hard those past Novembers were, and she didn't want to do it again.

"Do you, um, do you have any plans for Thanksgiving? Or are you working?" Blake asked.

"I usually work on Thanksgiving."

"Seriously?"

"Yeah," Eliza said it like it should've been given. "I've spent every Thanksgiving of my residency in the hospital. I haven't been home in nine years. Remember that baggage?"

"You really haven't spent Thanksgiving with anyone in nine years?"

"Allison's family once or twice. Other than that, no, I've been working. Why fight with other residents over the day when they actually have relationships with their families?"

Knowing that, Blake felt more confident in what she wanted to ask.

"Would you want to spend Thanksgiving with me? I don't want you to spend it alone and, well, I think it would be nice. Thanksgiving is always a hard time for us. You being there…well, it would seem less empty. I'd feel more whole. I usually do with you."

"I haven't done the schedules yet, but luckily, your girlfriend is in charge of them, so I'll be selfish this year and take off. Shake up everybody's world." She kissed her temple again. "I'll be there. I promise."

And just like that, Blake found herself looking forward to Thanksgiving for the first time since she was thirteen.

❖

"Okay, I have to be honest with you about something," Violet said.

Her tone was low and stern on Eliza's phone, and a million awful thoughts sprung to mind. It was a couple days before Thanksgiving, and this time of year always made her extra sensitive. "Is someone sick? Did someone die?"

Violet's eyebrows furrowed. "What? No."

Eliza covered her beating heart. "Thank God. Can you preface that next time your first words are something so vague and grim?"

"Yes, sure. No one's sick or dead. It's um, well, Emma had her Thanksgiving play yesterday."

"Oh, right. Those pictures of her were so freakin' adorable. I made it the background on my phone. It's seasonal and too cute."

"She was the cutest turkey, and it's not even a biased statement."

"It might be a little bit. So what do you need to tell me? Don't tell me that the rest of the pilgrims and Native Americans of her class chose her for their Thanksgiving dinner?"

"No, no, Emma and all her other turkey friends were spared. The pilgrims and Native Americans decided to do a vegan dinner this year."

"Great. Wonderful health benefits. Easy on their arteries."

Violet forced a thin smile that didn't reach her eyes. "There's this mother that I've been talking to. Well, you know, small talk when we pick our girls up. Nothing too deep. Hell, I didn't even know her last name until the play when I saw her daughter Chloe listed as one of the Native Americans." Violet paused and peeled her gaze from the phone screen. "She's, um, well…it turns out this mother is Matt Ware's wife. Matt Ware and his parents were at the play last night."

Eliza froze. Her body felt hollow in an instant.

Matt Ware was the middle child, two years younger than Tess. Eliza wasn't sure what she was more surprised about, that his daughter was in Emma's kindergarten class or that the sixteen-year-old Matt Ware who lived in her memory had a kid. If the twenty-nine-year-old Matt Ware had a five-year-old daughter, then he'd probably gotten married young, fresh out of college, living the very traditional—and extremely straight—life his parents wanted for their three children.

"Did they...did the parents recognize you?"

Memories of the Wares released like a broken dam, and Eliza had to suck in air before they completely drowned her.

"They didn't recognize me, but after the play, when all the parents chatted over pie, they recognized Mom and Dad."

Prickling heat burned her skin. Her chest compressed as the air in the room withered away. Her mind was doing that thing again where it was like a projector replaying the images on a giant screen, pulling Eliza back in time so she could relive all the deep-rooted anxiety and fears that took hold of her anytime she was in Mr. and Mrs. Ware's presence. They were relevant again, somehow indirectly crawling their way back to her life.

"His wife stopped me before the show, and he was by her side, introduced us, and I thought nothing of it. Not until we took our seats and I saw Chloe's last name on the program, and then his parents walked in and sat with them a few rows ahead of us. There's no way I wouldn't recognize them. Matt and Carly tried talking to us after the play, and that's when his parents recognized Mom and Dad."

"What...what happened?" Eliza couldn't help her curiosity.

Violet said that the Wares stood silently by Matt and Carly as they talked to her about how cute the play was, oblivious to it all. Then, according to Violet, Mr. Ware said, "Bill and Amy, it's been a long time," and the mood drastically changed after that.

"And then Dad said," Violet continued, "'Not long enough. Hope your family is doing well, though,' and then he grabbed

Mom's hand, and they went over to Emma, who was playing with her friends...and Chloe."

The resurfaced pain sank in her gut like a heavy brick, and Eliza was stunned yet again, imagining her father, who never did confrontation, stand up to the bullies. She couldn't imagine it, but at the same time, her heart swelled over the knowledge. She couldn't believe it. "Dad said that?"

Violet nodded. "I was stunned, and it was truly awkward when he and Mom left, and I was stuck with the Wares. I think Matt was able to put the pieces together, but Carly had no idea what was going on. I'm sure she knows everything now. But the story isn't even over. When I picked up Emma today, Matt was there getting Chloe, and he stopped me in the parking lot."

"Jesus fucking Christ." How were the Wares relevant again? She wished that they had stayed in her Before and were locked there. Quite honestly, she thought she'd never have to worry about them again. Until now.

"It wasn't like that," Violet said. "He was...well...sweet. He apologized for the awkwardness after the play. And he asked about you, actually seemed curious. He said that he hopes you're doing well, hopes you're happy, and that he thinks about you often."

"What?"

"I told him that you're a surgeon in California, about to take your boards. We talked for about ten minutes, and Eliza, it was a great talk. He's nothing like his parents."

"Wow...just...wow." Eliza shook her head, still in disbelief. "I thought they were a thing of the past."

"Yeah, me too. Look, I don't want this to bother you. I figured it was better to tell you than hide it, you know?"

"Yeah, I know. It's just...it brings back a lot."

"Try not to focus on the past. Remind yourself that you're safe, you're happy. Hell, I mean, I haven't seen you this happy in years."

"Things are going pretty well."

"With the girlfriend?"

The blush hit her cheeks. "Yes, with the girlfriend. I'm, um, I'm even spending Thanksgiving with her and her family."

Violet's smile faded, and Eliza knew why. Violet spent every year trying to convince her to come home. "Oh, you are?" Eliza recognized the disappointment and jealousy in her tone. "When do we get to meet her? You ever going to bring her around to us?"

"You? Yes. Come out here, and you can meet her."

"So you're going to hide your family from your girlfriend? You two sound pretty serious—"

"It is pretty serious."

"Then when does she get to meet your family? This is the perfect opportunity to show Mom and Dad that you're happy. Invite them back in your life again."

"I tried inviting them into my life when the Wares outed me, and that didn't really go over well. Mom and Dad printed off articles about becoming straight and left them on my bed. Mom asked me multiple times what she did wrong."

"Yeah, and that's awful, Eliza. I understand that. But the 2000s were a totally different time. Look how far society has come since then. Mom and Dad progressed too, you know."

"Doesn't take back all the hurt and betrayal."

"I'm not trying to diminish what you went through, okay? I'm the first person to tell them that what happened back then was messed up. You know that I defended you the whole time." Violet let out a deep exhale. "We talk about you a lot, you know. Mom and Dad are constantly saying how they hope you're happy. That they're proud of you and med school. Dad's always bragging to his friends that you're a surgeon."

"He doesn't know anything about what I do."

It was weird hearing that. A part of Eliza was so mad at imagining him boasting about her to his golf buddies over a beer. All the things they'd said to each other over the last nine years could be typed out on a single sheet of paper. But at the same time, the other half of her was relieved that there was still some love despite all the sludge that had fallen on their relationship.

"I really think you should think about coming home for Christmas," Violet said. "If you're as happy as you seem to be, I think this is the right time to let them in again. Show off your happiness, your new girlfriend. I mean, I'm sure she wants to meet your family."

"She hasn't said anything."

"Gee, makes me feel super loved and important."

"It's not my job to beg for my parents to accept me for being a lesbian. If they're not going to accept their kids for who they are, then they shouldn't have kids."

"The image of Mom and Dad you have in your head is fourteen years old. Again, I'm not trying to diminish your feelings, but people change, just like you and I have changed over those years. I think Mom and Dad have learned from their mistakes. They know you're dating someone. I told them."

"Yeah? And what did they say?"

"That they're glad you found someone and that they hope you're happy. You should think about it. You can stay with me and Jonathon. I'll be with you the whole time."

"I really don't want to."

"They're your parents. I think you would really regret not fixing your relationship if something happened to them tomorrow."

That really stayed with Eliza. Long after their conversation, she lay in bed and reflected on what her sister had said. She knew firsthand how fast life could change. She already had so many regrets with Tess, and their relationship was the best it could have been. She couldn't imagine if something happened to her parents, and she'd never reconciled with them.

Thinking about going home was already suffocating her. At least twice a month, she had dreams that she'd somehow ended up back in Tallulah, and she had no way out. She always ended up running into Mr. and Mrs. Ware in public, and in every dream, they stormed over and screamed at her. Usually in a restaurant, and all the customers watched, and no one did anything. Another recurring dream was that Eliza tried going to Tess's grave, but for some reason, she never made it there. She would always make a wrong turn or struggled to walk to get there, like gravity didn't exist, and she floated in the air, or she simply woke up right before she got to the cemetery.

It was a city that served as a time capsule. From the best moments of her life to the absolute worst. If she still struggled with her PTSD—like Blake asking about her ring necklace or telling a young patient's family that they'd died in surgery—how the hell would she be able to breathe inside the place that scared her the most?

She wasn't sure, but by the next morning, she had already convinced herself that it was time to finally go home.

CHAPTER TWELVE

Just like Adrian, Thanksgiving was Blake's favorite holiday. When she was a kid, she'd loved waking up to watch the Macy's Thanksgiving Day parade with Adrian and Jordan while her parents started cooking. When she was a preteen, she'd started showing interest in helping her parents cook as her love for food blossomed, and she occasionally snuck in breaks to watch the parade performances. While the turkey cooked to the perfect brown, the family would watch *A Charlie Brown Thanksgiving*. She and Adrian had seen it so many times, they'd quoted it from start to finish to annoy Jordan, who'd wanted to watch in peace. And then after they'd been stuffed with amazing food, they'd watched the football games.

She and Eliza spent Wednesday night at her parents'. She let Eliza catch up on sleep since she'd worked an eighteen hour shift the day before, but that was fine with Blake. She was in charge of the kitchen and loved the opportunity to boss her parents around.

By the time Eliza was showered, dressed, and came downstairs, the turkey was in the oven, rosemary and thyme perfumed the home, and her mother had made Nana's Swiss bean casserole ready for the oven, her mom's grandma's recipe brought down through three generations. Plus, Blake thought it was a somewhat elevated green bean casserole recipe that didn't use Campbell's cream of mushroom soup. She never understood that recipe.

"Oh, is that a green bean casserole?" Eliza asked. She rested her chin on Blake's shoulder, wrapped her arms around her, and stole a cornflake from the top of the dish.

Blake batted at her wrist and turned. "Hey, save the appetite."

"I am. It's all ready for the best part of Thanksgiving: the stuffing."

Blake placed her hands on Eliza's waist and pulled her in for a kiss. All the sleeping Eliza had to catch up on had delayed their first kiss of the day, and Blake felt cheesy for thinking it'd been too long since their last one. Eliza leaned into the kiss, pinning Blake against the kitchen counter and teasing her fingers underneath her sweater.

"Ew. Stop making out on the food," Jordan said when she walked into the kitchen. She covered her eyes dramatically and felt her way to the fridge.

Blake pulled away. "Are you ever not annoying?"

Jordan lowered her hands and grinned. "Nope. I take great pride in annoying you. Don't fuck up the food."

"Do I ever fuck up the food?"

Jordan looked skyward as she considered this. "Unfortunately... no. But it's okay, I'll insult you in all the other categories." She grabbed the bottle of Pinot Grigio that she'd brought over. "Eliza, want a glass? You'll probably need it."

"Well, I just woke up an hour ago, but it's Thanksgiving and five o'clock somewhere."

"I like her," Jordan said to Blake. "Can we keep her?"

"That's the plan. Shh, don't tell her, or she'll run away."

Blake was proud of her Thanksgiving meal. She was in charge of the turkey, stuffing, and mashed potatoes. Her mom made Nana's Swiss bean casserole. Hugo brought over Bela's pernil, a slow-roasted pork shoulder prepared in a green mole. Marc fixed cranberry salsa instead of cranberry sauce, as well as white rice and beans. Her dad made Tito's potato salad, and Jordan made the cornbread with jalapenos, onions, and bacon. Blake loved all the different plates of food passed down through the generations. She leaned back in her seat, watching her family and her girlfriend feast on all the dishes, and she loved the extra heaping of stuffing Eliza scooped onto her plate. She glanced across the table and stared at Adrian's marine photo that sat on the mantel along with the folded American flag in a walnut flag box—that also held all the shell casings from his twenty-one-gun salute—his dog tags draped around the flag box, and his Purple Heart case propped next to it. Her parents wanted those trinkets on the mantel so he was still part of the family for dinner. When the four of them had their Sunday meal, they always left his seat empty, in between Blake and her dad. At the table for Thanksgiving, Eliza sat in his seat, and her presence rooted Blake in place from drifting off to wherever Adrian was. Although his absence still filled the room, it might have been the farthest into the day without someone mentioning him, which invited a sullen, reflective moment at the table. Just because he wasn't mentioned until then didn't mean he was forgotten, but Blake wondered if having Eliza there helped patch up the hole punched out of her heart that always ached off and on during the holiday.

She snuck a glance at Eliza, who was on her third plate of stuffing, mixing it in with the cranberry salsa and pork.

"I have to say, cranberry salsa is a million times better than cranberry sauce," Eliza said.

Marc laughed. "Right?"

"Cranberry sauce is severely overrated. This cranberry salsa is everything."

"I would tell you to give her the recipe," Blake said. "But she might find a way to burn down her apartment, even though fire isn't involved."

Eliza playfully smacked her leg. "Hey!"

Eliza had fit right in with the family since day one, and Blake loved watching them interact as if they'd known her for much longer than four months. Instead of spending Thanksgiving floating between the past and present, the what-ifs and could-have-beens like she usually did, she floated between the present and future and what could be, and she had Eliza to thank for that.

❖

Eliza was beyond stuffed. She'd become one with her spot on the couch in the Navarro's living room after dinner. Three helpings of Blake's amazing stuffing did that, and even though the feeling was slightly uncomfortable, she had zero regrets.

Seemingly unaffected by all the food, Luis opened his record player, pulled out a Bennett and Sons album from his collection on the bookshelf, and placed it on the turntable. Out came songs that reminded Eliza of her dad. Seventies southern rock. It reminded her of summers as a kid. She and Violet would splash around in their small aboveground pool, and as her dad fired up the grill and the charcoal scented the backyard, Bennett and Sons would blast from his portable boombox, plugged in inside and pointed right against the window screen.

"This is a good song," Eliza told Luis.

"You love Bennett and Sons too?"

"My dad does. Joseph Bennett and Paul Simon were his two favorite songwriters. Reminds me of him."

"Your dad has good music taste."

He spun around and held out his hand to Sandra. She hesitated for a moment, almost as if she needed that extra second to forget the fullness of dinner, and pushed herself off the couch. He lifted her out of the chair and spun her around. Luis had dance moves, making Eliza wonder if he and Sandra used to go out dancing when they were younger because they seemed to know exactly what they were doing. She smiled as she watched the two wrapped up in their own world. Blake had told her that her parents had been married for forty years. Met when they were nineteen, married at twenty-two, and Eliza loved so much that despite four decades and so many ups and downs in between, they were still able to look at each other like they were their everything.

That was the kind of love she'd always wanted.

"My dad likes to dance off the tryptophan," Blake said with her arm around Eliza's shoulders. "He does this every year."

"You know that's a myth, right?" Eliza said. "Cheddar cheese contains more tryptophan than turkey. It's most likely the carbs and alcohol."

Blake elbowed her side. "Oh, don't get all scientific on us, or you're going to be forced into a solo dance."

"I'm just stating the facts."

Blake stood up and extended her hand. "Just for that, you have to dance with me now."

"Stating facts now warrants punishment?"

"Is dancing a punishment?"

"It is when you don't know how."

"As you can see, I know how to dance. Learned it from my dad. I'll lead. Come on."

"What about your cast?"

"Now you're making up excuses. I get this thing off in a week. I deserve a celebration dance. Don't you think?"

Eliza couldn't deny that. She was excited for the cast to be gone so she didn't have to wince every time Blake moved, wondering when the next tally on her long injury record would be. She was also excited that they wouldn't be interrupted with taking the damn cast off when they were caught up in the heat of the moment.

Graduating from the walking cast would be Eliza's early Christmas present, and because of that, she accepted, allowing Blake to pull her from her seat.

Eliza wasn't a fan of dancing, but with the Navarros surrounding her and all of their lively energy packed into one house, somehow, they all spent an hour dancing. It started with Bennett and Sons, and then Frankie Valli, Frank Sinatra, and other songs from the fifties and sixties once Sandra figured out how to use the Bluetooth speaker to play her favorites from her phone. The whole family danced, and Eliza got to share one with everyone, even Jordan, Marc, and Hugo. They loosened their stomachs dancing while Sandra got the tres leches pumpkin flan ready for dessert.

After a slice of the most delicious Thanksgiving dessert Eliza had ever had, she and the rest of the Navarros were defeated for the second time, sprawled on various chairs and couches around the house. As Eliza cuddled up next to Blake while Luis, Hugo, and Marc cheered and grumbled along with the Cowboys' game, she enjoyed the happiness that swaddled her. She couldn't remember the last time she'd had this much fun at Thanksgiving. Sure, the Thanksgivings with her friends were great, but they were nowhere near the level that the Navarros set. She wasn't even a part of their family, and the Navarros made her feel like she was one of them. They made her feel that way all the way back when they'd insisted on throwing a thank-you dinner for her. She barely knew them then, but she'd felt like she'd known them her whole life because that was the type of family they were. Filled with so much love that it suffused the whole house.

While the rest of the family struggled to pull their bodies off the couch, Eliza decided to check in on Sandra in the kitchen. Sandra had been avoiding doing dishes, and now, a nice collection of pots, pans, and plates littered the countertops and piled into the sink. Eliza decided to wash and rinse so Sandra could load her dishwasher accordingly. Her mom had her own specific way of organizing it, and Eliza didn't want to infringe on Sandra's technique.

"My technique is getting dishes over with," Sandra said with a laugh, taking the rinsed ceramic casserole dish out of Eliza's hands. "Don't spend too much time washing those down, hon. We can just throw everything in here. That's the greatness of this wonderful invention." She pointed to the dishwasher, and Eliza followed her orders.

"Thanks again for having me," Eliza said. "I'm so glad I was able to come. It's been a great day."

"Oh, honey, anytime. We are so glad to have you. Blake told us that you usually work on Thanksgiving?"

"Yeah. I usually take one for the team so everyone else can be with their families."

"But what about yours?"

Eliza hesitated for a moment, feeling the sadness of the holidays poke and prod at her for the first time that day. "I'm, um, I'm not very close with my parents."

Sandra glanced up, and her stare held Eliza's with great sympathy. "Really? I'm so sorry to hear that."

"It's all right," she said, even though it wasn't at all. "But I'm glad Blake invited me. It gave me something to look forward to. You guys have been very welcoming since day one."

Sandra smiled and took another dish. "I'm really glad you and Blake found each other. I haven't seen her this happy in a long time." There was a pleasant pulling in her midsection. "Really?" "I'm going to be honest with you, she's dated some interesting women. She was a little crazy in her twenties. Young, wild, and free."

"She's touched on that part," Eliza said through a laugh.

"She's been speeding through life a million miles an hour. She's always on the go, always has to be doing something. But I've always known that was a distraction. She took her brother's death pretty hard, and that's how she copes with it, I guess. Busies herself and her mind so she doesn't have to think about it. I don't know. What I do know is that once you entered the picture, her whole demeanor changed. You're a breath of fresh air, Eliza, to all of us. And Blake, well, she completely adores you. I haven't seen her face light up about any other woman that's been in her life the way it lights up when she talks about you."

Eliza knew that Sandra noticed the hot blush taking over her face and ears because when she looked back at her from the dishwasher, her smile grew.

Eliza glanced down at the dish, trying to hide even though she'd already given herself away. "I feel the same way."

"You're really good for her. You're grounded, you're very intelligent, sweet, just as passionate as she is. And you slow her down, make her appreciate what's currently around her. I really fear that she wasted so much of her youth trying to avoid, well, anything hard. I'm really glad she found someone like you. Luis and I are very grateful. We want you to know that."

All the love made Eliza's eyes sting. The Navarros had so much love to give, love she wished her parents had openly fed her as easily as the Navarro's did. "That really means a lot, Sandra. Everything your family has done for me...well, I haven't felt that in a long time. I'm really grateful for all of you too."

Sandra lifted herself from the dishwasher and offered her open arms. She gave Eliza a motherly hug, something she was so good at. She held her tightly, her embrace telling Eliza she was practically another daughter, that she was loved and welcomed whenever, and tears threatened Eliza. She wished so much that she'd gotten a hug like that from her own mother when she needed it the most. At the same time it deepened the wounds, the hug patched up the betrayal she felt from her own family.

Why couldn't she have this kind of relationship with her parents?

When Sandra pulled away, she kissed Eliza's cheek and continued loading the dishwasher.

As Eliza tried swallowing the lump, she felt two gentle arms wrap around her waist, a chin nuzzled on her shoulder, and the comforting woodsy smell greeted her.

"I miss you," Blake whispered and then kissed the back of her ear. "Come back to me."

Eliza loved so much how it didn't matter if Sandra was right beside them, catching a glance at them in their moment. She and Blake could hug and kiss in front of any Navarro, and they wouldn't have cared at all. In the Walsh household, Eliza couldn't even mutter Tess's name without getting some kind of look, as if she was committing a felony.

Eliza and Blake snuggled on the loveseat with her family, watching the last football game of the night. They snuck in kisses, and the worst that happened was when Jordan caught them and told them to get a room.

So they did. With all the wine, they'd already planned on spending the night in Blake and Jordan's childhood room. Luckily, the twin beds had been upgraded to a queen, and Jordan took Adrian's room.

After Blake closed the door, she peeled her sweater over her head, then tossed it at Eliza's face, completely ruining the sight. She quickly flung the shirt on the ground and soaked up the sight of a gorgeous and sexy Blake standing there in her black bra and skinny jeans. The sight of her flat, tan stomach did things to Eliza below her underwear. Every single time.

"Stop," Blake said, not at all serious. "We're in my parents' house, and you're eye fucking me."

"I can't help it. You're the one who stripped in front of me. You should have known better."

Blake unhooked her bra, and her perfect breasts fell into place, begging Eliza to walk over and cup them, maybe even suck them into her mouth. Blake pulled a pj's shirt from her suitcase, studied it for a moment, and then looked back with that infamous impish grin of hers. "Wanna know what I've never done before?"

Eliza followed Blake's lead. Once her top and jeans were off and tossed aside, she glanced up at the ceiling fan, thought about Blake's words, and then landed her stare back on Blake's exposed nipples. "God, I truly have no idea. I just figured you'd done it all."

Right as Eliza went for her duffle bag to grab her pj's, Blake said, "Wait. I haven't told you the thing I've never done."

She wasn't sure why Blake couldn't tell her while she changed into her comfy pj's that consisted of a baggy old USC shirt and plaid pants with an elastic band, emphasis on baggy and elastic. After eating three plates of food and a big slice of tres leches pumpkin flan, her body really needed baggy and elastic. But she went along with whatever Blake was up to.

"Okay, what haven't you done?"

Blake's grin turned salacious. "I've never had sex in my childhood room."

"What? Blake!"

Blake's breasts bounced as she crawled across the bed, and then she patted the empty space next to her. Eliza couldn't even deny that it was tempting. Trying to hold back kisses and touches all day, her frustrations were starting to reach a boiling point. Plus, Blake was topless on the bed, in only her hot pink boy shorts, which had become Eliza's new weakness. Just one look at Blake in boy shorts and she was done for.

She couldn't believe she was actually considering this. Sandra and Luis were kind enough to invite her into their home, allowed her to spend the night, gave their approval of her dating their daughter, and this was how she was going to thank them? By fucking their daughter a floor above them?

"Your family is downstairs," Eliza whispered loudly through her tightened jaw.

"Oh please," Blake said, waving her off. "My parents fall asleep down there every night and don't come to bed until well past midnight. And the first step on the stairs has a creak, so we'll hear when someone is coming up."

"But what if they hear us?"

"They're not going to hear us." She patted the spot again. "I know how this house works as well as I know how your body works, and I know you want to tear these boy shorts off me right now."

Eliza swallowed. Damn it, she hated—and loved—how much Blake already knew everything about her. "Yes, I really do."

"Then do it."

"But they're right downstairs. They've been so kind and hospitable and—"

"You look super sexy in your bra and underwear, you know that?"

Eliza paused, caught off guard. "You're trying to seduce me."

Blake wiggled her eyebrows. "Is it working?"

It wasn't like Blake had to try too hard. All she had to do was use her puppy eyes for a few moments while her naked breasts and her small, yet perfectly shaped ass taunted Eliza. She wanted one of those nipples in her mouth. She wanted to hear Blake whimper under her control. She wanted to kiss her all over like she'd been dying to since the beginning of the day.

"If I relent, you have to be quiet for once," Eliza said with a direct point while crawling over Blake in bed.

"I'll try my best. Not my fault you're so good at it."

"Blake, this is something teenagers do."

"I'm wine tipsy, you're incredibly sexy, and I want to scratch something off my bucket list. Please?"

Enough was enough. Eliza pounced on her...after she made sure the door was locked. If she was going to dive into this risky action, she was going to make sure the door was freakin' locked.

She hadn't fooled around with someone in their parents' house with their parents present since she was a teenager. Every footstep downstairs had them halting in place: mid-kiss, mid-nipple-suck, and right as Eliza was driving her closer to the edge, the bottom stair creaked, and she quickly tossed a hand over Blake's parted mouth. The footsteps wandered up the stairs, but even with one hand shutting Blake up, Eliza moved her fingers inside her. Blake whimpered into her palm as the family member walked past the door and down the hallway, and once the bedroom door was shut, Eliza removed her hand, crawled down lower, and rewarded Blake with her mouth.

After they both released each other, they cuddled naked underneath the blankets. Eliza spread her arm out so Blake could rest her head on her bare breasts.

"Thank you for being here with me," Blake said.

Eliza planted a soft kiss on her temple. "Of course. Thank you for giving this Thanksgiving orphan a home."

Blake traced invisible patterns on Eliza's chest, and the soft caress of her fingertips created goose bumps up and down Eliza's arms. "This is always such a hard time for us. It really means the world to me that you're here. It made the day a little easier."

She kissed her forehead again. "I'd do anything for you, Blake. You know that, right?"

"I know."

As the silence saturated the room, Eliza reflected on the day and how much she admired the Navarros for how they lived their lives after Adrian's devastating death. Despite it being a hard holiday for them, they were still able to have so much fun, and Eliza had even forgotten that it was a tough holiday for the family. They all were so optimistic, full of life and love, and God, were they accepting of a stranger. She knew she wasn't a stranger anymore, but she still thought back on the dinner at Mezcal and how she'd felt like one of them by the end of it.

Why couldn't her own life be like that? Filled with optimism, hope, and will? It was like she'd been stuck in a pool of mud for years, and instead of trying to get out, she just sat there helpless. Why did she allow herself to feel like that? Why didn't she try harder?

Violet's words hadn't stopped ringing in her mind. Being around Blake and her family made Eliza constantly think about her own parents and how she desperately wanted what Blake had. Although Blake filled up a lot of the holes in her heart, she could only do so much because Eliza needed her parents. It'd been long enough, and the more she was around the Navarros, the more she opened her mind up to the idea that she needed to go home for Christmas. Violet was right: she needed to show her parents who she was, show them that she'd found a woman who made her incredibly happy. But was it too soon for Blake to meet them? They'd only been dating for three months. Three months was nothing compared to nine years of not talking to her parents. Should she wait to bring Blake home until they lived together, even though she had no idea when that would be. Definitely not until it had been at least a year.

After a few minutes of ruminating, she decided to go with her heart and gut. She couldn't imagine going back home for the first time in nine years without Blake. Blake was confident and so patient, and Eliza needed all of that to face her biggest fear: her Before. Although going back home terrified her no end, it was a Band-Aid she needed to yank.

If she didn't, she would never fully heal.

"I've been thinking a lot...about my family...my parents."

Blake lifted her head. "You have?" Eliza nodded. "I hope you weren't thinking about them for the last half hour."

She nudged a laughing Blake. "No, I wasn't."

"Okay, good. Now continue."

Eliza sighed. "The more time I spend with your family, the more I really want that with my own. And I think the thing holding me back from fully healing from my accident is learning to forgive my parents."

"Oh, damn, you're really serious." Blake straightened her back against the headboard.

"It needs to happen, Blake. I haven't seen my parents in nine years. *Nine.* Almost a decade. If something happened to them tomorrow, I wouldn't ever forgive myself. I don't want to live with that regret. I don't want to lose them or, hell, my own life, without repairing some part of our relationship. It needs to happen."

"Yeah, I totally agree."

"I'm going to go home for Christmas."

Saying it out loud hit her straight in the gut. Her heart was set. She was going home.

Blake grabbed her hand. "Oh, okay, wow. That's a big decision for you."

"I'm ready to do it. Now's the time to do it. It's been long enough."

"Do you want me to come?"

Eliza hesitated for a moment. "Do you think it's too soon to meet them?"

Blake frowned. "Why would I think it's too soon?"

"We've only been together for, like, three months. We're still so new."

"Yeah, but I'm fully in this. I want to meet your family. If you want me there, I'll be there."

"I want you there."

She didn't care if they'd only been together for three months. She didn't know how to do it without Blake.

Blake kissed the back of Eliza's hand. "Then I'll be there. I promise."

Chapter Thirteen

Eliza lost so much sleep during the days leading up to going home. On the plane, she couldn't find a comfortable position, and the Dramamine and Xanax she took to pass out didn't even work.

What had she agreed to?

Six hours later, she and Blake landed in Cleveland. As Blake grabbed their luggage from the overhead compartment, Eliza felt the lack of oxygen on the plane, and the walls started closing in as her breaths became shorter.

"Eliza, you okay?" Blake asked and dropped her head so she could see. "You're white."

"Why am I here? Why did I do this?"

"Because you said it was time. Hey," Blake said, sliding back in their row and resting her hand on Eliza's bouncing knee. "I'm going to be right by you through all of this, okay? So is your sister. You're not going to be alone."

"I haven't seen them in nine years. This is going to be *so* awkward."

Right as Eliza was about to run her hands down her face, Blake grabbed her wrists and lowered them. "It might be awkward at first, but we have to try our best not to let it linger. We need to go into this with an open mind."

Eliza nodded, and Blake kissed her forehead. A simple kiss that she would have welcomed in California caused a different reaction in her home state. She tensed up, and she hated that her natural instinct was to do that. Luckily, Blake didn't notice, but knowing how open Blake was to sweet PDA like that, Eliza wondered if her liberal way of life would be hindered by the traditional minds of the Midwest.

Violet and Emma greeted them at baggage claim. Violet yelped when she saw them and pointed to Eliza so Emma would also notice. Once she realized it was Eliza, Emma scampered over with her arms wide and barreled into Eliza's legs.

"Aunt Wiza!"

Eliza scooped her up, spun her around, and kissed her cheek. One of the less intimidating things being home had to offer: her favorite little one. She couldn't believe how big Emma was. The last time she'd seen her, she was three, beyond her memory, but Eliza was grateful that their weekly FaceTimes made an impression. She wasn't expecting such a warm welcome.

"My favorite niece. You're so big." She tickled her sides, and Emma giggled. "How old are you now?"

She held up five fingers. "I'm five."

"Five? So you're all grown-up?"

"I think so." She looked over at Blake, becoming shyer and curling up in Eliza's arms. "Who's that?"

"I'm Blake," she said and held out her hand for a high five, and once Emma comprehended the gesture, she smiled and smacked her hand, laughing as she did so. Blake pretended Emma hurt her, which caused her to laugh even harder.

And just like that, Emma approved of Blake.

"Do I get a hug, or do you only care about little people?" Violet said.

"I only care about her," Eliza replied as she put Emma down so she could hug Violet. More like squeeze her. God, did she miss her older sister. She already knew that, but when she hugged Violet, she really felt how much she'd missed her. "And this is Blake."

Violet gave her a wide, obnoxious smile, held out her arms, and took Blake in. "It is so nice to meet you," she said and broke the hug. "I've heard *so* much about you."

"Oh, I can only imagine," Blake said.

"I'm so glad you're a real person. Now tell me, how do you manage being my sister's girlfriend?"

"I'm not going to lie, Violet, it's a lot of work."

Eliza smacked her arm as Violet rewarded her with a bellowing laugh.

"I like her already," Violet said.

Emma held Eliza's hand as they walked back to the car. She cautiously looked at Blake, asking questions like what her full name was, her favorite color, how old she was. By the time they got to the car, Emma had already warmed up, and the two of them carried on a conversation in the back about all her stuffed animals. How easy it was for five-year-olds to make friends. At that moment, Eliza wished she could use some of Emma's techniques on her parents.

She didn't have much to say on the thirty-minute ride from the airport to Tallulah, not as each mile that progressed on the odometer added another weight on her chest. In the back seat, Emma showed Blake how she could count to one hundred in Spanish, and Blake counted with her. Despite her immense anxiety, Eliza still was able to smile at how adorable the moment was. Then Emma rambled about kindergarten and all her friends, and Eliza cringed when Emma mentioned Chloe in passing, a reminder that she was going to be in the same vicinity as the Wares.

Violet attempted small talk by telling Eliza all the new things in Tallulah, but Eliza's mind was focused on how close they were to *the* exit. There were two exits on the highway for Tallulah. The exit she'd taken the night of the accident was the first one, Exit 22, the one she'd always taken. It probably only cut off a minute from the ETA as opposed to the next exit, 18. The air became warmer and thicker the closer they got. It squeezed her chest like a stress ball, and as they approached the sign, her breath caught. She closed her eyes, and Violet sped up. When she didn't veer to the right, Eliza opened her eyes and watched as they passed Exit 22. She turned to Violet. She and her family never got off at 18. It was a habit.

Except for now.

Once they got off, a sign that read, "Welcome to Tallulah. The Sweetest Place on Earth. Founded 1818," greeted them. Eliza scoffed at the irony of the sign as the familiarity of her hometown settled in her. The traffic was still the same. Eliza had endured years of LA traffic and was still surprised that a small town in Northeast Ohio had traffic that made her just as mad and swear just as much. Two-lane streets split the town, and they hit every stoplight on the main road, adding to Eliza's frustration and anxiety.

So much and so little had changed. The Super K-Mart that she and Tess had always met up at was now vacant, much like the whole strip mall. Back then, the parking lot was a teenager's loitering paradise, only a short walk to Taco Bell for a late-night snack after perusing the K-Mart aisles for fun. The Blockbuster that Eliza used to work at—and the place her family went to every Friday—was now a tire store, stripped of any remnants of the discontinued franchise. The Bennigan's that Tess had worked at during the summers was now a hibachi restaurant.

Then they drove through the center of town, which was still cute, the only redeeming quality Eliza would give Tallulah. Possessing small-town charm, a white gazebo sat in the middle, and residents always took pictures there for special occasions like school dances, weddings, or family photos. Since it was Christmas, a tree flickered with white lights, garland wrapped around either side of the railings leading up to it, and it was the perfect beguiling backdrop for family photos.

"Your town is cute," Blake said as they drove past the gazebo with groups waiting for a picture.

"This is the only cute part."

"Oh, Eliza," Violet said and patted her knee. "There are lots of good spots, Blake. Don't listen to her."

"Yeah, the K-Mart lot is a happening place right now. I'm sure it adds property value."

"It's been closed for eleven years," Violet said.

"And the building is still there? My point exactly."

Blake laughed and squeezed Eliza's shoulders from behind the seat. "Let's keep an open mind about the next few days, all right?"

"Listen to your girlfriend. You don't want to be in a bad mood during Mom's favorite holiday. It'll make things worse."

"If I get all the trash talk out now, I'll be less bitter about this place when I get to their house."

"Okay, fair. Air it all out."

A few miles later, Eliza's stomach sank when they hit yet another red light. But this time, it was in front of St. Teresa of Avila, the Wares' Catholic church, one of the main landmarks imprinted in Eliza's memory that encapsulated much of her emotional pain. Staring at the brick building with the white steeple reaching toward the bright blue sky, she remembered all the times Tess had talked about her parents forcing religion on her, how she had to go to LifeTeen every Sunday night during high school, where she'd learned about how to be a better Catholic, and that included not being gay. One time during their junior year, when Eliza had met Tess after her Bennigan's shift and treated her to a Crunchwrap Supreme from Taco Bell, Tess had sobbed in the passenger seat and asked if they were wrong for each other. Eliza's family never went to church unless it was someone's baptism or wedding. St. Teresa of Avila was the reason why Tess had deeply feared telling her parents the truth about her heart, about them, and the summer after their junior year, when the Wares had forced them to break up and stay apart, they'd also forced her to "volunteer" with the church, probably thinking that her volunteer hours would deplete all the "sins" that lived in her.

Tess didn't tell Eliza what had happened that summer until they'd gotten back together. She'd said that every day, the priest would bless her and pray that Tess would get back on God's path by the end of summer. Eliza still wondered if Tess had told her everything that had happened, besides the priests and nuns forcing Tess to place white crosses on the front lawn to represent the aborted babies or praying her gay away in the form of holy water, lots of prayers, forced weekly confessionals, and hours wasted in the church. She really wondered if they'd tried some conversion therapy on her, and whenever Eliza had the courage to ask, Tess had mowed it over like a weed, moving on to the next subject.

Eliza's conclusion was that they had tried to convert her.

"I'm sorry," Violet said softly as the seconds ticked longer at the godforsaken red light. She rested a hand on Eliza's bouncing knee. "I'll peel out of here the second it turns green."

Tess's funeral had also been at St. Teresa's. The side of the brick building, right next to the handicap ramp that zigzagged to the main entrance, was the spot Mrs. Ware had blamed everything on Eliza. On the other side of the road from the church was the cemetery. Tess was somewhere behind the pine trees and the rows of tombstones. Tess was right there. Her presence was the strongest it had been in thirteen and a half years, and it choked Eliza now.

Finally, the light turned green, and Violet did exactly as she promised. She sped up to forty despite the lower speed limit and zipped by the large cemetery. It wasn't until they reached the next stoplight with St. Teresa a half a mile behind that Eliza finally let out her breath.

When they got to Violet's, and after Eliza had given Jonathon a nice, long hug, she and Blake carried their bags up to the spare bedroom. She fell onto the bed, closed her eyes, and tried to breathe out the heaviness in her chest.

"Hey, you all right?" Blake asked and plopped by her side.

Eliza couldn't believe that after nine years of not seeing her parents, she would return with her girlfriend. When she'd made the decision, she'd thought it was bold and brave, and having Blake by her side kept a steady stream of confidence flowing through her. But now in Ohio, driving through all her pain and trauma, she started questioning it all.

She shook her head and hid her face inside her elbow. "This is hard. We passed the exit where we got into the crash, we passed her church where her parents blamed me, the cemetery where she's buried—"

She didn't want to cry. Not an hour after landing in Ohio. If she cried, her face would be red and puffy just in time for them to go over to her parents' house for dinner. The whole point of spending Christmas in Tallulah was to let go, to see if her parents had changed like Violet swore, to finally turn her After into something she wouldn't regret because as it stood, she regretted a lot about not having much of a life in her After. The only thing she didn't regret was Blake and her career.

The panic attack was brewing behind her sternum. She always knew one was about to take hold when she felt hot prickles starting in her neck that traveled up to her scalp at the same time her lungs rapidly shrunk. She sat straight up as her chest constricted with the panic of Blake having to witness another one of her attacks.

It was so embarrassing.

"Eliza?"

She shook her head and closed her eyes so she didn't have to witness the room spinning. The nausea crept up her throat and balled up. Sweat coated her hairline and the back of her neck. She remembered the breathing techniques she'd learned in her outpatient therapy and attempted to stop it in its tracks. Blake rubbed her back, and Eliza focused on that and how it made her feel. It brought her some relaxation and calm when her body was about to skyrocket into overdrive.

Blake pulled Eliza in and hugged her, and she caved into the force. "It's okay. I'm right here. You're safe."

Hearing those words cracked something inside her. She cried, and as embarrassed as she was for falling apart right when she got to Violet's house, she hoped that releasing the building tension would deplete her emotions so she could get through her stay without a panic attack waiting around every corner.

Afterward, she cuddled into Blake's chest, deeply inhaling the woodsy smell of her shirt to soothe the crying aftershocks that ran through her body, and enjoyed the arm rubs Blake gave. After fifteen minutes of quiet, Violet called them downstairs so they could go.

Her chest clenched yet again.

The drive over to her childhood home was only ten minutes, and luckily, they didn't pass any Tallulah landmarks. During the drive, she and Blake sat in the third row of Jonathon's Toyota Highlander, and Blake held her hand the whole time, rubbing her thumb along the soft part of Eliza's skin.

"It's going to be all right," she whispered in Eliza's ear and then kissed her cheek.

In the depths of her mind, Eliza knew Blake was right. Given the fact that it was Christmas, her parents weren't going to start any drama. She was positive because at the first sign of drama, they shut down and ran away, never people to partake in an argument. If they were too afraid to stand up to the Wares at Tess's funeral, there was absolutely no way they would try anything during Christmas. Eliza had to keep reminding herself of that.

She exhaled a long, warm breath when Jonathon parked in the driveway. Her childhood home sat in front of her. Her mom's Ford Windstar and her dad's Ford Explorer—the family cars she'd learned to drive in—were gone. They'd been replaced with a Chevy Cruze and a Ford Fusion, the open garage door barely recognizable with those cars inside.

Once she was out of her car seat, Emma ran to the front door that was still the same red of Eliza's childhood, adding a pop of color to the white aluminum siding and black shutters.

This was it. Her walk of shame. It was barely above freezing out, and Eliza felt hot and constricted in her peacoat.

"I promise it will be fine," Violet said with a pat on her shoulder. "They're really excited to see you and meet Blake. Just be yourself, all right?"

Easier said than done, Eliza thought. As a teen, she had been programmed to hide who she was just to receive some kind of acceptance from her parents.

Emma rang the doorbell and jumped when Eliza's mom opened the door. At the first sight of her mom, Eliza's breath caught around the ball in her throat, a mixture of joy and sadness. Her mother's friendly face looked the same, a few more wrinkles than the last time she'd seen her. Her dirty blond hair was still in a long bob, and her dark blue eyes hid behind glasses, a new addition to her appearance. Eliza was sad to see the aging on her face, proof of how much time had passed since she'd last seen her.

"Grammy, it's Christmas time. Santa is coming tomorrow," Emma said, raising her arms so Eliza's mom could pick her up. As she did exactly that, her eyes locked with Eliza's, and a thin smile formed.

"Have you been good?" her mom asked Emma. "Santa only comes to good kids."

"Daddy says I'm a perfect princess."

Her mom laughed. "Oh, did he?"

"Hi, Grandpa."

Emma waved, and when Eliza's mom let her down, Emma scampered inside the house. Violet and Jonathon gave informal greetings, proof that they saw her parents so often that they were beyond grand hellos.

"Eliza," her mom said, contentment in her tone. Her smile widened with her arms, opening up for a hug. Then she faltered, almost as if asking permission and fearing she would get rejected.

Eliza was shocked that all she needed to see was her mom in person for all her bitterness to unwind. She felt like she'd transformed into a kid, needing her mother's hug after an awful day at school.

"Hi, Mom," Eliza said and took a step up on the patio to give her mom a cautious hug, not ready to lower her guard to give her a warm hug she probably should have given her mother.

Her mom still smelled the same, the mixture of her warm natural scent and the smell of their house.

"It's so good to see you, honey." Her mom broke the hug and examined her from head to toe, and the tears brimmed.

"You too, Mom," Eliza said, swallowing the emotion that attempted to collect in her throat.

Then her father crept into the foyer and waved. He cautiously walked over as if warming her up for a hug. She accepted it with hesitancy, just like with her mom. There was so much uncertainty in the air that prevented her from melting into her parents' arms.

When she broke the hug, she turned and found Blake standing in the door, a big smile on her face as if she was unaware of the family drama permeating in the house.

"So, um, this…is my girlfriend, Blake."

Being in this house put Eliza's out-and-proud life in California out like water dousing flames. She heard the shaking in her voice when she said that. Saying "girlfriend," "Tess," or "gay," was taboo back then, more than "fuck" and "shit." But after saying the words out loud and directly to her parents, she felt a little proud, as if she'd accomplished an impossible task. It was weird saying girlfriend in her childhood home to her parents, but that didn't mean it didn't feel right.

Blake extended her hand. "Nice to meet you, Mr. and Mrs. Walsh."

It was as if she wasn't fazed at all, like all of Eliza's stories about her parents didn't affect her one bit. Blake's personality and confidence still shined as brightly as it did in California, and Eliza was envious. She wished she could have done the same.

Her mom gave Blake a friendly smile and shook her hand. "It's so nice to meet you too, Blake. You two had an okay plane ride?"

"It wasn't too bad," Blake answered and then looked at Eliza.

"Ready for all the family time?" her dad said.

"I'm always up for some family time."

Her parents smiled. "You look so grown-up, Eliza," her mom said.

"Becoming a doctor does a great job aging you."

"Can't believe you only have a few months left," her dad said, a smile on his face that hit her straight in the stomach.

She couldn't remember the last time her father had looked at her like that, like he was proud of her. She got a smile like that when she'd graduated from undergrad, but it was short-lived when she'd told them she wouldn't be coming home.

"I'm ready for it, trust me," Eliza said.

Her relationship with her parents was so strained, she felt like a stranger in her old home. It looked and smelled exactly the same, but that wasn't enough to cut through the tension and make her feel comfortable sitting on the living room couch. Her dad even had to offer her something to drink because she didn't want to ransack the kitchen and overstep her boundaries.

While her parents took turns checking on the dinner, Emma was a good distraction from the tension. She spread her four favorite stuffed animals on the living room floor. Her innocence was so pure while all the adults walked around the giant crater in the middle of the room. Eliza's parents stuck to talking about Emma at first, how great she was in her Thanksgiving play, of course, bypassing the miniscule details that were the Wares. But that was one time Eliza was glad her parents avoided an issue in conversation. They told Eliza and Blake how Emma's teachers couldn't stop singing her praises and then showed them some artwork Emma had drawn for them that hung on the fridge while everyone helped bring the food to the table.

"Eliza, have you given any thought about what you'll do after you finish your residency?" her father asked while passing the roasted brussels sprouts to Violet.

It felt more like an interview question than a dad casually inquiring about his daughter's professional trajectory. But it was all part of the small talk, the only conversation starters they had. She hated small talk. That was something she did with her patients. It wasn't something a kid and their parents should have been demoted to. But what did she expect, really? She was a whole different person since the last time she'd seen them. They had to get to know her all over again, just like they had to get to know Blake or any guest in their home. But the thing was: Eliza wasn't a guest.

How the hell did she allow herself to become a guest to her own family?

The severity of the estranged nine years sat right across from her at the dinner table. It was a reminder of why she was home. She had to get rid of it.

"I'm going to apply to several fellowships," she said, scooping the brussels sprouts on her plate. "Trauma fellowships. It's been my favorite rotation."

"What hospitals are you thinking?" Jonathan asked, more casually than her dad.

"USC, Cedars-Sinai—"

"The big leagues?" her dad smiled, finally relieving the tense interviewing disposition.

"I figured I'd reach high. I have Bellevue and USC med school on my CV, so that looks nice. But Bellevue is one of the top hospitals in the country, and I really like San Diego. So staying there is my first choice."

She hadn't really discussed the fellowships with Blake, and she tensed knowing that Blake was hearing this all for the first time. When Eliza snuck a glance at her, Blake almost looked disinterested in the conversation and instead sliced her porkchop. Eliza thought it was a little weird, and she hoped that applying to fellowships in LA didn't piss her off to the point where she ignored the conversation and focused on the porkchop. If it were reversed, if Blake was looking at venues for Vagabonds in LA without telling her, she'd be pissed off too. But it wasn't like Eliza had purposely kept it from her. With Dr. Norman's letter of recommendation and the fact that she was chief resident, her chances of getting a Bellevue fellowship were very high. LA was very much a backup plan.

"USC and Cedars-Sinai are backup applications," Eliza added, hoping that snagged Blake's attention. "I'd prefer to stay at Bellevue."

"It's always great to have several plans," her dad said.

Eliza checked on Blake again, and when their eyes met, Blake forced a grin and squeezed Eliza's knee before going back to her plate. It was a conversation she wanted to clarify, to assure Blake that she really didn't want to go to LA, not when they were going so strong.

But that conversation wasn't meant for the dinner table or any part of this trip. She would talk to Blake about it when they got back home.

When Emma darted from her seat to avoid eating her carrots, she ran to Eliza with Missy, her white unicorn with a rainbow horn. Eliza patted her lap to get Emma to sit with her.

"How's Missy's horn?" Eliza asked. "Did you tell her to rest?"

"She's sleeping right now. But now Sheeba is sick."

"Sheeba?"

She nodded as if Eliza knew exactly what stuffed animal she was talking about. "She has a temperature. I gave her a shot."

"In the head?" Emma nodded again, causing Eliza to laugh. Maybe she could teach her niece to stop giving her stuffed animals shots in the head. "How are we going to fix her?"

Emma shrugged. "I don't know. You need to fix her."

"I do? But you're the doctor."

"Nuh-uh. I'm your nurse."

Eliza smiled and kissed her head. "Okay, I'll take a look after dinner, all right?"

Blake shook her knee. Eliza faced her. "What?"

"Your dad asked how we met."

Right, her parents were talking to Blake, Violet, and Jonathon while she excluded herself for the important conversations of a five-year-old. This was the first test of letting her parents back in her life. She had to power through this. Having them ask about her relationship was a sign that they were at least trying.

"We met at my hospital," she said and took a bite of porkchop.

Her mom chuckled. "That's it? That's the story? I'm sure there's more than that."

Violet kicked Eliza from her other side, and right as Eliza gave her a scowl, Violet tightened her jaw and thinned her lips.

"She was in a motorcycle accident," Eliza continued. "I put her back together."

Blake and Jonathon chuckled, seeming like the only two people who got her humor.

"A motorcycle accident?" her mom said. "Oh my gosh. Were you okay?"

"Broken leg and a bruised ego," Blake said. "The worst part about it was that I was in a cast for five months and have been getting lectures about motorcycles from Dr. Walsh ever since."

"You might be overdue for one since you haven't sold it yet," Eliza said.

Her dad's graying eyebrows furrowed. "So she was your patient?"

Eliza wasn't sure if it was her paranoia or if her dad really did have a slightly judgmental tone. "My patient at first, but we ran into each other a month after the fact. Not my patient anymore."

"I left her a note when I was discharged, inviting her to my restaurant," Blake explained freely.

Eliza wanted to squeeze Blake's knee to signal her to at least withhold some details, really the juicy details. Her parents weren't anywhere near as open as her family. They couldn't delve into their story like a romance novel, cuddle up on the couch after dinner, or sneak in kisses. Blake could tell her family about the note she'd left behind, and Eliza could admit that it was that very note which eventually drew her to Mezcal. But her parents didn't need to know that. They'd be too focused on the fact that Blake was originally her patient. They were far away from the West Coast. Here in Middle America, time moved much slower. You could tell by the number of churches per square mile.

But Eliza stopped herself. As much as it made her uncomfortable, she knew she had to power through it to see how far they'd progressed.

"I didn't think she would come," Blake continued, oblivious to all the tension floating around Eliza. "It took her about three weeks."

"You own a restaurant?" her dad asked with piqued interest. Hopefully, that was enough for him to forget the whole patient-doctor thing. He'd always wanted his kids to be with someone who was successful, and it would be a quality he would really value in Blake.

"I don't own it. My uncle does, but I'm the head chef. It's a pretty cool gig."

"Wow, that's quite impressive."

"It's a great job. I love it."

"She's working on opening up her own food hall with her friend," Eliza said, knowing how much her father loved hearing about people's successes, as if that defined them. She wanted to make sure her parents knew Blake could provide for her, had a steady job and income, was passionate, and worked hard for a living. Those were qualities they would soak up like a sponge.

"A food hall?" her mom asked, confused.

"It's like the latest trend in food," Eliza said. "Like a West Side Market, but all the vendors are restaurant booths."

"All local," Blake added. "And hopefully, local shops and breweries. My friend and I have a couple places that are good contenders."

"Are you looking in San Diego?" Jonathon asked. "Or elsewhere?"

Eliza turned to Blake for her response. She'd just assumed Blake was looking in San Diego because why wouldn't she be? That was where her family was. That was where Eliza was. "Most of them are."

Most of them are? Eliza perked up. This was new information for her. *What about the ones that aren't in San Diego? Where the hell are they?*

"We'll be deciding on one after the holidays," Blake continued, "and after that, our goal is to open by next fall." Blake knocked on the wooden table.

Her dad also knocked on the table, pulling a grin from both Eliza and Blake. "Wow, that's really impressive. Good for you."

She'd table her concerns for later. Right now, she wanted to absorb the sight of her parents praising Blake. That was the thing she would cling to in order to get through the rest of the evening— hell, the rest of her stay. Were her parents approving? Was Blake passing the test?

"Eliza needs you," Violet said to Blake. "She doesn't know how to cook. I hear about her failures all the time."

"Oh, trust me, I'm well aware of this," Blake said. "We have an understanding that she's not to set foot in the kitchen."

Her family chuckled.

"You used to be my little helper in the kitchen," Eliza's mom said. "You always wanted to stir and measure the ingredients. I thought I was preparing you for success."

"Well, I failed," Eliza said. "I can do knee replacements and put a shattered leg back together but can't cook mac and cheese."

"So what you're saying is that we should have Blake cook the prime rib on Christmas Day?" her dad said.

Blake perked up at the idea. "I will gladly do whatever you want me to do in the kitchen. Obviously, I enjoy it."

"Well, we can't compete with a professional chef. We don't mind if you don't mind."

"If that's not getting in the way of any family dinner traditions, then I would love to."

Eliza's mom waved off her comment. "It's not a problem at all. I'm sure we could learn a few pointers from you."

"We'll talk about the menu after dinner."

"Sounds good, chef," her dad said.

Eliza hardly recognized her parents as they went over the Christmas dinner menu with Blake, all three of them sharing the living room couch. She wondered if Blake thought everything that Eliza had said about them was a lie because her parents were doing a good job of proving her wrong. But she wanted to be wrong. She wanted everything Violet said to be right, that her parents had changed. As elated as she was watching her parents laugh and chat Blake's ear off, she couldn't help but feel an immense amount of guilt and sadness for thinking that her parents were anything less than what they were in front of her.

Her parents told Blake everything they thought about cooking for Christmas, having most of the ingredients already to avoid the chaos of last-minute shopping. Eliza's heart swelled as Blake took notes and offered to brave the last-minute shopping crowd to pick up any extra ingredients.

"I think you're underestimating the grocery store," her mom told Blake. "We might live in a small town, but it feels like a city at the grocery store the day before Christmas."

Blake waved off her comment. "I've been bred to handle Southern California traffic. My tolerance for crowds is very high."

Violet took a seat next to Eliza on the other couch. "They're doing great, aren't they?" she whispered and nudged her arm.

She couldn't peel her eyes off the three in their own little world discussing food. It was a sight she thought she would never see, and a sight she wanted to see more of. "Yeah, they are."

"I told you they'd changed."

For the first time in years, Eliza truly believed it. She was watching it with her own eyes. The tension that had swaddled her at the beginning of the night had loosened, and her body fell into a steady pattern of breathing regularly without holding in a terrified breath.

Eliza smiled and then looked at her sister. "I'm glad we came."

And she meant it.

Every Christmas Eve, the Walshes went to the center of town and posed for a picture in front of the gazebo Christmas tree. It was a tradition her mom had started when Eliza was born. She included the picture in her Christmas cards to family and friends and saved a copy for the family to keep in an album, showing Violet and Eliza growing up throughout the years. She'd never missed a year, and every Christmas that Eliza had refused to come home since her undergrad graduation, Violet had made sure to point it out as one of the reasons why she *should* come home. Apparently, their mom hadn't been sending the pictures to family and friends, and Eliza wasn't sure if it was because Christmas cards weren't really something people did anymore or because her absence ruined the perfect family photo.

"I'm so glad you're going to be in the picture again," her mom told Eliza as they approached the gazebo for their turn in front of the tree. As dusk fell, the white lights on the tree twinkled, matching the lights wrapped around the lamp posts and store windows. As they waited their turn, Eliza checked her surroundings, making sure the Wares weren't one of the families waiting in line. Tallulah was a small town, and the gazebo tree attracted the residents like sugar attracted bees. In the past, they'd always run into at least one person the family knew, so the fear wasn't an irrational one.

"I can take the picture," Blake said when it was finally their turn. She reached into her coat pocket to pull out her phone. "Everyone, squeeze together."

"Oh, no, Blake you're going to be in the picture," her mom said and motioned Blake to join.

Even Blake appeared shocked, stealing a glance at Eliza. "What? No, it's fine—" Blake said.

Eliza's mom leaned in and whispered something to her. Whatever she said, Blake lowered her arms, turned to the people behind her, and asked if they could take the picture. After pawning off her phone, she positioned herself next to Eliza and slipped her arm around her back.

"What did she say to you?" Eliza whispered.

"I'll tell you later," she said through clenched teeth.

The teen behind them in line snapped several pictures and had her mom approve them. Eliza had to admit that seeing the pure smile claim her mother's face made her insides swirl with happiness. Just because their relationship was severely strained didn't mean that she didn't want to see her mother happy. Of course she wanted her to be happy. She loved her, and she was glad to know that something as simple as a picture in front of the gazebo made her smile like that.

Eliza's mom wanted everyone to stay the night so they could wake up Christmas morning as a family. Because the day was so special to her, keeping up the traditions were important. No matter the temperature outside, she always started a fire in the fireplace, had the Christmas tree on, and had classic Christmas songs playing from the Bluetooth speaker. When Violet and Eliza were kids, their mom had read "'Twas the Night Before Christmas," and apparently, Violet had upheld that tradition because Emma bounced up and down in her red plaid pj's, asking Eliza to read her the story.

"I want Blake too," Emma said when Eliza walked her to the staircase.

Eliza turned back to the living room where Blake was getting cozy on the couch with her parents, Violet, and Jonathon, seemingly content to manage the Walshes by herself. Eliza thought back on what Blake had told her on the flight over about how Eliza couldn't censor herself around her family. They needed to see who she was, and if Eliza wanted to call Blake "babe," hold her hand, or kiss her on the cheek, she needed to do it as if she were at the Navarro household.

"You've been summoned, love," Eliza said.

She could feel her parents watching as Blake got off the couch. For an extra measure, Eliza put an arm around her shoulder, kissed her check, and followed Emma up the steps.

And it felt damn good to show Blake affection.

Emma plopped in bed and handed Eliza the book so authoritatively, it made her chuckle. Blake pulled the covers over Emma and sat by her feet. For not having any little kids in her family, Blake was really great with them. Eliza had been secretly admiring her interactions with Emma, and for the first time ever, she understood when women said that their ovaries were flaring up. Eliza went back and forth about having kids, but watching Blake becoming Emma's new best friend, it really made her want them. With Blake.

It was jarring when it first hit her. They'd been dating for four months and already, she was considering their future? Did Blake want kids? As Eliza and Blake took turns reading a page while Emma dozed off peacefully, she imagined Blake reading to their kids and how she would be as a mother. She questioned if it was too soon to even think these things. It scared her at the same time because underneath her anxiety, she knew that the fact that she actually thought about their future—and cared about it—was a good sign. She'd only pictured her future with one other woman, and those thoughts meant something.

They were something.

When Eliza and Blake finished the story, they kissed Emma good night. Once they stepped out in the hallway, Eliza reached for the top of Blake's pj's pants and pulled her in.

"You're really great with her," she said and stole a soft kiss.

"She's really great," Blake said.

"You want kids?"

Blake pressed her lips together for a moment as if thinking about it. "Yeah, I really do."

"How many?"

She looked skyward. "Three. Two boys and a girl, or two girls and a boy. Actually, it doesn't matter to me. I just want a family."

Eliza skimmed her hands underneath Blake's shirt. "You'd make such a good mom."

"You think?"

She bit her lip and nodded. "Oh, I know for a fact," Eliza said. "You know, I never understood when women said their ovaries were flaring, but seeing you interact with Emma and picturing you as a mom, my ovaries are out partying."

She leaned in to kiss Blake's neck, and Blake let out a soft murmur, craning her neck to give Eliza better access. "You know, we can go try to make some babies right now."

"Hell, no. Not in my parents' house. One step at a time."

"I thought you weren't going to censor yourself? If you're in the mood, then you're in the mood—"

Eliza pulled away and playfully smacked Blake's arm. "No," she said, laughing. "I'm risking a lot kissing your neck in their hallway. Speaking of my parents, what did my mom say to you at the gazebo?"

Blake's smile faded into a thin line, and for a moment, Eliza's did too, scared of what the answer would be. She didn't want the truth to ruin the optimism flowing through her veins. But then Blake tucked a strand of hair behind Eliza's ear and held her face. "She said, 'If my daughter brought you home, you're part of this family.'"

The words plowed right through Eliza.

"She really said that?" she said, struggling to get the words out past the disbelief.

Blake nodded. "They've been really great. I haven't felt uncomfortable once."

"Neither have I. It's...weird."

"No, it's amazing." She kissed Eliza on the lips. "How are you feeling about it?"

Eliza thought about it. "I feel like they finally see me for me."

They went back downstairs to join the family. Eliza's mom started a fire, and the flames crackled against the old-time Christmas songs playing softly from the speaker. Blake turned into a child when quarter-size snowflakes fell outside, adding another layer to the cozy Christmas Eve scene. Since Emma was asleep, the magic of Christmas went to bed with her until the crack of dawn, when she'd wake the family to open presents from Santa. But Blake, staring out the windows and beaming over the dusting of snow, added the magic back into the living room. She even had Eliza's parents sharing a laugh when she said she always wanted to have a white Christmas.

"This is really your first white Christmas?" Jonathan asked.

"Yes. My first white Christmas, first Christmas when I needed to wear a winter coat. First Christmas without a palm tree sighting."

"It's one good thing about the crazy weather here. We get snow, which means sometimes we get magical Christmases."

"I can tell you that this beats a warm Christmas in San Diego. I'm sold."

"Lize, remember that one Christmas when the two of us couldn't sleep?" Violet said and cozied up against Jonathon.

Eliza had her legs on Blake underneath the blanket they shared. Blake rubbed her legs underneath her pj's pants, but the fact that Eliza had her legs on Blake in front of her parents was a big step, the biggest form of PDA yet.

As much as her reflexes told her to adjust herself, she didn't. Blake was too comfortable, and so was she.

"When it snowed a foot overnight?" Eliza asked.

"Yes, that one. It was four in the morning, and we couldn't wait to open our presents, and then freaked out when we saw how much it was snowing."

"We got our snow pants on and went outside to play," Eliza said and then looked at Blake, who stared at her with fascinated eyes that glowed in the white tree lights. "We made snow angels and attempted to build an igloo but failed. It was tragic."

"And then Mom came out," Violet said, and the two of them looked over at their mom, who sat there quietly, staring at them with the same smile she'd had all night, as if basking in the scene to preserve the memory, one she would treasure like the gazebo pictures of the past. "We thought she was going to yell at us, but instead, she started a snowball fight."

Eliza had honestly forgotten about the memory, and reflecting back on it, she realized how great that Christmas had been. She had been six years old; Violet was ten. The neighborhood was silent and peaceful, with candles in the windows, Christmas trees, and string lights lining their neighbors' homes flickering against the freshly fallen snow. They'd chased their mother around the house until their fingers couldn't take it anymore, and then they'd gone inside, burrowed underneath blankets, and their mom made a fire at five thirty a.m. The three of them had watched the first *Home Alone* movie by the time their dad woke up, and when their mom had filled him in on the fun he'd slept through, he made the family hot chocolate while they'd watched *Home Alone 2*. She and Violet had passed out by eleven in the morning and took a long nap as the prime rib scented the house, waking them up to the wonderful smell of roasting potatoes and rosemary. It was the meal her parents always made on Christmas, and the smell would forever remind Eliza of the day.

As the memory played in her mind, Eliza found herself absorbing the scene around her, the first time the family had been physically together in nine years, and the first time they seemed content in even longer than that. Despite being terrified of coming home for the holidays, the last several hours with her family had turned out to be the best Christmas she'd had since she could remember.

Like her mom, Eliza preserved the scene too, so it would stay a wonderful memory just like her sixth Christmas.

Blake had conquered some pretty impressive meals under enormous pressure before. Like her first meal at her externship, Axis LA in Downtown Los Angeles, when renowned celebrity chef and owner of the restaurant, Serena DeLuca, had been present. She'd worried the whole time that the sweat dripping down her face would fall into the halibut and marinate it an unwanted salty flavor. Another time was when the musician Blair Bennett had rented out Axis LA for her girlfriend, the biggest pop star in the world, Reagan Moore, and Blake and the other chefs didn't stop sweating until the five-course meal was finished. Even after they'd sent the desserts out, Blake's hands didn't stop shaking until she'd gotten back to her apartment.

Those high-stake meals competed against making the Walshes Christmas dinner. She wanted them to be impressed, she wanted their seal of approval, and she wanted to make sure the delicious meal solidified the great holiday they were having.

At first, she alone helped Bill and Amy. Eliza attempted to join them, but with Blake leading the anti-Eliza-in-the-kitchen movement, Blake banned her, and her parents jokingly went along with it.

"I still can't believe Eliza can't cook," Amy said while mincing the garlic for the mashed potatoes.

"Apparently, she burned Kraft macaroni and cheese," Blake admitted. "Not going to lie, it terrified me. But on our second date, she came to my apartment, and I coached her through making carne asada tacos with homemade corn tortillas. Turns out, she's fantastic at following directions. Only two tortillas burned. My kitchen is still intact."

Amy's thin smile didn't reach her eyes. Blake looked out of the kitchen window to find Eliza and Emma playing in the freshly fallen snow. Emma hit Eliza with a snowball, and she pretended to fall over dead. Emma jumped on top of her, and Eliza tickled her until she toppled into the snow.

"Can I ask you something, Blake?" Amy asked, her words soaked in vulnerability that Blake didn't expect.

The mood shifted in the kitchen, as if Amy finally acknowledged the crater in the house that everyone had been tiptoeing around.

Blake's stomach dropped but not with the same delight from surfing, motorcycles, or ATVs. "Of course," she said through her muted dread.

Amy stopped mincing and looked down at the chopping board. "Is she happy?"

The question spawned a million words tumbling over each other as she searched for an answer to give her girlfriend's mother, whom she'd heard many stories about, none of them good.

"Uh..." Blake said. It slipped right out of her.

Amy glanced at her with profound loss in her eyes, pleading for an answer. It was such a complicated question, one she didn't think should be directed at her. But Eliza had warned her that her mother hated confrontation. She avoided it at all costs, and maybe the question was because she was too terrified to ask her daughter. Blake was the shortcut, and as a guest in Amy's home, and given the fact that it was Christmas, Blake was going to somehow answer, even if she sounded awkward doing so.

"In what context?"

Amy blinked and thought about it. "I don't...I don't know. Do you think she's happy?"

"Uh, well..." Damn it, how was she supposed to answer this? There were so many levels of happiness. "I feel like she's happy when she's with me, if that's what you mean."

"Maybe. I, well, I really don't know what I'm asking," Amy said, shaking her head. She picked up the knife and started mincing again as if giving up on the question.

Blake sucked in a deep breath and braced herself for what she was about to say. "If you're talking about everything that happened with her accident, she still struggles a lot with it. She's gotten a little better since we met, but she still struggles." Amy's shoulders collapsed along with the knife in her hands, as if she'd run blindly into the truth she had been running away from. "She went through a lot. Survived something traumatic, lost her girlfriend, was blamed for it. It's emotionally and mentally affected her. I don't blame her for still thinking about it."

Amy nodded and quickly wiped her cheeks. Blake blew out the ragged breath, upset that Amy was upset. She hoped no one walked into the kitchen during this conversation.

"I lost my brother when I was fourteen," Blake said softly. "He died in Iraq."

"I'm so sorry."

"I think losing people so important to us is what really drew us together. You don't ever heal from that kind of loss. You just learn to live with it. A part of her is always going to be broken, but I know she's really committed to taking her life back. She talks about it all the time, and I think being here with her family is helping tremendously, in more ways than she expected."

Hope sparkled in Amy's dark blue eyes, and Blake enjoyed the sigh of relief that traveled through her. She didn't want anyone knowing about this moment, at least not until Christmas was over, and a new day started. Hell, if they were able to reconvene with the rest of the family with no evidence of tears or sadness, Blake didn't plan on telling Eliza about it until they were back in San Diego. Eliza was finally starting to get comfortable around her parents and being with Blake around her parents. Blake wanted that momentum to keep going, knowing how important this visit was to Eliza. She knew it would be the make-it or break-it for her relationship with her parents. If it didn't go well, Blake had no idea how Eliza would ever open up to the idea of allowing her mom and dad back into her life, and Blake so badly wanted everything to keep going the way it was. No drama, no dents from the past prodding through. She worried that Eliza would see the remnants of her mother's crying, and that would unravel all the progress that had been made.

"You think so?" Amy asked with a shaky voice.

Blake forced a reassuring smile. "I do. She told me last night that she thinks you guys finally see her."

Amy's eyes teemed with a new round of tears. "She said that?" Blake nodded, and Amy shook her head again. "We always loved her. We just...we were just so surprised when everything happened. When Tina Ware called us about her and Tess. We were blindsided. There wasn't a manual for that back then. It wasn't accepted as it is now, and Bill and I were so scared for her."

"My parents were too."

"She was so resentful after that happened."

"She wanted her parents to tell her that they loved her no matter what. That's what any kid wants. They just want their parents to see them and to try to understand them."

Amy wiped her eyes. "I love my kids so much, and I know that I'm not a perfect mom. I know I've made mistakes that I wish so much I could take back."

"Don't feel like you're the only parent to have regrets," Blake said, hoping that sharing some insight about her own parents would help Amy see that she wasn't an evil mom. Blake had never thought that. Eliza might have held a grudge, and Blake absolutely didn't blame her for being hurt, but Eliza never saw her parents progress through the years or try to progress. Blake had that perspective, and she planned on using it to encourage Amy to talk to Eliza. "My parents had their moments too. My mom didn't like that I wore boy clothes and didn't like it when I cut my hair short, but after my brother died, she changed."

Blake watched the words settle in Amy. She flattened her smile and slowly nodded as if she understood. "It's strange how horrible things make you wake up."

"A lot of changes beyond Eliza's control happened all at once. She was scared, she felt ashamed for who she was, who she loved.

And then in an instant, her whole life changed. She lost that one person who she felt saw her and listened to her, and then on top of it, she was blamed for the accident."

"I know." Amy's voice cracked, and more moisture streamed down her face. "I know, and it broke my heart when it happened."

"Look," Blake said and reached for Amy's hands, giving her a reassuring squeeze. "I know her accident must have been hard on you too. I'm sure you were as scared as she was during all of this, but you really need to tell her everything you told me. She really needs to hear it, to hear you apologize, and she really, *really*, needs to hear from you and Bill that you two love her the way she is. I don't think she can fully heal from her past without hearing those words from her mom and dad."

Amy squeezed Blake's hand. "Thank you for the talk, Blake. I really appreciate it."

"Not a problem. Just make it happen with Eliza."

Even though the conversation stopped there, the silence spoke volumes. She knew Amy was ruminating on her strong suggestion, and hopefully, a Christmas miracle would happen, and Bill and Amy would say all the things that had been left unsaid.

Hopefully, the holiday would stitch up the old wounds all three of them shared.

If Eliza knew how nice being at home was, she wouldn't have made sure to fly back the day after Christmas. She wanted so much more time with her family, and she craved alone time with her mom and dad. The tension had been relieved, but it hadn't disappeared. At least not until they'd finally uncovered the dreaded time capsule they'd been walking over. Eliza had already considered coming back home in late February to see her family again, which gave her enough time to reflect on Christmas, and hopefully, the reflection gave her the confidence to confront her parents.

"I'm really glad you came home," her mom said softly in Eliza's ear, hugging her tightly once she and Blake tossed their suitcases in

Violet's car. Right as Eliza flinched to pull away, her mom lingered and held her tighter. Eliza quickly sank into her mother's embrace as if it was the unknown remedy that she'd needed all this time. She'd missed her mom so much. More than they both even knew. "And we're so glad we met Blake." Her mom pulled away and rested both hands on her shoulders. "You'll keep us updated on the fellowship?"

Both parents looked at Eliza with hopeful stares and content smiles.

"Of course," Eliza said, and she meant it. She might not have gotten the full apology and explanation for why her parents did what they'd done, but as she'd learned in therapy, she couldn't change her parents. They had to do that themselves, and they weren't people who were liberal with the spoken apologies. She'd come to realize during her stay that even though they never said the words, she still felt the apology. They showed with actions and acceptance, and it was more than Eliza had expected. She was going to leave Tallulah with a little piece of her heart mended, and she was taking that as a win. "I'll call you once I know. Should know within the next couple of weeks."

"We're proud of you, Eliza," her dad said, and rested a firm hand on her shoulder. "No matter what happens. Just know that."

A lump grew in her throat. All she'd ever wanted was to make her parents proud.

"Thanks, Dad," she said, barely.

She couldn't believe that her eyes welled as Violet backed out of the driveway. She wished so much that they could stay an extra few days, especially after her dad told her that they were proud of her, a sentence that she'd desperately waited her entire lifetime to hear. For the first time since she was a kid, the indignation toward her parents diluted to almost nothing.

That was what she'd wanted for Christmas. Her parents and closure. Although she was on the right track of getting complete closure with them, there was still one more door that she needed to close, and she was finally ready to do it.

"Violet, can we make a stop at the St. Teresa cemetery?"

If Eliza left without visiting, she wouldn't forgive herself. She had to see her. She had to tell her everything.

She had to let her go.

She bought a bouquet of pink and white lilies from the store. Her lungs shrank as they drove closer to the cemetery, and when they finally got there, Eliza told Violet and Blake that she needed this moment to herself. While they stayed in the car, she walked along the asphalt path and dug up the memory like an old picture in the photo album of her brain, trying to remember the general area she'd seen the tent from across the street at St. Teresa's before the funeral. She felt like she was committing a crime, walking through the property and trying to find her tombstone. She worried that the Wares would be there, and she would have to endure another round of yelling and blaming. But luckily, when she found the tombstone, no one was in sight.

The weight of Tess's presence clenched a cry out of her. She covered her mouth when the tears leaked at the sight of her full name carved into the black marble with that date that had broken her whole life in two. A wreath with a red bow sat against the tombstone, along with two bouquets of flowers. There were fresh footprints in front of her tombstone, and Eliza wondered if they belonged to the Wares. She fell to her knees without caring about the snow soaking into her jeans. She could feel Tess wrapped around her. Her presence was so heavy, almost as if she was hugging her after thirteen years of being apart.

"Tess," she blubbered. The bitter cold made her damp face colder. "God, I've missed you so much." She put her hand on her tombstone and absorbed the cold of the black marble. She could feel her again. "I'm sorry I haven't been here to visit until now. It's been…" She blew out a trembling breath. "Really hard. So fucking hard. I think about you all the time, what our life could have been, and all the years that were erased from us. And maybe I've thought about it too much because I haven't really done anything since the last time I saw you." She wiped the steady flow of tears. "You'll always be my first love, Tessa Lynn Ware, and you'll always have a part of me, but I haven't been living my life the way I should have. I've been too scared to do anything, and I've seemed to waste away the last thirteen years. Well, except for the past four months.

Everything has changed. I, um, I met someone, and she makes me want to get out there and live, the way you made me feel. The world is so much less scary with her in it. It's like I can finally breathe again. She's amazing and wonderful, and she's so good for me, and if you're really somewhere in some afterlife, I'm sure you like her too. You taught me how to fall in love, and what it's like to be loved, and nothing will ever change that or erase all the memories we have together. But now it's time for me to take what I learned from you and give it to someone else. I have to let you go, Tess. Just remember, you're always going to be a part of me, and I'm going to love you. Always."

Eliza pressed her lips against her fingers and placed them on the tombstone, sending a kiss through the cold marble. After a few minutes of calming down and drying her face, she left the bouquet on the other side of the tombstone from the others, took a deep breath of cold December air, gave one last look at the name of the amazing girl who'd opened her heart, and went back to the woman who kept it beating.

After she got back to her apartment in San Diego, Eliza followed through on the promise. She slipped the necklace over her head and studied it in between her fingers, letting the memory of driving to Claire's and the moment in the Cavanaugh Park pavilion sweep her up, the last time she would let it do so.

Eliza had kept Tess so close to her heart over the years that it had prevented others from coming in. But now, it was time to keep her in her Before in order to make room for the rest of her life, the only part she had control over.

She kissed the ring one last time, plopped it in the jewelry box on her dresser, and closed it.

CHAPTER FOURTEEN

"How were your holidays, Dr. Walsh?" Dr. Nunez asked Eliza as they stepped into her office in mid-January.

Dr. Nunez had emailed that morning to set up a quick meeting during lunch, which had skyrocketed Eliza's heart rate. She knew it was regarding the fellowship, and she would leave Bellevue today with either her dream job or turning to her plan B and C hospitals... in LA.

As she walked to Dr. Nunez's office, the last thing she wanted to do was tell Blake that LA would likely be her new home for at least a year. She'd mentioned once after the holidays that USC and Cedars-Sinai were backup plans. Eliza really didn't want to move to LA. It was too materialistic for her taste, too flashy, too loud. She wanted quiet, simple, and under-the-radar. Blake hadn't shown any sign that she was upset about the LA fellowships. She'd said it was great Eliza had backup plans, and that was that. End of conversation.

She inhaled deeply before knocking at Dr. Nunez's door. Dr. Nunez smiled and motioned her in. Eliza's skin burned while she took a seat across from the Program Director of Surgical Critical Care. She was highly respected and educated, and Eliza knew she could learn so much from Dr. Nunez, someone who she admired, especially given the man's world of surgery.

"Dr. Walsh, it's great to see you," Dr. Nunez said. She put on her glasses and focused her attention on Eliza's CV and cover letter in front of her. "Thank you for taking the time to meet with me. This should be quick."

"Thank you for having me," Eliza said, silently gulping back the nerves lodged in her throat.

Dr. Nunez met her gaze and folded her hands on her desk. "I'll just get straight to it. No need to beat around the bush. I'm glad you applied for the fellowship. We had a lot of applicants, but as you know, we only accept two critical care fellows. Dr. Norman speaks very highly of you, even before he wrote his letter of recommendation. I believe you'll be a great asset to our team. I'm offering you the fellowship."

Eliza relaxed in her seat. She screamed in her head but choked back the elation so only professionalism came out. "Wow, thank you so much, Dr. Nunez. This is a dream job. It means so much. I'm very grateful for the opportunity."

"I'm glad, and we're excited to have you on board. I wanted to tell you in person. I'll be sending over the official offer sometime today. You can think it over—"

Eliza laughed. "I won't need time to think it over. I can send you the paperwork by Saturday morning when I'm back."

"That sounds great, Dr. Walsh. I love the enthusiasm, and I'm very excited to work with you."

It was painful to have to hold her excitement in during two back-to-back surgeries. She couldn't go ballistic until she got outside and sent texts to her family group chat with her mom, dad, and Violet, something she'd just started, but why not start a family group chat over the exciting news that she got her dream job working in one of the best hospitals in the state? She called Allison and told her they needed to meet at Mezcal for celebratory al pastor tacos and margaritas, and luckily, she didn't have to twist Allison's arm too much. And then she texted Blake, knowing she was working and would get a delayed reply.

Babe! I got offered the fellowship. I'm freaking out. Allison and I are going to stop by for tacos and margs. Come celebrate when you get off your shift.

Eliza had the next day off, and that meant she was going to give herself a proper celebration. All that time, studying, and long hours had paid off.

She was going to get drunk on a Thursday. Why? Because she could. Because she freakin' deserved it.

❖

Blake had no idea how to feel when she saw Eliza's text.

Her heart ballooned, and she was so fucking proud of her for getting the Bellevue fellowship. She knew Eliza wanted that so badly, and her badass girlfriend had gotten exactly what she wanted and worked hard for. Nothing was sexier than that. She was unbelievably proud.

But ever since the holidays ended, picking the venue for Vagabonds had weighed on her mind. Malai really wanted the Huntington Beach venue, and Blake didn't. She didn't voice her hesitancy about Huntington Beach because there was the smallest chance that Eliza would accept one of the fellowships in LA, and then they both could move. A part of her had hoped that the two hospitals in LA stood a chance. Malai wanted so badly to lease Huntington Beach, she'd practically salivated anytime she mentioned it. Everything would have been easier if her girlfriend and her business partner were in the same city.

Now, it was official. She had to choose between letting one of them down.

She sat in her back office and attempted to organize all the swirling thoughts. She wanted to put on a happy face and celebrate with Eliza on the other side of the kitchen, but she hadn't yet perfected a plastic smile.

When are you done? Come out, Eliza's text said.

She checked her watch. It was already past eight, and she'd told Eliza she would try to sneak out early. She'd been procrastinating and even made the order of tacos herself to give her an excuse to be late.

She balanced both plates of tacos on her palms and brought them to Eliza and Allison's table. Remnants of guacamole stuck to the sides of the molcajete, and the pitcher of margaritas was almost gone. Eliza's face lit up, and the red streak on her cheeks hinted that she was certainly celebrating…and feeling very good.

"Hey. There you are," she said as Blake handed them their tacos.

"Two orders of al pastor tacos, made by moi," Blake said.

Eliza reached for her hand and gently pulled her into the booth. When she sat, Eliza planted a kiss on her cheek. She already smelled like mezcal margaritas.

"Are you going to celebrate with us?"

"Of course," Blake said, grabbing her hand. "You got the fellowship. I knew you would."

"Well, this is one way we're celebrating," Eliza whispered against her earlobe. "And then, hopefully later, in one of our beds."

She'd never seen Eliza drunk before. A happy buzz, sure, but not to the point where her words slurred, and her reserved disposition dissolved. She would have fully enjoyed the moment if it wasn't for Huntington Beach weighing on her mind.

She forced a smile, hoping she did a good enough job to mask her worries. It was Eliza's night to celebrate. She wasn't going to ruin it with her dilemma. It could wait for the next day.

"How many pitchers in are we?" Blake asked and motioned to the empty one.

"Two," Allison said while wiggling her fingers. "We were thinking about getting one more glass."

"We should," Eliza said. "We haven't gone out and had a night like this since college."

"It's long overdue. I've been waiting for this for nine years," Allison said. "I'm so glad I have the day off tomorrow so I can fully enjoy Drunk Eliza, practically as mythical as a unicorn."

"Just be careful," Blake said.

Eliza laughed. "You're telling me to be careful? I never thought I'd hear that in my life." Eliza clasped Blake's face. "I will. I'm done after one more glass." She pulled her in for a kiss. "I'm just so freakin' happy right now."

Even her kisses tasted like mezcal. Seeing her this elated should have filled Blake with happiness, but it didn't. Blake hated so much that she couldn't shake the looming conversation with both Eliza and Malai. Maybe she should have ordered her own pitcher and joined in so the mezcal could numb the anxiety.

"I know, babe," Blake said and kissed Eliza's cheek. "You deserve to be. I'm so happy for you. You're a badass doctor."

"This fellowship is, like, my dream job. I still can't believe it." She studied Blake for a moment, and her smile faded. "Is everything okay?"

Blake painted on a wider smile. Apparently, her first attempt hadn't done a good job as a disguise. "Of course I am. My girlfriend got her dream fellowship."

"What's wrong?"

"Nothing's wrong. Why do you even say that?"

"Because I know you."

Even drunk, Eliza was able to read Blake perfectly, and she hated it so much. Now that she'd pointed it out, it was hard for Blake to continue the act. She tucked a tendril of hair behind Eliza's ear. "It's nothing important. We can talk about it later. Let's just enjoy the night."

Eliza's shoulders dropped. "I can't enjoy the night knowing that something is wrong."

"Here." Allison poured the remaining margarita into her glass and slid it across the table. "Finish it."

"Thanks," Blake said and took advantage of the opportunity. She pounded back the glass like a shot and hoped the buzz would kick in soon.

"Blake?"

"We don't need to talk about it right now. It's been a stressful day, that's all."

"I have to go to the bathroom, come with me?"

Blake had to get up to allow Eliza out. Eliza grabbed her hand and meandered toward the back of the restaurant, past the bathrooms, and out the back door meant for staff.

They stepped outside the back of the building, the spot employees deemed the smoking break section. Luckily, no one was out. Blake knew she wouldn't be able to avoid this talk until she gave Eliza a hint about what it was.

"You know, the bathroom is back there," Blake said. "Come on, let's go back in, get another pitcher, and focus on you. Tonight is your night, not time to worry about me."

Eliza crossed her arms, a sign that she was committing herself to this talk. "But you've been off since we came back from Ohio."

"That's because we're in the end stages of finalizing Vagabonds, and it's stressful. Seriously, it's something for another time. Let's go back in—"

"What about Vagabonds?"

"Eliza, please, let's go in—"

"If it's not a big deal, I don't understand why you can't tell me now. Put my mind at ease. You know how it works."

Blake rolled her eyes and ran a hand through her hair. "We have to nail down a venue soon, and I'm stressed about it."

"Why are you saying it like it's a bad thing? That's so exciting. You should be excited."

"Because Malai and I have different favorites. But the thing is, the one Malai likes is absolutely perfect. It checks almost everything on our 'want' list."

"Why isn't it your favorite, then?"

Blake sighed. She couldn't believe she was about to tell Eliza her anxieties. It wasn't so stressful keeping Huntington Beach on the back burner while knowing that Eliza had applied to two fellowships in LA. But as they'd waited for Eliza to hear back, Malai's hopes had continued to skyrocket.

"Because of the one thing it doesn't cross off," Blake said.

Eliza faltered for a moment, almost as if she knew the next words were bad news. "And what's that?"

Blake shook her head and glanced at the ground. There was no way she'd be able to save Eliza's celebration night. She was so upset she couldn't mask her feelings, and the guilt piled on her sternum likes bricks.

"Blake?"

"It's in Huntington Beach."

She couldn't even look Eliza in the eyes. She didn't have to in order to know her reaction. The silence spoke volumes.

"Huntington Beach?" Eliza asked. Her voice was flat. Blake nodded and picked at her cuticles instead of looking up. "As in, two-hours-away Huntington Beach?" Blake nodded again. Despite

Eliza's low voice, the disappointment screamed at Blake. "God, I'm so dumb."

Blake frowned. "What? Why?"

"You told my parents most of the venues were in San Diego, and it freaked me out, but I didn't want to say anything because I wanted to enjoy Christmas and focus on not being standoffish with my parents."

"Can we please talk about this at another time? You sound upset, and I don't want it to ruin—"

"Of course I sound upset because you never told me about those places. You've been hiding the fact that you've been looking at a place two hours away. It all makes sense now why you never told me."

"You applied to fellowships in LA. Just like those were backup options for you, Huntington Beach is one of the options—"

"Does Malai know that's a backup option for you? Because it sure doesn't sound like it."

Blake put her hands on the top of her head. She had no idea what to do. No matter what she decided, she would have to let someone down. Her best friend of twelve years? Or the woman she was falling in love with?

There had to be a way to avoid hurting both of them.

"I mean, I don't need to be at the food hall every day. I could commute," she thought out loud.

"From San Diego?" Eliza said. "You're going to commute for four hours every day?"

Blake ran her hands down her face. "I would move out of San Diego and live halfway in between."

"So you already have a plan? You've known about this long enough to have a plan? That doesn't sound like a backup plan. That sounds like you like the venue enough to make it work."

"I'm still thinking about the logistics, Eliza. I'm trying to make sure that everyone is happy and gets what they want. I wanted to ask you this at a better time, but since you're pressing the issue, I thought maybe we could move in together. Halfway."

Eliza frowned and crossed her arms. That wasn't the reaction Blake had expected when she proposed the topic, but then again, in her head, she would have proposed the topic when Eliza wasn't drunk, when the night wasn't about her, and definitely not in the smoking section next to the dumpster. The plan to ask Eliza to move in with her was so much more romantic in her head.

"Move in together? An hour away? On top of the eighty hours I already work? For one, I don't even drive. Two, I'm not allowed to live more than a twenty-minute drive from the hospital."

"Okay, then let's say Vagabonds stays in San Diego. What does that mean for us?"

"What are you talking about?"

"I want to live together. I want to take the next step."

Eliza pulled her gaze off Blake and looked at the ground, seeming lost in a tangle of thoughts. Each silent second that ticked away, Blake could feel another rip in her heart. She thought that when she asked Eliza to move in with her, Eliza would jump up and down, thrilled to take the next step. Blake didn't think it would be such a difficult decision. Was she an idiot for thinking—more like expecting—Eliza to jump at the idea? Throw her arms around her, kiss her senselessly, and say yes?

"I take your silence as a no?" Blake said, deflating.

"I need to think about it—"

"You need to think about it? We've been together for five months. I spent Christmas with your family. I thought that was a good indication that we were serious about this."

"I *am* serious about this. Blake, why can't we have this conversation when we've been together for a year? There's no need to rush things when they've been going great...or at least were going great. We've been together for five months. We're still new."

"We're still new, but you took me home to meet your parents? I think we're beyond casual."

"We are. Why are you putting words in my mouth?"

"Because I asked you to move in with me, and you still have yet to respond."

"Because you've been keeping all of this from me—"

"I didn't even hear about you applying to two jobs in LA until we were at your parents' house."

Eliza's mouth parted. "Oh, so you've been holding that in for three weeks, huh? For once in your life, can you not rush through things?"

The comment was like a slap in the face. Blake's mouth dropped as the burn stung deep. "Wow. Just…wow."

Even if she stayed in San Diego and disappointed Malai, her love life had just slammed into a brick wall. Well, actually, one of Eliza's brick walls. Blake thought she'd torn those down months ago, but apparently, all it took was to ask about taking the next step in their relationship for those walls to stack perfectly back in place and smack Blake in the process.

She was serious about their relationship. She was going to be thirty-one in a month. She was over the casual dating, had been for a few years. She wanted to settle down, get married, have kids. This whole time, she'd thought things were different with Eliza. Blake had been there and done that with plenty of women. She knew exactly what she wanted and needed, and it was Eliza. She was one-hundred-percent positive. She thought Eliza was too, given the fact that she'd brought Blake home to meet her family. And it cut her deeply that she'd been wrong this whole time. If the person she was dating wasn't serious about that trajectory, then why would she waste her time?

"If we're taking low blows like that, then I'm gonna head out."

"Blake—" Eliza said, much softer than the last time.

She reached for Blake's hand, but Blake pulled it away. All she needed to do was lie in bed, calm herself down, and think really hard about what the right move would be.

"I'm tired, and quite frankly, pretty pissed off right now, and you're drunk. This is a conversation we both need to have when we're in a better emotional state."

"You're seriously leaving?"

She didn't want to, but after this conversation, the zings they'd shot at each other, and after Eliza had to think about whether to move in with her or not even if Vagabonds stayed in San Diego, she couldn't plaster on a fake smile. Her heart was already hurting. She wanted to celebrate with Eliza, but it was a little too late for that.

"Yes. I need to go."

No matter where Vagabonds ended up, she had a feeling that she was going to lose Eliza. It would have been simple if Eliza had reacted well to the idea of them living together. Being firm with Malai and sticking to the original San Diego plan would have been so easy knowing that meant Eliza would be her roommate, and finally, they could see each other for more than just a few hours once a week.

But Eliza didn't like the sound of that plan. She'd shut down when Blake mentioned it, and it was too similar of a reaction—and too similar of a feeling—of when she'd dated Lindsey and wanted to take that next step. Hindsight was twenty-twenty, and looking back on her relationship with Lindsey, the clues were laid out there like crumbs. Four years down the drain, and there were warning signs Blake had chosen to ignore. She'd promised herself she wouldn't be that blind again.

Was this a sign that she didn't have a future with Eliza? Was she wasting her time again? She never questioned it until Eliza reacted the way that she did, completely blindsiding her with hesitancy despite bringing her home to her estranged parents. Was the wall Eliza had thrown up a reactive defensive move? Or had it been there the whole duration of their relationship, and it took her just now to notice?

Staying in San Diego was the easy part. Staying on the other side of Eliza's walls was the impossible part.

Eliza formally accepted the fellowship on Saturday, but signing the job offer shouldn't have left her feeling guilty, as if all her happiness and excitement swam around a boulder of guilt anchored in her gut. She didn't think they had any problems until the night at Mezcal. Not until Huntington Beach spontaneously appeared in their lives, and Blake used her LA fellowships as a rebuttal. Eliza should have talked to her more about it once they'd gotten back to San Diego after Christmas, but Blake had acted so normal, Eliza hadn't even thought it was a problem.

Sure, Eliza had been drunk when they spoke, but she was aware of everything that had happened and the ripple of hurt running through her when Blake decided to leave. Flat out leave on the night she was celebrating a huge accomplishment in her career. That was probably the thing that hurt Eliza the most. Her girlfriend couldn't even stay to celebrate her dream job.

Instead of letting the anxiety stew in her, filling in made-up answers to all the questions she had, Eliza texted Blake. They needed to talk and figure this all out, and it needed to happen ASAP.

They hadn't spoken since Blake had abandoned her at Mezcal, but Blake was quick to respond when Eliza said she wanted to talk after work. She went over to Blake's in the evening, and when she opened the door, Blake looked so different. There was the smallest oil stain on her powder blue LA Chargers crewneck sweatshirt. Her eyes were glossy and swollen, her hair was disheveled, and her smile seemed miles away.

"Hey," Blake mumbled and opened the door for Eliza to come in.

Usually whenever Eliza came over, Blake's apartment was like the home version of a cast iron skillet that had soaked up the smells and flavors from her latest meal. But instead of fresh scents, the smell of stale pizza scented the studio, coming from a box on the kitchen island.

Blake plopped on her couch. "What's up?" Her voice sounded tired, and it reflected in her eyes.

Not seeing Blake's usual vivacious smile kicked any lingering hangover out of Eliza. "I took the fellowship offer," Eliza said. "I signed the papers today."

"Good for you," Blake said but with zero excitement in her tone.

"It's an offer I can't refuse. After twelve years of school, all my student loan debt, all the time I've given to my job, it would be a huge mistake to turn down a fellowship at one of the best hospitals in the country."

"That's great. I'm proud of you."

But the sentiment didn't resonate with Eliza.

"You know, it really hurt when you left on Thursday. I was looking forward to celebrating with my girlfriend over something I wanted so fucking badly. And she just up and left."

"It really hurt when you made that jab at me."

"I'm sorry, Blake. You just blindsided me with Huntington Beach, and I was taken aback and angry and drunk. I mean, how long were you hiding this news?"

"I wasn't hiding anything. I told you it was a backup plan, and now we're here."

"Then how come Malai has her heart set on that venue?"

Blake opened her mouth and then closed it, proving Eliza's point exactly. She knew that she'd led Malai on with the venue. She could tell by how Blake reacted to her question. She couldn't even look Eliza in the eye.

"I don't want to go to Huntington Beach, Eliza," Blake said. "I want to be with you. But no matter what I want or decide, I'm going to disappoint someone. It's a lose-lose situation for me, and not only that, but no matter where Vagabonds ends up, I feel like I've already lost you."

"How have you already lost me?"

"Because I thought we were on the same page when it came to us, but I guess I'm more committed to the future than you are."

Eliza felt her mouth open as the brunt of Blake's comment gutted her. She couldn't believe that was how Blake felt. She'd thought about their future, starting at Christmas and ever since. Every day she was with Blake gave her more of an indication that Blake could very much be the one. Blake made life less scary. She made it easier for Eliza to breathe and look forward to the future instead of fear it.

How the hell didn't Blake know that?

"I think about our future all the time," Eliza said. "That's why I'm upset that you're leading Malai on with this venue because I don't know what that means for us. I want to take my time with something this important to me. This is a big discussion that we've never even had until it was randomly brought up the other night.

That's a huge step in our relationship that needs to be considered thoroughly. It's not something you just do on a whim."

"Okay, fine. Then let's have the discussion."

"While we're arguing yet again?"

"We can figure out logistics later. I want to know how the idea sounds to you. Right now, in this moment."

"Right now?"

"Yes, right now," Blake demanded. "If there are reservations about us forming a life together, I need to know now. If you're scared of taking the next step, I…I don't know what to do."

Blake glanced down at her fidgeting hands, and Eliza felt so numb. She wanted a future with her. God, did she want that. Blake had met and dated a lot of women. She'd had more experience with what she wanted and didn't want. Eliza had never given herself that time. Five months might have been long enough for Blake to know what she wanted and needed, but Eliza wasn't on the same page. She was falling for Blake. That part she knew, but falling for someone and planning a future together right then and there terrified her because the last time that had happened, she'd lost someone forever.

Eliza knew her worries were irrational, but that didn't stop her anxiety. Living together was a leap, and she needed time to think about it, formulate a plan, get herself ready for it. It wasn't something she could dive into freely like Blake could, like she seemed she could do with almost everything.

Eliza picked up and discarded so many things to say next. She had no idea what she wanted or what was best for her. All she knew was she was scared. "You might think I'm boring because I stay away from risks, but I've done them a few times in my life. I snuck around my parents to be with my girlfriend. We created an elaborate plan to move cross country to be with each other. I got engaged at eighteen, four hours after my high school graduation, dead set on marrying my first and only relationship. Where did all of that get me? Being heartbroken and gutted. So yeah, I don't move through life as fast as you, and I don't think there's anything wrong with taking my time or waiting until the summer when we've been together for a year."

"I'm fine with waiting until the summer. I just want to know that there's a plan, that you're really in this. I want to make sure we're heading somewhere."

"We are heading somewhere." Eliza's voice rose. "I took you home to my parents."

"I was with a girl who strung me along with no intention of having a future, and I want to make sure that doesn't happen to me again."

Eliza looked up, completely shocked that something like that had come from her. "You think I'm stringing you along? Because I think moving in together right now is too soon? If we're solid in our relationship, then there's plenty of time to do that. Needing more time doesn't mean I'm not interested. Why can't you respect that?"

Eliza had never seen Blake look so wounded before. Blake was supposed to be her rock. She wasn't supposed to be afraid of anything, and for the first time in their relationship, she looked terrified, like her biggest fears were sitting opposite her on the couch. Seeing her rock shatter made Eliza feel like she had no steady ground supporting her.

"See, I don't need any time to think about it because I know I want you," Blake said with a rattling voice as she swiped at her damp face. "I want all of you. I want more of you. I want a life with you. You spend all your free time with me, yet we only get to see each other for a few hours once a week. Hell, I'm lucky if you spend the night and go to work from here. I want more than a few hours with my girlfriend. If we live together, we can see each other before and after work. We can actually have a life together."

"I never said I didn't want a life with you. You blindsided me with Huntington Beach, and now you're accusing me of stringing you along and not wanting a future with you? I brought you home to my parents, for fuck sake, Blake. You don't think that was a serious gesture of commitment? You even said it the other day that it was a sign of us being serious."

Eliza was so angry. The tears brimmed as the silence and anger congealed in the studio. She'd fully let Blake into her life, and it meant everything to her. How didn't Blake see that? How could she even think that Eliza wasn't serious about them when she'd taken her home to the parents she hadn't seen in nine years?

"Okay, then," Blake said and slapped her legs in defeat. "Since you can't move, and you don't want to live with me, here are all the things I'll do for you." Blake wiped her face, but it did her no good because the tears kept streaming down her cheeks. "I'll tell Malai we won't move forward with Huntington Beach—"

"Blake—"

"And even if we did go through with Huntington Beach, I would stay in San Diego and commute up there when I had to. I'd do all of that if it means I get to be with you, if I know that in the next couple months, we can finally stop seeing each other once a week and live together, so we can spend more time together, so I can sleep in the same bed as you. Now it's your turn."

"What? You want me to say that I'll move in with you when I think we should wait a few more months? Break my lease with Allison and wish her luck with a new place—"

"Okay, you know what? I feel like I'm begging you to live with me, and clearly, that's not what you want." She got off the couch and ran a hand through her hair, but this time, it didn't affect Eliza like it usually did. Instead, the gesture numbed her as she watched Blake give up on the conversation. Give up on them. "I'm not sure how to bounce back if we're done with this conversation."

Just three days ago, they'd spent the night kissing, making love, cuddling each other to sleep naked. She felt safe in Blake's arms. The two of them felt indestructible. Never once did Eliza worry about an end in sight. But here it was, exploding right in front of them. As her heart broke in a million pieces, she couldn't help the anger starting to boil. Blake wasn't listening to anything she was trying to say. She felt like she was getting abandoned at the first rough patch of their relationship, and Blake was right. If the conversation was over, if Blake wasn't willing to listen and wait, she had no idea how to bounce back either.

Eliza stared up, pleading and begging that this wasn't the end, but Blake couldn't even look her in the eyes. Was she really done after barely trying?

"If you're not able to respect my feelings and wait to see where we are when my lease is up, I'm not sure how to bounce back either," Eliza said in defeat.

"Okay, if that's the case, then I guess we're done."

There it was. The end. Eliza couldn't control the yanking in her throat. The cry tore through her. As she stood, it rippled through her whole body and threatened to take out her knees, but she couldn't collapse in Blake's apartment. She had to wait until she got back home to do that.

"Wow, Blake. Half a year gone, just like that, because you're not willing to listen to me? I thought you understood me better than that, but I guess I was wrong," Eliza's voice rose as her words grated against her raw throat.

"Yeah, there's no way we can come back from this." Blake wiped her face with her sweatshirt sleeve. "You can leave now."

Eliza held everything in until the Uber dropped her off. She ran into her apartment, hyperventilated in the elevator, and sobbed on the kitchen floor once she made it inside. She couldn't even make it to her room to break. Holding it in for the last half hour used up every single bit of energy she had left.

Allison ditched the TV and sat next to her on the floor. She scooped Eliza up and allowed her to bawl in her arms.

This was why Eliza didn't get into relationships. Right when she fully welcomed someone into her life, right as it was about to soar, she lost them.

Chapter Fifteen

Who would have ever thought Eliza would need Tallulah to help her breathe again?

A month had passed since she and Blake had broken up, and zero text messages had been sent. Eliza thought that she would have been used to the silence in her inbox, but she still found herself checking her phone to see if today was the day Blake had reached out.

She'd needed a distraction. While one relationship crashed and burned, she'd decided to focus her energy on repairing another one. For her last vacation during her last year of residency, she went home and even decided to stay in her childhood room instead of staying at Violet's.

"You know, for someone who just got an amazing fellowship, you look awfully sad," her dad said.

Not even a bottle of champagne and a box of meat lover's pizza from her favorite Tallulah pizzeria could cheer her up. The pizza tasted like Friday nights in the Walsh household. Although she tasted the nostalgia, she couldn't help but think about the last time she'd seen Blake in dirty clothes with a box of stale pizza on her kitchen island. An accomplished head chef with old pizza was an image that was burned into her memory.

It made her stomach ache thinking about how much she'd hurt Blake and how much Blake had hurt her. She was nowhere and everywhere at the same time.

She hadn't told her parents about the breakup, only that she was coming home again to visit. Five hours after she landed, her parents seemed able to see the pain in her eyes, not like she tried at all to hide it.

She lowered her slice and focused on the stem of her plastic champagne flute. Eliza had never talked to her parents about her love life unless it had to do with convincing them to let her see Tess or the brief story of how she and Blake had gotten together. This might have been the first moment of her life when she let them into that part of her.

She exhaled a hot, ragged breath, the emotion crawling up her throat already shaking the words she had yet to say. "Blake and I broke up."

From her periphery, Eliza noticed her parents exchange a glance. She kept her stare on her flute and the bubbles still floating to the top.

"Oh, Eliza, I'm so sorry," her mom said, and her sympathetic voice pulled Eliza's gaze.

"What happened?" her dad asked. "You two seemed to be going strong."

They looked at her as if they understood her hurt, the very look Eliza had wanted when she was seventeen and had never gotten until now, and it broke her. She set her flute on the end table and wiped away the tears.

"Yeah, so did I."

"Oh, honey, I'm so sorry," her mom said, ditching her spot on the recliner to scoop Eliza up in her arms. "What happened?"

Eliza choked back the rest of the feelings and told them everything as if she'd never had a problem sharing her love life with them. The relief that hit her from being able to tell them everything and from all the comfort she got made her eyes leak.

They hadn't been there for her during her first breakup, but they were there to catch her as she fell after her second, and it felt so good to land on something as soft as her parents' embrace. It dulled the heartbreak for that moment, and any sort of relief allowed her to breathe without the weights packed in her lungs.

"I just…I just don't understand how it ended so quickly," Eliza said while wiping her eyes. "Christmas, when she was reading to Emma, that's when it clicked. Everything clicked into place. Blake was the one…or I thought she was."

"I don't think you should give up on her," her mom said softly. "I watched you with her. Your face lit up. I've never seen your face light up like that. You seemed…well…you seemed happy. I don't remember the last time I've seen you like that."

Her mother's words were a double-edged sword. The fact that she even hinted at Tess and the accident was an open door for Eliza to ask all the questions she'd been needing answers to.

"She's the first person in almost fourteen years to make me happy," Eliza said and then caught a glimpse of her dad, who made quick eye contact before dropping his gaze to his lap.

The lost but shared years were so present that it was like a ghost haunting the room. Eliza sat in her spot, raw and vulnerable, and when she glanced at her mom, the way she picked at her fingers and pressed her lips together made Eliza wonder if she wasn't the only one in the house who felt haunted.

"You know, honey, I have to tell you something. About Blake," her mom said without any eye contact. Eliza didn't need it in order to focus on her mom. The tone said it all: she was about to acknowledge it…everything. The crater they'd been avoiding for fourteen years. "Blake and I talked on Christmas. About you and how you've struggled so much since…since the accident."

Her heart plummeted, and the tears brimmed. Tess, the Wares, and the accident invited themselves in and sat right in the family room like a dysfunctional family reunion.

She'd envisioned this scenario so many times, and now that it played out right in front of her, she was at a loss for words. The words she'd practiced over and over again disappeared as if they never existed.

"She told me that I really needed to talk to you about everything that happened. And I'm so sorry, honey. I'm so sorry for everything you had to go through."

"Mom—" Eliza said, wanting to calm her down. But instead, a cry cracked through her voice, and she covered her mouth.

"I know you love her, Eliza. I know because I've had all these years to think about you and Tess. I know my little girl. I finally saw her again at Christmas, and I hadn't seen her since she was with someone who she loved and who loved her. We didn't do enough to protect you and Tess, so I'm not going to let us make that same mistake again. You need to call Blake."

"What? Mom," Eliza said through her raspy voice. She was still in the middle of processing her mom's words, and now she had to call the ex-girlfriend she hadn't spoken to in a month? "She broke up with me—"

"I don't care. We all know she loves you, and I'm almost certain you love her. Am I right?"

The sudden realization balled in her throat. It was the first time she'd admitted to herself that she was in love with Blake. She'd known back at Big Bear Lake that she was falling hard. And fast. The falling had never stopped. Blake made Eliza see colors that she'd never thought she'd see again, and without her, everything seemed to matter less. Eliza's world went back to black and gray.

"Blake is everything I've been looking for and everything I've been needing in my life," Eliza said, and the admission settled in her like a seed burrowing in the ground. Now that she'd said those words out loud, the realization started to blossom. "Yes, I love her. I want everything with her."

How could she have let such an amazing woman slip through her fingers?

"Eliza," her mom said sympathetically and pulled her close. Moments later, Eliza felt her dad's warm hand on her shoulder and the other rubbing her back. She couldn't believe she had both her parents consoling her. She wondered if they had any idea how wonderful it felt to feel them around her, protecting her from everything outside the living room. It was the feeling Eliza had been searching half her life for: being accepted and protected by them. She felt like a child running to her parents after a nightmare, but in that moment, she didn't care how infantile the scene was.

She needed her parents to stitch up the last wounds that needed healing.

"Eliza?" her dad asked quietly. Eliza turned. "Does Blake know that you love her?"

She thought about it for a moment and felt a pain swell in her when she realized that she'd never told her. God, how did that even happen?

"No, I don't think she does. Not when she told me I wasn't fighting for us and thinks I'm stringing her along."

"Then what are you doing back home?"

"I…I wanted to be around family."

Eliza's mom pressed her lips together as if accepting the answer. "If you love her, she's your family, and you need to go tell her."

"It's too late. We haven't talked in a month."

"Then you call her and tell her you want to talk when you get home," her dad said firmly in his fatherly voice, but this time, it didn't scare Eliza. She loved the tone because it was pushing her back into Blake's arms, and she truly never thought her parents would encourage her to be with a woman.

"It's not too late," her mom said. "You said she's everything you've been searching for. You need to fight for her, sweetie." Her mom snatched Eliza's hand. "She gave you your smile back. I think that's more than enough of a reason to try to make things work."

Eliza had messed up. She'd been scared of getting closer to Blake and losing her, so she'd run away. She'd put up a fight when she'd wanted everything Blake said they could have. She wanted to wake up and fall asleep next to her. She wanted Blake snuggled next to her when she was studying or on call. All the moments she wasn't working, she wanted to be with Blake. That was something that hadn't changed since August, and the need for her had grown each day they were together.

So why did she run?

She rubbed her face against her shoulder. Now that everyone had laid their emotions out there, she found the strength to ask her parents about Tess. They'd already mentioned her, and the shame had rattled their voices and soaked in their eyes. Eliza knew if she asked now, with all their guards lowered, she might actually get those answers that would patch her up. Finally.

"Can I ask you both a question?"

Her mom dabbed her eyes and then grabbed Eliza's knee. "Sure, honey."

"Why didn't you say anything to the Wares?"

They looked at Eliza with furrowed brows. The parental authority that had always shielded them was stripped away, and what remained wasn't her parents. Just two middle-age people looking scared and filled with much trepidation. For the first time in her life, Eliza wasn't afraid of them.

"What?" her mom said, as if she had no idea what Eliza was talking about.

Eliza wiped her face again to erase any sort of vulnerability. She was going to pull everything out of them. She'd spent almost fourteen years training for this very moment. She was ready. "At Tess's funeral, when they blamed me for the accident. You didn't say anything—"

"That's not true."

Her mom's slightly defensive tone would have scared Eliza when she was younger, but she was so tired of being mad, scared, and left in the dark about all the choices that had to do with Tess and the accident.

"The Wares really made me believe that I was the reason Tess died. They made me feel ashamed for loving their daughter so fucking much that losing her held me back for thirteen years. I guess I held back from Blake because I was scared of losing her."

"The Wares were completely out of line," her dad said in his authoritative voice, and the child in Eliza hushed for a moment when he spoke up. He hardly ever got angry, so when his voice intensified, it always stopped her in her tracks. "We weren't going to get into an altercation with them right after their daughter's funeral when they were burying her. The music from the funeral was still playing, for Christ's sake."

"So you let them yell at me and let me believe their words this whole time?"

Her mom reached for her hand and grabbed it. Eliza squeezed back. "Eliza," her mom said calmly. "Your father went over to the Wares a couple days later, you know."

"What? What are you talking about?"

Her mom had cried over Eliza losing Tess. Her parents had acknowledged the accident, and now Eliza was going to hear some story about how her dad confronted the Wares? She thought she'd known the entirety of Tess, the accident, and her parents' lack of involvement or sympathy. She had been wrong the whole time, and she could feel it painfully swirling in her stomach and rising up her throat.

Her dad leaned forward as if bracing for a lecture. "It wasn't my proudest moment," he said and shook his head. His ashamed voice caused a sharp heat to snake up Eliza's spine. "I'm ashamed that I went over and yelled at two grieving parents, but you know what? They really pissed me off." His voice rose as if he was getting lost in memory. "I told them that I was so sorry about their daughter, but they had no right blaming mine for any of this. That you loved Tess as much as they did and how disgraceful it was to yell at you at the funeral."

The truth cut Eliza so deeply that she felt herself falling apart. Everything she'd known and believed about her parents, the Wares, and the whole situation turned into something completely different. The truth shook her life up like a snow globe, and what fell back into place was a scene she'd never seen before.

Her parents *had* defended her.

"They screamed back at me, and I swear, I've never been so angry in my life," her dad continued. His rising tone hinted at what he'd used on the Wares all those years ago, and imagining it used on Ed and Tina Ware made something settle in Eliza. "God, I was so angry. I never had the urge to punch anyone until that moment when Ed was in my face—"

"He was in your face?" Eliza said, still in disbelief.

"He was. But I walked away. He wasn't worth a bruised hand or an assault charge. I just wanted them out of our lives and to stop harassing you."

She couldn't believe it. Her father—the sweet, quiet, laidback guy—talking about wanting to punch Ed Ware in the face.

A part of her wished he had.

"Why…why didn't you tell me this?"

"What good would that have done, Eliza?" her mom said. "The last thing you needed was an update on Ed and Tina Ware. We wanted them out of your life, our lives. Everything that happened stemmed from them and their bigotry and their hatred."

"And I was very embarrassed by my behavior," her dad said. He looked down at his folded hands before meeting Eliza's eyes. "I'm sorry I never said anything. I really am, and I'm so sorry that you believed this whole time that the accident was your fault. It was never your fault. Your mother and I never believed that for a second."

There was so much to process. It was like learning how to swim through a tidal wave, and Eliza had no idea which way was up or down.

"What about when Mrs. Ware outed me?" Eliza said. "You said that the Wares were hatful bigots, so why did you leave articles on my bed about how I could undo my gayness?"

"We're far from perfect parents, and we know that now, and we're so sorry," her mom said with a shameful head shake. Tears filled her eyes. "Times were different back then. We thought you were confused, but, honey, we know that wasn't the case. We know that now, and we're very regretful that we ever thought differently. You imagine a life for your kids, and when you find out they're on a path you hadn't imagined, it's shocking, and it was for us. You were also a teenager. We had no idea how serious it was because you were so young."

"I was with her for four years. Did you know we were engaged?"

Eliza said it much calmer than she'd always imagined. She wanted her parents to see her, to know her entire story, so she willingly opened herself up.

Both of their eyes widened as if they were taken aback by the truth she dropped in the room.

"You...you were engaged?" her mom asked, her grip around Eliza's hand loosening.

"Technically. She asked me on graduation night, and we were going to fly to Boston on our fifth anniversary. So, no, I didn't lose just my girlfriend that night. I lost my fiancée. You know I have PTSD? That I've spent years in therapy because of it? That I couldn't even date like a normal person? It wasn't until I met Blake that all of that changed. I'm thirty-one, and it's taken me this long to fall in love with another woman, and it took me until now to realize I pushed her away because of all the guilt and shame."

Her dad tightened his grip around her shoulder, holding and comforting her in all the ways she wanted.

"We love you very much, Eliza," her dad said. "Probably more than you know. We made mistakes in the past, but we never once loved you less. We just wanted to protect you. We want you to be happy."

Eliza felt so numb, and at the same time, she felt everything. Her heart ached while her parents' apology and "I love yous" patched her up.

"And Blake made you happy, sweetie," her mom said and tucked some hair behind Eliza's ear. She caved at her mom's gesture, feeling like a little kid needing to be swaddled by her parents.

"She did make me happy. So much."

"Then call her. Talk to her. Fight for her."

It was amazing how different Eliza felt with all the questions finally answered. Her parents had admitted their faults, and she knew they were genuine. She could see the hurt in their eyes mirroring everything she'd felt for the last thirteen years. Now that all the holes in her heart had been filled with her parents' love and acceptance, her insecurities dimmed. If her nonconfrontational parents found the strength to fight for their relationship with her, she was strong enough to fight for the woman she was in love with.

When she went to bed, she sucked in a ragged breath as she opened her text thread with Blake.

Blake, I've been thinking a lot about you and us. I think we need to talk again. I went back home, and I've had so much clarity, and I realized now that I made a big mistake. I ran away because I was scared of getting closer and losing you. There's so much more I want to say, but I want to do it in person. I'll be home next Sunday. Can we please find a time to talk? If it's not too late?

She didn't let go of that heavy breath until Blake texted back an hour later.

Sure.

Her text was short, bitter, and the fact that Eliza had plowed through all her doubts to send a text only to get that response made her want to regress as a reflex.

Eliza had spent her whole life running away from risks. The only ones she took were when she had Tess or Blake holding her hand. This was going to be the biggest risk she'd ever taken, and even though the thought of it shrunk her lungs to half their size, she was ready to do it. Blake was worth all of it.

CHAPTER SIXTEEN

Blake hadn't been out to the Ramos' house in at least five years, which was crazy to think about since her family used to visit the house multiple times a year to catch up and take advantage of their motocross track. Marc had suggested it. He said Blake had been moping for six weeks about her breakup and needed some cheering up.

"I haven't been moping for six weeks," Blake said on their drive out to Borrego Springs. "Malai and I filled up all our vendor spots. Construction broke ground a few weeks ago. I've been focusing on that."

After crying to Malai about her breakup and her stresses about Huntington Beach, they'd decided to go with the Ocean Beach venue right outside San Diego, an adorable bohemian neighborhood on the water, like Huntington Beach but only ten minutes from downtown San Diego.

It was more beneficial for them in the long run for sustaining vendors, and Blake really didn't want to live that far from her family. Even though she was ecstatic that Vagabonds had a home, she couldn't help but be upset with herself that she'd brought up Huntington Beach to Eliza. She should have put her foot down on it instantly instead of worrying about disappointing Malai because if she'd done that, maybe she and Eliza would still be together.

A part of her debated with herself about whether she should reach out to Eliza to let her know that Vagabonds was staying in

San Diego, but she'd ultimately decided against it. The damage had already been done. Eliza had built her walls in front of their relationship, preventing it from fully growing into everything it could have turned into. Texting her wouldn't change the fact that she didn't want to move in with Blake or reaffirm any sort of commitment.

And then completely out of nowhere, Eliza had texted her the week before to talk when she got back, and Blake's mind had been running on overdrive since.

"You're doing that thing you always do when you're upset," Marc said. "You overwork yourself so you don't have to think about it. You did it with Adrian too."

"Well, yeah. I have a food hall to start, and nothing is going to get done if I wallow. It's a great distraction."

"You're allowed to wallow. You and Eliza were together for like, what? Half a year?"

There was no denying that Blake was heartbroken and depressed. She'd missed Eliza every second since they last saw each other. She'd spent countless nights crying into her pillow; one time, she accidentally started crying in front of her mom and Jordan. It was such a bizarre time for her. She was elated that her dream was finally happening. She filled her days with watching it being built right in front of her. They'd secured their vendors faster than expected, which boosted their confidence about the community's excitement. They'd already gotten press coverage about it. She and Malai had gotten to pick out the decorations and decor while the construction company assembled the inside. Once a week, they checked on the progress, and their September opening date couldn't come soon enough.

But at night, when she didn't have Vagabonds to distract her thoughts, she realized how lonely she felt. It was hard to have so much happiness and no one to share it with. Sure, her family was supportive, but she wanted to share it with Eliza, and she hoped when they talked in three days, Eliza would tell Blake that she wanted to share her life too.

"Yeah, my longest relationship since Lindsey," Blake said.

"And you two haven't talked since?"

Blake shook her head and stared out the window at the desert surrounding them. "Nope. Well, except for the text message last week. We're talking on Saturday."

"Oh damn. How do you feel?"

"Extremely stressed, hence, the ATVs."

"You've been looking rough, cuz."

"Gee, thanks, Marc. You know how to charm a woman."

"I'm dishing the cold hard truth. I see through the facade."

"I'm not trying to have a facade. I really don't have anything to say to her."

"So, then, what do you plan on saying on Saturday?"

"Nothing. I said everything I needed to say. Ball's in her court."

"I find that hard to believe. I know you miss her."

Marc saying that made Blake well up. Her emotions had been all over the place for the past six weeks, and she hated crying, but now it was so easy for her to do. One mention of Eliza had her feeling heartbroken all over again.

She really needed to blow off steam, just like when she was a teen and experienced her first heartbreak and loss. She wanted to fly over the hills and speed around the sharp corners of the track to pump adrenaline through her body, something that made her feel anything but numb.

When they finally got to Ramos' house, Blake's mouth dropped when she saw the new and improved track. Anthony and his wife had a place of their own twenty minutes away from his parents' house, but the track still remained. Anthony had made improvements over the years to not only appease his skillset but for his ten-year-old son to learn as well. Apparently, his son, Elijah, was even better than Anthony when he was his age, zipping around the track like it wasn't a big deal. After watching Elijah show off, Blake was ready to suit up and get on one of the bikes.

The only question was, dirt bike or ATV?

She decided to do both.

She hadn't been on a dirt bike in ages and relied on Elijah to coach her through the first couple slow and steady laps around the track. After an hour of slowly speeding up, she felt much more comfortable and a little envious of Anthony and Marc getting air and cutting the turns so beautifully. That was exactly why she wanted to come out here. Of course to see the Ramos family, but the thrill of sharp turns, flying off the hills, the thump when she landed, mindlessly racing on the dirt track, it was all necessary for her mind to stop working on overdrive.

After tearing up the track on a dirt bike, they decided to take a break to drink a couple beers while watching Elijah show off. While drinking, eating, and laughing with Anthony and Marc, the heavy weight of stress dissolved. Blake leaned back in her chair and absorbed the hot, early March sun on her skin and the cold beer descending her throat.

At that particular moment, life was okay.

"We should race," Anthony said an hour later, waggling his dark eyebrows. "Just like ol' times."

Blake and Marc exchanged a glance as their lips curved upward. Back in the day, Anthony had challenged Blake, Marc, and Adrian to a race, and the four had pretended to play *Mario Kart* on the dirt track. Anthony had always won by a landslide, Marc and Adrian had alternated for second, and being the youngest by five years, Blake had always taken last, but it didn't matter to her. Being invited to hang with the boys had been her reward, a far better experience than Jordan and Gabriella inside the house playing with Barbies and dancing to the Backstreet Boys.

"Let's do it," Blake said, slamming down her third beer bottle. "I claim the ATV."

"Hey, Elijah. You ref the race. Watch your ol' man beat these two to a pulp," Anthony said, and Elijah's eyes widened with intrigue.

Elijah set the ground rules. Three laps, everyone had to ride an ATV. Blake expected to lose like when she was a kid, but she was ready to have an excuse to go fast and create a giant dust cloud. The three revved their engines, trying to intimidate the other, and when Elijah waved the white and black checkered flag from the sideline, the three were off.

As she zoomed around, Blake stared down the big booter, the largest hill on the track. At the beginning of the day, she'd taken it easy, and after each lap, she gained more confidence to let herself fly. Anthony, Marc, and even Elijah conquered the booter impressively, and Blake was ready to take it on and be part of the club.

Anthony was already half a track ahead, Marc was in the middle, and Blake was behind as usual. She watched Anthony climb the hill and fly through the sky and thought how awesome it looked. Eying the booter like the enemy it was, she twisted the right handle to maximize her speed. The warm desert air blistered through her shirt, airing out the sweat that stuck to her skin. She sucked in a breath as she climbed the hill and beamed as the ATV lifted off the ground, and her stomach plummeted. She loved that feeling, how her heart raced and how the adrenaline coiled in her. Her back tires finally made it off the ground, and right as the whole vehicle was airborne for a foot or two, it leaned forward, and she lost her grip on the handlebars. Her gut sank in a different way while she processed what was happening.

Fuck, oh fuck, she thought as her fingers slipped off the handlebars, and the ATV landed head first on the track.

Eliza's last surgery of the day was a hemorrhoidectomy. She would have preferred it as her first surgery of the day instead of the third and final, but scheduling didn't work in her favor. There were some surgeries she liked more than others. Actually, the further she got into her residency, getting out of general surgery excited her more. Hemorrhoidectomies were one of her least favorite, but at least with the trauma fellowship, her days of removing hemorrhoids were almost behind her.

After her evening rounds, she gathered her stuff and planned to go home, order Indian food, and dive nose first into studying. She planned on distracting her mind with studying until Saturday came, and she finally got to see Blake, apologize for everything, and fight to get her back. Without Blake to distract her for the last six weeks, her rebound had been her books. She'd become a studying whiz. With the first part of her boards less than four months away, she was getting down to the wire and had to dedicate as much time as possible going over everything she'd ever read.

When she checked her phone for the first time in four hours, she noticed she had four missed calls and one voice mail from Blake that spanned over the afternoon.

Her stomach bottomed out. Was she calling because she wanted to talk to Eliza earlier? Blake was the one who'd said she could do something on Saturday. If it were up to Eliza, they would have spoken the second she got back from Ohio.

She took a seat in her chair and braced herself as she clicked play. She just wanted to hear Blake's voice again.

"Hey, Eliza. It's Jordan…Navarro…calling on Blake's phone, obviously." Eliza could feel her heart hammering and the blood flowing through her ears when she heard Jordan's rattling voice. She possessed as much confidence as Blake, if not more, but the fear in her tone stripped it all away. Something was wrong, and it pricked at the back of Eliza's neck. "Blake was in an accident. They flew her out to Bellevue. We're here right now and thought you should know. We, um, she's in the ICU, and they haven't let us in her room yet, so if you're working, you should come down."

She didn't need to listen to the rest. She ran to the ICU as fast as she could. So many thoughts spiraled in her so fast and all at once that it made her dizzy. The hallway was never-ending and caved in on her. Goddamn it, it was happening again. Another accident. Another loved one hurt. She wasn't sure she could handle it.

She approached the nurse, Tanya, at the ICU desk as her ears started ringing and feeling like they were sinking into her head. Tanya gave Eliza a friendly smile, but it faded quickly. "Is everything okay, Dr. Walsh?"

"I need to know about a patient just admitted. Blake Navarro."

Without hesitation, Tanya looked at the computer, typing away, only making Eliza's pulse twitch faster. "Looks like she's in Room 104."

"Who's her doctor?"

"Dr. Duncan."

"Can I go in? She's...she's a family member."

Tanya walked Eliza to Room 104, and after getting permission from Dr. Duncan, she went in, and found an unconscious Blake in the bed. A nasal cannula delivered oxygen into her nose, a blood transfusion dripped next to the IVs, and a few small purple bruises spotted her forehead. Given the scene, Eliza put the pieces together that Dr. Duncan was treating her for internal bleeding.

The tears rolled down her face so easily despite her trying to hold it together. Even though Eliza was about to burst at the seams, terrified that she was going to lose someone else, she had to remain as professional and composed as possible in front of her colleague, one who she was going to be working closely with during her fellowship.

With a shaking voice and her words grating along her tight throat, she asked all the questions the surgeon ex-girlfriend of a patient would ask. What happened? What were her exact injuries? What procedures did they use? Were there any complications? What medications was she on? She was sure she sounded like the kind of frantic family member she had spoken to plenty of times before, but Dr. Duncan's professionalism and calm demeanor remained the same. He answered all her questions with enough detail to settle a blip of anxiety. Dr. Duncan was one of Bellevue Memorial Hospital's best trauma surgeons. When Eliza had seen him in the room, a huge part of her was relieved that Blake was being cared for by the best.

Eliza followed him to the family lounge where Luis, Sandra, Jordan, and Hugo sat. Sandra gasped, and Eliza hugged her and held her hand while Dr. Duncan went over everything. Blake had a broken collarbone, a dislocated shoulder, a broken wrist, a concussion, internal bleeding, and a pelvic fracture. Despite it being a mild pelvic fracture, it was still a serious injury that could potentially cause severe internal bleeding.

"Oh, Eliza, we're so glad you're here," Sandra said and dabbed her eyes once Dr. Duncan left the lounge.

"Me too. What the hell happened?" Eliza asked.

"Marc and Blake went to our family friends' house out in the desert—" Hugo began.

"The family friends with the motocross track?"

Hugo nodded. A stupid ATV. She didn't need any more details because based on Blake's injuries, she could piece together that the ATV had rolled over her. She'd seen patients come in with ATV rollover accidents a handful of times, and nothing about a four-hundred-pound vehicle rolling over a person was a minor accident. Blake was already small, and just imagining an ATV crushing her formed a large lump in her throat that made it hard for Eliza to swallow.

"They were all the way out in the desert?" Eliza repeated. "So she was flown here?"

Hugo nodded. "Marc said the medics transported her to the local hospital and then flew her out here since Bellevue can care for her better. Marc is on his way back now."

Borrego Springs was almost two hours away. The fact that the local hospital called for the nearest trauma one center—Bellevue Memorial Hospital—was a clear indication of how serious Blake's injuries were. Eliza hid her face in her hands as she finally had time to process everything that had happened, and the more she processed, the tighter her lungs became. Sandra rested a hand on her back while she attempted to stifle the cries. She knew the Navarros were leaning on her to be their rock through this, and she wanted to be that for them. But without crying out all her fears and worries, being a rock was merely impossible.

"She's going to be okay, right?" Sandra asked. The desperation was loud despite the softness in her voice.

Eliza lowered her hands and met Sandra's gaze, and the amount of pain and worry that rounded Sandra's eyes hit Eliza hard in her chest. No, Blake wasn't all right. This ATV accident was much worse than her motorcycle accident, and thinking about how extensive her injuries were boiled the anger in her. She wanted to scream at Blake for being so fucking reckless. Again. How hadn't she learned her lesson from her motorcycle accident? Sure, she hadn't ridden it since her accident but substituting it for an ATV joy ride, knowing how she loved flying over those hills? How could she still think she was invincible?

Blake had promised at Big Bear Lake that she wouldn't ride an ATV. Eliza guessed the promise was only valid when they were together.

"She has some really bad injuries," Eliza said and swallowed the emotion rising in her throat like vomit. No matter how delicately she framed the words, their meaning packed a punch to the rest of Eliza's body. She wouldn't get into the scary details about all the things that could happen, but the Navarros needed to know that Blake's injuries were serious and fucking terrifying. "A pelvic fracture is really serious. It can lead to a lot of internal blood loss, which means she's at high risk for shock and damage to her organs. But she's at the best hospital, and I'm not saying that because I work here. If I had to pick the doctors taking care of her, Dr. Duncan would be one of them. I trust him with her."

"But they're not you," Sandra said with a croak in her voice. "They don't know her and love her like you do."

Eliza's throat yanked and tugged as she kept swallowing back the tears begging to come out. She was so glad that Sandra knew how much she cared about Blake, and she hoped—and wondered if—that Blake knew the same.

"No, they don't," Eliza said and dabbed the corner of her eye. "But they're doing everything I would have done."

Then it was the waiting game. For Blake to wake up. For the ICU to allow visitors into the room. While Eliza waited, she stepped outside to breathe fresh air and process privately. She didn't want the Navarros to see her crying, but in order to be the rock she wanted to be for them, she had to let something out.

She found a dark corner in the parking lot and rested her back on the building before taking out her phone.

"Mom?"

"Eliza! Hi, sweetie. Bill, it's Eliza."

"Oh, hi honey. How are you?" her dad said off in the distance.

And that was when she broke. She blubbered to her parents to give her a second, and then she muted the phone to cry. She couldn't even speak; her throat was so raw from holding so much back.

"Blake's been in an accident," Eliza barely said through her cries. "And I'm so scared right now."

"What? What happened?"

Her parents sounded as scared as she was when she told them what had happened. The fear and familiarity squeezed more out of her. Her mother seemed so shocked that she struggled with finding the right thing to say, despite there being no right thing to say. Blake wouldn't be okay until the internal bleeding stopped. Once she was out of the ICU, Eliza would accept responses like, "She'll pull through. She's okay now."

But until then, she wasn't.

"I...I can't do this again. I can't lose someone else," Eliza said, gulping large sobs.

"Oh, honey, I'm so sorry," her mom said quietly. "Keep your head up. She's in the best care right now. You said it was only a mild fracture, right?"

"Yes, but that doesn't mean anything until she's out of the ICU."

Her parents were able to calm her down, reminding her it was okay to be upset and worried, and that they would keep their phones on them if she needed to talk or cry. Knowing that she had two people to fall on gave her an immense sense of relief that she didn't have to fall on the ground like she had the first time around.

While waiting for any sort of update, Eliza clung to that.

Two hours later, Luis and Sandra were finally allowed in Blake's room. The Navarros decided to take it in shifts during the time the ICU allowed visitors. After forty minutes, Luis came out and joined the rest of his family in the lounge, including Marc, who'd finally arrived from his trek from the desert.

Eliza cautiously stepped back into the ICU room. After she took a seat, she stared at Blake and all the cords and tubes connected to her. With almost eight years of experience working in a hospital, the sound of the heart rate monitor blended in with everything else in the background, like sirens and honking cars in a city or the crickets singing in the country. But now, Eliza was able to hear each inhale from the woman she loved through the beeping of the heart rate monitor and waited with a bated breath for the next one. She studied the vitals and tried to raise Blake's blood pressure telepathically. Low blood pressure was a sign that she was still bleeding internally. Eliza wanted to hold her hand, kiss it, smooth the hair out of her face, clean up the dirt under her eye. But she knew that if Blake were awake, the last thing she'd want was her ex-girlfriend doing that given all the things that they'd said and left unsaid.

"She's missed you so much, you know," Sandra said, low and soft, pulling Eliza's gaze to her. "She hasn't been the same since you two broke up."

"What do you mean?"

Sandra shrugged. "She wasn't my usual outgoing, carefree, happy baby girl. She was on edge, always busy with the food hall—"

"In San Diego."

The bitterness slipped out, and she felt bad for directing it at Sandra. Eliza had read online a few weeks after their break-up that the executive chef of Mezcal Cocina was going to open a food hall in Ocean Beach, and her heart had broken all over again. She was hurt because despite Blake staying in San Diego, she hadn't reached out at all.

Sandra thinned her smile as if she knew that a Vagabonds in San Diego—not Huntington Beach—packed a punch. "Yes, the one in San Diego. I'm sorry, sweetheart. I can't explain why she didn't tell you. The only reason I can guess is because she was so heartbroken over the two of you. I haven't seen her this upset in a really long time. She's seemed so lost and sad. My heart broke for her."

Although there was some relief in knowing that the heartbroken feelings weren't one-sided, it didn't comfort Eliza knowing Blake had spent all this time lost and miserable.

"I've really missed her too," Eliza mumbled. "An unbelievable amount."

Sandra's grip tightened around her hand. "I know, hon. If it makes you feel better, I know the feelings are mutual. She never really talked to us about it, and that's how I knew how hurt she must be because she tells us almost everything. Blake likes to keep herself busy when she's stressed. She's spent tons of time getting her food hall ready that at some points, it was obsessive. She even took a trip to Mexico City to visit her grandparents a few weeks ago, and then she and Marc planned this ATV trip. I've always had a bad feeling about those, Eliza."

Eliza pressed her temples and attempted to ease the pain stacking inside them. She wanted to shake Blake awake. Her patience was running on fumes, and she was terrified that there was a clock ticking.

There couldn't be a clock ticking. There was so much she wanted to tell Blake. Like how much she was in love with her.

This scene was all too familiar.

Waking up in a hospital and not knowing what the hell had happened. A large ball of pain anchored in the middle of Blake's head like a brick. Her dad and Uncle Hugo sat on either side of the bed, opening their drooping eyes at the sight of her.

Her father filled her in on what the hell had happened, and as he reminded her about being at the Ramos' house, the memories started sprouting.

She couldn't believe she'd gotten herself into another mess. What a fucking idiot she was.

The next time she opened her eyes, she found Eliza at the foot of the bed with her father. The woman she'd been desperately wanting to see and talk to for a month and a half was right there. They locked eyes for a moment, but Blake couldn't look at her longer. She already saw the fear glossing Eliza's eyes, so she closed hers because a new pain simmered in her, one of guilt. She could only imagine what she'd put Eliza through by being stuck in this hospital bed, and it was something she'd never intended. If every atom of her body didn't hurt so much, she would have started crying, so disappointed and mad at herself for putting her family and Eliza through another accident.

The morning light crept through the window, and she watched the back of her eyelids lighten as time passed. She kept her eyes closed for a while because she wasn't ready to talk to Eliza or see any more fear staring back. That one look they'd shared at least an hour before was plastered on the inside of her eyelids, haunting her to the point where she couldn't sleep it off. The emotion crept up her throat like bile, and she sucked in her lips to stop it.

Her father's hand landed on hers. "How are you doing, mija?"

He must have been watching very carefully because the only movement indicating that she wasn't asleep was sealing her lips together to hold back the sadness and guilt. That meant Eliza was watching her too, probably more meticulously than her dad.

It still hurt too much to speak, so she offered her dad a groan for an answer. He tightened the grip around her hand, and she did the same, letting him know she was doing okay despite how she probably looked and sounded.

"Eliza is here. Actually, she's been here the whole time."

Blake had no idea how to feel. Part of her was so happy to see Eliza. She'd missed her like crazy. Seeing her on the other end of the bed made her well up. If she was there, that meant there were still lingering feelings. At least, she hoped more than anything that was true. But the other part of her was still hurt from their break-up, mixing with the knowledge of putting Eliza through something she'd already dealt with years ago.

"Here, Eliza, take my seat," her dad said.

Blake lifted an eyelid just enough to catch a glimpse of Eliza taking her dad's seat but not enough for them to notice she was watching. Eliza kept her gaze on her, her blond eyebrows still high on her forehead. Blake looked away. Nope, she couldn't look at Eliza. It was still too raw.

"I think I'm going to go check on the rest of the family," her dad said. "Go back to the house for a bit to nap while Sandra, Jordan, and Marc come back over. We'll be back, mija. Just need a few hours of sleep but your mom should be here in a few." He leaned in and kissed her forehead. "When you're feeling up to it, you should talk to Eliza, all right? She's been here all night caring for us and looking after you. Love you," he said in Spanish.

When he left, the room felt so empty and so cramped at the same time. It was all too much for Blake. She was scared, angry, and disappointed at herself and felt horrible for putting everyone through this again. Her whole right side throbbed, and her chest burned. She pressed her lips together to stop the tears, but she couldn't. They freely rolled down her face and ruined her sleeping disguise. She attempted to wipe them away with her uncast left hand, but the pain still radiated throughout her whole body.

"Blake?" Eliza asked delicately, just above a whisper.

When she heard her familiar soothing voice rattling with trepidation, Blake tossed her left arm over her eyes and broke. "I'm...I'm sorry," she cried. "I'm so sorry."

"Blake—"

"I'm sorry. God, I didn't mean to."

Eight months after her last hospital visit and she was right back where it all started. Except this time, she should have known better. She should have tamed her overconfidence on the ATV. She needed to stop being careless and reckless. For her sake, for her family's sake, and God, by putting Eliza through this again, she was being so fucking selfish.

Eliza grabbed her hand, and the touch calmed Blake down a little bit. She'd missed her touch. "I...I don't know why you're even here," Blake said.

"Well, I work here, so it was convenient," Eliza said, attempting a poor joke, but it caused a twitch of a smile. Blake appreciated the joke to ease the tension and awkwardness making it feel so impossible to talk to her.

She studied Eliza, and even though the faintest smile was on her face, all the emotions collected in her stare. Nervousness. Fear. Heartbreak. Anger. Concern. Blake missed those dark blue eyes, and they stared at her so intensely, she felt like they wrapped her up in a much-needed embrace.

"Why wouldn't I be here?" Eliza said.

"Because we're not...because of everything."

"That doesn't matter."

All Blake wanted in that moment was Eliza. For the next few moments, she wanted to forget their last conversation and the month and a half that had punched a hole in their timeline. She wanted Eliza to put her back together again.

Eliza swatted at her wet cheeks. "Are you feeling okay?"

"No, everything hurts."

"Where? Does your head hurt? Are you dizzy? I can get the nurse if you need something."

Right as Eliza lifted herself from the chair, Blake tightened her grip around her hand, stopping her in place. "No, I just want you."

Eliza sat and pulled their intertwined hands to her chest. "Okay. I'll stay."

Her thumbs grazed Blake's skin as if trying to ease the pain, and it did. She sank into the bed and basked in the wonderful feeling of Eliza caressing her.

❖

"I come bearing gifts," Eliza said once she came back in the late afternoon.

She had stayed with Blake long after she fell asleep, until Sandra and Jordan came back.

By the time she'd returned to Bellevue, Blake was out of the ICU. When Eliza got the text from Sandra, the heavy weight lifted off her chest.

She was going to be okay. Eliza wasn't going to lose her.

In addition to Sandra and Jordan, there was an unfamiliar face in the room, but she guessed it was Blake's friend Malai. She presented the two blue Jell-O cups and some chocolate chip cookies from the bakery around the corner.

"Jell-O for the patient and some cookies for the family."

Blake lifted herself in the bed and focused on the treats. When she adjusted herself, she winced and then deflated.

"Don't move," Eliza said and walked to the side of the bed. "Save that energy for the Jell-O. Would you like one now or later?"

"Now please," Blake said, grunting through what Eliza could only assume was pain.

The fabulous, multitalented chef who traveled the world trying all different types of cuisines, who went to culinary school, who owned her own food hall, pulled up her battered body for a plastic cup of artificially flavored gelatin.

Eliza had really missed her and all the little quirky things that made her Blake.

After handing the bag of cookies to Jordan, Eliza peeled back the aluminum lid, dipped the plastic spoon in, and handed it to Blake. Blake scooped a large spoonful and closed her eyes happily.

"Are you five?" Jordan asked with a confused frown as she bit into one of the cookies and passed the bag to Malai.

Even with a healing pelvis, recovering from internal bleeding, numerous bruises, and cuts up and down her body, Blake still had the energy to flip off her younger sister.

"Apparently, she has a huge love for Jell-O," Eliza said to Malai. "Learned that from the first hospital trip. You know that, right?"

Malai looked at Blake and then back at Eliza, seeming mortified. "I did not. I…I don't know what to do with this information."

"If there's no alcohol in it, what's the point of eating it?" Jordan said.

"The flavoring is good," Blake said.

"It's fake. You of all people should know that."

"Let me eat in peace."

"Yes, you enjoy your animal collagen."

Blake lowered her cup and shot Jordan a glare. "That was an unnecessary reminder."

"It's the truth."

"She does have a point," Malai added. "I'm actually shocked how excited you seem about it."

"It's blue Jell-O," Blake said. "When you're in this bed, it's really the little things that make you better."

After introducing herself to Malai, Eliza took a seat between Sandra and Jordan, sitting back while everyone dragged Blake for loving Jell-O and warning her there would be none at Vagabonds. The mention of Vagabonds was a sprinkle of salt over the fresh wound that had never healed. It shouldn't have made Eliza uncomfortable because it was Blake's dream, and she'd made it her reality, and Eliza was so proud and happy for her. But it still picked away at her for being the catalyst to their break-up, and finding out it stayed in the San Diego area was one last zinger to her broken heart. It was like they'd broken up for no reason.

An hour passed, and as Malai gathered her stuff to leave, Sandra patted Jordan's knee. "Honey, how about we walk Malai out and then go for a walk? Give these two some time alone?"

Blake's eyes widened as if begging them not to leave her alone with Eliza, but Sandra shot her a look right back with a tightened jaw. Eliza's cheeks warmed up. She knew they needed to talk, but she was hoping the Navarros would help her stall a bit.

"We'll be back in an hour," Sandra said before she and Jordan left.

And then there was silence. Eliza waited for Blake to turn to her, but instead, Blake reached for her second Jell-O cup and peeled it back. Eliza knew that she'd turned to it to avoid the dreaded conversation. She wished there was one last cookie left so she could have a distraction as well. If she'd known Sandra would force the conversation on them, she would have waited to hand out treats.

A few hours before, Blake had gone from telling Eliza that she only needed her to now struggling to make eye contact once again. Her willingness to let her guard down in the morning was probably the pain medication. Blake could put up all the walls she wanted, but Eliza knew that, buried underneath, there was a part of her that wanted Eliza there. She wouldn't have asked Eliza to stay if that wasn't the case. At least, that was what Eliza told herself as a way to push through the thick tension. She was ready to get this over with and find out where Blake's mind and heart were at.

"Um, how are you feeling right now? Are you dizzy? Numb anywhere? Nauseous?"

Blake shrugged. "A little nauseous but I don't think that has anything to do with the accident."

The days of easy conversation, quick banter, and flirting were long gone, and what was left of their love was stuffy, awkward silences. It felt like Eliza was sitting on a bed of a thousand nails.

"What were you and Marc doing on those ATVs?"

"Oh my God," Blake muttered under her breath and lowered the Jell-O. "I woke up, like, eleven hours ago—"

"You asked me to stay with you this morning until you fell asleep, and I did. Are we not going to talk about it?"

"When I'm still in the hospital, and my body still hurts? No, it's not the first thing that comes to mind."

"You can't ask me to be with you and avoid the subject. That's not fair."

"I was in pain and on a lot of medication—"

"So, then, all of that was fake? Should I leave? Is that what you want?"

Blake was silent and focused on her broken right arm. The tension, anxiety, and heartbreak hung and stuck like summer humidity. Eliza had been so relieved when Blake had reached for her hand and begged for her to stay, and now she felt like she was being shoved out of the room, like the morning was a whole lifetime ago. She had no idea where Blake stood, but the fact that she struggled to look Eliza in the eye wasn't a good sign. She felt hopeless and useless, like there was no more room for her in Blake's life.

"Okay, I'll leave," Eliza said, standing up and grabbing her purse. "Clearly, you have nothing left to say to me."

Finally, Blake turned to her. "You broke my heart, Eliza. Completely broke it."

"The feelings are mutual."

"How? How is that even possible? I asked you to move in with me, you said no. I told you all the things I would give up to make this work, and none of that was good enough. You gave me nothing. You never tried."

"You never gave me time to think about a big move. And after all the drama that Huntington Beach caused, you stayed here, and I had to find out about it in the fucking paper. You don't think that hurt?"

"You ran so fast at even the thought of that venue. One mention and you were already out the door. I fought so hard during those two arguments, and you shut everything down. It was like our time together meant nothing to you."

"Meant nothing to me? You really think you meant nothing to me? I honestly thought I was going to lose you, Blake. You were… you…"

A cry burst out of her, and she covered her mouth as if trying to shove it back in, but the hot tears kept slipping out. She sat back down so she had the support she needed when her mind drifted back to an unconscious Blake from the night before.

"You…you were unconscious and hooked up to every single machine and a blood transfusion…and…" Eliza hiccupped cries in between her words. "I thought I was going to lose another woman I loved."

Just last evening, her skin had caught fire as she'd braced herself to lose another woman she was so very much in love with, and even though she didn't want to tell Blake she loved her this way—in a fucking hospital—it was already out there, and she was going to hold on to it and own it.

She stripped her heart from the words that had collected inside the last month and a half and laid all her emotions out there. When she finally heard her own admission, it smacked her hard in the chest but dissolved something wonderful and warm into her. Eliza knew what the aching in her heart was. It crossed her mind every day, but without Blake to catch the word and claim it as her own, Eliza kept burying it until she'd admitted it.

"You…you love me?" Blake asked, shy and cautious as if she was scared that Eliza might take it back.

"Of course I love you," she said.

"Then why are we here? In this situation? Why didn't you fight for us?"

Eliza scooted to the edge of her seat and grabbed Blake's hand with both of hers, and because both her hands were now out of commission, Eliza couldn't swat at the pesky tears slipping down her cheeks. "Here are all the things I'd do for you, Blake," she said through her hoarse voice. "I've been here by your side since I heard about your accident, waiting for you to wake up, even though you made it clear that I'm the last person you want to see. But I don't care. I'm staying right here until you get out of this hospital. And when you get home, I promise to stay with you as long as you need me because I know for a fact that no one can take better care of you than me. Then, after my fellowship is over next July, once I'm board certified, I'll go wherever you want to go. If you want to go to Huntington Beach, I'll go with you. If you want to move out to New York City and live in a closet in Brooklyn, I'll go with you. If you want to take a year off to travel Asia and visit all those cities you've wanted to visit, I'll go with you. If you want to live on the beach, in the mountains, in the desert, in the boonies, I will move anywhere as long as that means we have a life together. I'm in love with you, Blake, and this past month and a half has been absolutely debilitating without you, and when I got the call from Jordan, I...I thought I would never see you again. I thought it was too late to tell you how much I love you. I shouldn't have run away, and I'm so sorry I did. But I know what I want and need and that's you."

Blake tightened her grip around Eliza's hand. "I never meant to scare you or put you through that pain again, and I'm so sorry that I did." Blake let go and reached for Eliza's face to wipe away the moisture. Eliza caved into Blake's palm, and God, did it feel good to have Blake hold her again. "I'm okay, Lize. You don't have to cry anymore."

"Yes, I do because I'm scared that I'm so fucking in love you, and you're going to keep doing careless and reckless things. You out of all people should know that no one is invincible. When are you going to realize that?"

"Now. I've realized that now. I've been so lost that I had to take it out on ATVs to make me feel something, to make me feel as much as you did."

"Please don't compare me to an ATV. I'm not that dangerous."

Blake chuckled. "But you are dangerous, Eliza Walsh, because you have the power to either make me the happiest and luckiest girl in the world or the most heartbroken, and since January, I've been the most heartbroken."

Eliza kissed Blake's hands and held them against her lips. "I'm a doctor. Tell me how to fix it, and I'll do it."

"Kiss me. Please."

Eliza didn't hesitate for one second. She jumped off the chair and leaned against the bed, cautious of putting too much weight on Blake. She grazed her hand against Blake's cheek and studied her face for a moment with all her little bruises. She kissed each one delicately until she finally met her lips. The kiss started as careful, apologetic, and tender, but once Blake opened her mouth, begging Eliza for more, their tongues became acquainted again. She melted into the feeling of Blake's lips sensually dancing with hers. After a few moments, Eliza became fluent in the way Blake's mouth moved against hers. Once their rhythms were synced, they fell deeper into it. Blake cupped Eliza's face and kissed her so deeply, she could feel how much Blake loved and missed her.

Blake pulled away after a few moments. "Eliza?"

Eliza opened her eyes, and Blake's smile widened. "Hm?"

She couldn't talk properly. It was like kissing Blake for the first time all over again.

"I love you too."

Eliza smiled, and her insides ballooned. It felt so good hearing someone tell her they loved her. Those were words she never thought she'd hear again, and three words she would collect and hold on to for the rest of her life.

Eliza leaned back in to resume where they'd left off. She slid her tongue along Blake's bottom lip and sank right back into it.

"Oh, geez, okay, let's go back out," Jordan said, causing them to pull away and snap their attention to the door. "They're getting it on."

Eliza's whole body flushed as she straightened and watched Luis, Sandra, and Jordan cast glances between the two of them.

"Oh my God, did you two make up?" Sandra asked gleefully and clasped her hands in front of her chest. "Please tell me you did."

"Oh my God, Mom. Stop," Blake said, and a deep red blush spread on her cheeks.

"No, keep going, please," Jordan said and sat in an empty chair. "It's always great when Blake gets embarrassed."

"You all can go back out," Blake said, gesturing to the door. "We were enjoying the alone time very much."

Luis covered his ears and walked to the door. "I don't need to know anything."

Sandra hugged Eliza again. "I'm so glad you knocked some sense into her. We'll let you two resume your alone time."

"Good. Bye," Blake said and waved her family out the door.

Once they were alone again, she held Eliza's face and kissed away the lost six weeks.

CHAPTER SEVENTEEN

One year later

Eliza never expected her Always to start in Tokyo, but she'd learned throughout her life that spontaneous forks in the road happened, and it wasn't until she was older when she realized that not every one resulted in tragedy.

Hell, she had no idea that life could have an Always until the idea sprung in her head.

They were in the first city of their first trip together, the trip Blake had been dreaming about for years. They'd spent their first full day eating around Tokyo with Malai, visiting Sensō-ji Temple, and drinking their way through the narrow alleys of Shibuya Nonbei Yokocho. After trying all sorts of draught beer, sake, and shochu, Eliza and Blake stumbled into their hotel room, stripped each other's clothes off, made love, and after, while guzzling water, they cuddled naked under the sheets.

All these feelings had been accumulating in Eliza for the last several months, and she was ready to burst. God, was she happy. She was so incredibly happy with the life she and Blake had built within the last year. After Blake's second accident, Eliza had stayed with her until she was better. It made her realize that she and Blake worked so well together, and she was stupid to ever believe that living together was a mistake. So they lived in Blake's apartment for a year until Eliza was offered an attending trauma surgeon job at Bellevue. Then they bought a house together two months before their trip.

How couldn't she be happy? She'd bought a house with her girlfriend, her relationship with her parents had almost progressed to the type of relationship Blake had with hers. They both had their dream jobs, they were building a future together, and while Eliza snuggled her face into Blake's naked breasts, an idea popped into her head.

It was a crazy one. Hands down her craziest idea ever, but why did it feel so right?

She pulled away and glanced up. Blake smiled and plopped a kiss right on her nose. "What?" Blake asked with a wide, untamed grin, one that always colored her face after they had sex.

Eliza considered the thought, running through a quick pros and cons list before she proposed it.

"You're up to no good in there," Blake said and tapped Eliza's forehead. "You up for another round?"

"No, I'm just thinking—"

"No? Wow, you haven't said no since the day before your boards."

When Eliza had passed her boards and officially became a "board-eligible" surgeon, she'd celebrated her success and extra time with her girlfriend, naked under the sheets. Hell, sometimes they didn't even make it to the sheets and christened their kitchen island, their brand-new sectional couch, their walk-in shower.

Eliza lifted herself and rested her back against the bed. Blake stared right at Eliza's exposed nipples.

"Blake?"

She played with one of her nipples as a salacious grin grew. "Yes?"

Eliza grabbed Blake's twisting fingers and kissed both of them. "I have an idea. It's a wild one."

"You have a wild idea? Prove it."

"This might make up for the lack of bikes you've ridden since giving up Gisele and ATVs."

"You have my full attention."

Eliza slipped out of bed and paced back and forth before turning back to Blake.

"Should I be concerned?" Blake asked, her voice dipping lower, and confusion and intrigue crisscrossed her features.

"No, no, no. Quite the opposite, I hope." Eliza stopped pacing and found the pj's shirt Blake had stripped off her an hour before. She put it back on since the hotel air-conditioning formed goose bumps all over her, and she wanted to be comfortable for this. After slipping back into her underwear, she hopped on the bed. "Let's get married when we get to New Zealand."

Blake's mouth plummeted, one of the very few times she'd been speechless. "W…what?"

"We've been together for two years. We just bought a house together. We're stable. We're kicking ass at our jobs. We're happy. This is our first full trip together. Why not?"

Blake put the back of her hand against Eliza's forehead. "Are you really Eliza Walsh? What have you done to my girlfriend? Are you sick?"

"Your girlfriend wants to become your wife if you say yes."

Blake laughed, but her smile was as wide as ever. "Wait…so you put on a shirt and your underwear just to propose to me?"

"It would have felt weird if I'd proposed naked."

"And proposing in everything except pants is less weird?"

"You're not answering my question."

"I'm sorry. You caught me off guard. I mean, Jesus…" Blake stood. It was her turn to take a couple pacing steps before she stopped and let out a deep sigh. "You're stealing my thunder."

"How am I stealing your thunder?"

"Because!" She marched to her suitcase on the other side of the room, fumbled around until she picked up a Nike tennis shoe, and pulled out a small velvet box.

Now it was Eliza's turn to be speechless. What the hell was in Blake's hand? Scratch that. She knew what the hell it was, but why was she caught so off guard? How had she kept that little box such a huge secret?

And why the hell was it shoved in her Nikes?

"Oh, sorry, let me get on your level," Blake said, putting the velvet box casually on the foot of the bed while she threw her shirt and underwear back on. She knelt on one knee with Eliza perched on the edge of the bed. "See, you weren't supposed to propose because I was going to do that." She shook the box as proof.

"Blake, I…I had no idea—"

"I know you didn't, and that's why I'm mad at you for stealing my thunder because I was going to ask. In New Zealand. It's why I suggested adding New Zealand to our trip. So before I answer your question, you're going to have to answer my question," Blake said and opened the box to reveal a sapphire ring.

Eliza gasped. The ring was gorgeous, proof that Blake had this all planned for what had to be months. They'd booked their trip seven months ago. She'd kept a wonderfully dirty secret for that long, which meant both of their families knew and had somehow stayed silent. Most importantly, Allison had stayed silent, and Eliza was astonished.

"Eliza Grace Walsh, I had planned on asking you this question in New Zealand—"

She hid her face in her hands. "I'm so sorry. I had no idea."

Blake laughed and pulled Eliza's hands away. "And even though we don't have those beautiful blue waves crashing behind us like I imagined for the last seven months, the fact that we're in this predicament is honestly even better…because it reaffirms that we're meant to be together. I want to spend the rest of my life with you, loving you. Will you marry me?"

The tears hit her cheeks despite her heart soaring out of her chest. "Of course I'll marry you," Eliza said as a cry escaped her. She didn't think she could get any happier than she already was. "Will you marry me in New Zealand? Preferably with those crashing waves you imagined in the background?"

"Of course I'll marry you."

Blake jumped to her feet and slid the ring on Eliza's finger. Eliza cupped her fiancée's face and pulled her in for a kiss that led to Blake crawling on top of her. Right as they sunk back into the steamy kiss, Blake pulled away, leaving Eliza's body throbbing for her lips to come back.

"And if you hate the ring, blame Allison and your sister," Blake said.

"They knew about this?"

"Oh, honey," Blake said, tucking a strand of hair behind Eliza's ear. "Literally everyone knew about this except for you. I asked your parents back when we went to Cedar Point last September."

"You asked my parents at Cedar Point?"

Blake shrugged. "I guess it is better than Magic Mountain, but only because they said yes, and I got Bill and Amy to love me almost as much as they love you. Magic Mountain can't compete with that. And then Allison and I FaceTimed Violet, and those two told me this was your ring, and I hope they're right, or something's going to happen to both of them."

Eliza kissed both of her cheeks before giving her a soft sweet kiss on the lips. "The ring is perfect, and you're perfect, and I'm so glad that the most perfect woman is going to be my wife."

Blake found it almost impossible to concentrate on all the different tastes of Asia, not when her future bride was sitting next to her, and as much as she had wanted to visit Asia for years, knowing she was going to get married to Eliza pulled all her thoughts to New Zealand. Imagining Eliza in a white dress walking toward her made a tidal wave rush through her. While watching Eliza try chimaek in Seoul and fanning herself as she gulped ice water to tame the spice, Blake still couldn't believe that the beautiful woman with honey-mustard sauce on the corner of her mouth was going to be her wife. She fell even more in love with Eliza in Hong Kong when she agreed to try soy-braised octopus, despite warning Blake and Malai numerous times that she wouldn't do it.

They were going to have a wonderful, exciting life together. She knew it.

Tokyo, to Seoul, to Hong Kong, to Bangkok, to Taipei, to finally Auckland, the dessert of the trip. Malai joined them to be a witness to their marriage and helped them both pick out what they were going to wear. Since it was so spontaneous, they agreed they didn't want anything fancy. They weren't fancy people.

The morning of their wedding, Blake woke up with her heart ready to sprint out of her chest. She couldn't tame it. The adrenaline kept flowing through her veins, and it was the best rush she'd ever experienced. As the hours inched closer, her pulse quickened as she took a shower and spent too much time perfecting her hair. She'd come to realize that Eliza had a thing for her hair, and ever since she'd admitted that, Blake spent extra time on it. The more time she spent, the longer Eliza ran her fingers through it, and wouldn't it be wonderful if she got married and then her wife spent an hour playing with her hair?

By the time she changed into her white jacket and pantsuit, hair styled, cologne spritzed on her neck, her hands shook uncontrollably. "How do I look?"

When Eliza stepped out of the bathroom in her simple white maxi dress with a lace top, her hair perfectly tousled down to her collarbone, there wasn't enough air in the room to ease the tugging in Blake's chest. All she could do was stare for a moment, as if it was the first time she'd ever seen Eliza, and maybe in a way it was because it was the first time she'd actually seen her as her wife. She couldn't believe that she'd finally found her person, and she was absolutely gorgeous—inside and out.

How had Blake gotten so lucky? She wondered if she even deserved all the happiness in her or deserved someone as beautiful and incredible as Eliza Walsh. She was going to be her wife. Blake still couldn't believe it, and she wondered if she ever would.

Taking her in, the stinging hit Blake's eyes, and she tried shoving all her overwhelming emotions back down, but Eliza's beauty—her pull—was so strong, she failed. A few tears welled up, and she pressed her lips together, taking a moment to capture her breath and her words.

"You're absolutely beautiful," she said, hearing her wavering voice. "I can't believe I get to marry you."

She couldn't believe it the whole day. On the hour-long ride to the Tawharanui Regional Park, Blake had been lost in a daze, reminiscing about all the ups and downs of her life, her dating life, everything that she and Eliza had accomplished just within the last year. Eliza held her hand the entire car ride and didn't even flinch when Blake's palms started perspiring. She had no idea why she was nervous. It would just be Eliza, Malai, and the officiant, with both of their families watching on FaceTime. Eliza was going to say, "I do." There was no ceremony that would present them both with a chance to trip, fall, and humiliate themselves. But still, her heart wouldn't stop thrumming.

The Tawharanui Park offered a stunning view of the blue-green waters and golden sands. On the walk to the beach, bright green grass billowed in the wind. The beach was quaint and desolate. One look at it amazed Blake, and when she turned to find Eliza taking in the scene next to their officiant, her hair and dress blowing with the breeze, she lost her breath yet again.

"Are you ready?" the officiant asked, and the seams broke. She held it in as long as she could.

Malai stood a few feet away, recording it for both of their families back home. Blake was so grateful that Jordan wasn't there to laugh at her because she didn't have a dry eye at all, and their private ceremony only lasted five minutes. But the tiny beads rolling down Eliza's cheek eased her. At least they were both unstable messes throughout their vows.

When the officiant told them to kiss their bride, Blake barely registered the "woos" and the clapping coming from Malai's phone. She got lost in her wife's lips with the gorgeous water she'd been dreaming about for the last seven months crashing into the shore.

She pulled away and smiled when Eliza's eyes were still closed, savoring the kiss as if it was their first time. "I can't believe I just married the super-hot doctor who put my leg back together," Blake said.

Eliza opened her eyes and smacked her arm. "Blake, don't make this weird."

"It's true. Riding Gisele and getting hit by a car was hands down the best thing I ever did. Ten out of ten, would recommend." She leaned in to kiss her wife again. "Now, what do you say we ditch Malai and consummate this marriage?" she whispered.

"As long as you never refer to sex as that again, then yes. I'm for this plan. Poor Malai."

Blake waved her off. "She's a strong, independent woman. She can handle it."

They might not have had a traditional proposal or the traditional wedding, their families were on the other side of the world, and neither had spent more than fifty dollars on their outfit. Their fathers didn't walk them down the aisle. They didn't have a bridal party. Their "reception" was delicious New Zealand wines at a nearby winery. They bought a few bottles to bring back to their hotel room, where they drew a bubble bath, drank a glass, and finally consummated the marriage, but only after Blake said that word to Eliza, who cringed and playfully joked to divorce her if she used the word "consummate" one more time.

It wasn't traditional in any sense, but for both of them, the day was perfect. It was everything that Blake never knew she wanted for her wedding day, and she wouldn't have traded it for anything.

Even though their vacation had ended, Eliza wasn't sad about it. She hadn't expected to fly over the Pacific and come back a married woman. She never expected to have her honeymoon first and then her wedding second. She had never thought that flying home would excite her just as much as if she were to embark on another trip.

After a long and hectic flight back to California, forty-five hours of straight traveling, Eliza rested her head on Blake's soft breasts. They were home, in their king bed, in their new house, ready to tackle the rest of their lives.

Eliza played with the black tungsten ring on her wife's ring finger. She had to admit that it was a good look on her.

"Am I losing you to sleep?" Eliza whispered and kissed her cheek.

Blake nodded. "Traveling all over Asia and getting married takes a lot out of a woman." She pointed her finger upward. "And the sex. That does a lot too."

"If it's too much for you, then maybe we should stop."

Blake pointed her finger. "No. It's a good complaint. Like muscles hurting from a good workout kind of complaint. Ugh," Blake said before turning on her side and burying her face in Eliza's breasts. "I love you and this bed and this home."

Eliza kissed her temple. "We did it, babe. Can you believe it?"

Blake looked up and smiled. "I can. We're pretty great together, don't you think?"

"I do."

"You know, a part of me is glad I got into the ATV accident."

Eliza pulled her face back. "What's up with you being grateful for all your horrific accidents? Those aren't anything to be proud of."

"The first one, I met you, and the second one forced us to talk and get back together. You took care of me for those two weeks after, and then when I got better, you decided that you wanted to move in with me. There are huge silver linings to those accidents."

"I'm just grateful that you sold Gisele. Best day of my life."

"Better than our wedding day?"

Eliza thought about this. "Okay, it ties with our wedding day."

She wrapped her arms tightly around Blake, kissed her forehead, and felt Blake's breathing slow to a steady rhythm. Blake was always the first one to fall asleep, and Eliza loved cuddling her until her breathing became heavy, and her body started twitching. Her days would start and end with Blake, and knowing that, she couldn't help but be excited for the future. She couldn't believe there was ever a time when the future had terrified her to the point that living was almost impossible. Eliza felt like she'd conquered a mountain. On the top of the peak, looking down at the arduous trek she'd started when she was eighteen. She'd almost given up several times, and for a while, she'd lain in place as the rest of the world continued, and she'd allowed her past to paralyze her. She'd never thought she would make it out, find love, reconcile with her parents, find some glimmering hope in her After.

But ever since they'd met, Blake had pulled her out of the rubble, encouraging her every step of the way. In a way, Blake had saved her. She'd given her confidence, she'd believed in Eliza, she'd made Eliza realize how much she was loved, and helped her reunite and forgive her parents. Blake had helped Eliza open her eyes to all the wonderful things her After had to offer, if only Eliza turned on the light.

Now, they finally had a home to call their own, a place to capture the rest of their lives together. It would be in this home that they would start their own holiday traditions, a home to host their families, and Eliza was so excited for next month when her parents would come visit for the first time since she'd moved to California. It would be the home where they would become mothers, a home that would be a lockbox to their kids' wonderful childhood memories, a home where they would watch them grow up.

Her Always looked bright and hopeful, and Eliza was so ready to tackle it.

About the Author

Morgan Lee Miller started writing at the age of five in the suburbs of Cleveland, Ohio, where she entertained herself by composing her first few novels all by hand.

When she's not introverting and writing, Morgan works for an animal welfare nonprofit and tries to make the world a slightly better place.

She currently resides in Washington, DC, with her two feline children whom she's unapologetically obsessed with.

Books Available from Bold Strokes Books

A Woman to Treasure by Ali Vali. An ancient scroll isn't the only treasure Levi Montbard finds as she starts her hunt for the truth—all she has to do is prove to Yasmine Hassani that there's more to her than an adventurous soul. (978-1-63555-890-6)

Before. After. Always. by Morgan Lee Miller. Still reeling from her tragic past, Eliza Walsh has sworn off taking risks, until Blake Navarro turns her world right-side up, making her question if falling in love again is worth it. (978-1-63555-845-6)

Bet the Farm by Fiona Riley. Lauren Calloway's luxury real estate sale of the century comes to a screeching halt when dairy farm heiress, and one-night stand, Thea Boudreaux calls her bluff. (978-1-63555-731-2)

Cowgirl by Nance Sparks. The last thing Aren expects is to fall for Carol. Sharing her home is one thing, but sharing her heart means sharing the demons in her past and risking everything to keep Carol safe. (978-1-63555-877-7)

Give In to Me by Elle Spencer. Gabriela Talbot never expected to sleep with her favorite author—certainly not after the scathing review she'd given Whitney Ainsworth's latest book. (978-1-63555-910-1)

Hidden Dreams by Shelley Thrasher. A lethal virus and its resulting vision send Texan Barbara Allan and her lovely guide, Dara, on a journey up Cambodia's Mekong River in search of Barbara's mother's mystifying past. (978-1-63555-856-2)

In the Spotlight by Lesley Davis. For actresses Cole Calder and Eris Whyte, their chance at love runs out fast when a fan's adoration turns to obsession. (978-1-63555-926-2)

Origins by Jen Jensen. Jamis Bachman is pulled into a dangerous mystery that becomes personal when she learns the truth of her origins as a ghost hunter. (978-1-63555-837-1)

Pursuit: A Victorian Entertainment by Felice Picano. An intelligent, handsome, ruthlessly ambitious young man who rose from the slums to become the right-hand man of the Lord Exchequer of England will stop at nothing as he pursues his Lord's vanished wife across Continental Europe. (978-1-63555-870-8)

Unrivaled by Radclyffe. Zoey Cohen will never accept second place in matters of the heart, even when her rival is a career, and Declan Black has nothing left to give of herself or her heart. (978-1-63679-013-8)

A Fae Tale by Genevieve McCluer. Dovana comes to terms with her changing feelings for her lifelong best friend and fae, Roze. (978-1-63555-918-7)

Accidental Desperados by Lee Lynch. Life is clobbering Berry, Jaudon, and their long romance. The arrival of directionless baby dyke MJ doesn't help. Can they find their passion again—and keep it? (978-1-63555-482-3)

Always Believe by Aimée. Greyson Walsden is pursuing ordination as an Anglican priest. Angela Arlingham doesn't believe in God. Do they follow their vocation or their hearts? (978-1-63555-912-5)

Best of the Wrong Reasons by Sander Santiago. For Fin Ness and Orion Starr, it takes a funeral to remind them that love is worth living for. (978-1-63555-867-8)

Courage by Jesse J. Thoma. No matter how often Natasha Parsons and Tommy Finch clash on the job, an undeniable attraction simmers just beneath the surface. Can they find the courage to change so love has room to grow? (978-1-63555-802-9)

I Am Chris by R Kent. There's one saving grace to losing everything and moving away. Nobody knows her as Chrissy Taylor. Now Chris can live who he truly is. (978-1-63555-904-0)

The Princess and the Odium by Sam Ledel. Jastyn and Princess Aurelia return to Venostes and join their families in a battle against the dark force to take back their homeland for a chance at a better tomorrow. (978-1-63555-894-4)

The Queen Has a Cold by Jane Kolven. What happens when the heir to the throne isn't a prince or a princess? (978-1-63555-878-4)

The Secret Poet by Georgia Beers. Agreeing to help her brother woo Zoe Blake seemed like a good idea to Morgan Thompson at first...until she realizes she's actually wooing Zoe for herself... (978-1-63555-858-6)

You Again by Aurora Rey. For high school sweethearts Kate Cormier and Sutton Guidry, the second chance might be the only one that matters. (978-1-63555-791-6)

Coming to Life on South High by Lee Patton. Twenty-one-year-old gay virgin Gabe Rafferty's first adult decade unfolds as an unpredictable journey into sex, love, and livelihood. (978-1-63555-906-4)

Love's Falling Star by B.D. Grayson. For country music megastar Lochlan Paige, can love conquer her fear of losing the one thing she's worked so hard to protect? (978-1-63555-873-9)

Love's Truth by C.A. Popovich. Can Lynette and Barb make love work when unhealed wounds of betrayed trust and a secret could change everything? (978-1-63555-755-8)

Next Exit Home by Dena Blake. Home may be where the heart is, but for Harper Sims and Addison Foster, is the journey back worth the pain? (978-1-63555-727-5)

Not Broken by Lyn Hemphill. Falling in love is hard enough—even more so for Rose who's carrying her ex's baby. (978-1-63555-869-2)

The Noble and the Nightingale by Barbara Ann Wright. Two women on opposite sides of empires at war risk all for a chance at love. (978-1-63555-812-8)

What a Tangled Web by Melissa Brayden. Clementine Monroe has the chance to buy the café she's managed for years, but Madison LeGrange swoops in and buys it first. Now Clementine is forced to work for the enemy and ignore her former crush. (978-1-63555-749-7)

A Far Better Thing by JD Wilburn. When needs of her family and wants of her heart clash, Cass Halliburton is faced with the ultimate sacrifice. (978-1-63555-834-0)

Body Language by Renee Roman. When Mika offers to provide Jen erotic tutoring, will sex drive them into a deeper relationship or tear them apart? (978-1-63555-800-5)

Carrie and Hope by Joy Argento. For Carrie and Hope loss brings them together but secrets and fear may tear them apart. (978-1-63555-827-2)

Death's Prelude by David S. Pederson. In this prequel to the Detective Heath Barrington Mystery series, Heath discovers that first love changes you forever and drives you to become the person you're destined to be. (978-1-63555-786-2)

Ice Queen by Gun Brooke. School counselor Aislin Kennedy wants to help standoffish CEO Susanna Durr and her troubled teenage daughter become closer—even if it means risking her own heart in the process. (978-1-63555-721-3)

Masquerade by Anne Shade. In 1925 Harlem, New York, a notorious gangster sets her sights on seducing Celine, and new lovers Dinah and Celine are forced to risk their hearts, and lives, for love. (978-1-63555-831-9)

Royal Family by Jenny Frame. Loss has defined both Clay's and Katya's lives, but guarding their hearts may prove to be the biggest heartbreak of all. (978-1-63555-745-9)

Share the Moon by Toni Logan. Three best friends, an inherited vineyard and a resident ghost come together for fun, romance and a touch of magic. (978-1-63555-844-9)

Spirit of the Law by Carsen Taite. Attorney Owen Lassiter will do almost anything to put a murderer behind bars, but can she get past her reluctance to rely on unconventional help from the alluring Summer Byrne and keep from falling in love in the process? (978-1-63555-766-4)

The Devil Incarnate by Ali Vali. Cain Casey has so much to live for, but enemies who lurk in the shadows threaten to unravel it all. (978-1-63555-534-9)

His Brother's Viscount by Stephanie Lake. Hector Somerville wants to rekindle his illicit love affair with Viscount Wentworth, but he must overcome one problem: Wentworth still loves Hector's brother. (978-1-63555-805-0)

Journey to Cash by Ashley Bartlett. Cash Braddock thought everything was great, but it looks like her history is about to become her right now. Which is a real bummer. (978-1-63555-464-9)

Liberty Bay by Karis Walsh. Wren Lindley's life is mired in tradition and untouched by trends until social media star Gina Strickland introduces an irresistible electricity into her off-the-grid world. (978-1-63555-816-6)

Scent by Kris Bryant. Nico Marshall has been burned by women in the past wanting her for her money. This time, she's determined to win Sophia Sweet over with her charm. (978-1-63555-780-0)

Shadows of Steel by Suzie Clarke. As their worlds collide and their choices come back to haunt them, Rachel and Claire must figure out how to stay together and most of all, stay alive. (978-1-63555-810-4)

The Clinch by Nicole Disney. Eden Bauer overcame a difficult past to become a world champion mixed martial artist, but now rising star and dreamy bad girl Brooklyn Shaw is a threat both to Eden's title and her heart. (978-1-63555-820-3)

The Last First Kiss by Julie Cannon. Kelly Newsome is so ready for a tropical island vacation, but she never expects to meet the woman who could give her her last first kiss. (978-1-63555-768-8)

The Mandolin Lunch by Missouri Vaun. Despite their immediate attraction, everything about Garet Allen says short-term, and Tess Hill refuses to consider anything less than forever. (978-1-63555-566-0)

Thor: Daughter of Asgard by Genevieve McCluer. When Hannah Olsen finds out she's the reincarnation of Thor, she's thrown into a world of magic and intrigue, unexpected attraction, and a mystery she's got to unravel. (978-1-63555-814-2)

Veterinary Technician by Nancy Wheelton. When a stable of horses is threatened Val and Ronnie must work together against the odds to save them, and maybe even themselves along the way. (978-1-63555-839-5)

BOLDSTROKESBOOKS.COM

Looking for your next great read?

Visit BOLDSTROKESBOOKS.COM
to browse our entire catalog of paperbacks, ebooks,
and audiobooks.

Want the first word on what's new?
Visit our website for event info,
author interviews, and blogs.

Subscribe to our free newsletter for sneak peeks,
new releases, plus first notice of promos
and daily bargains.

SIGN UP AT
BOLDSTROKESBOOKS.COM/signup

Bold Strokes Books
Quality and Diversity in LGBTQ Literature

*Bold Strokes Books is an award-winning publisher
committed to quality and diversity in LGBTQ fiction.*